Copyright 2016

Fallout

Part 1

Prologue

It wasn't like the old days. You couldn't just use a hunting rifle to rid the world of problem people.

Perestroika ruined that for everyone. Satanic Soviets against God's Good Guys used to be a great gig. Simple. Effective. Resonated with everyone's innate xenophobia. The public would put up with just about any amount of gangsterism, as long as you told them it was a shootout between spies over nuclear secrets. And as long as you told them the good guys had won.

The assassin sighed. Bygone days turned a nostalgic sepia in the mind's eye. He knew it was so, yet he was still subject to the illusion.

Could he be blamed? It was a ballsy game, back then. Bullets and blades. None of this biological weapon bullshit, he thought wistfully as he patted the vial of biological weapon bullshit in his suit pocket, shaking his head ever so slightly and tightening his semi-permanent grimace.

They'd have never stood for it, back in the day. No room for hacks and poseurs. It was all about high-velocity cars and high-velocity women and high-velocity bullets.

Highballs, high heels, high stakes, and high times.

Then the goddamned wall came down.

It was tough to find work for a while. People momentarily lost the stomach for permanent solutions.

But statecraft recovered in due course, as did spy craft. The two were inextricably linked, the assassin reckoned.

He was glad he persevered. Glad to have survived. Happy to still be in the game.

Such as it was.

Goddamned drones, goddamned germs, goddamned pencil-necked pencil-pushers, MBA college boys playing at a man's game.

His mark showed up, taking her reserved seat a few tables over from him at the sidewalk cafe on Pennsylvania Avenue, just a block from the White House, saving the assassin from tumbling headlong into another bout of self-righteous self-pity.

He put his gloves on.

Then he felt the vial of biological bullshit again. Hepatitis? AIDS? Bird flu? Mad cow? He had no clue, and he didn't want to know. Sometimes staying alive meant staying dumb. Society lacked a clear enemy, which made people far more sensitive and far more litigious. Hence an even greater need for plausible deniability.

And all those goddamned video cameras these days. One surveillance camera for every ten Americans, he'd read.

It was yet another of the forces driving his profession into extinction. One wrong step and your face would be all over You-view, or whatever the kids called that internet video thing.

His mark's meal arrived. He didn't remember her ordering, but then he remembered that she was a regular, and a wannabe mover/shaker, the kind of person who would put in a standing order at a trendy restaurant, then look too stern and preoccupied and important to enjoy it.

Salad is what they brought her. Twenty-something dollars on the menu, for fifty cents worth of rabbit food.

The assassin humphed. As good a last meal as any, he finally decided after giving it more consideration than it deserved.

He shook his head, annoyed at the wayward thoughts. He was on assignment, after all. No time for fuzzy-headedness.

He was still the best around, as far as he would admit, but he feared he might be hearing the faint thrumming of bat wings up in his belfry. Wasn't getting any younger. Maybe time to remove the semi from semi-retired.

His B-team showed up. Right on time, for a change. An elderly couple. Even more elderly than the assassin. They checked in with the hostess, who nodded, smiled, grabbed menus, and walked toward an open table.

Right toward his mark.

Showtime.

The assassin donned his hat, grabbed his cane, palmed the sealed glass pipette in his pocket, stood up, and made for the exit, dodging tables and diners.

He passed the hostess going the opposite direction, then the elderly B-team woman walking behind her. Next was the elderly man.

On cue, vertigo set in, and the old man stumbled into the old assassin, who stumbled into the mark's table, upending glasses and clinking silverware against china.

Lost in the commotion was the sound of the sealed glass vial breaking open over the mark's salad, its clear, odorless contents draining neatly into the overpriced arugula as the assassin's gloved hand searched for a place to arrest his feigned fall.

"I'm so terribly sorry, ma'am," he said to his mark, regaining his balance, setting aright the molested flatware, looking straight into her forty-something-year-old eyes, which registered officiousness and severity and focus and genetically bitchy overtones behind clumping makeup. The assassin didn't doubt that somebody would want *this* particular DC muckety-muck out of the picture. She had that vibe about her, like maybe a few hundred people might like her better dead than alive. But maybe he was projecting.

She allowed a small wave and an unconvincing smile that never made it any further north than her cheeks, and let out a perfunctory "think nothing of it" in a tone that would have been much more at home in the company of a "bugger yourself," then joined her assassin in restoring order to the contents of her table.

Apologies from the clumsy B-team man for good measure, a polite tip of the hat to the mark, and the assassin was on his way.

And that was that.

He walked out of the cafe, took a right, waited for the light, and walked toward the park and the setting sun, just an old man on a postprandial stroll, taking his air, as they used to say.

Hell of a night for it. Beautiful breeze, beautiful sunset. His mind was already long beyond the killer bug already at work on the

Justice Department bureaucrat's innards.

Chapter 1

One year later.

Sam Jameson died once. In the line of duty. In the service of a not-terribly-grateful nation. Death by torture. It sucked.

Fortunately, her death didn't take.

But it did rattle about in her psyche, lingering neurotically, prompting uncomfortable questions.

To wit: what the hell am I doing with my life, and why the hell am I getting killed over it?

She lived a pretty full-throttle existence before her untimely but short-lived demise, busting skulls and catching spies as a counterespionage agent at Homeland, which always sounded too much like Fatherland for Sam's liking, with disturbingly similar overtones of xenophobia and aggression and totalitarianism. But beggars couldn't be choosers, and nobody else would employ a pinup girl with a mouth like a sailor and a mean left hook, unless there was first a disagreeable amount of reeducation.

But in her post-death life she'd taken a slightly different tack. She still followed her instinct, but no longer did she take the kinds of unreasonable risks she used to take.

That's what she told the man she loved, anyway, whose voice

she now heard, sexy and deep, intellect and testosterone adorably audible even through her tinny cell phone speaker.

"Why you?" Brock James asked. She heard notes of disappointment and anger. Dark clouds brought on by yet another ruined weekend.

Sam shrugged, a useless gesture in a phone conversation, but human wiring predated phones by a zillion eons. Plus or minus. "Born lucky," she guessed.

She heard him let out his breath. Dead giveaway for exasperation, in her experience as his live-in consort. "They're sending you halfway around the globe to view a case file," he said. "Can't they just email it to you?"

She shook her head, again pointlessly, eyes half closing as she let out her own sigh. "It's protocol in cases like this one."

"Like what one?"

"A guy died. Run over by a car."

"In Budapest?" An edge to Brock's voice. "Must happen a dozen times a day. Why do they need you there?"

"Because he was one of ours."

A long pause. The energy changed.

"Shit. Sam, I'm really sorry." More silence. "Anyone we knew?"

"Mark Severn," Sam said, conjuring her coworker's youthful face as she spoke his name.

Ex-coworker, to be completely accurate. As of yesterday.

"The bass player?"

"That's him," Sam said. "*Was* him, I guess." She recalled a few enjoyable evenings watching Mark Severn's rock band play in various Alexandria booze joints. The band was tight and well-rehearsed, and they were becoming kind of a thing around town. Sam and Brock enjoyed hanging out, tapping their feet, singing out of key, half-transported from the usual Washington DC manure for a few hours, overall an agreeable effect.

"Shit," Brock repeated, anger replaced by commiseration. "I liked him."

"Me too. He was going to be a good one." Implying a marked contrast to the rest of them. Sam often complained that the Department of Homeland Security was a behemoth among bloated DC bureaucracies, and she respected precious few of her fellow agents' skill and professionalism. The more ambitious among them were fat desk jockeys playing at cops and robbers. The less ambitious sent emails to each other about cops and robbers. Losing a rising star stung on personal and professional levels.

"Accident?" Brock asked.

"By all accounts."

"I'm sorry you have to go. I made plans for us."

Sam closed her eyes, feeling a tired burn inside her lids that accused her of working too hard yet again. "I'm sorry, baby. Really."

"Forget about it. Duty calls. Will I get to see you naked before you leave?"

An airport announcement blared, making Sam's response both inaudible and redundant. She repeated it after the harangue relented, just to fill the silence on the phone. "There were tickets in the file

Davenport gave me," she said. "My flight's in an hour."

More silence on the other end of the line. Brock was an understanding guy by nature — twenty years as a fighter pilot tended to give one a rather sanguine approach to non-lethal setbacks — but he was obviously several notches south of happy.

"But listen, an idea struck me." The corners of her mouth crept upward. "I have a proposition for you."

It took a moment, but he came around. "I love your propositions," he said, a small smile around his words.

"Join me."

"In Budapest?"

Sam chuckled. "If you're going to join me, then yes, it'll have to be in Budapest."

"Isn't that in Africa or something?"

"Europe, smartass."

"G'day."

"Close."

"Guten Tag."

"Getting warmer."

"I'll see what I can do."

"Just buy a ticket. For Saturday. Two days should be plenty of time for me to finish up the paperwork on Severn. Then we could both really use a week off."

"Strong offer," Brock said.

"I'll pick you up at the airport, and we'll bonk like bunnies on our hotel balcony."

"I'd fly to the moon to get in your pants."

"Don't. I won't be there."

"Europe it is."

"Then I'll see you Saturday."

"I love you painfully," Brock said.

"I love you worse."

Sam dropped her phone in her purse next to her Kimber .45 — being the living, breathing personification of Big Brother wasn't without its perks, which included, improbably, much less infringement on the Constitutional right to bear arms than the average US citizen enjoyed — and trudged wearily to her gate.

She sighed.

Long day behind her.

Long day still ahead.

Chapter 2

His mother named him Nero. She was aiming at power and strength. She got ruthlessness and megalomaniacal insanity instead. She must have been sick on history day.

He went by Jeff. Short for Jefferson, his middle name. After Thomas Jefferson. A philandering miscegenation-prone oligarch, if you dug too deeply. Best to admire the stern visage on the two-dollar bill and not ask too many questions.

He had never seen a two-dollar bill. He had, in fact, seen an insufficient number of bills in any denomination.

He blamed his name, at least in part. Some men got great, powerful, awe-inspiring names, which undoubtedly catapulted them to wealth and notoriety.

He got Nero Jefferson Chiligiris.

Thanks, mom.

He was born in Cleveland, Ohio, circa 1969. The city was deep in Rust Belt ruin by the time Nero came of age. Especially so on Nero's side of the tracks. Nothing to do for money that wasn't illegal.

He was a lifelong Browns fan, which was a perfect metaphor for the pervasive futility all around him. Even the good years weren't very good.

There were plenty of male role models in Nero's life, but none of them were particularly positive. He spent his youth in and out of juvie, mostly for petty crimes related to scaring up enough money to eat.

Then came his eighteenth birthday, a milestone significant in that it meant the end of juvie and the beginning of an adult criminal record. He became intimately familiar with a couple of state correctional institutions.

Then, one unlucky day, he crossed state lines during the commission of a crime. Blam. Federal offender.

Federal prisoner.

Fifteen years. Out on parole after ten.

Scared straight wasn't quite accurate, but Nero saw the wisdom of remaining on the outside.

And strange as it might have been for a tough street kid, he didn't like violence. He was big enough to survive relatively unmolested in prison, but his disposition was anything but outsized. He never picked fights, never intimidated people, and never joined the mutual blood-letting during the turf wars endemic to prison life.

He did his time, worked out at the prison gym, kept his nose clean, and researched opportunities to make a legitimate living on the outside.

Which amounted to jack and shit. Nobody was hiring. Qualified, college-educated workers weren't finding jobs. What hope did a felon have?

There was one industry that embraced Nero's ilk, however. Debt collection. It was an industry made of misfits and unemployables from all walks of life. Buffalo, New York was its capital. Browbeating deadbeat dads and down-on-their-luck homemakers into making just a single low monthly payment to set right all those thousands of dollars of debt wasn't work that anyone else wanted, so the work fell to the ex-cons, and they flocked to Buffalo by the thousands.

And it was one hell of a booming business. All you had to do was hustle. Start dialing debtors in the morning, work your "talk-off" technique all day, and rack up the payments. There was enough cash to insulate your big new house and fill the trunk of your big new Escalade.

But it was the wild west. The criminals working the phones resorted to shockingly criminal measures to extract and extort payments on old and long-forgotten debts.

Nero never had the stomach for that sort of thing, so he was never better than an average collector. But he was thrown out on the streets just like the rest of them when the federal regulators finally woke up to the madness. He had the rug pulled out from under him three times in less than a year.

Nero took it as a sign.

He managed to make a few acquaintances during his stint in the seedy underbelly of America's economic system. One of them was an irascible and almost unbearably arrogant gentleman of nondescript Middle Eastern descent whose real name Nero never learned, but who went by the moniker Money and paid handsomely in cash for services rendered.

They weren't difficult services, either. Mostly courier work, based out of Denver. Locked duffel bags, locked suitcases, sealed backpacks. Always heavy.

The deal was always the same: Nero was allowed to bring no cell phone, no pager, no GPS, no computers or electronic devices, and no weapons. He was always to drive an old car without a GPS tracking system. The exchanges took place in extremely remote locations, and absolutely no words were exchanged between couriers.

Sure, Nero had the vague notion that something slightly untoward might have been afoot. But he was making good money. He had people depending on him. Kids and a girlfriend. Wife, really, but they'd never bothered with a ceremony. Oldest boy starting high school.

He made sure his ignorance was absolute. He had no clue what was in the bags, and he worked hard to keep it that way. Prison sucked, and he had no desire to return. Money's business was no concern of Nero's. He went out of his way to make sure the boss knew it, too. Nero knew his place.

On this day, Nero Jefferson Chiligiris's place was several miles south of a rest stop on I-70 in Eastern Colorado, near the Kansas border. He was driving a Pontiac Grand Am, old enough to have the cheesy plastic bumpers and no On-Star on board.

The air smelled much less like Colorado and much more like Kansas. Nero hated Kansas. The bugs and the humidity got to him. And the bovine slack-mouthed look most Kansans had about them. At least, most of the ones in his tax bracket, which was admittedly less impressive than it might have been had he bothered to report all of his income.

Nero looked around. Not another car in sight. Corn fields on either side, getting on toward the harvest, Nero figured, judging by their size.

Out of habit, he looked overhead as well. Nothing but a couple of birds circling, riding thermals up from the two-lane blacktop road that ran straighter than a laser beam as far as the eye could see.

No traffic, no cops, no bug-smasher airplanes buzzing around. Perfect conditions.

The other car approached from the highway side. Another beat-up old shitbox, ready to give up the ghost if the engine's wheezing was any indication.

Nero found the trunk button, heard a clunk as the latch released, and stared straight ahead. He had long ago mastered temptation, and was no longer even curious about who might have been on the other end of the transaction. He didn't want to know anything about them. Not even what they looked like.

Nero felt the suspension lighten as the other courier lifted the large red duffel from the back of Nero's Grand Am.

Then there was a thunk, the replacement bag, ostensibly the *pro quo* to his *quid,* either greenbacks or goods, Nero didn't know which. And didn't want to know. Not his business.

The trunk slammed shut. Nero stared straight ahead, heard the other courier's footsteps in the gravel, started his Grand Am, and put it in drive.

And all hell broke loose.

Nero heard a low, thrumming buzz. The air vibrated. The

sound grew more intense, more insistent. It became overpowering, hammering Nero's chest, battering his car, shaking the earth around him.

The noise grew unbearably loud. It assaulted his ears, robbed him of breath, scared him witless.

A helicopter appeared, impossibly huge and deafening, pounding the air into submission, skidding to a hover just above corn height. Then another, and one more, surrounding him, angry and ominous and in his face.

One blocked the road to Nero's south and a second blocked the north, trapping him on the narrow road.

Nero stared wide-eyed, pulse pounding, insides clenched with fear and dread, adrenaline slamming his veins.

Strapped in each chopper's doorway was a man in a black jumpsuit wielding an assault rifle.

The third helicopter took position overhead and just to the west of the road. It was the one with the loudspeaker, Nero later realized. Get out of the car with your hands above your head. Instructions he'd heard before, but not in a very long time.

So much for the straight life.

Chapter 3

Uncle Sam didn't spring for business class — bad optics, they said — so Sam tried to get comfortable in her coach seat, an obvious impossibility for anyone over five-three. It was one of the low-grade annoyances that added up over time, contributing to the general angriness Sam sensed inside and around her.

She was more acutely aware of those things in her post-death incarnation, because the notion had crept into her mind that peacefulness ought to be a priority on some level, which she thought to be much more related to subtracting things from one's life than adding.

Like airline travel. She could permanently subtract *that* from her existence and be forever happier.

And she would undoubtedly have to subtract work as well. Not entirely, but substantially. It was likely the only way to remedy the constant fatigue that plagued her, and the scowl on her face most mornings, and the preoccupation that had come over her.

She could tell it was taking its toll on Brock. He understood, of course. He'd been awakened in the middle of the night countless times during his own career, sent off to foreign lands to fly circles over petulant dictatorships or dodge surface-to-air missiles and drop bombs on rogue states. But she could see the tiredness in his eyes.

And her death had taken a remarkable toll on him.

How could it not? He had been forced to watch the whole thing, strapped horizontally to a wall while his shattered ankle dangled at a grotesque angle, his heart and psyche breaking just as completely and painfully, unable to turn away as a deranged killer had his way with her battered body.

And for what? For truth and justice? For good to triumph over evil? Laughable.

Existential questions welled up often from deep in her consciousness, more bitter each time. Justice was a farce. She worked for fools and charlatans.

But she couldn't stop. Trouble had a way of finding her. New bastards presented themselves to her with frightening regularity. And once on her radar, she didn't have it in her constitution to simply look away, to leave them for someone else to handle.

Because they would mishandle it. And the bastard would walk. And that conjured in her the image of her helpless little self, cowering under the hard glare of the biggest bastard she'd ever met, powerless to give him what he deserved and restrained from hurting him by the invisible bonds of a twisted love-hate thing.

To hell with all of them, she thought. Finding and stopping the bastards would be somebody else's problem for a change.

She bounced her knee, restless, wrestling.

Then she decided. She was going to ask for a transfer out of field work. She'd had enough, had given enough. The costs were just too high.

She would ask for an administrative job, put up with

bureaucrats and senseless meetings for a few years, then put in for early retirement.

They'd travel. She'd give Brock random and deeply satisfying head when he least expected it. She'd maybe have children with him.

Maybe.

After she exorcised a few more personal demons.

But it would all have to wait.

Mark Severn's death deserved the department's full attention, and she resolved to set her weariness aside and go about her business with dignity and respect.

Then take a vacation.

Then quit.

She looked at her watch. 3:45 pm DC time. Six hours to Brussels, and with the time change it would be 4:50 am by the time she got out of the noisy aluminum tube. Then a two-hour layover, followed by a two-hour flight to Budapest.

Restlessness struck. She got up and walked to the lavatory as much out of a need to move as a need to pee. She chose the far lavatory, the one in the middle of the plane, to afford more time out of her seat. She took her time strolling up the long, narrow aisle, watching with idle amusement as heads bobbed and shifted in unison with the mild turbulence.

She looked at her face in the bathroom mirror. Tired. Older than she wanted to look. Younger than she felt. Red hair and green eyes still blazed back at her. Still the spark of life, still the slightly defiant arch of her eyebrow. Time to figure out what you want to do with your life, she thought.

Business completed, she wandered back down the aisle toward row forty, still contemplating fate and future.

She was miles away when a familiar feeling brought her instantly back to the present.

An uncomfortable feeling.

Eyes.

Someone was looking at her. Studying. Evaluating. It was a sixth sense she had developed over years in the field. It had saved her life countless times. Her adrenal glands were already at work before her eyes darted to her right.

A man. Professional but not very. His eyes lingered on her, even as hers bored through him. A seasoned pro would have smiled, played it off, even come on to her. Maybe even looked down at her figure with a smile. Anything to hide the operational assessment going on behind the eyes.

This guy wasn't that smooth, but he was definitely on the job. His cheekbones were high and Slavic, mouth slightly too small, eyes tilted slightly upwards at the outer edge, containing an operator's interest and an American-style knowingness despite the decidedly foreign heritage.

All of this Sam gathered in an instant.

Then just as quickly she smiled, affecting a look as if she might say something, as if she might have known the man, like maybe they had met somewhere before.

Then she pretended to think better of it, turned her head, and continued onward.

She noted the man's seat number as she walked past. 32A.

She found her seat. As she turned around, she took an extra second to survey the passengers. Tails traveled in pairs. At least, the serious ones did. Sam wondered where the other guy might be lurking.

A few more questions popped to mind, the kind that were hard to answer while trapped on an airplane, smelling-distance away from three hundred other people.

She looked again at her watch. Still six hours to go, minus three minutes. A long flight just got infinitely longer.

* * *

She tried to sleep. Nothing doing. Her body needed it badly, but the sardine-like accommodations and the compulsion to survey her surroundings kept her awake.

As was often the case during air travel, the hours passed like months. She took notes on the Severn case to stay occupied. The captain's cool-guy voice finally announced their impending arrival in Brussels.

Four millennia later, the airplane came to a stop at the gate. The seatbelt sign went off, causing nearly everyone on the plane to stand up simultaneously.

Sam couldn't see the guy in 32A. He was eight rows in front of her. Might as well have been eight miles.

When she walked up the ramp and onto the concourse, he was nowhere to be found. She found a quiet corner to pretend to check her messages while scanning the crowd for any hint of him.

No luck.

Maybe he was more professional than she gave him credit for.

Maybe she should figure out what the hell was going on.

She took out her government-issued Blackberry. She hardly ever saw Blackberries anymore, except in the hands of US government employees, which made Sam wonder whether the company was being propped up for political reasons.

She did the time-zone math, grimaced, then auto-dialed a number she'd called a thousand times before. It belonged to Dan Gable, the most capable deputy a girl could wish for. It was a quarter to eleven in DC, and she knew he'd be awake.

"I thought I was rid of you for a few days," Dan said instead of hello. A squealing baby was surprisingly loud in Sam's ear.

"I wasn't going to call you at this hour, but then I did," she said.

"No worries. I was just contemplating jumping out the window."

"You make fatherhood sound so dreamy."

"Who's dreaming? That requires sleep."

Sam laughed. Her relationship with her second-in-charge was easy and informal. Strictly business — no overtones or undertones — and Dan was as competent as they came. He was one of two men she trusted, and the only other human at the Department of Homeland Security with whom she'd entrust her life.

To call him a lifesaver was a gross understatement. He'd helped her through countless impossible situations.

And he had brought her back from the dead.

Dan had arrived too late to save her from the madman, but early enough to bring her back to life. He had pumped her heart for her, and breathed life back into her lungs, while Brock watched broken and helpless. The doctors had made clear to her that she owed her continued existence to Dan Gable.

He was five-eight, two inches shorter than Sam, built a little bit like a bowling ball but with very little fat, with thick, beefy arms and stubby fingers that pecked away at a computer keyboard with the best of them.

Dan was beyond competent in the field — rock-steady aim, rock-steady disposition — but his real value was in his otherworldly mastery of espionage via computer. There were very few who could hold a candle to him, and it was those skills that Sam intended to invoke.

"Please give my apologies to Sarah for calling so late," Sam said.

"I would, but it wouldn't do any good."

"Still mad?"

"Perpetually. Mostly at me."

"This shouldn't take too long. It should leave plenty of time to kiss and make up."

"Lay it on me."

"I made a new friend this evening. Bulky guy, Slavic bones, definitely watching me."

"Sure he didn't want to ask you on a date?"

Sam chuckled. "No. He was unmistakably on the job."

"I thought this was supposed to be a milk run, followed by a week's vacation."

"Me too."

"But you do have a long list of people pissed off at you," Dan said helpfully.

"Thanks. I didn't feel exposed enough already. Seat 32A, on Brussels Airlines flight 1850."

"Got it," Dan said. "Do you know who Brussels code-shares with? It'll make the hacking a little easier."

"United Airlines."

"Great. Shouldn't take long. Call you when I have something."

Sam thanked him and signed off.

For the first time in a long time, she wanted a drink.

It was a strange sensation, with a few years of sobriety behind her. She fought the urge, of course. That was one genie she could never let back out of the bottle.

Chapter 4

Nero Jefferson Chiligiris assessed his situation. He'd been arrested by some kind of a SWAT team, bound in chains, and flown to a detention center on the outskirts of Denver.

He had no idea how long ago that had been. They'd confiscated his watch, along with his wallet, shoelaces, and belt, and put him in a windowless holding cell.

It wasn't like a prison cell. There were no bars. It was just a six-by-eight room, no bigger than a broom closet, with concrete walls and a chair and a fluorescent light overhead that hummed and buzzed. There was no switch in the cell, and the light stayed on the whole time. Nero was certain there was a camera in the light fixture as well, keeping tabs on him.

He still had no idea why they'd taken him. Nobody had said a word about it, and all of his questions went unanswered. "You'll find out in due time, Mr. Chiligiris," one of the men in black had said.

Which had Nero thinking. Sure, he didn't work for a great guy. Even the name was a little bit off-putting. Money. Like, I'm The Man. Arrogant to go with it, and a pretty dangerous temper.

Not that Nero had ever given Money cause to lose his temper. Nero was a model employee. He never skimmed, never peeked, never asked questions, never moonlighted, never screwed up. Nero was pretty much a perfect hire for a guy like Money.

And Nero was a model citizen. Family man. Even had a minivan. He hadn't knowingly dabbled on the sketchy side of the line for eons.

So the current mess had to be on Money.

And Nero's recent rationalization to Penny, who was concerned that Nero couldn't really describe what business Money was in, felt a little bit silly in light of his new circumstances. "Maybe Money's not doing anything illegal at all," he'd said. "Maybe he just doesn't trust bankers and guards. Maybe he just likes to do security his own way."

"And maybe I'm Miss America," Penny had said.

And maybe she was right about Money, the way she was right about almost everything.

Not like him. He was a little bit too stubborn. You could always tell Nero, his mom used to say, but you couldn't tell him much. Good advice usually didn't stick except in hindsight.

This was one of those hindsight-type situations, Nero figured. He alternately cursed his deliberate naiveté, then defended the Money decision by asking himself rhetorically where else he could possibly have found a job that paid enough to keep a roof over their heads.

Anyway, how the hell did they find him? He left his cell phone at home — a serious risk, given that there were no pay phones around for an emergency — and he drove a shitty 1990's car without any GPS tracking on it. Just like Money insisted on. He had no pager. He didn't even use a burner phone. He didn't use a credit card, ever. Way too easy for people to track your movements and stake out your regular haunts. He didn't have anything to hide, but you couldn't be too careful.

He was as clean as clean could be, yet they'd swooped in on him almost as soon as the transaction took place.

Could they have tracked the other guy, the one who showed up to exchange duffel bags near the Kansas border? Definitely a possibility. They arrested that guy, too, but it could have just been for show, to protect the other courier's identity as a stooge. You could never rule anything out.

Still, it seemed weird. He had taken so many precautions to keep his nose as clean as possible, to make himself as hard to track as possible.

Could it be some tax thing? He was a W-9 employee, which meant he had to hire a guy for an arm and a leg to figure out all the wherefores and therefores. And there might be a few stacks of bills — cash bonuses for jobs done well and with minimum fuss — that Nero might have neglected to mention to the IRS.

But the cash was in coffee cans, in holes, often on public land, with nothing but GPS coordinates to point the way, which were themselves on a yellow sticky in a safe deposit box, all of which would have required The Man to have a serious burr up his ass to go after.

And seriously, what did the IRS care about fifty grand? It probably cost that much to send the helicopter team after him.

Besides, wouldn't they need a warrant for all of that, anyway?

And why hadn't they read him his rights?

Which brought him back to where he started: where am I, and why the hell am I here?

The door opened, breaking the unproductive mental loop in Nero's head.

In walked a Special Agent America looking guy. Big barrel chest, veins like a geography map carved in bulging forearms, thick neck, short haircut, 9mm sidearm strapped to his trim waist, clipboard clenched in a beefy paw.

Nero saw a second guy positioned just outside the door. The two agents could have been twins.

Nero stood up. He wanted to be polite. He wanted to be helpful, and get to the bottom of things, and demonstrate that he didn't know the first thing about anything that any law enforcement-types might be interested in.

"Mr. Chiligiris," Special Agent America said. "Please have a seat."

Nero sat back down on the chair.

"Do you know why you're here, Mr. Chiligiris?"

"No, sir. I was hoping you could tell me."

America looked disappointed. "Cooperation is always best, Mr. Chiligiris."

Nero nodded. "Trust me, sir, I'm willing to cooperate. I got a job and a wife and kids to get home to."

"You're married?"

Nero blushed a little bit. "Well, not technically, but me and Penny have been together for years."

America made a note on the clipboard.

"You're a convict, Mr. Chiligiris."

Nero bristled. "Ex-con. I'm past all that now. Like I said, I got a family. Responsibilities. Can I call home?"

"Do you know why you're here?" America repeated.

"Like I said, sir, I was really hoping you could clarify that for me. And maybe you could tell me where I am, while you're at it."

America eyed Nero. The agent's jaw muscles worked. His eyes seemed preternaturally clear. Hard. It had a spooky effect.

"You're in Denver," America said. "In a holding facility belonging to the Department of Homeland Security."

"Can you tell me why I'm here?"

"What do you think, Mr. Chiligiris?"

"What do *I* think? I think I'd like to know how I can help you, so I can get out of here and go home. Has anyone called Penny, let her know I'm OK?"

"No calls have been made on your behalf, Mr. Chiligiris."

"Can I call her, please?"

America shook his head. "Not at this time."

"Am I arrested? Are you charging me with something?"

"You are not under arrest."

"So you're releasing me?"

"No. Your present status is as a detainee."

"Detainee? What the hell is that?"

"Don't raise your voice, Mr. Chiligiris."

"Don't you have to read me my rights? And what about that Habeas Corpse thing?"

"Corpus."

"What?"

"*Corpus*," America said. "It's Habeas *Corpus.* Your right to be brought before a judge and formally charged."

"Exactly! That's what I mean. What are you charging me with?"

America wrote on his clipboard. "Mr. Chiligiris, The USA Patriot Act and the Military Commissions Act set aside Habeas Corpus in cases like this one."

"Case? You have a case against me?"

America shook his head. "Not like you're thinking. Not with clerks and lawyers and a judge."

"Then what?"

America clicked his pen, lowered his clipboard, bored through Nero with those freakishly clear eyes for another long moment.

He rose. "Mr. Chiligiris, you are being detained on suspicion of conspiracy to commit acts of terror against the United States of America."

Nero's jaw dropped.

"You're insane."

"I'm afraid not, Mr. Chiligiris."

"You're absolutely out of your mind."

America shook his head. "Not in the slightest," he said. He rapped on the door. The latch clacked. The door opened. America turned to leave.

Nero rocketed out of his chair. "What the hell? I'm a US citizen! I'm clean! I have rights! I want a goddamned lawyer!"

A giant fist shoved Nero back into the seat. A small smile

crossed America's face. "You're not getting it, Mr. Chiligiris. Involving yourself with terrorists takes you off the citizen list. We take the gloves off for cases like yours."

America left. The door slammed shut in his wake.

Nero trembled with fear and rage. His hands balled into fists. He rose, paced, cursed.

He smacked the wall with his hand. Timidly at first, then again with more force.

Then a flurry of fists, flying with an irrational, helpless abandon. He pounded the walls, hands numbing with pain, a howl leaving his throat, like a caged animal.

He collapsed back into the chair.

"I'm fucking innocent."

He was certain no one heard him.

Chapter 5

Sam found a seat at a bistro in the Brussels airport. She fired up her government laptop, a big black paperweight sold by Dell, and it began its lengthy startup sequence. The space shuttle booted up faster than that damn thing. She watched the spinning blue wheel with growing impatience.

Maybe the desk job wasn't a great idea.

Despite a queasy feeling in her stomach, she ordered breakfast. Eggs, bacon, vegetables, and coffee.

She switched her iPhone back on after its long in-flight slumber. It woke up, then ting-tinged with a message from Brock: "Just bought my tickets (ouch!). Can't wait to see you on Saturday!"

She smiled. She was beyond ready to climb on top of her man and ride him until they were both spent. All work and no play was bad policy, and it was catching up with her. She and Brock badly needed some time away together, to rediscover and revel in their ferocious mutual need, to reconnect with their primal humanity. They were going to get reacquainted in Budapest, no less, one of Europe's most gorgeous cities. It was going to be a glorious week.

Her food arrived about the time her government laptop finished its boot sequence. She ate while she wrestled with the airport Wi-Fi connection.

She had finished her meal by the time she'd established a remote connection to the Homeland server. Email slowly stacked up in her inbox. Cortisol built in her body as she read the subject lines and senders.

Sexual assault awareness training. Mandatory, of course.

Computer security procedures training. Overdue. The IT admin threatened account suspension unless she got her act together.

Performance summaries on Dan Gable and two other direct reports needed revisions. Due next week.

A thunderstorm warning. Sam chuckled at the ridiculousness of an emailed weather warning.

And a note from Tom Davenport. It had a red exclamation point next to his name. Sent with high importance. The subject line just said *Urgent.*

Tom hadn't been her boss for more than a month or two, but already there was tension. Tom replaced Francis Ekman, who ate a bullet in Caracas. Ekman's only crime was an unreasonable crush on his subordinate, and maybe a little too little operational savvy to stay alive in a hostile environment. Self-critiquing on both counts. Sam had once been discovered by her boyfriend with her boss's love-lever buried to the hilt someplace the boyfriend felt was exclusive territory. That was back when she was drinking. Years of sobriety hadn't dulled that particular lesson, and she no longer played where she worked. Plus, Ekman wasn't her type. Too much milquetoast in him for Sam's liking.

Tom Davenport was a different animal altogether. Political down to his very mitochondria. Tom made no decisions. He merely relayed news up and down. You couldn't be fired if you were never wrong, and you'd never be wrong if you never decided anything.

Plus, he was a true believer. Those were dangerous people. They did what they were told, even when what they were told made no sense, and even when it could get people killed.

Against her better judgment, Sam opened Tom Davenport's note.

Special Agent Jameson,

I'm afraid I have some bad news. I'm sorry to have to tell you that Deputy Director Farrar has canceled your leave. He has a priority eyes-only tasking for you. Please book a return flight as soon as the Mark Severn fatality case permits.

I'm sorry, Sam. Nothing I could do about this one.

Sam read it three times. By the third trip through the message, the words had become difficult to see. Tears welled. Her hands trembled. This kind of thing happened all the time in her line of work, but it somehow felt different, more injurious, more painful, more costly this time.

Why her? Why now? Why the sudden emergency? There were floors full of idle DHS agents. None of them would fill the bill?

It felt personal, like a betrayal, like she was being jerked around. Sam hated being jerked around.

Even if her bosses had a good reason, it wouldn't be good enough.

She hammered out a reply that began with the words "Are you

out of your damn mind?"

Then she reconsidered, erased, retyped.

"I quit."

Reconsidered again. Erased again. Hovered over the keys, fingers flexing into fists, hands still shaking with rage.

She deleted her reply and slammed the laptop shut with far more force than necessary. Heads turned at adjacent tables, but Sam didn't notice.

She considered calling Brock. She considered pretending not to have read the message. She considered turning around and going home. She considered tendering her resignation.

Her flight to Budapest was announced. She walked on wooden legs to her gate, phone in hand, Brock's number called up, hovering over the call button.

Then she found Davenport's number. She stopped short of dialing.

She took a deep breath. She needed to calm down before she talked to anyone important in her life, she decided. The phone went into her purse.

Sam stood in line to board the sardine can. She stared straight ahead, lost in her conundrum, mind whirring through alternatives and alternate realities.

Her turn came. She handed her boarding pass to the attendant. She barely managed a smile as the attendant wished her a nice flight, as if such a thing were possible.

She was committing a cardinal trade craft sin, Sam knew. Being knotted up in your own private drama was a great way to miss important things. A great way to get hurt, maybe. But she lacked the energy or inclination to keep her senses sharp.

She found her seat, closed her eyes, and tried to relax.

Chapter 6

Sam calmed down to a slow smolder during her flight. She began thinking clearly enough to formulate a plan.

Direct confrontation was usually her style, but she had long ago discovered the hard way that direct confrontation via email usually backfired.

So Sam decided to passively resist. She decided that the Mark Severn thing would probably develop unforeseen complications requiring her extended presence in the picturesque European gem of a city. Brock's presence alongside her would remain their little secret. What the douchebag desk-weights in her chain of command didn't know wouldn't hurt them.

But forewarned was forearmed. She availed herself of the in-flight Wi-Fi, courtesy of her government credit card, to start a static-laced voice-over-internet conversation with Dan Gable.

It was just before midnight DC time. The first sound Sam heard as Dan answered was of a screaming child. Her hunch was right: the youngest, who'd been inflicting a vicious case of colic on Dan and Sarah for the better part of a month, had kept everyone in the Gable household awake yet again.

"Sorry to bug you again," Sam said.

"Don't worry, you'll see it on my time card."

"Reminds me, I need to sign yours."

"It would be nice. They're going to turn off our power."

"Burn your furniture for light and heat."

"You're a solutions-minded boss. I'll be sure to include that on my employee satisfaction survey this year."

"I need a secretary to keep all this crap straight," Sam said.

"Or you could use a calendar. Works for seven billion other people."

"I'll take it under advisement. Anyway, I just got the long-distance bend-over from Farrar and Davenport. Leave canceled, come home ASAP, eyes-only case, blah blah. Have you heard anything about this?"

Dan laughed. "By definition, 'eyes-only' means I haven't. Isn't that the point?"

"But you hear things. And you're a network administrator."

"What are you suggesting?"

"Nothing. I was just hoping you'd know something."

"So this is really a deniable request for me to dig around?"

"I'll deny that if anybody asks."

"I'll see what I can do."

"I don't know what you're talking about. And did you learn anything about the asshole in 32A on the Brussels flight?"

"Yes. The asshole's name is Gertrude Annalise LeJeune. She's a sixty-four-year-old grandmother from Verviers, Belgium."

Sam shook her head, lips pursed in frustration. "He switched seats."

"Or you're hallucinating."

"Or that," Sam said.

The seat belt sign illuminated, and the "sit down, shut up, and strap in" speech ensued over the PA system, delivered much more politely than Sam was used to hearing on American carriers. Mutually-assured bankruptcy evidently hadn't yet taken hold of the European airline industry as it had in the States.

"Thanks, Dan," she said after the announcement ended. "And maybe try some Jack Daniels."

"What?"

"For the colic. I hear it works wonders."

"That's barbaric," Dan said.

"I meant for you. I don't know how to help the baby."

* * *

The plane broke through the European undercast on its approach to Budapest. Sam's window seat on the west side of the jet afforded her a spectacular view of the Danube River and one of Europe's most spectacular cities, cast in an angelic sunrise glow.

Even from the air, there was a sense of permanence and significance about the place, all stone and gentility and gravitas, not like the endless miles of shitty strip malls and pop-up suburban houses she was used to seeing in her native land.

Maybe the Europeans had figured a few things out, she mused.

She strengthened her resolve to find a way to spend some quality time in Budapest.

The plane landed and taxied to the gate. As the flight crew prepared to open the door, Sam let go of vacation thoughts and prepared herself. She was pretty sure that she had been under surveillance on her earlier flight. There was no reason to believe she wouldn't be surveilled in Budapest as well.

She wasn't wrong. She disembarked, a weary expression on her face that was only partially feigned, and casually scanned the crowd gathered at the gate.

She saw him.

32A.

Looking right at her, with intent in his eyes. He looked away, but much too slowly.

Sam's pulse pounded. She felt adrenaline hit her stomach.

The familiar rush overtook her, the sensation of danger, of cold reality, of heightened stakes. It was clarifying and terrifying and intoxicating all at once. She felt absolutely, outrageously *alive*.

Her instincts kicked in.

She was utterly alone in a foreign city. Someone else's home turf. She had a gun in her purse, but they — whoever *they* happened to be — had home field advantage. And they also had an information advantage. 32A couldn't have been following her unless he had a serious jump on her. She'd received her tickets just a couple of hours before departure. How had they known her travel plans before she did?

Outnumbered and playing the away game. That really only left one arrow in her quiver: surprise.

Sam walked up to 32A, stuck out her hand, and said in a loud voice, "It's great to see you again! I thought that was you on the earlier flight, but now I'm positive. How have you been?"

32A looked bewildered, flustered. His eyes darted forty-five degrees to his left. Sam took note. Undoubtedly the man's backup. Her gambit had worked, and he was looking for help.

"I'm sorry," 32A said. "I don't believe we're acquainted." Thick Russian accent. Precisely the Eastern European overtones his obvious Slavic features would have suggested.

Again, Sam took note, yet didn't pause a beat. She put her hand to her mouth, feigning a loud, embarrassed laugh. She tossed her head back, turning as she did so to find 32A's partner.

Female. Unusual, but not unheard of. Brown hair, high cheeks, dark eyes. Gorgeous. Started fishing in her purse for something, almost quickly enough to avoid Sam's notice. Almost.

The slender brunette also had that operational vibe about her. A hardness, a precision in the way her eyes moved, a quickness and intelligence that took even more years to hide than it did to develop.

Sam repeated her apologies to 32A, let her phony but genuine-sounding laugh ring a few seconds longer for effect, and made her way to the airport exit. She walked quickly. She donned a pair of oversized sunglasses, her eyes never resting as she walked, scanning left and right, checking for nothing in particular except that one particular thing that would give away another operative.

She glimpsed the throng at baggage claim and made the difficult decision to abandon her suitcase full of sundries and lingerie. It wasn't smart to wait for baggage in a foreign city with operatives sniffing around, Sam decided. Maybe waiting would be harmless. But maybe not. And mistakes were often lethal. She shook her head, but brightened at the prospect of a shopping trip with Brock to replenish her supply of sweet nothings.

As she approached the taxi stand, her pulse quickened again. Changing transportation modes was always a terribly dangerous time.

She reached into her ridiculously expensive Prada handbag, felt the comforting heft of her .45 semi auto, and thumbed off the safety lever. She had one in the chamber and seven more in the clip. Eight more in her spare magazine, tucked into her purse's side pocket.

Enough heavy metal for serious head-banging, if it came to that.

Welcome to Budapest.

Was this some sort of cold war hangover? She was manifested as a Homeland agent, so it wasn't unheard of that the Hungarian government might put a set of eyeballs on her. Uncle Sugar wasn't as well-loved across the globe as he thought he was.

That might explain the surveillance in Budapest. But it sure as hell wouldn't explain the tail on her flight from DC to Brussels. The tickets had been bought just a few hours earlier.

Her turn came in the cab line. She gripped her .45 inside her purse as she settled into the backseat of the cab. "Rendőrkapitányságok," she said to the driver, foisting on him what was undoubtedly horrid Hungarian.

The driver raised his eyebrows.

Sam repeated her request, altering her pronunciation slightly.

"I understood you the first time," the cabbie said in nearly perfect English. "But I thought you were a little crazy. Nobody goes there unless they absolutely have to."

Sam smiled. "I absolutely have to."

The cabbie shrugged. "Police headquarters it is." He pulled out of the cab line and joined the rush of traffic leaving the terminal. "It's not every day I'm asked to drive there," he said, eyeballing Sam's cleavage in the mirror. "And most days I alter my route to stay away." He had a toothy smile and a smoky chuckle.

"Sounds like smart policy," Sam said. She smiled politely, hand on her pistol, heart rate settling down a little, senses still on full alert.

It definitely felt like game time.

But who were the players? And what game were they playing?

She felt that familiar, inexorable pull, away from normalcy and safety and routine and into the abyss of an evolving situation, exactly opposite the direction she'd resolved to move her life.

She took a deep breath. She was definitely along for the ride.

Chapter 7

The cell door opened. Nero awoke with a start. He was momentarily disoriented, then reality descended with a brutal weight.

This time, it wasn't Special Agent America. It was a lackey. Some slovenly looking guard with a weak chin and a spare tire around his midsection. His face looked mean and stupid. Nero knew the type well. What did losers do when they wanted to feel permanently superior? They became prison guards. The recognition brought back a long-dormant dread and loathing in his gut.

"Get up, Chiligiris," the guard said.

Nero didn't. "I want a lawyer."

"It's three in the morning, tough guy."

"I don't care what time it is. I demand to speak to an attorney."

"You're not really in a position to make demands," the guard said with a smirk.

A second guard walked in with chains. "We're taking a little trip. You're not going to be a problem this morning, are you?"

"Where are you taking me?"

"Stand up, Chiligiris. Hands out in front, fingers open, palms up."

Nero knew the warning signs of a guard about to flex muscle.

Or flab, as the case may have been. He complied.

The guards shuffled him out of the cell and down the long, blank hallway.

The chains were a visceral reminder of his prison years. His feet were chained together, forcing him to walk in unnatural, halting steps. His arms were bound to his feet, preventing him from raising them above his waist.

Bile rose within him. He had vowed never to put himself in this kind of situation again. He had kept his nose clean. He hadn't hurt anybody.

He was wicked angry, but he kept his composure. Resistance would have been ill-conceived and ill-advised. And it would have put him on the wrong side of karma.

They led him out a set of double doors onto a loading dock. A white prison transport truck awaited, rear doors open and tailgate backed up to the loading dock. "Watch your head," the guard said.

Nero ducked into the van. The benches ran the wrong way, forcing him to sit sideways. The air was still and stuffy. "Buckle up," the guard instructed.

The van doors shut. The engine started, a new diesel, much more power than the van needed, but it was public money so why the hell not.

The driver lurched the van forward, jerking Nero sideways. "Easy, man," Nero said through the open window to the crew cab. "I get carsick."

The driver eyed him in the mirror. "Not in this van, you don't."

"I'm not messing. Turn that AC on or I'll be blowing chunks in five minutes."

The driver complied. Soon a blast of cool air dried the sweat on Nero's brow. "Thanks, man. Really appreciate it."

No reply.

"Where we going?"

No reply.

"Seriously, man. Where are you taking me?"

No reply.

The van jostled, turned, stopped, started again, accelerated, kept accelerating. On the highway now. I-25, by the looks of it. Heading south.

Nero settled his head against the side of the van. He closed his eyes, felt the hum of the road deep in his skull, tried to clear his mind of the fear and rage.

Penny. What must she be thinking?

* * *

When Nero awoke, the sun was up. The air conditioner blasted cold air. He shivered. He debated whether to ask the driver to lower the setting. He decided against it.

He heard the click of the turn signal, felt the van decelerate, felt it turn off of the highway. Colorado Springs, a sign said. Another sign advertised a police station, with an arrow pointing the way. The prison van turned to follow the arrow.

"Where are we going?" Nero asked again.

He got no answer.

The driver pulled around to the back of the police station and stopped the van. He turned to face Nero. "Place your hands on your lap, palms up, fingers extended. No sudden movements."

The back doors opened. Two more guards. One more prisoner, a thin, brown, Middle-Eastern-looking guy, maybe in his early twenties. The prisoner took a seat on the bench opposite and offset from Nero. He looked angry. Dangerous, even.

The doors slammed, and the driver put the van in gear. Moving again.

Nero looked at the young prisoner across from him. The man didn't make eye contact.

"You know where they're taking us?" Nero asked him. "They wouldn't tell me anything."

"Florence," the man said.

"Where?"

The Arab man looked at him. "Supermax. In Florence."

"The federal joint?"

A nod.

"You serious, man? The big house, with no trial?"

The young prisoner sneered. "Trial? This is America, bro. You're the wrong color for a trial."

Nero didn't know what to make of the statement. "Seriously, do you know what's going on?"

"We're being taken to the federal maximum security facility in Florence, awaiting the disposition of our cases." The young Arab made air quotes around disposition and cases. His chains rattled as he put his arms back in his lap.

"You been charged?" Nero asked.

A derisive laugh. "Charged? With being a sand nigger in a white man's land, maybe."

"Seriously, what did they get you for?" Nero asked.

The young man shook his head. "Skin color, man. Serious as a heart attack. Me and a few other guys from my mosque."

"You have a mosque?"

"I go to a mosque."

"I didn't know how it worked," Nero said.

"Infidel."

Nero arched his eyes.

The young man laughed. "I'm just kidding, man. I'm not a radical. I'm a college student. Engineering. I happen to be Muslim. I don't have any ties to the Middle East. I was born here. But nobody listens."

"There's a lot of that going around," Nero said. "What's your name?"

"Robert." A strange name for a Muslim man, Nero thought. But then again, what did he know about Muslim men?

Nero offered his name and his hand.

The young man shook it, their chains making the gesture awkward.

A few more miles passed. No words passed between them. Then Nero's curiosity got the better of him. "How'd they nab you?"

The young man snorted and shook his head. "Like some kind of a movie, man. I was out running. I'm training for a marathon. It was a long run, fifteen miles. I was way out in the middle of nowhere. I like to clear my head sometimes, just get out on the trail, no cars around, no phone, no civilization."

Nero nodded.

"I had to have been three miles from the nearest person," Robert went on. "Just got to the top of a big hill."

"Let me guess," Nero said. "Helicopters."

Robert nodded. "I really thought I was going to piss myself," he said. "I mean, they scared the living shit out of me. Completely out of nowhere, and then they were right on top of me."

Nero nodded. He knew the feeling.

"I thought it had to be a misunderstanding. I figured it would get straightened out, and I'd have a good story to tell." Robert shook his head. "But that was three days ago. No lawyer, no charges, no nothing. Not even a phone call."

Chapter 8

It was a glorious late summer day. Sam's taxi drove northwest from the Budapest airport on Highway 4. The driver had his window down. Sam could smell the water of the Danube, off to the west. Budapest was split into two halves and two personalities by the ancient river. She was on the flat side of town, the eastern side, driving northwest into the center of the city.

The cab driver seemed to sense her state of mind, as the good ones did, and gave her space. None of the obvious questions, none of the hackneyed banalities. Just A to B, with a fresh breeze and a view to die for.

She was thinking about how nice it would be to take a week off. Or maybe how nice it would have been. She wasn't quite certain how things would play out, but the sight of Budapest at street level strengthened her resolve to spend some quality time, taking it slow and deep with Brock.

Work felt distant. The immediacy of the surveillance team she spotted at the airport seemed to fade into the slow pace of the city. It wasn't a terribly slow pace, but almost anything was more relaxed than the DC grind.

Her government Blackberry buzzed. A text from Tom Davenport. "Did you get my email?" Her stomach churned, her jaw clenched, and she flexed her hand in and out of a fist.

But she didn't reply.

She looked at her watch. Midnight in DC. Somebody clearly had Davenport hopping. The sackless bastard was probably dancing for a good performance report.

The Budapest Central police station was a round building situated several blocks east of the river, with a huge spire on top, with platforms at various intervals on the way up to the top, almost like guard stations. Sam had no idea how old the building was, but she envisioned counterrevolutionary Stalinist hard-liners with sniper rifles picking off agitators from atop the minaret-like structure during the ill-fated revolution in the fifties.

She got out at the police station, walked briskly but unhurriedly through the first set of double doors, and waited between doorways for a couple of minutes, hiding in glare and shadow while watching for a tail, pretending to check her phone. She didn't spot anything unusual.

She went through the second set of double doors and announced herself at the front desk. She made her best attempt at greeting the desk sergeant in Hungarian. He smiled benignly at her accent and said hello in English.

"Special Agent Mark Severn of the US Department of Homeland Security died in an accident here yesterday," Sam said. "I'm told there's some paperwork I need to take care of?"

"Of course. Right this way." The desk sergeant led her through a grandiose entry hall into a cubicle farm. It looked like a standard office warren, though somehow more Byzantine.

Through no visible means of navigation, the desk sergeant guided them to a particular cubby. In the cubicle sat a short man with glasses. The man looked the way clerks looked all over the world. Bookish, glasses drooping down his nose, annoyed at the interruption. "Yes. Come," the clerk said.

The desk sergeant took his leave, and Sam followed the small, slight clerk deeper into the bowels of the headquarters building.

They walked out of the cube farm and into an elevator lobby. The clerk pushed the down button. Sam found that strange, because they were on the first floor already. As they waited for the elevator, Sam noticed a stairway door to their immediate left. Half a minute later, the elevator arrived. They rode down one floor to the basement. The doors took forever to open. Sam shook her head. Walking would have been faster by a factor of twenty. The clerk must have been paid by the hour, she decided.

The bookish little man led her down a dank hallway. It smelled like stagnant water and extremely old paper. He unlocked a door off the main hallway, held it open for her, and motioned toward a wall of lockboxes, not unlike the inside of a bank vault.

The clerk produced a key and pulled open one of the lockers, then unceremoniously dumped its contents onto the table.

A wallet. A service pistol, a government-issue 9mm Beretta. A fine weapon. Never fired in anger. Sam would have heard about it otherwise. Along with Severn's DHS badge, which looked very official, the weapon was the reason the police station had ahold of Severn's belongings, rather than the hospital where his body was taken after the accident.

Severn's wallet, government-issue Blackberry, and personal iPhone were also in the pile of belongings. A hotel key, a receipt for lunch with two entrees and two sörök — beers — among the charged items, a rental car key, and three condoms rounded out the pile.

Two beers, two entrees. Three condoms. Sam wondered whether a little pleasure might have found its way into Mark Severn's business trip. He was single, employed, a musician, and attractive, after all, and Hungarian women were notoriously aggressive.

Maybe he died happy, she thought.

"This everything?" she asked, placing the belongings in a bag provided by the clerk.

He nodded. "Everything left," he said.

Sam cocked her head. "Everything *left?*"

"Igen." Yes. "Everything the other agent did not take."

"Other agent?"

"Igen. From America Homelands Department. Just like you. Only man. Tall. Blue eyes. Very strong." The clerk made fists and flexed his little clerk arms for emphasis.

Sam knew no one at Homeland matching that description. But Homeland was a giant organization. "Do you remember his name?"

"Nem." No. "I ask don't." The clerk's English wasn't nearly as proficient as the desk sergeant's, but Sam was following along okay.

"Did you get a look at his badge? Did it look like this one?" She flashed tin.

The clerk shrugged. "I don't check badge. Door man check badge."

Sam's brow furrowed. She ran through the timeline. She was dispatched to Hungary within hours of Mark Severn's death. By law and by convention, Homeland agents weren't stationed abroad. And she was completely unaware of anyone else having been detached to clean up the paperwork. So it made no sense for another Homeland agent to have asked after Severn's belongings.

And why the hell would they have flown her all the way to Hungary if there was already someone else available to take care of things? Homeland was big and slow and stupid, as far as bureaucracies went, but that would have been a new low.

She shook her head. There wasn't any angle that made a great deal of sense to her.

She looked back at the clerk. "When was this man here?"

"Yesterday. Later. Almost dark."

The same day Severn was killed.

"You said he took something when he left?"

"Backpack. It had papers. In a…" He searched for the English word. "File," he said, a proud look on his face. "Big man take blue backpack with file."

"Did he sign for it?" Sam made a writing motion with her hand.

"Of course." The clerk produced the ledger. An unintelligible scrawl adorned the line beneath the clerk's thumb.

"Did he say anything? Where he was going, who he was meeting?"

"Nem. He say no words. He make no smile." The clerk donned a demonstrative scowl. "He just take backpack. He say someone else come for rest."

* * *

Sam emerged from police headquarters into the sunlight, Mark Severn's earthly possessions in a satchel under her arm, minus his hotel key, which she examined closely. Room 327 at the Hotel Danubius Gellért.

She hailed a cab, eyes darting behind dark sunglasses to check for any signs of a tail. Nothing out of the ordinary, but she gripped her Kimber inside her purse just the same.

The cabbie nodded wordlessly at her destination and pulled abruptly into the flow of traffic. A perfunctory honk expressed mild displeasure, and the cabbie waved a halfhearted apology.

Sam took a deep breath. She couldn't put it off any longer. She called Tom Davenport.

It was one in the morning in DC, which explained Sam's bleary-eyed exhaustion despite the brilliant midmorning sunshine, but Davenport sounded wide awake. "You need to get back on a plane, Sam," Davenport said after muted pleasantries.

"I just got off a plane, Tom."

"I'm sorry about that. This one is well above my pay grade."

"Someone else was here already, Tom. Do you know who?"

"Someone from the US?"

"From Homeland."

"Why would we send you to Hungary if there was already someone there?"

"The same question occurred to me. And why would he take a backpack full of files, and nothing else?"

Silence. "Sam, please come home. The deputy director was pretty adamant that you be the one to work this case."

"What case?"

"I can't tell you over an open line. You know that."

"You don't spend two thousand dollars to fly me over here just to fly me back again the same day. Tell me what's going on, Tom."

"You'll get it all when you get home."

"All of what?"

Silence.

"Why was I followed?"

Davenport was taken aback. "You think you were followed?"

"Yes. I *think* that because I *was* followed. Starting with my flight from Reagan."

"Jesus, Sam, that sounds a little…"

"A little what, Tom?" Sam thought she might've sounded a bit truculent, but she didn't care.

"I mean, are you sure you're not overtired?"

Sam snorted. "I'm definitely overtired, Tom. But I know a goddamned tail team when I see one. Twice. This is not my first week on the job, remember."

"So I'm told."

"A few answers wouldn't kill you. And they certainly wouldn't kill *me*."

"Listen, Sam, let me ask a few questions about what you just told me. Meantime, please go straight to the airport and buy a ticket home."

"I've been up for two days, Tom. No chance I can get a hotel and take a nap?"

"I'm sorry, Sam. Eyes-only, priority one, credible threat, Deputy Director Farrar with his mouth and ass-cheeks clenched shut. I don't have any latitude here."

"Did you ask for any?"

Silence.

"Thought so."

"You know how he is, Sam."

"I know how *you* are." Dickless yes-man, she didn't say. She shook her head. "Can you at least tell me what case Severn was working when he died?"

"I can't tell you over an open line."

"No hints?"

"You know better."

She shook her head, pursed her lips, thought a moment, looked at the hotel key.

"At least let me check out Severn's hotel room."

"I'm sorry, Sam."

"Great, thanks, Tom. I'll let you know what I find."

"I said no, Sa—"

She hung up. "Up yours, Tom," she said to no one as she threw her phone in her purse.

* * *

The Hotel Danubius Gellért sat on the west side of the river, the Buda side. The Szent Gellért Tér, a cobblestone lane barely wide enough for a car and a frightened bicyclist, sliced an arc around the hotel's entrance lawn. A glassed portico, its lines reminiscent of the

Roman arches that dotted the continent from a millennium before, shielded guests from frequent European rain showers.

Across the street and beyond a waist-high wall flowed the Danube, that dark, eternal, meandering causeway, witness to a million dreams, and maybe as many nightmares.

A slightly wider cobblestone lane led northwest, away from the river and up a gradually steepening hill. The buildings lining the street looked old, genteel, stately. Directly across the street from the hotel sat a street cafe with a view of the river.

Gorgeous. A universe away from DC. Sam felt an irresistible urge to stay.

"You will see the caves while you are here?" the taxi driver asked before pulling to a stop in front of the hotel portico.

"Caves?"

"Yes. Miles and miles. On the Buda side only. Hospitals, churches, bunkers, everything. All underground. Very interesting. Maybe you take a tour."

"Maybe I'll do that," Sam said.

"I will drive you there," the cabbie said.

Sam smiled at the enterprising driver. "That's very generous of you," she said. "But for now, would you mind waiting for me?"

The cabbie smiled and nodded. He gestured to the running meter. "Long as you like."

Sam entered the hotel lobby, smiled at the desk clerk, strode to the elevator, punched the up button, waited patiently, stepped in after the doors opened, pressed 3.

She disembarked on the third floor, which was nothing but

guest rooms. The decor wasn't new, but wasn't quite overdue for an overhaul, either. The carpet featured a rich pattern in mostly burgundy, slightly faded. Wainscoting adorned the walls, dividing antiqued paint and tasteful wallpaper.

It was a nice hotel. It was probably above the government's cost limit, which meant that Mark Severn was paying the difference out of pocket. He had probably wanted to make the most of the European trip, even if it bit into his personal budget a bit.

Sam found room 327.

Severn was ostensibly killed by a car. But the hair was standing up on the back of Sam's neck, so she took no chances. She examined the door for signs of forced entry.

She checked the hallway for passersby, drew her weapon, and opened the door.

She charged in, gun leveled, knees flexed, covering and clearing each potential hiding spot in the small room.

Nobody home.

She repeated the procedure for the small, cramped bathroom. Same result.

The room was empty. The bed was made, ready for the next inhabitant. The linens smelled fresh.

It was as if Mark Severn had never been there.

Or the fixers had already done their business. If so, there wouldn't be much point to what she was about to do, but she did it anyway.

Sam fished in her purse for her multi-spectral camera. It looked largely like any other digital camera, but it cost seventeen times as much, and it was bought by the government. She took a dozen photos of the empty room. Each time she snapped a photo, the camera captured visible, infrared, and ultraviolet information. The other spectra held information that visible light couldn't communicate. The technology wasn't without limitations, though. The information had to be processed by computer.

But she had a guy for that. She pulled the memory dongle out of the camera, clicked it into her phone, and emailed the photos to Dan Gable back at Homeland. She wasn't expecting Dan to find much, but she felt she owed it to Mark Severn to do the job right.

Sam used the fisheye lens in the door to survey the hallway before exiting the room, then walked briskly to the stairwell entrance. She figured any surveillance team worth its salt would have someone posted in the stairwell.

She saw neither hide nor hair. The stairway was empty all the way to the ground floor, where she exited through the door and walked to the front desk.

It was manned by a middle-aged lady still hanging on to illusions of beauty. Sam asked whether she'd seen Severn recently.

"Mr. Severn," the clerk said. "Very handsome. He was booked until Friday." Booked came out *boookt*. "But the maid asked me today if he had checked out. All his belongings were gone this morning."

"Everything?"

"Completely empty."

"No personal effects whatsoever?"

"Nothing."

"What time did the maid clean the room?"

The clerk shrugged. "Half eight, maybe?"

Sam nodded. "Guess his plans changed."

She thanked the clerk and walked outside toward her waiting cab.

But she got that feeling again. The hair stood up on the back of her neck. Like she was being watched.

She looked around as she walked toward the cab.

She saw an elderly couple walking toward the sidewalk cafe, arm in arm.

There were a few people in the outdoor bistro, all of them ignoring her.

Further south were two teenage boys, laughing.

And an old man walking a ridiculously small dog.

And an operator.

Middle-aged man. Oversized suit jacket. Probably armed. Sunglasses. Tight jaw. Watching her. *Evaluating* her. Forced nonchalance as he glanced back at his newspaper. Made a show of looking at his watch, then turned away and began walking, as if it were time for an appointment. He walked northwest. Uphill, away from the river. Toward the metro station.

Decision time.

She was outmanned and outmaneuvered on someone else's home turf. She had nothing going for her, and the conservative option would have been to retreat and regroup. No telling how many agents were on the surveillance team shadowing her, and no telling what they had in mind.

Sam didn't take the conservative option.

She threw a wad of bills at the taxi driver and hustled on foot up the hill after the man in the oversized jacket.

Chapter 9

David Swaringen took a deep breath. It was a big day.

His security clearance paperwork was finally finished. A messy divorce a few years back had ruined his credit. Bad credit meant you were potentially vulnerable to financial exploitation, which meant that you were a security risk. You could be tied over a barrel, forced to tell secrets. In theory, anyway, which was why it took nine months for some pencil-pusher in some dark cubicle in the guts of the National Security Agency to finally okay his clearance.

He'd just signed on the dotted line a few moments earlier. On pain of prison or death, I swear never to say anything to anyone. Ever. No matter what.

It took a lot of faith and confidence to sign a piece of paper like that. What if NSA were doing something untoward? What if they were crossing the line again? As an employee of the National Security Agency, who would he tell? Who *could* he tell?

Rhetorical questions, of course. There was nobody *to* tell, unless Swaringen wanted to go to prison. Sure, he could maybe voice concerns with his superiors. But they were all in on all the secrets. They were the foxes, charged with watching the hen house.

Was he the only one who felt nervous signing a piece of paper like that? Didn't matter now. It was a done deal. He was fully authorized to view the details of the program to which he'd been assigned.

It was an unacknowledged program. Not even the program's code name — Penumbra — could be spoken, except in highly secure spaces. Even mentioning the name in the wrong crowd could cause his security clearance to be revoked. They didn't mess around, and Swaringen wasn't sure he trusted himself not to screw something up. He hoped his paranoia would keep him out of trouble.

But there was no denying that the whole thing was über cool. It was Tom Clancy shit. Hollywood spy movies had nothing on the NSA. Electronic door locks, magnetic badges, seven-digit personal ID numbers typed into keypads on the wall. James Bond. Ethan Hunt. Jason Bourne. Just needed the exploding pen.

He was lucky, he knew, to have landed this kind of gig. He had no government service experience. He used to work in the electronics industry, on the sales team of a giant computer chip manufacturer, selling shiny objects to jaded executives. He got bored, got a Harvard MBA, met a few military officers in his public policy classes who were destined for bureaucratic greatness and were getting all of the damns and shits and hells buffed out of their vernacular before pinning on their stars.

One thing led to another. One of the military officers had experience working for the NSA. He knew of a vacancy in a fairly prime posting. Swaringen applied to be the executive assistant to Clark Barter, the NSA's Deputy Director of Operations, and to no one's surprise more than his own, Swaringen was offered the position.

He looked at his watch. Five a.m. Barter was an early riser, so everyone in Barter's organization had to rise early, too.

Swaringen badged into the room. He stepped into a dark chamber full of computer monitors. Every monitor displayed a different video feed. Every video feed was an overhead view of the terrain beneath, obviously from several thousand feet up. Afghanistan? Iraq? Horn of Africa? Swaringen couldn't make out where the footage was coming from. It seemed to cover the gamut — cities, deserts, forests, towns, mountain ranges, cars driving on highways, cars driving on dirt roads in the middle of nowhere.

"David!"

Swaringen's back stiffened. Clark Barter's was an intimidating presence. Swaringen turned to take Barter's outstretched hand. More paw than hand. Big, rough, hirsute, with a grip like crocodile jaws. It was all Swaringen could do to keep from wincing. "Sir," he said, with a short, respectful nod typical of subordinates greeting their betters in a military-type organization.

"Welcome to CC-Bravo," Barter said. The CC stood for command center, Swaringen recalled.

"Honored to be here, sir," Swaringen said.

"Cut the ass-kissing. You already got the job."

Swaringen didn't know how to respond.

And he wondered again what he might have gotten himself into. Maybe the NSA wasn't the best move for a man of his temperament. He suddenly felt like the only child in a very adult world.

But it was one hell of a cool world.

Barter must have caught the look on his face. "You'll be fine. Have a seat." The big man motioned toward what must have been the only empty seat in the room, right next to the big executive chair that Barter himself occupied.

Swaringen sat. His body was tense. He felt self-conscious. Then he felt foolish for feeling self-conscious. He was a Harvard MBA, after all. Nothing he couldn't handle.

"I know they read you the security riot act this morning," Barter said in a low rumble, "but it bears repeating. You can't breathe a word of this shit to anyone. Not your wife or your mother or your hooker or your gay lover or your dog or your goldfish. And the same goes for Congressional committees, nosy senators, staffers, journalists, and other dirtbags you'll find poking around all the time. This program doesn't exist."

"Yes, sir," Swaringen said.

"They ask you easy questions, you play dumb."

Swaringen nodded.

"They ask you hard questions, you lie."

Swaringen's eyes widened involuntarily.

"I'm serious as a case of the clap," Barter said. "Don't say anything to anybody."

Swaringen nodded again. "Yes, sir."

"Good man. Welcome to the team. We're doing God's work. Days are long and hard, but we're making a difference. Saving lives."

"Yes, sir," Swaringen said. "That's what I signed up for."

Chapter 10

The taxi sped up Szent Gellért Tér in front of the Danubius Hotel. Sam followed behind, her pace deliberate but unhurried, her gaze out to the west, following the man in the oversized suit coat out of her peripheral vision.

The taxi passed Suit Coat. He looked inside the cab as it passed. He did a double-take. He evidently hadn't expected the backseat of the cab to be empty. His head whipped around to find Sam.

Amateur move. Dead giveaway. Sam smiled.

Suit Coat turned his torso back around and resumed his march up the hill. His pace quickened.

Sam pulled her phone from her purse and pretended to futz with it. But she was really watching the watcher, again out of the corner of her eye.

Her phone made a noise.

The man turned around again.

Sam kept her eyes down at her phone. Text message from Brock. "Couldn't wait to see you, so I changed my tickets. I leave tonight. :)"

Sam had mixed feelings about that bit of news. She was more than game to roll around naked with Brock, yet Suit Coat's presence in her life was compelling evidence that things were a long way from copacetic in Budapest.

The man turned right at the first intersection, halfway up the hill.

Sam followed fifteen paces behind, cursing the timing of Brock's text and the way it had taken her mind from the task at hand: figuring out who the hell was following her, and why.

There had to be another agent on the surveillance detail. Probably more. Find the others, she told herself.

She looked around, hoping she looked a lot more casual than she felt. She surveyed passersby. Old lady in a red scarf. Old man in a crazy Hungarian hat, complete with a feather. Young mother with two ankle-biters in tow. No eye contact from anyone. Almost as bad as DC. Maybe the Soviets had beaten the friendliness out of everyone.

The man with the oversized suit coat ducked into a haberdashery.

She still hadn't located the backup man, and she became more seriously concerned that maybe there wasn't a backup *man*. Maybe she was being followed by an entire surveillance *team*. Maybe she had made one of them, but the rest of them were playing it cool and professional.

She cursed beneath her breath. Her instincts clashed with each other. The survival instinct told her that the situation was getting out of control. She should abort, regroup. Fly home, maybe.

An equally cogent voice hounded her. It said that these kinds of situations didn't tend to age well, left to their own devices.

Surveillance teams didn't usually lose interest. They inevitably brought drama of some sort. The tails on the airplane, in the Budapest airport, and again outside of Severn's hotel were best not ignored.

And surveillance could turn to a much bigger problem in the blink of an eye.

Plus, she had them on the run. She had seized the initiative. She had spotted the tail and forced him to react to her.

She was forcing Suit Coat and his cronies — wherever they might have been at the moment — to move deeper and deeper into their contingency plan. Why quit now?

She wasn't itching for a confrontation, but she needed to know what was going on. It would have been far too easy to blunder into a buzz saw otherwise. It happened all the time in the counterespionage world.

She took a deep breath and ducked into the store, now ten paces behind Suit Coat.

The shopkeeper greeted her. She forced a smile, waved, and walked past.

Suit Coat was already three-quarters of the way to the back of the haberdashery. He clearly wasn't shopping. He didn't look back at Sam, but she saw his reflection in a fitting mirror as he passed.

It was definitely him. The chase was still on.

She didn't have a plan. She didn't speak Hungarian. She was probably outnumbered. She didn't have much going for her, other than a strong desire to figure out who the hell was following her.

Suit Coat opened a door in the back of the hat shop. The

shopkeeper's sharp protest needed no translation. Suit Coat ignored the shopkeeper and strode out into the daylight, turning left immediately outside the door.

Sam followed into a blind alley between two ancient buildings. They were still pockmarked, possibly from one of the many wars that plagued Hungary in the last century.

Suit Coat's pace quickened. He found a stairway cut into the alley and descended.

Sam kept pace.

He disappeared down the stairway.

Sam broke into a jog. She spotted the top of the man's head as she approached the top of the stairs. The rest of his body came into view a few steps later. He was working a key into a lock in a wide, low, heavy-looking door at the bottom of the stairwell.

"Sir?" Sam called out, hoping the man spoke English. "Sir, you dropped something," she lied. "I picked it up for you."

No response. He didn't even look at her.

She was on the fourth step when the man finally got the door open. He charged through the opening. He slammed the door shut.

Sam's foot stopped the latch from catching.

Suit Coat threw his weight against the door. Sam felt her shoe give, crushing her foot. She gritted her teeth and pushed back. "Sir, I have something of yours," she lied again. "You dropped it."

Suddenly, the door sprang open. Sam tumbled inside a low, dank, dark hallway, barely keeping her feet.

Suit Coat's footfalls echoed down the corridor. He was running away into the darkness.

Sam righted herself and followed.

She found herself in a dark corridor with a low ceiling. More cellar than basement, with hunks of scrap metal and steel rebar scattered about. Sam was careful not to trip over the debris as she followed Suit Coat at a run.

He rounded a corner, moving deeper into the subterranean gloom.

Sam followed, again questioning the wisdom of the whole enterprise. Perhaps her questions about who was following her and why could be answered at some other time, in some less dangerous way. The voices in her head argued with each other. Press the advantage. Retreat and fight another day. Stop. Don't stop.

Indecision was a de facto decision. She charged onward, making up ground.

Plastered walls and ceiling gave way to bare stone. Sam's legs were moving somewhere between a jog and a sprint to keep up. Suit Coat was much faster than he looked.

One more corner loomed. The light grew worse, the ceiling lower, and Sam had to stoop to keep from bashing her head against supports set in the rough stone ceiling.

Sam gritted her teeth and ran, bent over uncomfortably at the waist and neck.

She was no longer in a corridor. She was now in a cave.

Guess I won't need to take that tour.

The ceiling was just a couple of inches above her tall frame, and the walls were just wide enough to permit her arms to swing as she ran. It wasn't a large passageway.

It couldn't go on forever, Sam thought, passing through regions of light and shadow between dim bulbs spaced unevenly at shoulder height.

Another corner appeared. Suit Coat slowed, his feet slipping on the earthen floor. He slapped his hands against the far wall to make the corner, pushed off again at a run, and disappeared into the side corridor.

Sam rushed headlong after him.

She turned the corner.

And impaled herself on a long metal rod, gripped on the other end by thick, strong hands.

White hot pain seared her side. Her body curled up around the steel shaft. Her momentum pushed the rod deeper into her flesh. A shriek escaped her lips. She fell to the floor, gasping for breath, hands groping for the rod, desperate to pull it out of her side.

Suit Coat was on the other end of the rod. He jabbed it forward, plunging it further into her body. Sam looked up at him, saw the snarl on his face.

Slavic. High cheek bones.

Just like 32A.

He drove his weight, the force of his thrust overcoming Sam's grip and driving the rod deeper, tearing muscle and guts and sinew. She screamed, a loud, piercing, anguished howl amplified by the stone passageway.

The man pushed harder. The rod drove further into her side.

Sam's eyes rolled back in her head.

She knew what had to be done. To make it stop, she first had to make it worse.

She gritted her teeth. Then she let go of the rod. It moved ever deeper through her innards. She felt like she was going to pass out, but she forced herself to stay awake, to focus on her right hand. She forced it to find her purse, forced it to find the heavy metal object within, forced it to find the right grip, to check the safety was still off, to point it at the man's heart, to pull the trigger.

The explosion was unbelievable. The gunpowder flash lit the man's shocked face. Crimson goo exploded out a gaping hole in his back. The giant bullet tore his heart out and splattered it against the wall and ceiling.

He fell. He was dead long before gravity finished with his body.

Sam panted, fighting panic and hyperventilation and shock.

Was the man alone?

Or were there others?

She listened for footfalls in the earthen cave. She couldn't hear anything but the sound of her ears ringing in the aftermath of the gun blast.

She looked down the short corridor. No movement.

She turned her head, saw the corner leading to the long corridor, the corner where she had made a rookie mistake.

A deadly mistake.

She saw shadows dancing on the far wall.

Someone was rushing down the long hallway.

More than one person.

She could shoot the first, but the second would have plenty of time to return fire.

She looked again at the shadows. She grimly surmised that there might even be a third person.

It wasn't a good situation. She needed to find cover, and quickly.

She looked down at her side, regarded the thick metal rod jammed through her guts, cursed silently. It was clear she wasn't going to make it far with four feet of steel protruding from her innards.

That left her with one option.

Sam dropped her weapon and gripped the steel rod with both hands, sliding upward along the shaft to find raw metal unslicked by her own blood.

She tightened her grip, gathered resolve.

The shadows loomed larger, closer. She was running out of time. Her heart thudded in her chest. Sweat dappled her brow. She held her breath, clenched her jaw, steeled herself.

Then she ripped the poker from her side.

She felt intense, immeasurable, otherworldly pain.

The animal howl she heard was her own. It seemed far away from her consciousness, like somebody else's problem, or someone else's universe.

The pain wouldn't stop. It was deep and vicious and inexorable. It overtook her. Darkness came in its wake. She passed out.

Chapter 11

The morning unfolded uneventfully for David Swaringen. His feelings of unease dissipated as he spent more time next to Clark Barter, the National Security Agency's Deputy Director for Operations. Barter ran a tight ship. People on the floor moved with a purpose. It was all business.

Swaringen still felt out of place, but had the sense that he would rapidly catch up. He was, after all, a Harvard MBA. There's nothing he couldn't figure out, given enough time and resources. He took copious notes. Barter told him in no uncertain terms that the notes had to remain inside the secure facility. "No classified information leaves this room, unless you want me to saw your nuts off." Not the kind of admonishment Swaringen was soon to forget.

By seven, a sort of dreariness had settled over Swaringen's brain. The luster of the classified environment was wearing off, and it had begun to feel much like many of the office jobs he had held in his prior life.

Then something extremely interesting happened.

It began over in a far corner of the operations room. A buzz began. Swaringen could feel it before he was fully aware of it. He turned to look. Two operations personnel had gathered around a third. They all stared intently at a video monitor.

Swaringen looked at the monitors. Three screens showed three separate angles of the same scene, of a car, driving on a dusty road, out in the middle of nowhere.

"Got them, chief," one of the technicians said.

"Are you sure this time, numb nuts?" Barter rocketed from his executive chair in the front of the operation center. The floor creaked beneath his heft as he half-ran to the front of the room. Technicians parted to make way.

"Sure as I'm ever going to be, chief."

"I'm ready to hear your verification checklist," Barter said.

Swaringen didn't follow the litany of cryptic, terse verbiage that flowed from the technician's mouth. Clark Barter seemed to understand all of it. He nodded intermittently, asked a question or two, which Swaringen again didn't understand, and then nodded his head with finality. "I authorize action," Barter said.

All conversation in the room ceased, and a low hum of intensity emerged, its locus in the front corner of the room, centered on Barter and the three video technicians.

"Inbound, sir," one technician said.

"How long?"

"ETA in five, sir."

Barter nodded. He looked at his watch. He pointed at an otherwise-idle technician, a hefty woman in her mid-forties. "Notify the Director."

The woman picked up a telephone, punched a single button, and spoke in hushed tones.

Barter returned his attention to the video screen. "Armed?"

"Unknown at this time, sir," the third technician intoned. The man's voice was calm and even, but Swaringen heard distinct undertones of tension.

"Switch to millimeter-wave."

The technician toggled a computer setting. The hue of the video display changed noticeably. Where there was once nothing but the solid rooftop of the car, Swaringen was now able to see details of the contents beneath. The driver was a surreal, organic blob in the upper left of the picture. There were no passengers. There were articles strewn about the car, but Swaringen couldn't make them out.

Evidently, the technicians could. "Passenger seat, sir. Assault rifle, with the clip in."

"Got it," Barter said. "Tell the Director that, too."

The woman at the phone nodded.

"ETA?"

"Three minutes until the helicopters arrive."

"Zoom out. Any oncoming traffic?"

The technician adjusted a video setting. The view expanded. The car shrunk in size, and the surroundings grew to occupy an increasingly large portion of the video screen. There were no other cars in view. "Looks clean, sir," the technician said.

Barter nodded. He looked at his watch. He fished an antacid from his shirt pocket and popped it into his mouth. He looked at Swaringen. "You picked a good day to have your first day."

Swaringen nodded. He was aware that his eyes were inordinately wide. He felt every bit the befuddled neophyte, but the excitement of the room was contagious. Clearly something serious was going down.

"Zoom out further," Barter commanded.

The technician complied. The camera backed out again, and Swaringen guessed its picture encompassed four or five square miles.

Three shadows became visible in the video display. Helicopters. Flying close to each other in an arrow formation. They advanced rapidly toward the car.

"Tactical audio," Barter commanded.

A hiss of radio static filled the room. The noise was punctuated by occasional radio transmissions, over-amplified but still unintelligible to Swaringen's uninitiated ears. A technician handed a microphone to Barter. "You're hot, sir."

Barter snatched the mic and pressed the transmit lever. "All units, Charlie Charlie Bravo online," Barter said.

The speakers crackled in the command center. "Roger, sir," Swaringen made out from among the static.

"Execute," Barter said.

"Roger, Charlie Charlie Bravo. I copy, execute on your orders." The helicopter pilot's voice beat in time with the rotors, like someone kicked him in the chest a dozen times a second.

The helicopters caught up to the car in a matter of moments. "On my mark," the helicopter pilot said over the radio. Swaringen found his pulse pounding. His palms felt sweaty. He had no dog in this fight, yet he was on the edge of his seat.

"Three…Two…One… Mark."

There was a flurry of activity, a cacophony of radio calls.

Swaringen was unable to follow what they said. He watched the video monitor intently.

One helicopter circled around in front of the speeding car. The remaining two helicopters flanked the car, favoring the rear. The road was arrow-straight, and there was no place for the car to go. Swaringen thought he saw a rifle protruding from a door in each of the helicopters.

"Zoom in, millimeter wave. Now, people!" Barter yelled.

The camera view changed again, along with the hue, and Swaringen was again looking through the roof of the car.

The driver's right hand reached for the object in the passenger seat.

"Gun!" Barter yelled into the microphone. "He has an assault rifle."

"Copy gun." The pilot's voice sounded calm and cool. Swaringen wondered how that was possible under the circumstances. "Request permission to engage," the pilot said.

Swaringen watched Barter closely. Sweat had formed on the deputy director's brow. He looked unwell but resolute.

Barter clicked the mic. "Engage."

On the video screen, smoke erupted from the guns protruding from the helicopter bay doors.

The organic blob in the driver's seat slumped over, stopped moving. The car veered off the road, crashed through a low bramble, and came to rest in a shallow ditch.

"Status?" Barter asked over the radio.

"Standby," the helicopter pilot said. A long pause ensued,

during which nothing much appeared to happen. Swaringen found himself holding his breath.

The chopper pilot's voice crackled over the radio again. "Target neutralized."

Barter nodded. "It looks that way from here as well," he said. "Nice work."

Barter handed the mic back to the technician. "Standard protocol from here," he said. "Have the assault team establish a perimeter until the ground forces arrive."

The DDO walked back across the room and sat heavily in his executive chair. "Now for the fun part," he said. "Damn paperwork."

He looked at Swaringen and laughed. "Need some help getting your jaw off the floor?"

Swaringen smiled sheepishly. "No, sir. But you have to admit, you don't see that every day."

Barter nodded, a wry smile on his face. "You're right. It's usually every other day."

Swaringen smiled again, trying to hide his discomfort. He would get used to it, he hoped.

It occurred to Swaringen that he still didn't know where the events had taken place. Afghanistan? Horn of Africa? Iraq, even? Any of the above was plausible. The United States was involved in open hostilities on three continents. "Pardon the rookie question, sir," Swaringen said, "but what theater was that?"

Barter looked hard at him. "That's classified."

"Aren't we in a secure space?"

"*We* are in a secure facility. But *you* are not briefed."

Swaringen was confused. "I was just briefed this morning."

Barter shook his head. "This is a tiered program," he said. "Not everyone needs to know every detail. So not everyone *does* know every detail."

Swaringen wasn't sure he knew what to make of Barter's answer. "Who does know?"

"Know what?"

"Every detail."

Barter eyed him again. "None of your goddamn business."

Chapter 12

Sam awoke in a darkened room. She heard the creaks and cracks of an old building settling in its foundation. Her mind felt muddy, slow, sluggish. She had no idea where she was. The room smelled old, damp, well used, full of a vague, permanent human stench.

She heard footsteps outside the door. Heavy footfalls, made by a large man, pacing back and forth in front of the doorway.

The fog in Sam's thoughts lifted slowly, as though an anesthetic were wearing off. She moved to sit up in her bed, but a searing, stabbing pain seized her. Her hand shot to her side. She felt bandages.

She moved her arm, and something tugged against her wrist. An IV. The tube led up to a bookshelf, where a bag of fluid was perched precariously atop books and sundries.

She had no idea what time it was, or how long she had been asleep. Events came back to her in a flood: the surveillance team on her flight from DC, again in the Budapest airport, and then again outside of Mark Severn's hotel. The civilized chase of her tail that ended in the savage stabbing of her midsection. The gunshot blast, the dead man, the ungodly pain she felt as she pulled the iron rod from her gut, the men approaching down the dark hallway as she slipped from consciousness.

Sam rubbed her head. Her hair was matted together. Blood. Whether hers or the dead man's, she didn't know. Her heart beat fast. She tried again to sit up in bed, this time using her arms to support her torso. The pain in her side was intense, insistent.

She surveyed the dark room, searching for a doorway, hoping for an adjoining restroom, but finding nothing but old furniture, cracked plaster walls, ancient windows, musty curtains.

She sat up on the edge of the bed, swinging her legs gingerly until her feet touched the floor. Her toes felt hardwood, polished by decades of use. She stood. Her side protested as she straightened to a standing position.

She took several unsteady steps forward, emitting small gasps with each step, fighting against the searing pain in her side. Her mind felt sick, heavy, as if she had spent the weekend on a bender. She was undoubtedly suffering the aftereffects of sedation. She had obviously been tended to, but by whom?

The door latch rattled. The handle turned. The door opened. A giant of a man stepped through the dark opening, arms like oaks, legs like tree trunks, jaw chiseled in stone.

Sam assumed a fighting stance out of fear and reflex.

The giant man regarded her. He smiled. "Don't hurt me." His voice was like gravel. His face was hard, but his eyes were amused and kind. His English had a Hungarian accent, but something else too. Undertones that felt familiar to Sam, but she couldn't place them.

He motioned back toward the bed. "You should rest."

Sam relaxed, then obliged, setting herself gently back atop the musty covers.

"Where am I?" Her voice sounded small and thin.

"You're in my apartment. Welcome."

"Thank you. Where did you find me?"

"Someplace you shouldn't have been. In a pool of blood, next to a dead man."

"Who stitched me up?"

"My father. He is a doctor. Very respected."

"How did you know where to find me?"

"We received a phone call, from a man we know well. He told us where to find you, told us to follow you."

"Why?"

"You are a friend of a friend. You needed protection."

"We have a mutual friend?"

The giant man nodded.

"Who?"

He shrugged. "I never ask."

"Who are you?" Sam asked.

Hesitation. A smile. "Sebastian."

It wasn't quite the answer Sam had in mind, but she went with it. "Sebastian, it sounds as though I owe you a debt of gratitude."

Sam saw him smile in the darkness. "You may stay here as long as you wish."

"Where am I?"

"Budapest. Just upstairs from where you killed the man."

Sam nodded slowly, reconstructing the geography in her mind.

She must have followed Suit Coat into this very building. The experience felt eerily distant from her, like it had happened to a different person. "That was an unfortunate sequence of events. I just wanted to talk to him."

"His kind are not much for talking."

"Who are his kind?"

"I think you know already," Sebastian said, a knowing look on his face.

"All too well," Sam said. "But why was he following me?"

"That I cannot answer. Maybe nobody can, now. And for now, you should rest."

"I'm not sure that's such a great idea," Sam said. "It seems someone is unhappy with me at the moment."

"You are among friends," Sebastian said.

"I would feel much more comfortable about the situation if I happened to know who those friends were."

Sebastian's reply was drowned out by a loud, harsh conversation in the hallway. It was a heated exchange between two people in a language Sam didn't understand. It didn't sound like Hungarian.

The door burst open. A small, slight man, graying at the temples and frothing slightly at the mouth, marched up to Sebastian and placed a finger in his chest. A clamorous one-sided conversation ensued. Sebastian nodded intermittently. The small man's gesticulations included forceful index finger jabs in Sam's direction.

Sam got the distinct impression that she was not necessarily among friends exclusively. Some of Sebastian's crowd were not thrilled by her presence.

The small man left in a huff. He slammed the door behind him.

Sebastian looked at Sam, a sheepish expression on his face. "My apologies. It appears we are not all of one mind."

"So I gathered," Sam said. "I should really be on my way, anyway."

Sebastian shook his head. "Nothing to worry about. He is just a little concerned."

"Evidently. About what?"

"Local matters. Beyond your concern. He will be fine, and you must rest."

"Who are you people?"

Sebastian smiled. "Concerned citizens."

"Concerned with what?"

"In Hungary, mistrust is a virtue."

Sam shook her head. "I'm thoroughly confused."

Sebastian nodded. "It is like this. We have many friends and many enemies, and sometimes they are the same."

"Why are you helping me?"

"Favors are currency. The formal economy is hopeless for people like us. So we survive on the informal economy."

"Who asked for the favor?"

"I don't know."

"Jesus."

Sebastian smiled. "It wasn't him."

Sam laughed, then winced as her wound protested the exertion. A thought struck, and her face turned grave. "What time is it?"

"Nearly dawn."

"Balls. Where is my stuff?"

Sebastian pointed to a shabby dresser. Her purse was perched on top. She looked through it. Nothing was missing but her weapon. "My gun?"

"Later. When you are well enough to leave."

Sam nodded. She picked up her Blackberry.

Three messages from Tom Davenport. Her jaw clenched. It couldn't possibly be good news. She didn't bother to listen to them.

One message from Dan Gable. She listened. He had processed the multi-spectral images from Mark Severn's hotel room. "Sam, the UV shots showed blood spatter everywhere, consistent with a very long blade. There's no doubt in my mind. Someone was slaughtered in that room."

Chapter 13

Sam sprang into action. The file Tom Davenport had handed her on Mark Severn's death had certainly said nothing about a stabbing. Death by motor vehicle accident, the report said. Not death by slaughterhouse knife work. That was the kind of discrepancy that couldn't be ignored.

She removed her IV and began gathering her belongings. "I need to leave as soon as possible," she told Sebastian.

"You received interesting news?"

"Interesting like the Chinese curse," Sam said.

"Are you strong enough to leave?" Sam noticed his accent again. It didn't sound completely European, but Sam wasn't sure what other flavors might have been mixed in.

"Thank you for your help, and for your concern," she said. "I'll manage."

"In a bathrobe?"

"Good point. Would you mind showing me to my clothes?"

Sebastian shook his head. "Burned. Too much blood. Too much evidence."

Sam nodded. "Know any place I might find some clothes at five o'clock in the morning?"

Sebastian eyed her tall, athletic frame. "One minute," he said.

He left the room and closed the door behind him.

He returned moments later, bright colored clothes in his arms. "These might be a little small," he said. "But I think they will do."

Sam thanked him, and he left her alone to change. She donned a shapeless knee-length denim skirt and a ruffle-shouldered blouse that suffered from a fatal overdose of paisley. Her own shoes were folded up in the clothing, along with a pair of dark blue knee-length socks and a paisley headscarf.

She regarded herself in the mirror. She looked like a cross between an Amish refugee and hired help at a dude ranch. Ridiculous by any standard. She shook her head. Any port in a storm.

She exited the small, dark bedroom into a small, dark hallway. The air smelled slightly fresher, but not by much. Sebastian met her halfway, and pointed toward an open doorway. "The back door?" He asked.

Sam nodded. "That would be best."

Sebastian led her through a warren of small rooms and narrow hallways. The apartment was clearly constructed during a time when the average human was much smaller, and the average human's expectation of privacy and personal space was much less developed. The walls felt close and tight around her, and Sam felt slightly claustrophobic.

Sebastian led her through another short, narrow hallway and opened the door at the far end. Light and conversation spilled from a larger room. Sam followed him in.

The talking ceased at the sight of her, and Sam felt five pairs of eyes bore through her. She scanned the faces: blue-collar, rough, dirty, hard, genuine. Most wore neutral but wary expressions. One smiled weakly. Sam sensed open hostility from another, the same man who had done all the hollering and finger-wagging earlier. She smiled sweetly.

"Thank you so much for your kindness and hospitality," she said, making eye contact with each of them. "I hope someday to repay you."

Sebastian translated. There were nods and murmurs.

The angry old man with the loud bark broke the subsequent silence. "He says your leaving is repayment enough," Sebastian translated.

Sam laughed. "Right back at you, buddy."

Sebastian didn't translate.

He continued through the room and opened a door on the opposite side. It led through a tiny kitchen, barely wide enough to stand in. At the far end was a low window. Sebastian opened it and motioned Sam through. "Fire escape."

Her denim skirt and angry wound made climbing into the window problematic. Sebastian helped her through. She stood unsteadily on the narrow steel catwalk outside. She was relieved to find a zigzagging staircase leading down to street level, instead of a ladder. The stairs would be easier to navigate with her injury.

She took a step toward the stairs, but felt Sebastian's strong grip on her shoulder. In his other hand was her handgun. She smiled sheepishly. "Thank you. Never know when you'll need one of these," she said with a small laugh as she tucked her gun in her purse.

"Clearly. But I would be careful with it," he said. "It is rumored the police are treating the man's death as a murder."

"Thanks for that cheery bit of news."

Sebastian smiled and extended his hand again. A bottle of pills. "You will need these, I think."

"I sure as hell will." She gave Sebastian a hug. "Thank you again."

"Go with good fortune," Sebastian said.

"Won't you tell me who you are, so I can thank you properly, when the time is right?"

Sebastian shook his head, a cloud coming over his mien. "I'm afraid it's not possible." His eyes were suddenly a long way away, as if he was thinking of distant taskmasters and unfortunate alliances.

Sam nodded, planted a small kiss on his cheek, and started down the fire escape.

* * *

Sam descended from the fire escape and found herself in a narrow alleyway. Garbage cans and detritus littered the cobblestone.

She saw a faint orange glow in the east, dawn's harbinger. It gave her an uneasy feeling. The clock was ticking on Mark Severn's death. The odds of getting to the bottom of the situation dropped dramatically with each passing hour. Forty-eight hours was the magic number. Two days. Sunrise marked the start of day three.

Sam fished in her purse for her notepad. She had used the long flight from DC to consolidate salient notes from the file Davenport had given her. Written on the first page was the name of the hospital that contained Mark Severn's remains.

She typed the address into her telephone. Three miles. Thirty minutes on foot. Sam decided to walk. It wasn't a terrific choice, but neither was stealing a car. And she wasn't about to hail a cab. She would have been better off wearing a "Dismember me and stuff me in a suitcase" sign around her neck.

She checked the messages on her personal phone. She had two from Brock. "There was a slight delay in Frankfurt," one of them said, "but I should be landing on time in Budapest."

Brock's other message said, "I'm a little worried that I haven't heard from you, but I know how you get when you're working. Can't wait to hang out with you in Budapest!"

She smiled. The sound of his voice warmed her insides. She couldn't wait to hold him.

But there was a lot of the real world standing in the way at the moment.

She checked her watch — five a.m. in Budapest meant ten p.m. in DC — and dialed Dan Gable.

"Holy shit, boss, are you in trouble," Dan said in lieu of a greeting.

"Terrific," Sam said. "What have you heard?"

"Dereliction of duty, absent without leave, disobeying a direct order."

"Davenport?"

"Yes, but I think he's just parroting what the deputy director said."

"Great. Do they know what happened?"

"I guess that would depend on what happened," Dan said with a chuckle.

"I was attacked. Stabbed in the gut with a length of rebar."

"Holy shit."

"You should see the other guy," Sam said. "He really fell apart."

"How to win friends and influence people," Dan said.

"Right. Turns out I wasn't just being paranoid, I was actually being followed. I spotted another tail outside Severn's hotel, right after I sent you those multi-spec pictures. I thought I'd try to ask him a few questions. Things went a little sideways."

"Not your brightest idea."

"Evidently."

"Are you okay?"

"Yeah, I am. Thanks to a very strange collection of people."

"Come again?"

"Apparently, I passed out in a pool of the dead guy's blood. I woke up a little while ago, stitched up and with an IV in my arm."

"In a hospital?"

"No. In an apartment. Three stories up from where I shot the guy."

"Small world."

"They were very cryptic about who they were and why they helped me. I never got a straight answer."

"Any ideas?"

"I was hoping you could help me out with that," Sam said. "They said I was the friend of a friend."

"Helpful. Did they give you anything else to go on?"

"Not much," Sam said. "They clearly didn't want to be involved more than they already were, and I didn't press them for details. The situation seemed a little tenuous as it was. Not all of them were happy I was there."

Sam arrived at an intersection. She eschewed a narrow two-lane thoroughfare in favor of continuing down the narrower, darker alley. She felt safer in the smaller space. The avenues of approach were much more controlled, and there were fewer hiding places.

"Something else," she said. "They had exquisite knowledge of where to find me. I was in the cellar of a building, actually in a cave attached to the cellar. These guys arrived just a few seconds after the whole thing ended. They said their orders were to watch me, to keep me out of trouble."

"Spooky."

"I'm glad they were there. I might have bled out otherwise."

"Holy shit, Sam. It was that serious?"

"My side is killing me. I'm afraid to look at the stitches."

Dan was quiet for a moment, churning the facts over in his head. "Anything else they said?"

"They were very coy," Sam said. "But the accent was strange. They were definitely fluent in Hungarian, but there were overtones. The consonants were familiar in a strange way. Out of context, maybe. But I couldn't place it, and I couldn't tell you why it sounded familiar."

"Non-native Hungarians in Budapest, secretly playing for the good guys," Dan said. "With such a running start, I should have this figured out in a minute or two."

"Smartass."

"Seriously, that's not very much to go on. Are you sure you need to know who they are?"

"I think so," Sam said. "Somebody told them exactly where to find me. I'd like to know who."

"You make a compelling point," Dan said. "But it's going to be tough. There's not much of anything to work with."

"I'll text you the coordinates of the building. I don't know how useful the location will be, but it might help you to cross-reference a database somewhere."

"Sure. I'll ask the Great Database in the Sky," Dan quipped. "The all-seeing, all-knowing Cloud."

"Something like that."

Another thought struck. "The guy who attacked me was Slavic," Sam said. "Just like the guy in 32A."

"Perfect. Another nonspecific clue. That should keep me running in circles for weeks."

"Sorry," Sam said. "But if I knew more, I probably wouldn't need you."

"Touché."

"And I need a favor."

"Another one?"

"Are you keeping track?"

"Yes. Christmas bonus. Sarah wants a new minivan."

"Lucky you," Sam said, peering into a darkened entryway as she passed. "I need you to talk to Tom Davenport for me, please.

Bring him up to date. Tell him about the blood stains in Severn's room, about me being tailed and attacked, and about the mystery team coming to my rescue."

"Why can't you tell him all that?"

"I can. But I don't want to."

"Why not?"

"Because it's hard to disobey orders you never receive."

"What are you talking about?"

"He's going to order me home, for that eyes-only thing. But the situation here is a long way from right."

Dan laughed. "You're something else. You're alone in a foreign city, and someone's got a target painted on your back. Don't you want a little help?"

"From Davenport?" Sam snorted. "With my taxes, maybe. But with this? No fucking way."

* * *

Sam's senses were on high alert. The sun had just peeked over the horizon in the east, and the light was poor for picking out tails and overly interested eyeballs.

Dan was right. Rogue and alone wasn't a winning combination, especially five thousand miles away from home.

But she had an extremely important question to answer, so she pressed on as quickly as her sore side would allow. She rounded a corner and caught sight of the hospital.

It was named after Dr. Rose Magánkórház, someone Sam had never heard of. She had envisioned a giant American-style medical megalith, so the small, squat structure caught her off guard. It looked as though the building had been a small European barn in an earlier incarnation.

Her side hurt as she walked up the front stairway. The anesthetic was wearing off. She wondered how much speed and stamina she would have available in case of another encounter with her new fans, who were undoubtedly less than pleased about their ranks having been thinned by one.

A tired-looking reception nurse greeted her. Sam asked whether she spoke English. The nurse's expression grew more tired. "Of course," she said.

Sam displayed her Homeland badge and did her best to explain the situation. She needed to see Mark Severn's body.

The nurse was less than impressed. "Family members only in the morgue," she said.

"I'm Mr. Severn's colleague," Sam said, "and I've been sent here to take care of the details. I won't be able to return home until I've had a look at his remains."

The nurse sighed. She turned, pulled open a file cabinet drawer, leafed through reams of paperwork, and produced a form, which she handed to Sam.

The form was written in Hungarian, with small English subtitles. The English translation seemed to have been done by someone who didn't speak English, Sam thought. It made no sense to her. She prevailed upon the nurse to help her fill in the blank items. She wrote illegibly and fabricated answers to a few of the more obscure questions.

The nurse lost patience halfway way through the form. "It's

okay," she said. "Come with me."

Sam followed down a long hallway. There must have been an annex not visible from the street, Sam surmised, because the hallway appeared too long to be contained inside the small barn-like structure she had seen from the front. She wondered if there was a parking lot in the back of the building. She wondered if it was visible from the roadway. She was already thinking tactically about her exit.

The nurse swiped a badge through a reader on the wall. There was a beep and a green light, then an audible click as the latch released. The nurse held the door for Sam, then repeated the procedure at the next doorway, which opened into the refrigerated morgue. Sam asked about the heightened security measures. "Organ trafficking," the nurse said.

"It's a messed-up world," Sam said.

The nurse shrugged. She cross-referenced the sheet on a clipboard dangling from a nail, then pulled open one of the long, heavy steel drawers lining the long wall. She unzipped the body bag, and opened it to give Sam a view of the head and torso.

Sam steeled herself. She had seen plenty of corpses, but that didn't mean she enjoyed it. She looked into the drawer.

A senescent face greeted her. Gray hair, wrinkles, a double chin.

It was certainly a dead body.

But it was certainly not Mark Severn.

Chapter 14

David Swaringen felt groggy when his alarm went off. There was no way he was going to get used to the early mornings, he figured.

He started a pot of coffee, climbed into the shower, and let the hot water spill over him.

Yesterday wasn't quite the first day he had wanted. He wasn't sure what his boss thought of him. Clark Barter, the grizzled, crusty old DDO, was tough to read. Swaringen wasn't sure whether he was going to fit in at the National Security Agency. More specifically, he wondered whether he was going to fit in on the Penumbra operations floor.

And he wasn't sure he wanted to.

Something bothered him about Barter. There was something broken, Swaringen thought, something not quite right. He wasn't sure what, but behind bluff, bluster, and bravado inevitably hid a scared person. Swaringen wondered what Barter was scared of.

Swaringen knew what *he* was scared of. Swaringen was scared of Barter.

He hoped things went a little more smoothly today.

He finished getting dressed, straightened his tie, grabbed his briefcase, and began his commute. Today was a new day, he decided. It was going to be a better day.

And all things considered, Swaringen thought as the first rush of caffeine-induced optimism hit him, his first day on the job hadn't really been all that bad. Sure, he would have hoped for a more auspicious first impression, but in light of everything going on, it hadn't been heinous. In the history of first days, this one wasn't the worst, he decided.

Swaringen made his way toward the gigantic NSA complex in Fort Meade, Maryland. It was early enough that the normal DC-area madness had not yet begun. Swaringen almost didn't know what to make of it. It seemed like a different town than the one he was used to, a much better town. Maybe the early mornings weren't going to be all that bad.

He felt a sense of opportunity. How many people got to be involved in the kinds of things he was getting to be involved with? How many people knew the things that he knew? Maybe a few hundred, he surmised, out of seven billion people on the planet. It was certainly a privileged and rarefied crowd. Swaringen didn't feel as though he belonged yet, but it felt good just to have his foot in the door.

He hoped that Barter would warm to him over time. He hoped the environment didn't turn out to be quite as hostile as it first seemed.

Something nagged at him. Why had everything gone sideways when he asked where yesterday's events had gone down? It was as if he had asked permission to sleep with Barter's daughter. It had seemed a colossal faux pas. Had he missed the memo?

Swaringen shook his head. At least the first day was in the books, he thought. And today's a new opportunity.

The drive took less than half an hour. He parked his car in the shadow of the gigantic, gleaming NSA cube, grabbed his briefcase, and walked inside, fresh resolve in the set of his jaw.

He got lost on the way to Command Center Bravo. Just for a little while. Just long enough to make him late.

He badged into the secure room, walked across the operations floor, set his briefcase atop the desk, planted his backside on the seat next to Clark Barter. The old man made a point of glaring at his watch, a stern expression on his face.

Swaringen apologized "I should have left breadcrumbs when I went home yesterday," he said.

His apology earned a chuckle from the old man. Swaringen considered it a small win.

He perused the monitors, moving his eyes methodically from screen to screen, taking in details. Each view was from above, at varying degrees of magnification. The scenery varied from sector to sector, and varied to a lesser degree from screen to screen. He surmised that each operator was responsible for a particular area.

He looked for a pattern, a common thread. There must be one, he reasoned. *Something* had to tie everything together. Everything in front of him had to make sense, from the right perspective. So it was just a matter of figuring out the right frame of reference.

He saw urban scenes, but he didn't recognize any of the cities.

He saw rural scenes, but he saw no distinguishing landmarks.

He saw forests and bodies of water, but he didn't recognize

any of their shapes.

When there were cars, they were familiar-looking, but Swaringen didn't place much stock in that. The same cars were sold just about everywhere in the world, with a bit of regional variation. It was the nature of globalization and consolidation.

His mind wandered and his eyes unfocused. His thoughts turned existential. Have I made the right career move? Am I enjoying this? Will I make it long enough to qualify for retirement?

Will I wind up an asshole like Clark Barter? A small smile crossed his lips.

And that's when he noticed. It was a small thing, but momentous. It was barely noticeable, but once noticed, it couldn't be ignored.

When viewed from a distance, the images revealed their coherence.

All the shadows pointed the same direction.

West.

All of the videos showed someplace in the Western Hemisphere.

Swaringen sat up. Was the US at war someplace in Central America? South America? Was it the war on drugs? Did anybody still call it that? Was there terrorist activity this close to home? Swaringen had no idea. And he had more sense than to ask.

But he resolved to find out.

Chapter 15

Nero Jefferson Chiligiris sat glumly next to Robert the Muslim. They had spent the night in a putrid police station holding tank in Pueblo. Some kind of bureaucratic mix-up at the Florence facility prevented them from being accommodated as originally planned. The guard's word, *accommodated.* Like he was some kind of concierge.

"Don't worry," the prisoner transport driver had said. "We'll get it sorted out. You'll be in there first thing in the morning." There was a bit of wickedness to his smile.

Nero spent the night shoehorned between a drunk and two gang bangers. He half expected a shank between the ribs in his sleep. The drunk spared him by snoring too loudly to permit any shuteye whatsoever.

As each new guard passed by on watch, Nero asked the same question: "When do I get my phone call?"

The answer was always the same. "No phone call for you. You got a problem with it, take it up with the feds."

Nero's despair deepened. His hope of successfully pleading his case diminished with each passing hour. He worried about Penny and the kids. What must they be thinking?

And would it kill anybody to let him have just one phone call?

He felt drained. Losing hope was enervating.

Sunlight peeked through the high, narrow windows at the top of the holding cell. Nero's eyes burned with exhaustion, and a low, dark mood settled over him. He saw the prison transport driver approach the cell with the local guard, and he sank into deeper despair.

"On the road again," the driver sang with inappropriate glee. Nero cursed beneath his breath.

He and Robert shuffled in their manacles down the long hallway from the holding cell. They both noticed where the driver placed the keys to unlock their chains. Right front pants pocket. Not a terribly secure location, but it wasn't like they were going to overpower the guard with their hands and feet shackled together.

The driver led them out into the early morning light. The fresh air taunted them. They struggled to climb into the van, arms and legs shackled together. "We're burning daylight," the driver prodded, with that slightly malicious laugh again.

The van bumped and jostled, stopped and started through a few intersections, then accelerated onto Highway 50, heading west to Florence. The sun peeked through the rear window of the van, first a bit of faint orange, then a blazing ball of crimson.

It reminded Nero of the outside world. The world he was no longer part of.

They continued westbound, away from the Pueblo gloom, past crack house after crack house, out again onto the Colorado plain.

"I guess this is it," Nero said.

"Home of the free."

Nero nodded glumly. He rested his head against the van frame, again feeling the hum of the road rattle through his skull, hoping for a few minutes' rest before the nightmare continued.

The van swerved. Tires squealed. There was a thump, as of metal meeting flesh, and curses from the driver's seat. Nero's body was tossed against the seatbelt. The driver cursed loudly, manhandling the oversized steering wheel. Nero's body lurched and lunged with the driver's overcorrections.

There was a horrendous squeal of brakes, a loud, violent impact, the sound of twisting metal, then the ear-splitting screech of metal on pavement. Another vicious impact brought the van to an instant stop, slamming Nero's weight against his lap belt.

An eerie silence settled over them.

Nero looked at Robert. No visible signs of damage. Just a stunned expression on the kid's skinny face.

Nero unbuckled his seat belt, leaned forward, and looked through the window into the driver's compartment.

The driver's face was a bloody mess. One of his arms was bent and twisted at an impossible angle. Nero felt suddenly ill. His stomach threatened revolt. He was always squeamish around blood and guts. He turned away, looking out the side window instead, gathering himself.

What had they hit? If there was another car, Nero couldn't see it. Had the driver just run off the road? Texting? Dodging an animal, maybe?

He looked out the windshield. He saw blood and fur. Maybe they'd hit a deer.

"What a trip, man," Robert said. His voice was faint and far away. The wiry Muslim man still wore a shocked expression on his face, but there was no sign of blood or trauma.

Nero examined his own arms and legs. He felt no pain, except where the seatbelt had dug into his lap. He was suddenly worried about an explosion. Everybody made fun of the way it happened all the time in the movies, but Nero was suddenly concerned that there might have been an element of truth to it. He didn't want to have his skin roasted off if the van caught fire.

"Let's get out of this thing," he said.

Robert pointed to the back doors. "No door handles," he said.

Nero cursed. He leaned forward and tried the window in the bulkhead separating the forward and aft compartments of the prisoner van. Locked.

He leaned back on the seat, raised both legs, and mule-kicked the window. The glass was thick, and reinforced by wires enmeshed between panes. Nero's kick barely registered.

Nero cursed, clenched his jaw, and unleashed a fury of successive kicks. Hot pain flashed in his feet and heels, but he kept going. Finally he prevailed, sending shards of glass flying forward. The he used his shoe to dislodge the sharp edges lingering near the window frame.

He righted himself, leaned through the window, and checked the driver's pulse. Weak and faltering. Nero was no doctor, but he didn't like the driver's chances.

He reached with both hands further down the driver's body, searching for the pocket containing the manacle keys. He had to unbuckle the driver and manhandle his limp form, shifting the man's weight to the left to access the pocket.

Nero shoved his hand inside. Pay dirt.

He pulled out the keys.

They dropped between the seats. Nero cursed, jammed both hands between the seats to retrieve them, and pulled the keys back through the shattered window.

He tried them on his handcuffs. Success. The same for his shackles, and then for Robert's. They were no longer bound and chained.

"What do we do now?" Robert asked.

Nero looked at him. "Bro, we run," he said.

Robert smiled. "I was hoping you were going to say that."

There was no way to open the back door from within the prisoner van. The glass was bulletproof and wire-reinforced. Nero's feet wouldn't stand another onslaught. He motioned toward the small window.

Robert went first. His wiry frame slipped through the opening with little hassle.

The same could not be said for Nero. His bulk fought every attempt to sneak through. "Help," he exhorted Robert.

Robert grabbed his hand, braced his feet against the seat, and pulled.

Nero felt glass shards dig into his side as he squeezed through the narrow opening, first his torso, then his waist, then his legs.

Then he was through. He gathered himself on the front seat, picking glass from his clothing. "Thanks, bro," he said.

"Don't mention it."

The front of the van was crumpled by the impact, and there was no getting out the passenger door. It was bent and twisted, held fast in place.

Nero looked at the bloody driver, the way his arm was twisted and broken, like there was an extra elbow. His stomach turned.

But there was no choice. They were going to have to climb over the comatose man.

"You first," he told Robert.

The younger man crawled gingerly over the mangled driver. He found the door latch, pulled the lever, then pushed the door open. He crawled the rest of the way over the driver, then tumbled out onto gravel and scrub.

"Help me move him," Robert said.

Nero shook his head. "His arm's wrapped up in the steering wheel."

"Then climb your big ass over," Robert said.

Nero grunted and strained with effort. He held his breath and winced as he let his weight settle momentarily on the wounded driver. He heard bone grind against bone in the man's arm. Nero felt dizzy and nauseous.

"Come on, man," Robert said. "Get off him."

Nero leaned forward and reached for Robert. The young man did his best to lift Nero's weight from the stricken driver. Robert pulled. Nero felt his body slide over something slick and gooey. He shuddered, then abandoned caution, suddenly frantic to be free of the bloody mess beneath him.

"Chill!" Robert yelled, straining under Nero's weight. "Stop fighting."

But Nero had edged beyond reason. He clawed and kicked, trying to outrun panic and revulsion. He finally disentangled himself from the van and the steering wheel and the mangled driver. He fell in a heap on top of Robert, then sprang to his feet, wiping nondescript gore from his torso, his breath coming in gasps.

"Help me," Robert said. "His pulse is fading."

Nero turned to see the younger man reaching back inside the van, struggling with the comatose driver's heft.

"He needs an airway," Robert said. "I need something to keep his head up."

Nero looked in the door, his stomach turning again. He felt bile creeping upward.

But he had an idea. He took off his shirt. It was bloodied from his recent entanglement with the gravely injured driver. He rolled it into a ball, gritted his teeth, and wedged the shirt between the driver's chin and chest.

He steeled himself again. He grabbed the driver's bloody head and pulled it backward. The man's mouth fell open. Nero wedged the keychain between the driver's teeth, then let go.

"It worked," Robert said, palm of his hand next to the injured man's mouth. "His breathing is stronger."

Nero nodded. The driver's face was a bloody pulp and his arm would never be the same, but at least he had a fighting chance at survival.

Nero suddenly found tears coming from his eyes. He had no

idea why. Exhaustion, shock, fear, revulsion, relief. Maybe all of them. He caught Robert looking at him, and he wiped his eyes. "Don't know what got into me, man," he said.

Tire noise brought things back into focus. There was a car coming. It was heading west out of Pueblo, the way they had come.

"Get down!" Nero commanded. "Behind the van!"

They scrambled around to the far side of the van and flattened themselves against the earth. Nero held his breath as the noise grew louder.

What if they stopped? They would surely call the cops.

What if it *was* the cops? Nero's heart pounded.

The car grew louder, the tire noise growing harsher, meaner, more vicious, until it felt deafening. Nero was surprised by how loud and frightening it seemed.

Then it blew past. Nero listened, breathless, for the telltale signs of slowing. But there were none. The driver continued west, as if there were no accident, as if nothing at all had happened by the roadside.

"We have to get away from this road," Nero said unnecessarily.

"No argument here," Robert said. "Closest town looks to be that way." He pointed to the west. Toward Florence.

Nero shook his head. "Prison town," he said.

"What do you mean?"

"I mean, no sane resident is going to help a hitchhiker. Not with a federal supermax nearby."

Robert nodded. He turned to the east.

"We gotta split up," Nero said.

Robert's eyes narrowed, as if he had been insulted. Then realization dawned. "They'll be looking for the pair of us."

Nero nodded. "And no matter what else, we gotta get away from this highway," he said. "It's too busy. We'll be caught in a minute."

More tire noise grew from the distant silence.

"We gotta get out of here," Nero said. He began walking south, away from the road and the wrecked prison van.

Robert followed him.

"Bro, you have to go the other way," Nero said. "We're sitting ducks otherwise."

Robert looked at him. "I guess this is it, then."

Nero returned his gaze. "I guess it is. May the force be with you, or whatever they say in the mosque," he said, a wry smile on his lips, his hand extended.

Robert shook Nero's hand. "Don't take this the wrong way," the young man said, "but I hope I never see you again."

Nero gave Robert a closed-fisted, two-pat man-hug, turned on his heel, put the rising sun on his left, and trudged into the wilderness.

Chapter 16

"Are you one hundred percent certain?" Sam asked.

"Yes," the hospital nurse said in thickly accented English. "I check the paperwork two time."

"It's not him," Sam said, shaking her head. "It's not Mark Severn."

"Yes, it is," the nurse said. "It say so, right here, on death paper."

Sam held out her hand. The nurse handed over the paperwork. It was written in Hungarian. She had no idea whether it was a death certificate, but it had Mark Severn's name all over it.

"How do you know this is him?" Sam asked.

"His identification cards." The nurse produced another folded piece of paper, this one with photocopies of Severn's identification. The *real* Mark Severn's face smiled back at her from the page.

The ID looked authentic.

Sam pointed to the dead man on the slab. "You've got to be kidding me," she said. "This guy looks nothing like the ID."

The nurse snatched the paper from Sam's hand, examined the photocopied identification, and studied the face staring up from the morgue drawer. She shrugged.

"Are you serious?" Sam asked. "You didn't even check to

make sure the picture matched the face?"

The nurse shrugged again. "Somebody signed."

"What do you mean?"

"Somebody was here, to look at the body," the nurse said. "He signed papers."

Sonuvabitch. "Let me guess," Sam said. "Tall man, blue backpack."

"Yes. You know him?"

Sam shook her head, disgust on her face. "I'm getting to know him better by the minute."

She looked more closely at the body. "May I unzip the bag a little further?"

The nurse shook her head. "Nobody may touch the bodies," she said.

Sam smiled with exaggerated sweetness. "Then would *you* please unzip the damned bag?"

The nurse did as she was asked. Sam examined the dead man's exposed torso. There were no evident injuries of any sort.

There was no bruising, as might be expected from a fatal automobile accident.

There was certainly no butchery, as might have been made by a long blade, long enough to fling blood on the walls at high velocity, like in Mark Severn's hotel room.

The dead man was in his fifties if he was a day old. He didn't look like he had taken great care of himself. Sam figured he could have died by natural causes. Maybe a heart attack. Maybe he had engaged in sexual activity without his doctor's permission.

Impossible to say.

But he certainly wasn't run over by a car, and he certainly wasn't murdered with a knife.

"Thank you," Sam said. She stepped away from the morgue drawer. "Did he have any belongings with him?"

The nurse shook her head.

"Nothing at all?"

"Nothing. Just identification."

Sam nodded, lips pursed. Obviously a red herring, meant to throw her off the trail. She wondered where they had found the dead man. She wondered maybe if they hadn't killed him themselves. Poison, maybe. Or asphyxiation.

She wondered where the hell Mark Severn was.

"You said there was a man here earlier to identify the body. Did he sign any paperwork?"

The nurse nodded, and motioned for Sam to follow. The nurse trudged back toward the front desk, found a file cabinet, opened a drawer, hummed softly while she leafed through papers, and pulled a single sheet from the drawer.

Sam couldn't make heads or tails of the signature, but the printed name was clearly legible.

John Q. Public.

How clever.

"Were there any other fatalities around the same time? Any stabbings?"

The nurse flipped through a folder on the admissions desk. "No. Not here. But Budapest is big city. Maybe ten hospitals."

Sam nodded grimly. It would take a team of detectives all day to canvas the hospitals. She didn't have a team, and she didn't have a day. Because she had someone chasing her.

She reflected on the situation. Yesterday's play to force their hand had certainly stirred things up. But it had not worked nearly the way she had hoped. She had undoubtedly changed the rules of engagement for her pursuers. No professional organization in the world took kindly to losing one of their own. The remaining members were bound to prosecute any and all opportunities with vigor and enthusiasm.

Sam felt exposed.

John Q. Public. Someone was toying with her.

She wondered for a moment how they had such perfect intelligence, how they knew with such precision where she would be, and when she would be there.

Then she realized that her move had been completely obvious. Anyone investigating Mark Severn's death in an official capacity would eventually have to identify the body. So it wasn't a question of whether Sam would make an appearance at the hospital. It was only a question of when.

And she had walked right into it.

Dread. Fear. Adrenaline. Her pulse quickened.

Sam took a few steps toward the front door of the hospital, pausing to peer through the windows and glass doors. The sun blazed brilliantly outside, and Sam shielded her eyes. She scanned the front of the building methodically, from left to right.

Her vigilance was rewarded. She spotted a watcher. A woman

this time. She couldn't tell whether it was the same woman from the airport, 32A's cohort, but the odds seemed better than even.

Sam felt vulnerable. The sun angle meant the woman watching the hospital entrance couldn't see into the building. That was helpful. But the woman was undoubtedly accompanied by one or more additional agents.

And it was entirely possible they were already inside the building.

Sam fought the desire to run, to hide. She needed to keep her head about her.

But she needed to get the hell away.

She walked back to the reception desk. "Thank you for your help today, ma'am," she said to the nurse. "Is there a restroom nearby?"

The nurse pointed down the long hallway. "On the left," she said.

Sam nodded her thanks and walked briskly down the corridor, surreptitiously checking for open doors along the way.

She found an unlocked lounge. She ducked inside. It smelled of smoke. Evidently, the worldwide ban on smoking had not made it yet to Hungary. Either that, or enforcement was not quite what it might have been.

She glanced around, looking for anything useful. She found a bank of lockers along the far wall. She padded over to them, being careful not to cross in front of the window in the hallway door.

There were locks on only about a third of the lockers. It was usually best to try things the easy way first. She began opening unlocked locker doors.

The first five were empty. She hit pay dirt on the sixth. A leather jacket, a pair of sweats, a wallet, a set of car keys. BMW. Nice.

She donned the jacket. She peeled off the denim skirt and threw it in an unused locker, and pulled on the sweats in their place. She had to cinch the ties tightly to keep them from dropping to her ankles.

She stuffed the car keys in the jacket pocket, and left some money on the shelf in the locker she had just pilfered, for karma's sake. And she'd claim it as an expense on her travel voucher when she got back home.

If she got back home.

She snuck back to the hallway door and peered out the window into the long corridor.

The early hour worked to her advantage. The hospital wasn't yet crowded with employees and patients. Sam craned her neck as far as possible in either direction, looking for an opportunity to leave unseen.

Seeing no one, she pulled the door open a smidgen and peered through the opening.

A nurse emerged from an adjacent room, a preoccupied look on her face.

Sam held her breath and slowly closed the door to the lounge. She felt her heart thumping in her chest.

The nurse scurried past, lost in her thoughts. Sam exhaled, reopened the door, and made her way toward the restroom.

She had a hunch, and sincerely hoped it proved correct. It was an old building. Old buildings usually used old ventilation technology. Windows.

Above the far stall in the women's bathroom, Sam found her escape plan.

She worked the window latch, applied a little force, and was rewarded with nothing but recalcitrance. The window didn't move.

She used a little more leverage. The window creaked open an inch.

Sam curled her fingers around the edge, braced her foot against the wall, and pulled. Her wounded side protested angrily, and she stifled a gasp.

She tried again. The window broke free of friction and slammed open, banging loudly into the frame. Sam cursed the pain and the noise.

She listened for anyone coming. Only the sounds and smells of early morning greeted her through the open window.

Sam stood up on the throne and checked in both directions beyond the window. Finding no one, she punched out the window screen. It clattered to the pavement below.

She adjusted her stance on the toilet seat, gritted her teeth, placed both hands on the window frame, and counted to three in her head.

She leaped on three.

The pain in her abdomen was amazing. Her eyes instantly teared. She wondered if she hadn't ripped the stitches out. A little howl escaped her lips, and a small sob. It sounded pathetic. She felt grateful no one was around to hear it, especially not anyone she knew.

Her body was balanced on the window ledge. There was no turning back now. It would hurt just as much to climb back into the bathroom as to climb through to the outside. She set her jaw and twisted onto her right hip to protect the left side of her abdomen, where 32A's twin brother had plowed a steel rod through her insides. Then she half rolled, half fell to the pavement below.

The pain was extreme. She stood with her hands on her knees for the better part of a minute, composing herself, breathing into the pain, clearing the tears from her eyes, fishing the painkillers from her purse, doing her best not to cry out.

She stood slowly. The pain subsided. Walking wasn't a picnic, but it wasn't unbearable.

She got her bearings. The bathroom window had let her out into a small paved alleyway between wings of the hospital. To her right was a dead-end. Trash had accumulated in the corners of the building.

She looked left. The small alleyway opened up. A walkway intersected the mouth of the alley, forming a T. She crept forward, keeping her body against the far wall, ducking to avoid windows as she advanced toward the alley exit.

She peered around the corner. A small smile crept across her face. She saw a parking lot.

She fetched the stolen car keys from the pocket of the stolen jacket. She thumbed the key fob. Nothing happened.

Sam steeled herself. She was going to have to walk through

the lot to find the right car. She had a bad feeling in the pit of her stomach.

She put the hideous paisley scarf over her head and tucked her flaming red hair inside. Details mattered. Hiding her hair might buy her a few seconds. A few seconds might make a live-or-die difference.

She walked deliberately through the rows of cars, doing her best to look as though she belonged, trying not to limp or dawdle. She pressed the unlock button on the key fob every few seconds, searching for the telltale flash of parking lights.

She grew increasingly uncomfortable as the seconds passed. She began to wonder whether the car wasn't parked somewhere else. The thought gave her a panicked feeling in her stomach. She was on borrowed time. They knew she was going to show up at the hospital, and she had obliged them by waltzing in the front door, alone, half-drugged, and wounded.

What had she told Brock? No more unnecessary risks?

She figured that *necessary* was in the eye of the beholder, but Brock would likely see that argument as quibbling. And he would be right.

She rounded the third row of cars, and her blood froze.

She saw a man sitting in the driver's seat of a small sedan. The motor was off. He wasn't playing with a cell phone, or listening to the radio, or smoking a cigarette.

He was watching.

He saw her.

It was too late to turn back. If she ran, the man would simply catch her. She wasn't going to set any land speed records with an angry wound in her side.

Sam walked past the sedan, pulse pounding, hands vibrating with adrenaline.

She heard the car door open as she passed.

She moved the key fob to her left hand, stuck her right hand into her purse, clutched her pistol. She quickened her pace, hoping the headscarf was enough of a distraction to buy her a few paces, a few meters, a few seconds.

She quickened her pace yet again as the man stepped out of the sedan. She resisted the urge to turn and look at him. She didn't want to give him a good look at her face.

She also resisted the urge to run. It would just invoke the man's chase instinct. Like a feral dog.

She mashed the unlock button manically. Her thumb hurt from the unnecessary pressure.

Finally. The flash of yellow lights. She had found the car. A BMW sedan, a five-series. She must have stolen a doctor's jacket.

She resisted the temptation to run toward the car, opting instead to walk at a brisk, deliberate pace.

She was ten steps from the car when the man called out to her. "You! Stop!" His voice was low, guttural, raspy.

He yelled in English. Not a good sign. It suggested he recognized her.

Sam pretended not to hear. She kept walking. Six paces to go.

"Stop!" he shouted again. He sounded closer, meaner, more insistent.

Fear coursed through Sam's veins. She lunged toward the driver's side door, jerked it open, thrust herself into the seat, and slammed the door shut. She used the key fob to lock the doors. She jammed the key into the ignition and twisted. The big, powerful BMW engine came to life.

Motion caught the corner of her eye. She turned. He was right outside the window.

"Police!" the man shouted. "Open up, now!"

He wasn't wearing a uniform.

He wasn't holding a badge.

But he was definitely holding a gun.

Chapter 17

Sam jammed the big sedan into reverse. She cranked the wheel to the right. She mashed the gas pedal.

She saw the man, the gun, the snarl on his face. He became a blur as the car pulled out of the hospital parking spot.

She saw him lurch out of the way, but not far or fast enough. She felt a thump as the sedan sideswiped him.

After that, she couldn't see him. She had no overt intention of grinding him up beneath her tires, but she wasn't opposed if that was what the universe had in mind. She cleared the other cars, threw the transmission into drive, whipped the wheel back to the left, stepped hard on the accelerator.

The car lurched forward, rocketing toward the parking lot exit. She felt no more thumps. He must have gotten out of the way.

She saw motion in her rearview mirror. The man was standing up, pointing the gun at the back of the car. Sam rounded the corner, narrowly missing an early morning commuter on the cross-street. She looked back into the parking lot. More motion. The attacker, sprinting toward the back of the parking lot.

Then he was lost to sight.

The road arced in a long, lazy curve, and the hospital soon disappeared around the bend. Sam spent more time checking her mirrors than looking forward. She was certain there would be more of them.

Time to change the game up.

She took the next left, and then the first left after that, sending her back toward the rising sun. The maneuver displaced her one block south of the hospital road, and she was now heading opposite the direction she had turned leaving the parking lot. It was an old trick, but a pretty good one. She hoped it had worked.

She looked at her watch. Thirty minutes until Brock's flight landed. She wondered if there was enough time to shake her tail.

She wondered if it mattered. If they knew her flight details in sufficient time to place an agent or two on her trans-continental flight out of DC, it was no stretch to imagine that they'd know about Brock's flight, too.

The thought made her shudder. Brock was two hundred pounds of sexual tyrannosaurus, but he wasn't a trained spy.

She thought again about the woman standing outside the hospital entrance. Her features had seemed familiar. Sam wasn't certain, but her instincts told her it was the same woman from the airport. If so, it implied a resource limitation. It was a fundamental rule of trade craft. If you're spotted, you're pulled from the op. It was just too risky to have a field agent running around who was known to the target. So maybe the opponents weren't as well-resourced as Sam originally thought.

Her thoughts snapped back to the present. The goon in the parking lot. Had she shaken him? Were there others?

The question answered itself, and in unambiguous fashion. As

Sam approached an intersection, two cars pulled forward and stopped in the middle.

Instant gridlock.

Sam cursed.

There was no road space to drive around the two cars. But there was a sidewalk. Sam cranked the wheel to the right, jumped the curb, and narrowly avoided a newspaper stand on the corner. A startled pedestrian dove out of the way. Sam floored the accelerator, and the big sedan leaped off the sidewalk, tires chirping as they contacted the roadway.

As Sam rounded the corner, the two cars blocking the intersection maneuvered to give chase. The first was already on her bumper. The second was turning around, to a chorus of angry honks.

It was on. The Wild Damned West.

Sam matted the accelerator. The big BMW responded. She felt her body sink into the cushion as the powerful engine rocketed her forward. Thank God for midlife-crisis cars. She was soon doing a hundred and fifty clicks per hour on the narrow two-lane road.

It gave a whole new meaning to the term defensive driving.

She checked her rearview mirrors. Both cars from the intersection were in view. A Saab and a Volvo, at least from what Sam could tell. They evidently had plenty of power to keep up. It was going to be down to the driver and, unfortunately, the driver's knowledge of the city. Sam didn't like her odds.

The road intersected a cross-street. A busy traffic circle conjoined the perpendicular roads. Sam dove into the fray, narrowly missing an angry commuter. She forced herself into the traffic loop.

She heard long horn blasts and saw an obscene gesture. She nudged her way over to the leftmost lane of the traffic circle and accelerated again, tires squealing with the force of her turn.

She didn't exit the traffic circle at the first, second, or even third exit. Instead, she went all the way around. She ended up heading the opposite direction on the same road she'd just left.

She had lost sight of her pursuers, both of them. She had no clue where they had gone, but she didn't linger to find out. She took the first side street, turning a hard right to make the corner. Her tires chirped with the turn. She scanned her mirrors frantically.

Then she looked forward.

A dead end.

She cursed loudly and slammed her fist against the steering wheel. She'd just proven again why car chases in strange cities were rarely advisable. Another crazy risk she'd forced herself into taking.

She drove as far forward as possible, still spewing obscenities. A long, low wall brought the narrow side street to an abrupt end. There was enough room to turn the big BMW around, but just barely. Sam jerked the transmission into reverse.

She was halfway through her turnaround, the big car awkwardly perpendicular to the narrow roadway, when she saw them. First the Volvo, then the Saab. They rounded the corner onto the side street.

It was over.

There were a few options, Sam figured, but none of them were terribly savory.

So she opted for brute force. She left the keys in the ignition, jammed the car into park, threw the door open, and leaped free of the car.

She stood in the Weaver stance. She pulled her Kimber .45 from her purse and leveled it at the approaching car.

The threat had no visible effect. The driver was undeterred. He accelerated toward Sam, engine growling with malice aforethought. Evidently, her pursuer doubted her willpower.

Sam aimed for his center of mass, hoping the windshield wouldn't deflect the slug on its way to the man's heart. She pulled the trigger, first once, then again, and was rewarded by the familiar boom and mule-strength kick of the big handgun.

The windshield was no match for the big slugs. They punched through, leaving concentric rings in the glass in their wake.

Hit.

Center of mass, Sam guessed. Maybe a little high. She blamed the windshield.

The car lurched. The engine sound changed, and the nose drifted. It slammed against the side of the building on Sam's left. It came to a halt, blocking the narrow lane. The trailing car skidded to a halt behind.

Sam didn't wait to see what happened next. She leaped over the low wall, gritting her teeth at the sharp pain in her side, wondering vaguely about the status of her wound. She hadn't checked it since the eye-watering experience of leaping out of the hospital bathroom window.

Her foot landed on a steep downslope on the opposite side of the wall. She lost her balance. She fell headlong down the hill, ass over teakettle, twisting and rolling, until her legs slammed into the ground at an awkward angle, ending her tumble.

She cried out with pain. Her side hurt with an unbelievable intensity.

There was no time to recover. She stood, unsteady at first, dizzy from her fall, woozy from the pain. Then she took a deep breath, clenched her jaw, and took off again at the closest thing to a run that she could muster.

Before her flowed the Danube River. Behind her, the sound of heels clicking against the pavement on the roadway above.

Her stomach constricted. Where was her gun? It had been in her hand when she leaped over the wall. It was gone now.

She turned around, frantically scanning the steep slope leading up to the dead-end road. The path of her fall was clearly marked by flattened weeds and grass.

Sam backtracked the trail with her eyes. A third of the way up, she saw it, the blued steel barrel gleaming in the early morning sunlight. She scrambled up the hill.

Her pursuer leaped over the wall.

She saw his eyes widen as he realized the severity of the downslope on the other side. But his landing was more athletic than her own. He arrested his fall in just a couple of steps.

He raised his weapon.

Almost there. Sam dove the last few feet, arm and fingers extended, reaching for her gun. Her body slammed into the side of the hill.

The air rushed from her lungs. Her side erupted in electric

pain.

But her fingers closed around her gun.

She heard the telltale *sssip* of a silenced slug as he loosed his first round. She heard an angry *crack* as the bullet tore into the concrete riverbank behind her. She had to find cover.

But there was no cover.

She rolled to her left, came to rest on her stomach, adjusted her grip, leveled the sights, and squeezed the trigger, letting loose another thunderous boom that rolled up and down the river.

She hit him. Nowhere vital. But a .45-caliber bullet entering one's body at any spot tended to have a profound effect. Her assailant howled. He clutched his leg. He cursed.

But he didn't go down. He raised his gun again.

Sam's training kicked in. Slow down to get there faster. Aim small to miss small. The muzzle of his gun stared her in the face, but she forced herself to relax. She inhaled, held her breath, willed her index finger to move backward slowly, steadily, calmly.

The explosion and recoil surprised her, just like it always did when she let loose a bullseye hit.

Center of mass.

Game over. He fell in a heap.

Sam stood, unsteady, body shaking from adrenaline. She retched. She had no idea if it was due to her anesthesia, or due to the adrenaline, or due to the pain in her side, but she emptied her meager stomach contents onto the hillside next to the Danube.

She wiped her mouth on the stolen leather jacket. She safed her weapon, put it back in her purse, and moved forward to examine the body. All the noise was certain to attract gawkers, and then police. She didn't have much time. Searching the body was a risk, but Sam needed something to go on, anything to point her in the right direction. Even a tiny morsel could help her figure out who was chasing her, and why.

She walked on rubbery legs over the dead assailant. High cheekbones. An angry, small, thuggish mouth. Eastern European.

Slavic. Just like 32A.

She saw instantly that her bullet had pierced his heart. Just like the last guy.

She'd let loose three rounds, all from her personal handgun, the same gun that had gutted the man in the cave the day prior. She wasn't exactly keeping a low profile. All of that forensic evidence was bound to catch up with her. She needed a break, and fast.

There wasn't anything in the man's pockets, other than his car keys. Sam pocketed them. She was suddenly in need of a ride, she realized, and the assailant's wheels would do as well as any. For the moment, anyway.

She kept his silenced handgun, a Hechler and Koch. Nice piece. She vowed that the next time she killed a guy in Budapest, it would be with the goon's gun, and not her own.

She frisked him, finding a large knife inside of one sock. She put it in her purse for a rainy day.

She heard a crinkling sound as she patted down his other leg. Like a piece of paper. Sam lifted his pant leg and pulled down his sock. A business card fell out. Weird.

Sam couldn't read the writing. There were no pictures to help her out. She had no idea whether it would be useful or not. But she figured that a sock was a strange place to carry around a business card. She pocketed the card.

She trudged back up the hill.

She looked over the low wall as she neared the top of the rise. Her heart leaped into her throat again. A small crowd had gathered. They were peering into the window of the first assailant's car.

Indecision seized her. Should she turn around, march back down the hill, and make her escape on foot? Felt like a low-percentage play, especially with a gaping wound in her side. She needed mechanical transportation, and pronto.

She took a second to compose herself, then walked toward the growing crowd.

Nobody noticed her. They were all too busy staring at the dead guy, hunched over in a pool of his own blood. Several were snapping photos with their cell phones.

Sam thought that was a damn good idea. She did the same, cursing herself for not remembering to photograph the other guy, down the embankment. In a flash, she emailed the photo to Dan, hoping it would produce a hit in a database someplace.

Sam walked to the second assailant's car. She climbed inside, put the key in the ignition, put the car in reverse, backed out of the narrow side street. If any of the gawkers noticed her leaving, they didn't give any indication.

She turned out onto the main road just as the first police car arrived. A lucky break, getting out before the cops showed up.

Her hands shook. She still tasted bile. Her side was killing her.

But she felt alive.

Post-combat euphoria set in, a potent cocktail of endorphins and post-adrenal alertness. She felt a familiar elation, an awe and wonder at being alive. The world had a sharpness, a crispness, a colorful, welcoming friendliness. She wondered vaguely whether she had traded alcohol for adrenaline. Addicts only had the power to choose their poison, she remembered from her recovery days.

She shook her head. She had cheated death again. But she was still very much in play. She was tooling around a foreign town in a car belonging to her pursuer, a man she had just sent howling into the afterlife. Obviously, hers wasn't a life-prolonging predicament.

She needed to search the car to glean any available information, and then she needed to find a new ride. Immediately, if not sooner.

Her iPhone buzzed.

A text from Brock. "Hi, baby. I just landed in Budapest!"

* * *

Sam's heart raced. She feared for Brock's safety. She responded to his text. "So glad you're here! Small situation…"

Brock's reply arrived instantly. "Tell your boss to pound sand."

"Wish it were that easy. Remember our flight to Caracas?" It had only been a few months since their trip to Venezuela, and it had been an extremely eventful flight, so she was sure Brock would get her meaning. There were watchers. Sam and Brock had given them the slip, but Francis Ekman hadn't been so lucky. Or proficient. Ekman's punishment had been a bullet between the eyes.

"Oh, shit," Brock texted.

Sam smiled. "Right. Ask for a wheelchair, cover yourself with a blanket, and I'll meet you outside of security."

"Are you sure about this?"

"No, but I don't have any better ideas yet," Sam typed.

She had no idea where she was. The car chase had left her completely turned around, so she asked her cell phone about her whereabouts, and how to get to the airport. The little glowing box obliged, providing a roadmap and spoken real-time driving instructions. Miracles never ceased.

Twenty minutes to reach the airport, the phone said. Sam figured it hadn't accounted for her lead foot. She hoped to make it in fifteen.

Along the way, she called Dan Gable. It was midnight in DC. Sarah was going to hate her even more.

"Sam, you have to stop calling me at home," Dan said.

"But that's where you are," Sam said. "How else would I get ahold of you?"

"Ha ha." Dan sounded tired.

"I made some more new friends," Sam said. "I sent you a picture of one of them."

"I got it," Dan said. "He looked permanently relaxed. Your doing?"

"Unfortunately," Sam said. "But he started it."

"I suppose you want me to run a search."

"Anytime in the next few minutes would be great," Sam said. "He had a friend who ended up in the same condition. The friend had a silenced H&K pistol and business card on him. The card was tucked into his sock."

"Strange place for a business card," Dan said.

"I thought so."

"What did it say?"

"Something in a foreign language. I'll send you a picture of it. Maybe you can work some internet magic."

"Magic is what I do," Dan said. His voice turned serious. "Sam, seriously, three bodies in less than two days. Somebody is bound to notice."

"I hope they do, and I hope they learn their lesson," Sam said.

"The tough guy routine gets a little old, Sam. You take too many risks. You're going to get killed again."

She ignored the admonishment. "I'm told the first guy is being investigated as a murder victim. And when I left the scene with the other two goons a minute ago, the police were just arriving. I'm driving a dead guy's car."

"Smooth. They'll have an APB out on you in a nanosecond. I don't suppose you picked up your shell casings?"

"Shit," Sam said. She wasn't thinking like a fugitive.

"Smooth," Dan said again.

"I suppose this probably warrants a call to Tom Davenport."

"You think?"

"I have other news, too. The dead Mark Severn looks nothing like the live one."

"What?"

"It was a dead guy," Sam said. "But it wasn't *our* dead guy."

Dan whistled. "The old switcheroo?"

"Unbelievable. They couldn't have expected to gain more than a few hours with such a brazen fraud."

"Maybe a few hours is all they needed."

"Maybe so. I'd really like to know if there were any stabbing victims treated in Budapest over the last couple of days," Sam said.

"Your wish is my command."

"That's what I like to hear," Sam said. She followed her phone's directions and merged onto the highway, working through the Saab's gearbox and enjoying the turbocharger en route to the airport. Was there a speed limit in Hungary? She had no idea.

"Speaking of wishes and commands," Dan said, "I was able to do a little sleuthing about that eyes-only thing Farrar and Davenport want you to investigate."

"Do tell."

"Rumor has it Homeland is compromised."

"Say it isn't so." Perhaps the sarcasm wasn't necessary, but Homeland was compromised once a week, in Sam's estimation. "Is it a bullshit tasking?"

"If it quacks like a duck…" Dan said.

"I was afraid of that."

"Sam, you could spend your whole career looking for moles. Who was that guy who gutted the CIA?"

Sam nodded. She remembered the story. Everybody in the counterespionage world did. "James Jesus Angleton."

"That's right. He hobbled them. And how many moles did he catch?"

"Not one. So you're saying the bosses are putting me on a snipe hunt?"

"I don't know. But smart money says if they had any credible evidence, they'd be making an arrest, not reassigning agents from active cases."

"Good point," Sam said, taking the highway exit specified by the talking box in her hand. "So I should resist coming home for as long as possible?"

"I don't know what you should do, Sam," Dan said. "They don't seem terribly happy with you at the moment. Davenport thinks you should have gone straight to the airport, and not stopped at Severn's hotel."

"Yeah, that might have been a direct verbal order," Sam said. "Then again, it wasn't the clearest connection in the world. Maybe there's some wiggle room there."

"I'd play up the wounded-in-the-line-of-duty angle."

"I won't mention that I might be wanted for murder. Speaking of, have you made any headway learning who my mysterious benefactors were?"

"Maybe. What kind of accent did they have again?"

"I don't know for sure. Their consonants came from a little bit too far back in their throats, like they were talking around their teeth. It sounded familiar, but I couldn't place it."

"Is there any chance it was Israeli?"

Sam slapped the steering wheel. "Holy shit. That's *exactly* what it was. I had an Israeli instructor during training. I could never really understand him. What the hell are the Israelis doing in

Hungary?"

"Same thing they do everywhere else."

"Mossad?"

"My money's on Shin Bet."

"Even better. How did you find them?"

"The coordinates you gave me corresponded to a safe house in the archives. I tracked the financials. The records dated back to a Cold War op."

"Cold War?"

"Soviets. Nukes. Remember?"

"Yes, Dan, I remember the Cold War. It's just a little hard to believe."

"The agency divested the place in 1972. Right after the Munich Olympics massacre."

Sam pursed her lips. "Hence your Shin Bet wager."

"No pun intended, I'm sure," Dan said. "My gut says the Agency gave it to the Israelis to use while they tracked down the Munich terrorists. It was a Shin Bet op all the way."

"But that still doesn't explain why the Israelis were helping me out, or how they knew where to find me, just in the nick of time."

"I have no theories there," Dan said.

"This is turning into one hell of a yarn ball."

"Doesn't it always? And here's another little something," Dan said. "My wife swears she saw Mark Severn yesterday."

Sam laughed. "Are you sure it's not lack of sleep playing tricks on her mind?"

"I'm sure that's exactly what it is, but I would have to be a damn fool to suggest it."

"Good point. I'm scared of Sarah, and I'm not even married to her."

"I don't know what you're talking about. It's pure bliss. As long as I keep the kitchen knives hidden."

"I'll try to stop calling in the middle of the night."

"No, you won't."

"I said I'd try. Who knows if I'll succeed."

Chapter 18

Nero Chiligiris assessed his predicament. He was shirtless, wearing only shoes and pants trousers, walking south through scrub and scrabble, gaining distance between himself and Highway 50, which ran east-west with varying degrees of straightness across the entire width of the state.

Half a dozen miles to the east was Pueblo, a little slice of the Third World right in Colorado. Nero had made several exchanges in Pueblo in his capacity as messenger for the sour-tempered Arab, and he never enjoyed his time there. Globalization had decimated the industrial sections of town, and Pueblo only had industrial sections.

Trafficking was the major remaining commercial enterprise. Humans, narcotics, weapons, desperation. It was a grim business, but it was booming.

The recollection made Nero wonder again what kind of business Money was really in.

The recollection also made him realize that Pueblo was probably the perfect place to begin clearing his name. Almost everyone in Pueblo had something to hide, even if it was just an undocumented relative. Nero would fit right in. At least long enough to get a plan together.

He continued south until the road noise from the highway had dissipated to a low murmur, then turned toward the midmorning sun.

He wasn't certain how far it was to Pueblo, but he was certain he was up to the task. It would be slow going, through fields and bramble, over an occasional barbed wire fence, avoiding the ubiquitous dirt roads that transected the flat sections of the state.

He had no illusions. Setting things right wouldn't be easy. While they weren't exactly extreme right-wingers, the local population was certainly well-trained to avoid helping strangers so near the federal prison. It was full of murderers and rapists, so the locals wouldn't likely hesitate to drop a dime on him. People with immigration problems usually had little stomach for criminal involvement. He had to be very careful, or he would find himself back on the inside.

And his experience over the last two days had demonstrated clearly that working from within the system to clear his name was not going to be possible. The game was rigged in a new and different way than it used to be. The scales were never really in the little guy's favor, but The Man had somehow developed a vice grip that worked on a guy's balls like no tomorrow.

No phone calls. No lawyers. No trial. No Habeas whatever-it-was. We suspect you, and therefore you're guilty.

He wondered when the justice system had gone off the rails.

Nero had done hard time, an entire decade in a gray cell, fighting despair and buggery, counting the days and months and years until he got his life back.

But he had done the crime that earned the time. He had been tried by a jury of his peers, and had been found guilty. Rightfully so. In his case, the system had worked. Sure, it didn't go down the way he would have wanted it to, but justice was served — to the extent that losing one's liberty over transporting a few plants across some line on a map could be called "justice."

But that's how the game was played. You drove on their roads, lived in their cities, paid for shit with their dollars, lived under the protection of their Army. You were very much in their world, and you had to play by their rules. That's how it had always been, since people began writing things down. Big people made big agendas, and little people either followed suit or got ground up in the gears.

But this was different. This was a new game entirely. They could throw your ass in a cell, call you guilty, lock you away, throw away the key, and strip you of any ability to prove them wrong.

And exactly how would you go about proving your innocence, anyway? It meant proving a negative, proving that something didn't exist. You couldn't prove what wasn't. Proving the non-existence of a sequence of non-events was a total impossibility. Not nearly the same thing as proving a fact, a relationship, a payoff, a murder, a crime. Something that existed could be proven. But if you didn't do it? How the hell were you supposed to prove that?

There was no presumption of innocence these days. That was the gut punch of it all.

Nero walked east, the sun beating down on him, a heavy weight gathering in his chest, a seething anger festering within him.

He had to figure something out, and fast.

* * *

Nero didn't have to walk very long or very far.

Opportunity met him more than halfway. A farmhouse. Low,

sagging, gray, empty.

Farm consolidation. Only the big guys were left. At least, that's what Nero had heard. He had no agricultural experience or aptitude. He could barely grow mold.

He cased the exterior of the house, looking for any signs of inhabitance. He peered through the windows, using his hands against the glass to block the sun's reflection.

Graffiti covered the walls. Drug paraphernalia was strewn about. He walked around to the front door. Unlocked.

"Hello?" He called. He didn't want to surprise anyone, especially anyone with jangly druggy-nerves and a weapon. He heard only the harsh echoes of an empty house.

"Hello!" Louder, and with more confidence this time.

Again, silence. He stepped in, looked around. The stench of human waste assaulted his nostrils. There was sweat mixed in there as well, and rot. He had smelled it before, a long time ago. He was grateful his life had never come to this.

He padded slowly and carefully through the small rooms of the small house, taking mental inventory of any potentially useful items left behind by the tweakers.

There weren't many. Disassembled appliances littered the kitchen, victims of the crack addicts' strange inclinations. It didn't matter. Nero didn't plan to do any cooking.

The bathroom was awful, worse than the worst truck stop disaster he had ever seen in his life. The smell was overpowering. He closed the door, fighting a wave of nausea.

He checked the bedroom. There was just one. It was a small

farmhouse, probably belonging to a small farm, probably a small-time guy who didn't have the cash reserves to survive a bad crop or two.

Nero smelled rotting flesh.

He looked in the closet.

He immediately wished he hadn't. A junkie lay curled up, dead, leathery flesh taut around his skinny arms, stomach contents adorning his torso.

It was more than Nero's stomach could take. He was sick, adding fresh bile and acid to the disgusting odors.

He stumbled from the bedroom and took a minute to gather himself.

Maybe he should have kept walking, he thought.

He took deep breaths, but the stench in the farmhouse added to his misery. He retched again, then put his hand over his mouth and nose, trying to block the stench.

He wandered through the remainder of the house, storm basement included. He found a long knife wedged in a crevice between basement stairs. It had a long blade, not very sharp, but if things turned sour, a dull blade was better than no blade. He tucked it into his pocket.

He found a dirty work shirt balled up in the basement corner. He shook it out, kicking up an indoor dust storm. It looked to be about his size. Providential, but smelly. He donned the shirt, fighting a sense of revulsion at putting on someone else's garments. He walked back upstairs, picked his way through the house, and found the door to the garage.

He opened the door and walked down the two wooden steps leading from the house.

What he saw made him smile.

* * *

It didn't look to be in terrific shape. There was rust, dust, and mud. But nothing major looked out of alignment. Upon first inspection, Nero could see nothing terribly wrong with it.

It was a motorcycle. Probably thirty years old. With a relatively recent license plate. Which meant that it probably ran, or if not, it probably wasn't going to be too difficult to fix. Old engines were designed for simplicity and reliability.

Nero wondered how the motorcycle had survived the deadly disassembling clutches of the tweakers who had made the abandoned farmhouse their temporary home. Perhaps it was only by a random act of kindness on the part of the vast, dark, cold universe that Nero was able to find the motorcycle relatively unmolested while kitchen appliances lay strewn about the house in various stages of disassembly.

It was a lucky break. Nero was damn glad for it. Lord knew, he needed one.

He cleared away debris, an old blanket, a tire iron, and an anvil from around the motorcycle. He raised the bike up off of its kickstand. He clicked the gear shift into neutral, rolled the motorcycle backward, twisted the handlebars, and backed the bike away from the wall, giving himself some space to work.

He opened the gas tank. Half full. He wondered whether the gas had sat long enough to denature. He didn't know what that meant chemically, but he knew it was a bad thing for engines. He moved the motorcycle back and forth, sloshing the tank. It looked and smelled like gas.

He checked the oil next. It was tar black, but again half full.

He squeezed the clutch. It squeaked and groaned. He wondered whether anything was happening inside the engine. He figured he would find out soon enough.

The spark plug seemed okay, and the ignition wires looked to be in good shape as well. Nero wasn't a professional mechanic, but neither was he a slouch around engines. He liked his chances of getting the old motorcycle running.

He swung his right leg over the motorcycle seat, pressed his weight down against the cushion, felt the springs and shocks compress beneath him, flexed his fingers against the brake lever.

The moment of truth. He flipped the kick-starter out to the side, double-checked the transmission was in neutral, pulled the clutch in anyway, and jumped on the starter.

The motorcycle lubbed, coughed once, and stopped well short of starting. But it did turn over, and that was a great sign. It meant all the moving parts were still in decent shape, and nothing was rusted solid inside the engine block. He liked his chances even more, and set about figuring out what had prevented ignition.

Simple stuff, he recalled. Gas, air, and spark. The atoms took care of everything else.

It took less than a second to figure out why the motorcycle didn't start.

No key.

Nero searched the garage, looking for a nail with a keychain hanging from it. No luck. Debris was strewn about, but there was little else of value remaining in the garage. He wandered around the house again, searching through piles of appliance parts for a key.

No luck.

He looked out the window. The sun was high in the sky. The prison van driver's words returned to him. Burning daylight. There would be a search party forming soon, and it wouldn't take any quantum physics to figure out the few likely hiding places in the vicinity. This part of Colorado featured a whole lot of nothing. He had to get that motorcycle running.

He went back into the garage, looked again at the motorcycle. The ignition box didn't look all that sturdy, and an idea struck.

Nero opened the side door, walked outside the garage, and found a fist-sized rock beside the house. He brought it inside, got a sturdy grip on it, took aim, and bashed the ignition box several times. The box was made of sheet metal, but the cover was plastic, and Nero soon exposed the ignition wires within.

He smiled. There was only one wire coming into and out of the key receptacle. Simple. Old-school. Easy to hotwire. "Yeah, baby," Nero said with a smile. He ripped the wires from the key receptacle, stripped the insulation a bit further with his teeth, and twisted the wires together.

No key necessary.

Nero mounted the bike again. He tried the kick starter again.

Again, the motorcycle didn't start. But the motor did turn over, and it did sound to Nero as if it were trying to engage.

Encouraged, he tried again. And again, giving it a little more throttle each time.

It turned over, burbled and sputtered for a second, then died.

Nero checked the accelerator on the right handlebar, wondering if the cable was loose.

Sure enough. He used his fingers to tighten the cable. He tried again.

The motorcycle started.

He revved the engine, and it sang to him, unsteady and out of tune at first, then strong and steady.

* * *

Nero drove away from the abandoned farmhouse. He figured it was best to avoid Highway 50, with all of its traffic and all of its state troopers. He turned south on a dirt road at the end of the abandoned farmhouse drive, accelerated, and worked his way through the gears with his left foot.

He had no sunglasses, and the wind dried his eyes, blowing tears backward toward his ears as he bounced up and down in the dusty, dirty Colorado scrub.

It felt damned good not to be chained up in a box. But he had his work cut out for him.

Before long, he came to an intersection with a paved road. Just a little two-lane job, untrafficked, with narrow shoulders and a faded stripe down the center. Exactly what he was looking for.

He turned east, toward Pueblo. He was aiming for the southern edge of town. Nothing there but dust and despair. Perfect for his needs.

Soon an expanse of dilapidated mobile homes, boarded-up shops, and a faded 1960s sparkle announced that he had reached Pueblo's outskirts. He was surprised how short the trip had been. The van wreck really hadn't been too far out of town.

Time to get to work. He needed gas to get where he was going. He needed money to get gas.

Or ingenuity.

Nero turned into the Dandy Deal Mobile Home Park and drove around. It didn't take long to find what he was looking for. He spotted a pickup truck parked in the weeds outside a ramshackle mobile home. Eighties vintage, judging by the truck's body rust and uneven lines.

Nero smiled. Trucks had gas. Old trucks had unlocked gas caps.

Nero looked around, searching for a hose, or anything he could use as a siphon. Nothing presented itself, so he drove around the trailer park again, looking for anything that he might use to pull gas from the truck's tank and siphon it into the motorcycle.

An old man peered from a trailer window. Nero smiled and waved. Best to be friendly. Human psychology. Nobody expected a friendly, courteous criminal.

He rounded the corner and made his way up the adjacent lane, looking around and behind each mobile home as he passed.

The third house from the left prominently featured a disused clothes washing machine in its final resting place at the side of the trailer, next to a rusting water heater. Nero got off the motorcycle, climbed through waist-high weeds, and examined the washing machine.

Bingo. Two black hoses, still attached to the hot and cold water inputs on the washing machine. Nero smiled. It was one hell of a lucky day.

The knurled hose caps dug into his fingers as he twisted them free. It took no small amount of doing, but Nero liberated both hoses from the washing machine. He only needed one hose, but they said you only needed one kidney, too. Redundancy was insurance.

He hopped back on the motorcycle, drove back around to the far side of the trailer park, stopped his bike several houses down from his target, and separated the ignition wires to kill the engine. He didn't want the sound of his motorcycle to alert the truck owner several addresses away.

He slung the washer hoses over his shoulder and pushed his bike nonchalantly down the narrow lane, just a guy taking his motorcycle for a walk through a trailer park, a nothing-to-see-here expression on his face.

He parked his bike next to the truck and looked around the mobile home for signs of occupancy. There was no motion inside the small, run-down trailer. Nero looked up and down the street, as well. He was the only thing moving on this particular block.

Satisfied he wasn't under surveillance, Nero snuck to the rear quarter panel of the pickup truck, pressed against the gas cap cover, and pumped his fist in victory when the cover sprang open.

He unscrewed the gas cap, inserted the hose in the tank, stuck the other end in his mouth, and sucked until he felt gas coursing through the hose. He pulled away to avoid a mouthful of petroleum.

Too late. Nero gagged and sputtered. Gasoline tasted terrible.

He quickly shoved the hose into the motorcycle's tank and watched as it filled up. It only took a few seconds. He hoped it would be enough gas to get to where he needed to go. He didn't like stealing from people, and he didn't want to have to do it again.

He put the gas caps back on the truck and motorcycle, flung the hose into the bushes, reconnected the ignition wires, and jumped on the starter. The bike revved to life, and Nero made his way back to the main road.

He was tempted to go home. Denver was just a few hours away. He was betting he could make it on a single tank of gas. In fact, he was certain he could make it.

But he had been around long enough to know that going home would be a colossal mistake. The feds would be all over him. In fact, by now, the feds were probably all over Penny and the kids, pressing them for details about his whereabouts.

He longed to touch them, to hold them, to talk with them, to reassure them, tell them that everything was going to be all right. But he knew that doing anything of the sort would be catastrophic. They would swoop in and snatch him up again, maybe with those damned helicopters.

And they would be much more careful with him this time around. He'd already escaped once, and they would want to make sure it didn't happen again. They would truly tie him by the balls.

He had to work out a way to get a message to Penny, to tell the kids he was okay.

But that would have to wait. He had more pressing needs at the moment. Money topped the list, both the green kind that bought things like gas and food, and the unbearably arrogant Middle Eastern kind, who Nero was sure held the key to understanding why the Department of Homeland Security had crawled up his ass.

Nero followed signs for I-25. He headed north, a plan forming in his mind.

Chapter 19

Sam followed her phone's driving instructions to the airport. She didn't take the exit for passenger parking. She followed the signs for employee parking. Throw the opposition a curveball at every opportunity, she figured. If she added enough of them together, she might even survive the day.

As she pulled toward the employee entrance, she saw a gate. There was a metal box on a post to the left. A card reader. The driver in front of her swiped a badge, and the gate opened. Easy.

But Sam had no badge. She pulled over to the side of the road, knee bouncing impatiently, checking the time on her phone.

It only took a few minutes for another car to appear. It drove confidently toward the gate and the box. Sam tucked in behind. When the gate lifted, Sam mashed the accelerator to make it through before the gate slammed shut behind. It was close, but she made it. She ignored the slightly put-off look from the driver she'd tailgated through the entrance.

She wound her way around a circular drive leading to the employee parking lot. All of the employee spots were numbered, meaning they probably used an assigned parking system. But the spots were not all full, so Sam chose an empty stall, parked, got out of the car, and threw the keys into the bushes. She was tempted to hold onto them, to keep them as an option for later in case things got dicey, but she knew that driving a dead assassin's car around town was a beautiful way to get pinched.

She had another problem to solve. She needed to get into the airport. She followed signs toward the employee shuttle bus, merged with a small crowd gathering at the bus stop, tucked the scarf tighter around her head, making sure none of her bright red locks were free to wave around in the breeze. There was no use drawing any unwanted attention, and she tried to blend in as much as possible, which was difficult for someone with Sam's looks and dimensions. She slouched, giving the world her impression of a downtrodden wage laborer, reducing her height and changing her vibe.

She performed a cursory scan of the crowd, noticed no threats, and cast a blank expression on her face, just another worker starting another day on the job.

The shuttle bus arrived. Sam shuffled on. The ride lasted just a few moments, and the shuttle emptied at the employee entrance. Sam merged with the flow of people. The first worker in line badged the door open and held it for the next guy, who held it for the next, all of them ignoring a printed sign exhorting everyone to badge in individually for anti-terrorism reasons. Courtesy continued to displace security, and Sam flowed with the crowd inside the employee center.

She noticed half the workers wore uniforms, while the other half didn't. The uniformed half went straight to work. The non-uniformed half went into a locker room. Sam followed a couple of female workers, of North African descent, by Sam's estimation, into the female locker room. The room was surprisingly large, filled with rows of lockers, most with locks.

Sam began her work in a far corner, away from the other laborers, who chatted drearily in a foreign tongue while changing into their work smocks.

She reached into her purse, retrieved two small, thin metal instruments, selected a locker at random, and picked the lock. It didn't take much time at all.

For her effort, she was rewarded with a gray cleaner's smock. The locker also contained a pair of gray pants. Sam donned the clothes. Too big in the waist, too small in the shoulders, arms and legs too short, and not by a little. Not ideal. But who really noticed cleaning people, anyway?

She rolled her other outfit — stolen from the hospital an hour earlier — into a ball and tucked it under her arm. A change of clothing might come in handy later. Little things made a big difference.

She still needed a badge to access the various doors throughout the airport. This proved trickier. Workers needed a badge to get through the automobile gate on the entrance road, so nobody left their badge in their locker.

Except by mistake. Sam surveyed the row of locks, took a deep breath, and went to work.

She felt grateful for her misspent youth. Picking each lock took only a few seconds. Picking two dozen locks only took a few minutes, even counting the time spent hiding in the bathroom stall while a fresh wave of workers changed clothes.

That was the magic number, it turned out. Two dozen. An

unfortunate worker had left her badge in the twenty-fourth lock Sam picked. She smiled. It could have been a long morning. She was grateful for her good fortune.

She needed props to complete her disguise. Cleaning people used cleaning supplies. Sam exited the locker room and joined a gaggle of workers heading toward the airport door. A row of cleaning carts lined the hallway near the exit. Sam watched as one of the workers in front of her carefully selected a cart, evidently for the quality of its rolling casters, and pushed it through the double doors and into the airport area.

Sam followed suit. Nobody cast an askew glance in her direction, and nobody spoke a word to her.

She looked at her watch. Thirty minutes had passed since Brock's text had announced his flight's arrival. She hoped he was okay. She hoped he followed her instructions.

She checked her phone for his flight details, then cross-referenced the flight arrival board to find the concourse and gate. She studied an airport map, found the right concourse, and set off, being careful not to walk faster than a real cleaning employee might walk on her way to start a long day scrubbing toilets.

Sam kept her eyes on a swivel. But she did so surreptitiously, staying in character. She saw no signs of trouble.

Until she got to Brock's concourse.

Three men. Two looked Slavic. A third looked Greek. They weren't standing together. They were milling about, but doing a poor job of blending in. They were not the kind of people you would find in an international airport wing, because they had no luggage.

Amateurs, Sam thought. They might as well have walked around with a sign taped to their foreheads.

But knowing who they were and getting around them on the way out of the airport were two very different things. She felt for her purse, slung around her shoulder beneath her cleaning smock. She felt for the familiar heft. Even heftier now, with two handguns stashed inside. She hoped she wouldn't need them. An airport was a terrible place to have to shoot somebody quietly.

Sam trudged toward Brock's gate, calling on every ounce of self-control not to break into a run, to sprint to him, to make sure he was okay. The trek took an excruciatingly long time.

She scanned the small crowd at Brock's gate. Most were sitting down, likely waiting for the next flight. Brock was not among them, and Sam felt her pulse rise. She looked around, far less nonchalantly than she would have desired.

Then she spotted him. He had folded his tall frame into a wheelchair, just like she had asked. He sat hunched over, a dull, bored expression on his face, a blue airline blanket pulled up to his chin, his carry-on bag perched on his lap.

Sam's heart fluttered. Even in his awkward affectation, she just loved him on sight. Her diaphragm spasmed with a bit of pent-up emotion, and her eyes misted.

Then she got herself together. Her eyes scanned the area. She was looking for any of the three goons, or any goon-like person whom she hadn't previously spotted.

She saw no one suspicious, but that didn't mean they weren't being watched. Maybe the rest of the surveillance team just sucked less than the first three clowns.

Sam strolled up to Brock. "May I help you sir?" she asked.

Brock did a double take. His eyes lit up. "Holy shit! Sam!"

"Baby," she said *sotto voce*. "Am I glad to see you. But we need to play it cool for a minute."

She maneuvered behind Brock's wheelchair, unlocked the wheel locks, and pushed him forward down the concourse.

The team following Sam was expecting to find two tall, athletic people. Wheelchairs, hunched-over postures, and cleaning smocks were details that did not fit. Sam hoped the incongruousness would buy a little time.

She scanned the side of the concourse for an exit sign, one marked for employees only. Her impatience grew as she walked past gate after gate, shop after shop, restroom after restroom, spotting no employee exit.

She fought the urge to charge down the concourse, to find an exit and get the hell out of sight as soon as possible. She knew that the fastest way out was to slow down and not attract unwanted attention, uncomfortable as it felt.

Finally, an exit appeared, just beyond a set of restrooms on the left side of the concourse. She wheeled Brock up to the door, swiped her stolen badge against the key card reader, and held her breath.

The door beeped, and Sam heard the clack of the latch. She opened the door.

She gasped.

A large, muscular security guard stood in the doorway on the other side. He eyed her. He looked at Brock in the wheelchair. Sam held her breath.

The guard asked her something in Hungarian.

Sam didn't have to feign ignorance. She had no idea what he'd said. She spoke in rapid-fire gibberish, throwing in an Arabic word or two, gesturing occasionally toward Brock. She stopped and looked up at the guard expectantly, as if her brief monologue should have cleared everything up.

The guard shook his head. *Damn foreigners*, his expression said.

He held the door open. Sam wheeled Brock through. "teşekkür ederim," she said. Turkish for thank-you, if memory served.

She quelled the sudden and irrational feeling of panic caused by the thought that the guard might, in fact, speak Turkish.

He didn't, evidently. He just waved and went back to doing nothing.

Sam's heart rate settled. She pushed Brock around the corner, and they found themselves alone in a long, narrow hallway. She stopped the wheelchair, locked the wheels, moved around to the front, and planted a long, hard, wet kiss on him.

She felt the usual stirrings in the usual places, and it brought a smile to her heart. "You have no idea how glad I am to see you," she said.

* * *

Their reunion was short. Brock stayed in the wheelchair. Sam followed signs for the employee center. If anyone thought it was unusual for a cleaning employee to be pushing a passenger around in a wheelchair, nobody said anything. Testament to human nature. If you looked like you belonged, people just assumed that you did.

But that didn't stop Sam from being nervous about it. She moved quickly, but was careful not to move too quickly. Her eyes surveyed her surroundings carefully, but she worked hard not to appear skittish.

They left the wheelchair parked next to the row of cleaning carts in the employee center. Sam ditched her cleaning uniform and changed into her stolen street clothes.

Next problem: transportation. Sam wasn't keen on stealing cars. Always problematic, especially with all the video cameras in the world. The average time needed to catch a car thief had dropped dramatically over the past several years. Sam didn't want to push her luck.

But neither did she want to walk, and renting a car was out of the question. There would undoubtedly be someone watching the airport rental counter.

She returned to the employee locker room, cursed her lack of foresight at not having stolen a set of keys earlier, and set to work yet again while Brock watched the door.

A Volkswagen this time. She smiled. The car would have a friendly little beep when she pushed the button on the key fob. She hoped it would cut down on the time they spent wandering around the parking lot looking for the car.

It took fifteen minutes. They wandered up and down the rows looking for a Volkswagen, pressing the key fob, searching for flashing lights, listening for the friendly little beep. Sam felt horribly exposed. It was déjà vu all over again. Just like earlier in the morning, in the hospital parking lot. Two corpses earlier.

Finally, they heard it. "Over there," Brock said. They walked briskly, reaching the car in a few strides.

It was relatively new, nice, a Passat. They climbed in. Brock tossed his carry-on bag into the backseat.

Sam leaned over and kissed him again, drinking in his scent, feeling the warm, pleasant tingle of his presence.

He reached his arm around her waist to pull her closer. She barked in pain. He looked at her face, then at her abdomen. "Jesus, Sam! You're bleeding!"

"I imagine quite profusely by now," she said. "I ran into a bit of trouble."

Worry and anger crossed Brock's brow. "Who did this to you?"

"Don't worry. Karma already kicked his ass." She started the car and backed out of the parking spot.

"You've got to knock this off, Sam," he said. "I can't take the strain and worry."

"Neither can I," she said, slowing to allow the automatic exit gate to raise.

"What now?"

"Damn good question."

"Who's following you?"

"Another stumper."

"What the hell is going on, Sam?"

She looked at him. He was upset. She touched his cheek with her hand. "Here's what I know," she said. She told him about 32A.

She told him about someone else having been after Mark Severn's things at the police station. She told him about the wrong body in the hospital morgue.

"Tell me about your side," he said.

She gritted her teeth and told him the truth.

"Jesus Holy Shit Christ, Sam! You spotted a guy tailing you, so you decided to chase him through the city? You've already died once — wasn't that enough?"

She shook her head. "I didn't have much choice, baby."

"What are you talking about? You couldn't call someone? Ask for help? I can't believe you went after these people by yourself, with no backup whatsoever."

"Where would I have gotten help from? The United States? Five thousand miles away? If I hadn't stirred the pot, I might very well have been taken out. My body would be cold by now."

She knew instantly it was the wrong thing to say. A dark cloud came over Brock's face. His fists clenched, and a long silence ensued.

"I can't keep doing this," he finally said. "Every time you leave the house, I wonder if it's the last time I'll ever see you. It's no way to live."

Chapter 20

Sam checked the map on her phone, exited the E71 that circumnavigated the south side of Budapest, took a few surface streets, and came to a stop at the banks of the Danube. The ancient river was home to infinite secrets, and Sam intended to add a few more to the list. "Hand me your cell phone," she said to Brock, grabbing her iPhone and government-issued Blackberry from her handbag.

"Want to read the texts from my girlfriends?"

"Funny," Sam said. She got out of the car, walked to the river bank, and threw all three cell phones into the water.

"A rather extreme solution, don't you think?" Brock asked as she sat back down in the driver's seat.

"Extreme but necessary," Sam said. "They can track your phone even with the power off these days," Sam said.

"Creepy," Brock said.

"Extremely," Sam said. "Anyway, it's kind of nice not to have that distraction all the time."

"I'm going to bill your employer for the phone," Brock said.

"Feel free. He has deep pockets."

"What's our plan?" Brock asked.

"Great question. We need to put some distance between us and this town, unfortunately. But they're tracking our movements somehow, and it wouldn't be smart to travel on your passport. You need a new ID."

"Don't you need one, too?"

Sam shook her head. She pulled her makeup case from her purse, opened the hasp, used her fingernail to manipulate a tiny lever. A spring-activated compartment revealed itself. Sam dumped a passport, identification card, and driver's license onto Brock's lap. The name on all the documents said Molly Rose Hillman. "I never leave home without a little documented schizophrenia," she said.

"Nice. I needed that trick when I was in high school, trying to get into bars."

Sam smiled. "You couldn't find any hot cougars to buy drinks for you?"

"No comment," Brock said.

"I don't have any idea how we're going to get a new passport," she said, brow furrowed. She drove as fast as she felt prudent, just ten clicks over the speed limit. Best not to attract unwanted attention while driving a stolen car.

"We need to talk to Dan," she said after a few moments of silence.

"Says the girl who just threw all our phones in the river."

Sam smiled. "Desperate times. You have your laptop in your carry-on, right?"

"Good thinking," Brock said. "A little voice-over-Internet."

Sam nodded, scanned for the nearest exit, looking for the ubiquitous Starbucks logo.

Sam found a medium-sized town. They drove around, finally spotting a coffee shop. Not a Starbucks. Maybe the franchise hadn't infested Hungary like locusts before mega-expansion turned into mega-contraction.

The coffee shop was closed, but Brock had a hunch the Wi-Fi would still be on.

He wasn't wrong. When his laptop booted up, he selected the free internet option. Provided by Google. In a post-Iron Curtain country. Brave new world, Sam thought. She used an Internet chat application to dial Dan's number. She woke him up.

"You again," Dan said.

"Hi, Dan."

"What do you have against your employees getting a good night's sleep?"

"Sorry," Sam said. "Brock is here with me."

"Seriously?"

"Yeah, this little trip was supposed to be a milk run, if you'll recall, and we were going to take a little vacation after."

"The best-laid plans of mice and men."

"You don't say. There were three thugs at the airport when I picked him up. Waiting for him, me, or both of us."

"So they've connected the dots."

"It sure looks that way," Sam said. "I think all of that means Brock needs new travel documents."

Dan was quiet for a moment, thinking. "That's going to be difficult. He's not a Homeland employee."

"We may have to outsource."

"You mean, commit a felony?"

"Not to put too fine a point on it," Sam said. "Unless you have better ideas."

"I might," Dan said. "Brock's still in the Air Force, right?"

"He is. Colonel Brock James to you and me." She gave Brock a playful pinch. He shook his head.

"I have a friend in the travel department," Dan said. "He's a friendly guy, and he has a lot of other friends. Give me just a sec."

Sam heard Dan walking through his house. Then she heard the click of keystrokes.

"We have that small matter of the Atlantic Ocean hampering our logistics," Sam said while Dan typed.

"We have embassies everywhere," Dan said.

"Run by the CIA, with the State Department acting as shill. We aren't exactly the closest of friends, and there was that scandal about State issuing false passports a while back, so I'm not sure how much help we can expect."

"You're right, in general. But espionage is a people business."

More typing. "Can you get to London?" Dan finally asked.

"You know someone there?"

"The queen."

"Very funny."

"Seriously, I think I can get a new passport for Brock from the London embassy without too many questions. Can you get there?"

"I don't know. Do we need passports to get from the Continent to the Isles?"

"Can't you just take that tunnel under the channel?"

"In a stolen car?"

"Jesus, Sam. You stole a car?"

"Two, actually."

"You are completely out of your mind."

"It was either that or hitchhike," Sam said.

"Jesus, Sam," Dan said again. "I'll leave you to figure that one out. Send me Brock's picture, official-looking. I'll have his new credentials ready to send to London first thing in the morning."

"You're a lifesaver," Sam said.

"Literally."

"Don't let it go to your head. Do you have any information on the dead assholes from this morning?"

"Strange you should ask," Dan said. "The business card you found in the dead guy's sock was written in a Russian dialect. The business is a floral shop in Boston."

"As in, Massachusetts?"

"As in the United States of America. And it gets better. The extremely relaxed gentleman with a hole in his chest went by the name Igor Kurilyenko. He was clearly of Russian descent. But he was a naturalized US citizen."

"Shit," Sam said. "I killed a US citizen in Budapest?"

"It looks that way."

"I'm sure that muddies the jurisdictional waters. It could work to our advantage trying to get out of here if things go south."

"I wouldn't count on it," Dan said. "Europe is a very small place these days."

"What the hell is a US citizen doing chasing me around

Budapest?"

"One does wonder," Dan said. "It might explain how they were able to put a man on your flight out of DC on such short notice. The US citizenship angle, I mean."

"Good point. We need to figure out who they were working for."

"It's on my to-do list already," Dan said. "I have a few feelers out, and I'm hoping to learn more soon."

Sam was silent, stirring things around in her head.

"You can say it," Dan said after a moment.

"Say what?"

"I'm awesome."

"And humble. Now get some sleep, and I'll pester you again in a few hours."

"Sounds like a plan," Dan said. They ended the call.

Brock let out a little whistle. "The plot thickens," he said.

Sam nodded. "I'm beyond confused."

"Glad I'm not the only one."

They got back on the road. Sam looked at her watch. Nine a.m. on a Saturday in Hungary. How many hours to London? A thousand miles, maybe? Twelve hundred? She had the instinct to look at the map on her phone, then remembered she'd sent it to sleep with the fishes. "It's going to be one hell of a long drive," she said.

"Maybe not," Brock said. He fished around in his wallet and produced a small, light green card. The Federal Aviation Administration insignia was emblazoned across the top. His commercial pilot's license. "Maybe we can travel in style."

"I like the way you think," Sam said. "Are you sure the Euros will let us buzz around their continent on the strength of a US pilot's license?"

Brock shrugged. "I'm sure there will be some hassle. But I think we're far enough east that policy takes a backseat to economics."

"I don't follow," Sam said.

"I brought cash."

"For bribes?"

Brock smiled. "No, love. For the requisite European airspace familiarization training. Form and substance at the discretion of the desk clerk at whatever airplane rental counter we happen to find."

"For bribes, then."

"That's what I said."

* * *

Life without telephones was damned near impossible. For example, where in the modern world would one discover the name and location of a suitable private aircraft rental business near Budapest, if not by using one's telephone?

Would one look in a phone book? Those were usually found near a phone, the kind that gobbled coins and gathered graffiti. Which were extinct. Gone from the face of the earth, like the dodo. Or extremely endangered, at least.

The Internet knew all about aircraft rental businesses in central Hungary. And the Internet was everywhere, except when it was nowhere to be found, such as when driving like a bat out of hell — at a medium pace — away from Budapest in a stolen vehicle.

Stopping was hazardous.

Driving a stolen car was hazardous.

Not knowing where you were going while driving a stolen car was good epitaph fodder.

They picked a town named Tata. "Moral imperative," Brock proclaimed. "A town named after tits. We have to stop here. And we have to take a picture next to the sign."

"Seriously, doesn't adolescence ever get old?"

"I don't know what you're talking about."

"And it's only one tata, anyway. Not a pair of them."

"All the more reason to stop. It's probably lonely."

Sam shook her head, a laugh on her lips. Brock's affected imbecility was self-mocking and charming. She loved him all the more for it.

Sam exited the E60 onto Hungary's Highway 1, drove north a few clicks, crested a promontory, and caught her breath. A medieval castle presided over a collection of neoclassical mansions perched on the edge of a sapphire lake. Sidewalk cafes and open-air shops straddled the strand. It appeared to exist in an era all its own.

"This place is unreal," Sam said.

"Makes me want to quit America," Brock said.

Sam chuckled. "Good luck. But I could definitely spend a few years in a place like this."

"We'll have to settle for a few minutes."

"We'll have to come back someday," Sam said.

Not if you keep getting killed, Brock didn't say.

His silence was plenty. The unmade point was made well

enough, and Sam's expression soured. A frown dug its way into her brow. "First things first, I suppose."

Brock nodded. It wasn't the time or place for that particular discussion. They both lacked the energy. He pointed to a Wi-Fi sticker in the window of a cafe.

Sam rounded the corner, parked the stolen Volkswagen behind the long row of shops, cafes, and restaurants, and threw the keys into the bushes.

"What'd you do that for?" Brock asked.

"Europe has almost as many cameras as the US. We need to distance ourselves before the license number hits the APB list."

Brock grimaced. "Nice day for a walk, I guess."

They chose a table at the cafe. Heads turned. They stood out immediately as Americans. It made Sam nervous. She hustled Brock along as he set up his laptop. The cafe's Wi-Fi password contained Hungarian characters, and Brock had to fish around in the computer's settings before he figured out how to enter them into the browser window.

Sam's leg bounced with impatience. She was worried about being recognized by surveillance, and she also began to worry about using Brock's laptop. It had its own IP address, akin to a digital fingerprint, and it wouldn't take anywhere close to Dan Gable's über-geek prowess for someone to start tracking their movements.

"We're in luck," Brock announced after entirely too long. "Aviation rental place right here in Tata. On the outskirts, I mean."

They hailed a cab, a dangerous undertaking, but Sam didn't feel comfortable breaking into a car and stealing it in such a cozy little town. Too many leisurely watchers with nothing better to do than take note of suspicious activity.

She held her breath as the cab pulled away, her hand wrapped around the silenced handgun she'd taken from the guy whose ticket to the Great Beyond she'd punched earlier in the day.

She eyed the cabbie suspiciously. He was all smiles and laughs. It was either great trade craft, or the sign of a non-operator. Sam reserved judgment, which didn't stop her from quietly clicking the safety lever to the off position.

She felt fatigue announce itself in her life as the cab wound its way up the hill away from the lake and toward the plateau behind the castle. Her eyes burned. Her wound started to throb again. She gulped a pain pill to take the edge off the ache in her side, to let her mind focus on more pressing matters.

Her mind felt slow and muddled. Her thoughts sauntered lazily to her consciousness when summoned, a telltale sign of sleep deprivation. She needed to rest, and soon. Before she made another mistake. This time, it was more than just her life at stake.

Sam had the cab drop them off at the hotel adjacent to the airport. Misdirection always helped and never hurt. She nudged Brock to pay the cabbie while she kept the weapon ready in her purse. If there were going to be any shenanigans, now would be the time.

The cabbie took Brock's money with more ebullient good cheer and drove away. Sam felt herself breathe a sigh of relief. She felt far less than ready for any further physical confrontation.

They walked the quarter-mile between the hotel and the

private aviation office, itself perched uncomfortably close to an uncomfortably short runway. Brock's F-16 career exposed him to nothing shorter than eight thousand feet of concrete. Ten was much better. Those jets liked to go, and they didn't like to stop. He still marveled that anything could take off or land from dinky little runways like the one above Tata.

They walked inside. "I'd like to take out one of your Cessna 172's for the weekend," Brock announced with a smile. "One with retractable gear, if possible."

The clerk eyed Brock's American flying license. A worried look crossed her face.

"I would be happy to take any local training that you think would be necessary," Brock said, subtly but noticeably sliding a short stack of greenbacks beneath the registration form.

The clerk's worried look disappeared. "We are always happy to accommodate our international friends," she said.

Brock smiled. "Thank you for your hospitality."

The desk clerk asked, "Would you like help preparing a flight plan?"

Brock shook his head. "I think we'll just see where whim and fancy take us. But I do need a bunch of sectional charts."

The clerk pointed over to a stack of shelves on the wall. Brock selected a handful of maps, and the clerk added them to the bill. Sam produced the American Express card belonging to the pretty redheaded non-person named Molly Rose Hillman.

The clerk used an old-school credit card swipe machine to make an impression of the card number on a three-color carbon-copy receipt. Circa mid-eighties. Sam smiled. There was evidently some truth to the adage that most parts of Europe lagged America by no less than two decades. She felt less worried that someone might trace the transaction.

Brock gathered the pile of maps, the aircraft's maintenance records and flight manual, and a fuel tester. Nothing would kill an engine quicker than water in the fuel, and the Cessna's gas caps were on the top of the wings. If the caps weren't fastened tightly, rain and condensation could ruin the day. Hence the fuel tester, which was nothing more than a clear plastic container. The clarity test was highly sophisticated: pour some gas from the fuel tanks into the container, and look for bubbles.

Sam strapped into her seat while Brock performed his pre-flight inspection. She scanned the area a dozen times, looking for anything or anyone that tweaked the antennae she'd developed in her years in the spy business. She saw nothing shifty, shady, or even mildly suspect. Which made her nervous.

Brock finished his walk-around, strapped into the seat next to Sam, ran through a few more checks, and started the engine.

Ten minutes later, they departed the surface of the earth, turned toward the big W on the compass, and followed the propeller as it clawed its way west.

* * *

They would have preferred an earlier start, but things just didn't quite work out that way. Eleven hundred miles. Eight hours, as the crow flew. And Brock planned to fly as the crow flew, making as close to a straight line as possible between Hungary and England.

They re-debated the wisdom of their decision to rent an airplane and fly across Europe. But the debate didn't last long. European rental car agencies all had Interpol on speed dial. It would be very difficult, even under an alias, to get all the way across Europe in a rental car.

And Sam was tired of stealing cars. It carried even lower odds of long-term success.

So they planned to make several refueling stops at small, out-of-the-way airports, hoping to rely on the relatively lax civil aviation oversight at local flight operations centers. The authorities simply didn't watch recreational aviation the way they watched other transportation methods.

They bumped along at 140 nautical miles an hour, or "knots" in aviation parlance. Brock kept the airplane low to the ground, and took every opportunity to descend below the tops of ridge lines, peaks, and hills to make tracking them by radar as difficult as possible. The flight plan he'd left on file at the rental office said something about heading south, toward the border with Serbia, which was obvious madness. Nobody from Hungary went to Serbia. In fact, almost nobody from anywhere went to Serbia. He wasn't sure the misdirection would be meaningful, but he felt it was worth a shot.

Once he left the Tata control tower's airspace, Brock switched his electronic beacon off. Extremely illegal, but one could always blame equipment failure. Without a beacon, they became a thousand times harder to track by radar, overall an agreeable effect and a worthwhile risk, they decided. Brock planned to stay away from airports and cities, and to stay below a couple thousand feet above the ground. Few air traffic controllers would notice, and fewer still would care.

Brock expertly trimmed the aircraft for level flight. It was an intuitive thing, after all of those years, as natural as putting the left foot in front of the right. The F-16's flight control computer trimmed itself, which was nothing short of luxurious, but Brock had stayed proficient flying small aircraft that required more constant attention. He was most at home with air under his ass.

The rhythmic throb of the aircraft engine and the vibration of flight lulled Sam quickly to sleep. She dozed fitfully.

Bratislava came and went. Then it was on to Salzburg. The miles disappeared beneath them, and the gas disappeared at a commensurate rate. They had to make a refueling stop.

Sam awoke as the sound of the engine changed. Brock had been given permission to land at a small regional airport beyond the outskirts of Salzburg. The scenery was mind-blowing, absolutely gorgeous. Castle remnants dotted the hills, vestiges of a more romantic millennium. And only slightly more feudal than the current millennium, Sam surmised groggily. Everyone was someone's bitch. Or serf, as it were.

Brock set the flaps, lined himself up on the runway centerline, adjusted his glide path, and made small corrections all the way down the chute. When the aircraft wheels crossed the threshold, Brock pulled the power all the way back, eased back on the yoke, and settled in for landing.

The small aircraft hopped a little bit, then settled down nicely.

Brock let it decelerate, exited the runway, found the right taxiway, and pulled to a stop in front of the small flight business office.

He parked between two similar light aircraft, ran through the shutdown checklist, and watched as the propeller slowed to a halt. Brock did his post-flight walk-around inspection while Sam went to buy more fuel.

The desk clerk was officious, playing into the Austrian stereotype, Sam thought with a small, tired smile. She tried a few words of German to break the ice, but it was thick ice. In the end, the credit card belonging to Sam's alias was good for a full tank of fuel, but nary a smile from the man behind the counter.

Sam inquired about food, and the clerk pointed to a refrigerator on the far wall. She bought a pair of day-old sandwiches for fifteen Euro. She reckoned that airport prices were the same everywhere, regardless of the airport's size.

She rejoined Brock at the airplane. Refueling took ten minutes, start to finish. Ten minutes more and they were airborne again, heading west, with Nuremberg on the nose.

The miles passed. They had long conversations over the intercom. Mundane, existential, and most points in between.

Sam enjoyed the view, and enjoyed Brock's company, but found it hard not to mull over the situation.

Where was Mark Severn's body? Who hired a gaggle of goons from Boston? Who hired the Shin Bet to look after her in Budapest? The waters were frustratingly muddy.

Russians in Boston. Not unheard of, obviously. But American Russians from Boston in Budapest — with guns and bad intentions

— were another matter entirely. She made a mental note to ask Dan to research the travel history of the dead Russians' known associates, if there were any known associates. Maybe seeing a list of plane trips taken by the dead guy's inner circle in the recent past, particularly with a Russian or European destination, might give insight into who else was involved.

And it might give her a chance to get one step ahead, which would be a refreshing change of pace. She'd been no fewer than two steps behind since the whole mess began, seven million hours ago on Wednesday. She had been on her heels the whole time, reacting, responding to threats. It was no way to stay healthy, and it was time to change the game up.

Heidelberg soon appeared in the distance. "Don't they have a castle there?" Sam asked.

"One of the largest and most famous in the world," Brock said. "I'm going to take us as close as we can get without attracting attention. It's one of the most amazing sights in Europe."

He wasn't wrong. A long bridge spanned the Neckar River, leading the way to the Heidelberg Castle, a fortress of yellowing stone, an accessible anachronism amidst the modern world of cell phones, computers, and satellites.

It was equal parts history and romance, mystery and mystique, and Sam was entranced, her mind racing to imagine the battles and intrigues the ancient walls must have witnessed.

She saw a thick, squat parapet. The wall had been blown out, heaving a gigantic chunk of castle structure into the grass nearby. Even from the air, Sam could see that the shattered parapet wall was impossibly thick. She had no idea how anything that stout could have been broken. "That was their weapons magazine," Brock explained. "Where they kept all their gunpowder. It exploded centuries ago, maybe more. The force blew the whole thing apart."

"Hard to imagine an explosion that powerful," Sam said.

"Given the right amount of internal pressure, even the strongest vessel shatters," Brock said, looking pointedly at Sam, the serious arch of his eyebrow balanced by a wry grin.

Sam nodded. She didn't need help connecting the dots. The internal pressure had certainly been mounting in her world.

"I'm still more than a little bit concerned about you," Brock said.

"What's to be concerned about?" Sam asked with a smile. "Russian muscle ain't what it used to be."

Brock smiled, but it was short-lived, and it never quite reached his eyes. He looked tired.

A long silence passed.

"I love you, Sam," he said, his voice soft and quiet, barely audible over the propeller. "But you need to understand that I can't do this forever."

Chapter 21

They landed and refueled just west of Heidelberg, at another small airport whose name Sam never bothered to learn. The stop took longer than previously, and they used the opportunity to stretch their legs. Sam bought more shrink-wrapped sandwiches, and they were on their way again.

They skirted Luxembourg City, peering down into the steep river valley that had been turned into both a fortress and a town. "There's an amazing Thai restaurant at the bottom of the canyon wall," Brock said. "It's built into the side of the cliff. It's an incredible atmosphere."

"Next time, maybe," Sam said.

"Provided someone isn't trying to kill you," Brock said. Sam thought she heard an edge. She felt a bit of anger flare, but it was short-lived. Who could blame him? Her life wasn't exactly conducive to peace and harmony at home, and she imagined it wasn't easy for him to watch her cheat death on a monthly basis.

She let out a long sigh. She had some hard choices to make.

But first, she had to extract herself from the center of someone's crosshairs. Existentialist musings would have to wait.

Charleroi was next, another fuel stop, followed by Calais. Then they crossed the channel to London. They had been following the sun all day, but it vastly outpaced them, and it was long past dark when their wheels finally kissed the earth for the last time. Just shy of midnight local time. It had been a long day, one that seemed to last a week.

"We need a real night's rest," Brock declared, eyes bleary from sustained concentration.

"No argument here." They inquired at the flight counter about a nearby hotel, relieved to speak with someone who spoke their native tongue. The night manager at the flight office gave them a brochure for a small bed-and-breakfast nearby, and they called for a cab.

They checked into the B&B, and not a moment too soon, as fatigue dominated their movement and thoughts. Brock showered, and Sam sat idly on the edge of the bed, debating with herself. She had a phone call to make. Tom Davenport. She was dreading it, and she considered extending her already-lengthy incommunicado period with her boss.

But bad news rarely aged well. She dialed from the hotel room, using her alias's credit card to pay the long distance charges, which she knew would be exorbitant.

Calling from the hotel was a risk. Maybe even an error. Phoning home on an un-sanitized line, from one's hotel room, no less, wasn't even close to pristine trade craft. But Sam concluded it wasn't any worse than stumbling around at midnight searching for a phone, half-drunk with exhaustion.

As if by some cosmic folly mocking all of her rumination and cogitation over the phone call, Davenport didn't answer. Sam left a message, something about things having gone a bit sideways, a few operational complications having arisen, and the like. Not her best performance, but she was relieved she didn't have to talk to him.

She took off her clothes, stood under the weak British shower for a few moments, climbed into bed next to Brock, and fell asleep nearly as quickly as her head hit the pillow.

* * *

Sam awoke. She had no idea what time it was. Her side was killing her. She got up gingerly from the bed, stumbled to the bathroom, and gulped a painkiller.

She peered out the bathroom window. Daylight. Still morning, but not quite an early start.

She walked back into the bedroom, crawled back in bed, and roused Brock. "We shouldn't stay in one spot for too long," she said.

He wrapped his arms around her waist, stroked the small of her back, kissed the curve of her neck, and let one hand venture playfully south on her anatomy. "I think we can stay here eight more seconds," he said.

Sam felt his growing arousal. She drew her leg across him, rolled him onto his back, kissed his mouth and neck, rubbed against his erection, felt the thrilling rush of blood to her sex, and let out a small gasp of pleasure as she took his full length.

It lasted nearly as long as Brock had predicted. Afterward, they lay in each other's arms, breathless, tired, content.

In those moments, all was right in the world. Everything else dissolved. There was only the moment, the communion of souls, the confluence of lives, the perfection of a matched pair. "I need more of this in my life," Sam said.

"I'm not the one who's flying around the world, impaling myself on steel shafts," Brock said with a wry smile.

Sam kissed his neck. "Something should be done about that."

"Yeah. How do I talk to the person in charge of your life?"

"Great question. I'll let you know when I find out."

Brock tightened his grip around her, kissed her neck, caressed her shoulders. "Maybe elevate it on your agenda," he said. "I'm even more game for a bit of adventure than the average guy, but this death and near-death business gets old."

Sam rose, peeled back the dressing on her wound, winced as the tape tugged at a stitch, and cursed as she saw the blood and pus. "Tell me about it," she said. They both agreed that she was going to need serious medical attention as soon as possible. But they had no idea when that might be.

They availed themselves of the breakfast that came with the bed-and-breakfast fee. A steaming cup of tea washed it down, and Sam allowed herself a sweet roll as a reward for surviving the past few days.

They made their way to a library on the outskirts of London where Sam used Brock's laptop and the free Internet connection to place another phone call.

Tom Davenport answered this time. He sounded mellow and relaxed, a marked difference from his high-strung demeanor the last time they had spoken. "Sam, how wonderful to hear from you."

"Tom, sounds like I caught you after cocktail hour."

"Is it that obvious?"

"I'm not complaining. You sound like you're in a good

mood."

"Conditionally, that's true."

"Contingent upon what?"

"Where you are at the moment," Davenport said.

"Brock and I are in London."

"I understand there's an ID issue."

"That's right. Dan's on it."

"Good man, that Dan. Always great in a pinch. I'm glad you feel you can trust him."

Clearly a barb. Sam didn't take the bait.

"All you had to do was ask," Davenport said. "I would have saved you the trip across Europe. I would have overnighted your new passports to Budapest."

"Budapest had worn me thin. Besides, I thought people were cracking down on that kind of thing," Sam said.

"I'm not 'people'," Davenport said. "And you were in play, in an evolving situation. I would have exercised my latitude not to inform the uptight parties."

Sam was quiet. "Thank you, Tom. I suppose I owed you a call earlier."

"I suppose you did."

"I'm sorry. I didn't quite know who to trust."

"I'm only your boss. Why would I possibly want to look out for you?"

"Once bitten…"

"I can't change what happened to you before I took over," Davenport said. "But I'm not those assholes, for one thing. And for another, a bad experience or two doesn't give you permission to disobey orders. I told you to come home."

"I'm sorry about that, Tom. It's just that things were obviously moving fast, and something was obviously way beyond wrong."

"Sam, you don't know the half of it."

"I have a long row of stitches in my gut that says I do know the half of it."

"Yes," Davenport said, a bit of sarcasm in his voice. "So I understand. I hope we can have a discussion about a few of your tactical decisions. And then there's the body count. Where does it stand? Three? Or have you killed someone else in the last twelve hours?"

"Sounds like you know quite a bit about what's been going on over here, Tom."

"Yes, I do. Come home, and we'll talk about it."

"Why didn't you just tell me earlier? Maybe all of your knowledge and wisdom could have saved me a few pints of blood."

Davenport laughed. Sam heard an edge of exasperation. "I did tell you, Sam. I told you it was classified. I told you I couldn't discuss it with you over the phone. I told you to come home as soon as possible. The order still stands. I want you on a plane, today."

"That's our plan, Tom," Sam said. "As soon as Brock's new ID is ready. Until then, we're going to lay low."

"I don't know what you mean when you say 'lay low,' but I imagine we might have different ideas on the subject. So I'll be as clear as possible. I'm giving you a direct order not to pursue anything further in the Mark Severn case."

Sam didn't know why that angered her. It wasn't like she was going to learn a lot while hiding out in London. But her hackles raised. "What the hell, Tom? We're just going to walk away from the situation?"

"Yes, Sam, we are."

"Don't we owe it to Mark Severn to figure this out? I mean, what reason could we possibly have to abandon this case before we figure out what the hell is going on?"

"Sam, the investigation into Mark Severn's death is officially closed."

"Goddammit, Tom, what is the matter with you? The wrong stiff is on ice in Budapest, and there's a gang of Russian pipe-swingers from Boston running around Europe right now, looking for us. They were a few seconds away from throwing me into the river yesterday. We have no idea who they're working for, and we have no idea what their angle is. Why the hell are you closing this thing down?"

Davenport chuckled. "Because Mark Severn walked into the office today," he said.

Chapter 22

A dull boredom settled over David Swaringen. The luster and excitement of the command center environment had worn off a bit, and Swaringen had settled into a restive workaday lassitude. He scanned a wall full of monitors that showed absolutely nothing going on. This wasn't going to be his life for the next decade, he hoped, hours and days of mind-numbing boredom punctuated by seconds of vicarious, voyeuristic excitement.

The phone rang. NSA Deputy Director Clark Barter answered, grunted a few times, hung up, and left the command center without a word.

"Looks like you're in charge now," a technician watching a bevy of video screens told Swaringen with a sideways tilt of the head.

"How do you figure?" Swaringen asked.

"You're the boss's right-hand man," the tech said. "You get to make all the calls in his absence."

Swaringen was taken aback. Barter had mentioned something along those lines during his brief indoctrination, but Swaringen had dismissed it as a comment relating to a distant, far-off future, as something to view with hopeful aspiration, and not relating to anything either proximate or pressing.

He smiled and nodded, hoping the unease and sudden spike in

his heart rate hadn't flushed his cheeks. He felt slightly panicked. Not uncommon for someone assuming a responsible role while still oblivious of the exact nature of his responsibilities. He pondered the precise scope of his position, and how it might relate to the "small war" Clark Barter and his gang were conducting from the DC-area office building.

Half an hour passed. Barter didn't return. Swaringen asked the nearby tech about the old man's absence. "This happens a lot," the clerk said. "He gets called away by high rollers. Congressmen, the White House, people in the administration, all sorts of interesting people."

"That so?"

"That's the rumor, anyway. He doesn't say much about it, which is rare. Most people brag about stuff like that, but Barter is pretty tight-lipped."

Swaringen nodded thoughtfully.

"Anyway," the clerk went on, evidently grateful for a diversion from the rack of intelligence feeds in front of him, "I'd say it was his wife calling to dictate the grocery list to him, but she's not in the picture anymore."

"That's too bad," Swaringen said. "She passed?"

The clerk laughed. "In a manner of speaking. She got fed up and left."

Swaringen nodded. It was probably a tough life for a wife. Barter practically lived at the NSA facility. Swaringen couldn't imagine there was much room for anything else in the old man's life. He knew with clarity that he wanted something different for his own life.

A yell broke the silence. "Situation!"

Swaringen snapped his head forward to the video monitoring station in the corner of the room.

"Subject vehicle is heading westbound toward a major population center."

A dozen pair of eyes turned to Swaringen. Evidently the video monitor technician's summary was also a request for direction.

Swaringen's heart rate soared. Were they serious? Did they seriously think he was remotely qualified or inclined to be the decision authority?

"Subject vehicle is speeding up," the tech said. "ETA to the city, three minutes. This is our window, sir."

Swaringen felt his face flush. What word had Barter used in this kind of situation earlier?

It came to him. "Investigate," he said, doing his best to sound confident and authoritative. He wasn't sure that it worked, but the technicians turned back around and got busy at their consoles.

"Sir, there is an airborne unit in the vicinity."

Airborne, as in the infantry unit? Or airborne, as in currently in flight? Swaringen wasn't quite sure what he was supposed to make of the information. "What kind of unit?"

"Two assault choppers on the outskirts of town. Maybe five miles away, sir."

"Are they otherwise tasked?"

"Negative, sir," the tech said.

"Use them," Swaringen said.

He looked back at the video screens. The picture was from directly above the scene, maybe offset slightly south, judging by the shadows.

A question formed in his mind, one that had gnawed at him earlier and had never been asked or answered. If the nearest helicopters were five miles away, where was the video feed coming from? From space? If so, the resolution was fantastic. And there were hundreds of individual views available. How many billion-dollar satellites would that have taken? An impractical number, even for a nation overly fond of printing money.

Which left drones. He surveyed the video screens again, with fresh eyes. A hundred monitors, maybe more, each one cycling through three to five separate views on a timer. Which meant there had to have been five hundred drones airborne at any one time. Which meant there had to be at least that many more on the ground. How many diplomatic agreements would that have required? Or, if Uncle Sam had blown off miles of red tape in dozens of foreign bureaucracies, how many countries' sovereignty was Swaringen flagrantly disregarding at the moment?

He took a breath. He felt perched on a precipice. People were looking to him for leadership, to direct force and firepower, and he didn't even know where the hell the video feeds were coming from.

Barter was still gone. Swaringen looked at his watch. He felt grossly unqualified to even participate in a scenario like the one he was in, much less be in charge of it. "Does Barter have a pager number?"

"No," a tech said. "Nobody uses those anymore. I'll try his

cell."

"Ask him to please hurry," Swaringen said.

A brief eternity passed, during which nothing happened. Swaringen felt the weight of expectation upon him but he didn't know what he should be doing. The helicopters were on the way to the suspect's car, which the overhead footage showed to be speeding toward the edge of the nameless city on the western edge of the video view. Swaringen felt pressure to do something before the driver reached the populated area.

"The team is on-station," the tech said. "Awaiting orders."

"Investigate."

The tech looked quizzically at Swaringen. "Sir, don't you want to hear the ID confirmation?"

Swaringen's face turned red. "Yes, please," he said, trying hard not to look sheepish.

The technician recited a litany of confidence factors leading to a single conclusion: "positive non-friendly ID. What should I tell the on-scene team to do?"

Swaringen breathed deeply. His heart rate accelerated. He felt very warm. "Investigate," he said.

"In these situations, sir, it has been our procedure to prosecute."

Swaringen nodded, sweat breaking out on his forehead. He looked at the car speeding westbound on the video monitor. Inside the car was at least one human. That human's life was in his hands. And there might be more.

"Sir? We need to make a move, or call it off. We're running

out of time."

Swaringen took a deep breath. "Prosecute," he said, his voice quiet and tense.

The tech relayed the command to the on-scene team. A flurry of activity erupted. Like before, radio chatter was broadcast over the room's PA system. Swaringen was better able to follow the action with a little experience under his belt, but there was much he still didn't understand.

The choppers bracketed the car. Armed men hung in the choppers' open side doors. The helicopters descended until the skids were eye-level with the car's driver.

The car stopped in the middle of the narrow two-lane road.

One suspect emerged from the passenger's seat. Swaringen saw his arms waving surrender on the video monitor.

The driver didn't surrender.

The driver ran.

"Permission to engage! Request permission to engage!" Swaringen knew the shouted request had come from the helicopter pilot. He could tell by the way the man's voice vibrated in time with the rotor blades.

Swaringen was silent, indecisive. The technician's laundry list of ID criteria seemed convincing, seemed genuine. But something held him back.

"Sir?" The technician asked. "The suspect is fleeing on foot near a population center. The pilot has requested permission to engage."

All eyes were on Swaringen. Sweat beaded on his brow. His

knees felt weak. He felt slightly woozy. This was not at all what he had signed up for.

"Sir!"

Swaringen wavered. On one side of the internal battle was the weight and momentum of business as usual in Command Center Bravo, a proclivity toward active engagement and lethal force.

On the other side was his conscience. What if the intelligence was wrong? What if they weren't "non-friendlies," and were just two people in a car driving to town? Could he live with taking innocent lives?

But what if the intelligence *was* correct? What if these were bad people, on their way to do bad things?

Swaringen needed to make a decision. Time was running out, and he was starting to look like a fool.

Too late.

A voice boomed from the back of the room. "Engage!"

Swaringen turned. Clark Barter's imposing form darkened the doorway. The boss had returned, and the boss had spoken.

It was over in an instant. The machine gun cut down the fleeing driver with a single long burst. Then the command center busied itself with its list of post-engagement duties.

Barter glared at Swaringen. "I didn't hire you to play patty-cake with those bastards," he said. "We're here to do a job."

He opened the door to the hallway and looked again at Swaringen. "Follow me," he barked.

* * *

Barter was a big man, not fit by any stretch, but he moved

quickly. Swaringen had to hustle to keep up.

Barter led him to the elevator, mashed the button for the top floor, and said nothing while the car moved them up from the bowels of the NSA building to the rarified air of the executive offices. Swaringen felt like a kid on his way to the school principal's office.

The elevator doors opened, and Barter charged out into the hallway. Swaringen stayed a respectful half-pace behind his boss.

The old man stopped at a door midway down the executive wing, swiped his badge, typed his PIN, and waited for the latch to unlock. He threw the door open and made straightaway for the wet bar.

Swaringen hadn't ever seen Barter's office. The job interviews had taken place in an executive conference room. Swaringen had stayed put while a parade of new faces asked him awkward questions. It had been just a few weeks ago. But it seemed like ages, like more than just time had passed. Like maybe innocence had passed as well.

"How do you take yours?" Barter asked.

It was a question totally devoid of context in Swaringen's mind. "Take my what?" he asked.

"Whisky. An Islay. Eighteen years old. Just like the best hookers."

Swaringen's eyebrows arched.

Barter chuckled. "Relax, David. I'm only kidding. About the hookers, that is. Not the scotch. I'm deadly serious about that, and I don't give a damn what time it is."

Swaringen smiled, his unease dissipating a bit. "Neat, please."

"Good man," Barter said. He handed Swaringen a glass and motioned toward a plush leather couch, arranged with a view out floor-to-ceiling windows into the lush Maryland forest below.

Swaringen swirled, sniffed. He loved the smell of the earth in a good scotch. It felt honest, good, and maybe even true. He took a sip and enjoyed the burn, relished the instant mini-buzz.

He had no idea what he was going to say. But he felt like he had to say something. He had struggled to stomach the events of the past few days, especially without a great deal of background information on why they were doing the things they were doing. And he didn't like the non-answers to what he considered to be legitimate questions. Sure, security was important, and all that. But it felt like something was wrong. Something was going on behind the veil of secrecy.

And he felt embarrassed by his indecision, emasculated by Barter having to take the reins in the critical moment on the ops center floor.

He opened his mouth to begin, but Barter beat him to the punch. "Let me tell you a story," the old man said, sitting down in a leather armchair adjacent to the couch.

Barter looked out the window. His eyes took on a weariness that Swaringen hadn't seen before. "It's about my son," Barter said. "Brad."

There was a knock at the door.

"Go away!" Barter barked.

The door opened anyway. A tall, lanky, bald man walked in. He wore thick glasses. He had on a short-sleeved button-down shirt, with a pocket full of pens. He looked like he had been plucked from IBM in the 1950s.

"Ahh, James," Barter said. "I nearly forgot." He rose, walked to a large metal security safe on the floor, and worked his combination into the dial, talking as he did so. "David Swaringen, meet James Alcorn."

"Pleasure," Swaringen said, extending his hand.

James Alcorn shook weakly. Like a dead fish. "New here?" he asked. His voice was gruff, nasal. Not terribly friendly.

"Started last week," Swaringen said.

Alcorn grunted.

Barter pulled open the safe drawer, grabbed something from within, sealed it in a bright red envelope with the words TOP SECRET written across the top, and handed it to Alcorn.

Alcorn left without another word. Swaringen wanted to ask what that was all about, but he knew better.

Barter sat in the leather armchair again. He motioned for Swaringen to take his place on the couch. "Where were we?" Barter asked.

"You were going to tell me a story about your son," Swaringen said.

Barter's face darkened. He took a drink. "Right," he said. He took a breath, looked out the window, and started talking.

Bradley Barter was a sophomore at William and Mary, kicking ass on a football scholarship. Then 9/11 happened. Spending his time playing a boy's game and getting a business degree seemed like the height of narcissism in the aftermath, and Brad enlisted in the Navy a week later.

He was a strong, smart kid, and he did well in boot camp and in his first assignment. He applied to BUDS, the basic underwater demolition school, which was the gateway to becoming a SEAL. He was accepted, and was one of the rare recruits who made it through on the first try.

Swaringen could tell Barter was proud of his son's accomplishment. And who wouldn't be proud to have a SEAL as a son?

"He did two tours in Afghanistan, and then one in Iraq," Barter said. Swaringen noticed the old man's hands were trembling slightly.

Barter inhaled deeply. He didn't look at Swaringen as he talked. His eyes looked out the window, but Swaringen got the sense they saw things years in the past and thousands of miles away.

"He went missing," Barter said. Swaringen wasn't certain, but he thought Barter's eyes had misted a bit, and that the old man's voice had constricted. Swaringen looked away out of respect.

"Halfway through his tour in Iraq," Barter continued. "We got a call from his SEAL Team commander. My wife took the call. I was away on business."

Barter pulled a pack of cigarettes out of his shirt pocket and offered one. Swaringen demurred. "Not supposed to smoke in here, but who the hell's going to turn me in?" Barter struck a match and inhaled deeply. "This is some of the shit that's killing me, by the way. Can't live with it, but I can't seem to kick it."

Swaringen nodded.

Barter picked up the story. "Anyway, we got that call from

Brad's commander, and you can imagine it was the usual sob story, only it was happening to us. Nobody had any idea where he was. His team was ambushed on a convoy. He was escorting a truck full of gasoline, so the army could run a generator to air-condition a thousand canvas tents in the middle of the goddamned desert.

"The lead truck ran over a land mine. Blew the driver away instantly. I mean, blood and guts splattered everywhere. With my security clearance, I saw the pictures. Grisly." Barter shook his head, pulled a long drag from his cigarette, and polished off his scotch.

"A firefight followed, and it dragged on into the night. Crazy firefight, with hajjis running back and forth between positions, lobbing grenades and Molotov cocktails at friendlies."

His eyes grew distant again. "When the dust settled, nobody could find Brad."

A long silence.

"They sent another team back into the same spot, looking for him. Those guys got shot all to hell, just like Brad's team.

"We waited for an eternity to hear something. With my clearance, I was privy to a lot of the details. They pulled out all the stops. Even had helicopters overhead around the clock for a few days. They really worked their asses off to find him."

Another long pull on his cigarette.

"But they never did."

Swaringen regarded Barter as the old man stared out the window. His huge frame seemed to have shrunk. The energy and bravado that propelled his persona were gone. He looked deflated, worn through.

"We tried to get back to our lives, but it never really worked. I mean, how the hell do you do that, anyway? There was no news, no closure. He was missing in action. That was it."

Swaringen felt pain and sorrow. He had kids of his own, and Barter's experience seemed utterly unimaginable. "I'm terribly sorry," he said.

Barter looked at him and nodded. "We slogged through our lives like zombies for a while," he said. "Like I said, the usual sob story. A million people experience this all over the world, so why are we special, right? But it's no picnic. Like you're in this state of suspended animation."

Swaringen nodded.

Barter lit another cigarette. "And then, the other shoe dropped."

He got up, grabbed the bottle of scotch, and poured another round. Swaringen nodded his thanks.

"I was walking in this park near our house," Barter continued. "Maybe fifteen minutes from here. By myself, just clearing my head. Trying to gather my thoughts, get my mind around the fact that Brad's gone and probably not coming home. What are you going to do, right? I mean, we could curl up and die, I suppose, or get back to living. Neither one sounded terribly appealing."

Swaringen watched while Barter took another drink.

"Anyway," Barter went on, "I was walking on the path around this pond, lost in my thoughts, when this guy came up to me. Black guy. Thin, thirty-something, scholarly glasses on his face, like the kind Malcolm X used to wear.

"He looks at me and says, 'Alhamdulillah.' That's hajji for 'praise be to Allah.' I'm thinking, what the hell? Do I look like I give a damn about Allah? But I notice he has his hand out toward me. He's holding something, offering it to me. Without even thinking, I just grabbed it. Reflex, you know?"

Swaringen nodded. Human nature.

"It was a little computer drive. With a keychain attached to it, only there's no key. Just the chain, looped through the little hole on the end of the thumb drive."

"Strange," Swaringen said.

Barter nodded. "Right. I was already getting pretty high up in the pecking order here, so I figured it was one of those intelligence-gathering ploys by some rinky-dink third-world outfit."

He took another mouthful of whisky and another lungful of smoke.

"Next day," Barter went on, "I took the thumb drive to the security people, down on the first floor. Told them what had happened. They asked all the usual bullshit questions, like did you know the man who gave this to you, do you still pleasure goats, all the normal stupidity.

"Anyway, they told me to wait outside while they ran a scan on the disk."

He brought the cigarette to his lips. His hands shook.

"It drags on," he continued. "I'm standing there in the hallway with my dick in my hands for maybe half an hour. I have work to do, so I'm getting antsy. I called them on their desk phones, but nobody answered."

Another drink, another drag.

"I'm about to leave when my boss walks in. 'Heya,' he says, or some shit. The DDO, the guy who was my boss's boss at the time, was right there with him. The DDO told me to keep waiting, and said it would only be a couple of minutes. They both walked into the security office."

Barter swallowed.

Swaringen realized his insides were tensed up, and his hand hurt from gripping the arm of the couch. He forced himself to relax.

"Finally the DDO came out," Barter said. "His face was ghost white. He looked like he was about to puke. 'I called the chaplain,' he told me."

More scotch, more smoke. "The goddamned chaplain. That's when I knew."

Swaringen felt dread and vicarious anguish in his chest. They pressed down on him like a weight.

Barter threw back the rest of his whisky, poured another, gulped half. "It wasn't a virus or a goddamned spyware thing on this thumb drive," he said.

His eyes misted and unfocused. His voice tightened.

"It was my son," he said. "A video. Those fucking animals strapped his head down to a board. Then they sliced his forehead and peeled the skin off his face. It took thirty minutes. Then they pulled off his pants and sliced his balls off."

Swaringen sat in stunned silence.

Barter took another drink. "He screamed and wailed and fought and suffered for a goddamned hour before they finally sawed his head off."

Swaringen felt a tightness in his chest. He couldn't speak. His throat constricted.

Barter looked out the window. "All I could think about was the way he looked as a little boy, crawling around with a big smile on his face, bringing me toys to play with."

Swaringen fought back tears. And he felt something else, too. White hot anger.

"I had this sense," Barter went on. "I knew for sure that watching him die like that, seeing the way he suffered, I had just died with my boy. I mean, it totally hollowed me out."

Swaringen shook his head, but said nothing. He couldn't fathom what it must have felt like to watch your own flesh and blood suffer such an unimaginable death.

Barter gathered himself. "Anyway, when they'd finally put him out of his misery, this goddamned coward in a mask held my son's head up in one hand and the Koran in the other," he said.

Swaringen felt sick, deflated.

Barter raised his glass in a bitter toast. "Alhamdulillah. Praise be to fucking Allah."

Barter topped off their whiskeys. It was a blistering pace of alcoholic consumption, and it likely accounted for the permanent red patina on the old man's nose. "My wife blamed me, my job here at NSA. She figured they would have let Brad go if I wasn't such a high-profile infidel."

He snorted. "But they would never have let him go. They were always going to take his life to make a statement."

Swaringen swallowed. The knot was still in his throat.

Barter smiled. "Seven years already, and I still can't talk about it very well."

"That's more than understandable," Swaringen said. "I can't even imagine."

Barter eyed him for a long moment. "I didn't tell you that so you'd feel sorry for me, or so you'd think I was less of an asshole than I really am."

Swaringen nodded, tried to smile.

"I told you all of that because I wanted you to know who it is we're dealing with here. These are not people who respond to peaceful overtures. They are barbarians, and they don't give a shit about human life. They are up to their eyebrows in bullshit religious dogma, and they fulfill their deeper purpose by killing us and making videos of it. It's that simple."

Barter stood. He had an air of finality about him. He motioned toward the door. The meeting was evidently over, and Swaringen was being dismissed.

Swaringen rose and extended his hand. "Mr. Barter," he said. "I'm completely at a loss. I'm so sorry."

Barter's giant paw crushed Swaringen's hand. "I'm not a healthy man, and I don't have much time left on this earth," he said. "But I'm going to spend my remaining days doing my damnedest to make sure no other parent has to go through what my wife and I went through."

Swaringen nodded. He couldn't argue with the sentiment.

"That's what Operation Penumbra is all about," Barter said,

showing Swaringen to the door. "Saving lives. But sometimes you have to pull the trigger to do it."

He clapped Swaringen on the shoulder. "So next time, son," Barter said, "don't hesitate to pull the goddamned trigger."

Part 2

Chapter 23

Nero Jefferson Chiligiris drove north on I-25. He was almost to Denver. The city had grown so quickly that it now almost connected to the town of Monument, halfway to Colorado Springs. The highway could be beset by a traffic jam at any given time on any given day along the front range. It was a sign of the times. There were nearly seven billion humans, and Nero figured that at least half of them had moved to Denver from California.

At least traffic was moving. It helped his frazzled nerves. Being alone on the road gave a man's mind plenty of time to conjure up all sorts of dire scenarios. Nero's waking nightmares involved recapture and reentry into whatever kind of messed-up system could lock him up and throw away the key without so much as a court hearing.

Nero had a safe deposit box in Denver full of cash. He wasn't stock market savvy — no matter how many fancy equations you used, playing stocks was ultimately little more than soothsaying, Nero thought, and he loved his money too much to watch it go up in smoke — but he wasn't a spendthrift. He saved his money, and even invested some of it in a little rental property. And he kept a big pile of it stored away for a rainy day.

But the safe deposit box required a key. The United States Department of Homeland Security currently possessed that key, along with the key to his grunge-era Pontiac Grand Am, which, Nero presumed, Homeland also possessed at the moment.

No problem. Nero would just present his identification to the clerk, and ask for a new key.

Except that his identification was also in the hands of the Department of Homeland Security. Nero didn't have so much as a library card on him.

He had no money. Other than the clothes on his back and the motorcycle he had liberated from the farm-cum-crack house outside of Pueblo, just a leisurely morning's stroll from the site of the fortuitous prison van crash that had freed him, Nero had nothing to his name.

Less than nothing, actually. Because he was a wanted man. In the Great Ledger of Life, Nero Chiligiris's name most definitely had something written next to it: detain on sight.

He couldn't exactly lay low at home for a while. He was beyond certain that the feds would have his house and family under surveillance. If they had spent the resources to send three helicopters full of storm troopers to collect him from a dusty road seventeen miles from nowhere, he was sure they could afford to pay at least one flatfoot to keep an eye on his front door.

In fact, Nero reflected, there was probably a flatfoot watching the home of every person Nero had ever met. The department's name said it all: homeland security. It was a narrow mandate with astronomically large latitude for interpretation. An infinite number of threats existed, real and imagined, which brought an equally large number of pork-roll projects and programs. Money was therefore no object. Nero surmised there was no shortage of resources to keep tabs on him, and anyone he'd ever known.

Which brought him to that asshole Money. If Uncle Sam thought that Nero was a terrorist of some sort, it was undoubtedly due to the cranky Arab. Any effort to figure out why the feds wanted Nero for terrorism had to start and end with Money. There was no way around it. Nero was squeaky clean otherwise. His only indulgence was cable television. He didn't even surf internet porn, because it made Penny feel insecure.

So Money was going to get a visit, Nero decided.

Unless Money had *already* gotten a visit, Nero suddenly thought. From guys with badges.

It brought up an interesting question, one that Nero hadn't fully considered. What if Money was already in custody?

What if Money had been on the receiving end of a coercive conversation, and some Special Agent America guy had squeezed him for names? Nero would be easy to implicate, if even one of the hundreds of duffel bags Nero had exchanged over the past few years had contained anything remotely shady.

Maybe that was it. Maybe Money had blown the whistle. Maybe the arrogant little prick was already in custody, had already struck a deal, and was singing like a bird to get his sentence reduced.

It made no difference that Nero had taken such great pains to keep himself oblivious of the true nature of Money's transactions.

Nero realized now, with the benefit of painful hindsight, that proving his ignorance would be a very difficult thing. As he'd realized earlier, proving a negative was impossible. And trying to prove his ignorance in front of a jury — provided the feds even bothered with any due process at all — would sound a lot like quibbling.

It was, in fact, pretty damn unbelievable. Nero could imagine the prosecutor's question: "You mean you worked for this guy for years, and you never bothered to ask what was in the bags you were delivering?" Nero would not have had a convincing answer, he was sure.

He would only have had the truth, which was that he truly *was* ignorant of Money's dealings. Because Nero was a man with a record, and he wanted no part of anything that could land him back in prison.

All of which might have suggested a little more due diligence on Nero's part, he thought with a grimace.

But it wasn't like he went into the whole thing completely blind. Sure, he didn't know the specifics, but he had been around enough criminals in his life to recognize one when he saw one. Money fit the description. But Money also paid pretty damn well, and Nero had fiscal needs, just like the next guy. Mouths to feed, and a life to rebuild.

And as a man with a ten-year prison sentence on his record, he wasn't exactly a hot hiring prospect for the six-figure jobs out there in the world. Money's money was good money, and Nero had used it to build a good life for his family. That was all the motivation Nero had needed to stay as ignorant as his conscience permitted.

Which accounted for why Nero was, at the moment, completely screwed.

Nero moved over to let a car pass him on the highway. Traffic was heavy but fast, a good thing. He scanned above the horizon, paranoid about another helicopter incident. He had no idea what the feds had on him, why they had used so much force to apprehend him, but if they had done it once, there was nothing to stop them from doing it again. Nero needed to get out of the open.

He needed money, clothes, transportation, and shelter.

And he also needed to find Penny, to talk to her somehow, to tell her he hadn't done anything, to tell her he was innocent, to tell her that he loved her and the kids, and that he wanted nothing more than to come home and continue their life together.

Nero was sure they were all things that Penny would doubt in the aftermath of his sudden and total disappearance. He wanted desperately to talk to her, to tell her what had really happened, to set her mind at ease about him.

Nero felt this need, the need to reconnect with his family, even more acutely than he felt the need to stay out of the grip of the feds. Nero loved the life they had built together. It wasn't mansions and yachts, but their house was full of laughs and contentment. He felt a physical ache when he thought of them, at home without him, wondering what had happened to him, wondering whether he had abandoned them.

But Nero was no fool. He knew that most criminals were caught trying to contact friends and family members. There was no smart way to approach Penny or the kids without giving himself away, Nero feared.

Which left him completely, crushingly alone.

He shook his head. There was nothing he could do about it at the moment. Other matters were more pressing. Nero was starving. He couldn't remember the last meal he had eaten. He was also parched. The long, dusty drive north from Pueblo had taken its toll.

Nero had no real idea where to begin putting his life back together. He believed he now understood what it might be like to be an immigrant, alone and afraid in a foreign country, particularly an unwelcoming country.

Like America.

He thought about all the immigration debates in the news over the years. The white man wanted his floors mopped and his tomatoes picked, and he wanted it done cheaply, but he didn't want to budge an inch on border controls. Messed up, Nero thought. But then again, Nero's skin was brown. Politics smelled a lot more like exploitation on the brown end of the spectrum, he mused.

Nero shook his head, focusing his thoughts. There had to be someplace newly-arrived immigrants went to get on their feet. Like a shelter or soup kitchen or something. Those were generally no-questions-asked kinds of places, at least from what Nero had heard. He'd never visited a shelter himself, and he didn't know whether the camera-happy surveillance apparatus had extended its reach to homeless shelters and hostels. He decided that given the kind of taxpayer money in play, it probably did.

He discarded the shelter idea.

Where could he turn?

He had a dozen close friends, and maybe three dozen in his inner circle. But Nero was certain all of them would be under electronic surveillance, and most of them would be subject to physical surveillance as well.

At least, that's what he imagined would be the case. Nero was not prone to delusions of grandeur, and he would never have figured himself to be worth a second thought, from a national security perspective. But three assault helicopters and a bevy of close-cropped Homeland agents had changed his mind about the situation. In light of those factors, Nero had to assume that he was under constant surveillance, and that the resources deployed to recapture him were indeed unlimited.

Which left him back at square one.

Nearly square one, he corrected himself.

There *was* something he could do.

He just hadn't given the idea any serious air time before. Because it was a terrifically stupid idea. Foolhardy. Desperate.

Suicidal, maybe.

But so was every other crazy notion he'd come up with so far.

So he decided it had to be done.

Chapter 24

Sam and Brock arrived exhausted in DC. They deplaned and stopped at a coffee shop in the airport concourse. Sam ordered a latte, and Brock got the house decaf. They wanted nothing more than to get home and get cleaned up, but there was a more pressing matter.

They sat at a table with a view of passersby. They watched. They had taken great pains to leave Europe unnoticed, but there was no guarantee they had been successful. They needed to know whether they were still being followed.

They had traveled under aliases, but Homeland's computer system had been compromised on numerous occasions, and there was no guarantee the opposition didn't have exquisite knowledge of their travel plans.

International flights being what they were, neither Sam nor Brock slept much on the trip across the pond from London. They sat bleary-eyed across from each other at a small table, but their eyes scoured the concourse, looking for people with that operational look.

Brock pointed out several candidates, people who he thought were paying undue attention. Sam checked them all out, and while she hadn't ruled any of them out completely, she didn't get a strong suspicion. After half an hour, they collected their belongings and made their way to the parking lot.

From there, the first stop was the hospital. Sam wanted to have a conversation with an English-speaking doctor about the hole in her side.

Sam remembered the hospital vividly. It was the scene of a vicious attack by a Venezuelan criminal known as El Jerga. El Jerga shot up the wing where Sam had convalesced. In fact, El Jerga had put her in the hospital in the first place. He had actually killed her, albeit briefly. Sam had ultimately returned the favor. So the world had one fewer hideous bastard in its ranks.

One or two of the nurses recognized Sam. "You should consider a new occupation," one of them told her.

"Maybe she'll listen to you," Brock said with a pointed look at Sam. "I keep telling her the same thing, but so far without effect."

"Maybe I'll go to nursing school," Sam said.

"I like that idea," Brock said. "You have to promise to wear the skimpy outfit."

The doctor arrived moments later and examined Sam's stitches. "Who did the work?" he asked.

"I have no idea," Sam said. "It all happened without my knowledge or consent."

"Well, you had pretty good luck, in that case," the doctor said. "The surgeon did a nice job. But it looks like you haven't quite been a model patient."

"I haven't exactly been able to get the kind of rest I would have hoped."

"I can see that," the doctor said. "You have two stitches that look like they've been pulled out. Honestly, it looks pretty painful."

"Accurate assessment," Sam said. "I've been gobbling pain pills like an addict."

"What've you been taking?"

"I have no idea," Sam said. She handed him the pill bottle from her purse. The label was written in Hungarian.

The doctor examined the label and made a face. "Do you always take unknown drugs?" he asked Sam.

"Only in a foreign country," Sam said. "When in Rome, right?"

"Why not?" the doctor said, a wry smile on his face. "What could possibly go wrong? I'm just going to keep these." He dropped the pill bottle into his lab coat pocket. "Liability. I have no idea whether these will react with what I'm going to give you. But I'm going to give you something that I know will work."

The doctor wrote a prescription, tore the sheet, and handed it to Sam. "I must insist that you take a couple of days off," he said.

"No argument here."

* * *

Sam followed the doctor's orders. She and Brock spent two days wrapped up in the sheets, wrapped around each other. It was glorious. The kind of thing that made life worth living, in Sam's estimation.

Truth be told, however, it wasn't entirely Sam's idea to take both days off. She had a strong desire to figure out what the hell was going on, and that involved a candid conversation with Tom Davenport, and his boss, Deputy Director Farrar. She was more than mildly curious about why Russian-born Americans had tried to kill her in Budapest, and about how Mark Severn had performed a miracle by waltzing into work three days after his death.

Those were questions that Sam was very eager to answer. She was willing to trade a day off to get those answers, but her bosses would have none of it. "If you won't look after yourself," Davenport said, "we will have to do it for you. You're persona non grata around here until Wednesday."

So she'd convalesced. And engaged in therapeutic sex.

Then, on Wednesday morning, while Brock stayed at home, still on vacation, Sam went to work. Her first stop was at IT, to get a new Blackberry. Her old one was making bubbles.

Then she walked into Tom Davenport's office.

"Welcome home, Sam," Davenport said, arms extended, inviting an embrace.

Sam wasn't sure their relationship had quite progressed to the point where hugs were appropriate, but she played along, feeling a bit of her residual low-grade angst and consternation dissolve. Just a little bit. Oxytocin, she remembered. Love, labor, and lactation, they said. An involuntary byproduct of human contact. Maybe it was also good for feeling less distrustful of one's employers.

"So this is the part where you tell me what the hell is going on," Sam said.

Davenport smiled indulgently. "Actually, this is not that part," he said. "But it's close. First, we're going to march down the hall to Farrar's office. And then you'll get to peek under the tent."

Farrar sat behind a sprawling desk. He rose, shook Sam's hand, wrapped his other arm around her shoulders, and welcomed her home. Everyone was touchy-feely. Maybe there was something in the water.

"So, what were you supposed to have told me last week?" Sam asked with a pointed smile when the pleasantries had ended.

Farrar smiled, a paternal look on his face. "I'd be happy to tell you what we were not permitted to tell you last week," he said. "Right after you apologize for being a loose cannon."

Sam laughed mirthlessly. "Merely responding to operational exigencies," she said with feigned friendliness. She felt herself getting riled up. "And a strong case can be made that you two threw me to the goddamned wolves. So yes, bureaucratic obedience took a backseat to survival."

Farrar shook his head. "There were certain realities to the situation that we failed to realize at the time," he said. "And there was a security barrier. We couldn't talk about things over an open line."

Farrar's gaze hardened. "But if you had returned home as you were ordered to do, rather than chasing after a foreign agent like a dog after a passing car, you might not have added to your collection of permanent scars."

Sam shook her head. "It wasn't possible," she said. "They knew everywhere I was going before I even started. If I hadn't shaken things up, they'd have had me stuffed in a footlocker at the bottom of the river by now."

"Highly debatable," Farrar said.

"I'm happy to play armchair quarterback with you," Sam said. "But the bottom line is it wasn't your ass on the line. It was mine."

Farrar's jaw clenched. "Field discipline is indispensable and non-negotiable."

"You're absolutely right," Sam said. "Luckily, I exercised exceptionally good judgment and field discipline. That's why I'm here right now, and why you're not organizing a funeral. But you're not talking about trade craft. You're talking about obedience to a guy sitting in an armchair five thousand miles away from the nearest sign of danger. Those are not even remotely the same things."

Sam sat back in her chair.

Farrar's face flushed.

Davenport filled the awkward silence. "Either way, you're here, and only a little worse for wear," he said in a conciliatory tone. "So now, it's all open-kimono. We're going to tell you what we know."

They knew a lot, it turned out. They knew Sam was in danger, and they knew it almost from the moment she landed in Budapest. Because a decidedly non-dead Mark Severn had told them so.

They also knew that once she caught a whiff of anything remotely untoward in Budapest, nothing would stop her from flipping rocks to see what crawled out from beneath. So they told her to come home.

And they knew that the odds of her coming home were less than good, so they had taken precautions on her behalf, to save her from herself.

They had called the Israelis.

Tom Davenport had cut his teeth as a young intelligence officer over in the Middle East. Anything happening in that region of the globe usually came to the attention of the Israelis, and Davenport had made acquaintances, both Mossad and Shin Bet. He called in a favor. He asked an old friend for help looking after Sam, and the home office reached out to the Budapest Shin Bet chapter.

The Homeland system tracked every agent's phone, all the time, a bit of privacy invasion that had undoubtedly saved Sam's life, because Davenport gave the Shin Bet agents the coordinates in Sam's phone. It was the reason they had arrived so quickly after her stabbing.

"Why the hell couldn't you just tell me that he wasn't dead?" Sam demanded. "It would have saved me a ton of trouble."

"Because I wasn't home yet," a voice said from behind her.

Sam turned to look. Mark Severn. Tall, athletic, attractive.

Alive.

Sam gave him a hug. "What kind of asshole fakes his own death?" she said.

Severn laughed. "A very scared asshole. It got a bit dicey."

Sam nodded. "I understand completely. I really wish I had known you weren't dead, though."

"They couldn't risk telling you over an unsecured phone line," he said, "because it would have jeopardized my egress."

"Aha," Sam said. "So you were on your way home while I was on my way to view your body?"

"That's about the size of it. I'm really sorry for all the trouble, but I was in deep shit."

Sam smiled. "Yeah, they seemed like serious people. How'd you figure out they were onto you?"

"It wasn't hard. Finesse doesn't seem to be their thing."

Sam laughed. "Not by a mile."

His face darkened. "They slaughtered a woman in my hotel room."

"Jesus."

"A woman I was… fond of."

Sam recalled the lunch receipt she had found in Severn's belongings. Two beers, two entrees.

"I assumed they were looking for me," Severn said. "So I ran."

"I'm sorry, Mark," she said.

"I am too. She didn't deserve that."

"How the hell did you pretend to be dead?"

Severn shrugged. "Wasn't hard. The traffic accident was easy enough to stage. After they took me to the hospital, it was just a matter of throwing around enough cash to make it work."

"You bribed your way dead?" Sam asked.

"Pretty much. A dollar still goes a long way that far east. I had plenty left over to pay for my passage home."

"Incredible," Sam said. "How'd you get home?"

"Private jet," Severn said. "I don't care how many TSA employees we have standing around at airline terminals picking their noses. If you want to sneak into the US, just charter a jet and fly to a small airport. Easy as hell."

Sam pondered, imagining Severn's escape. "How did you know who to trust in the Hungarian charter business?"

"I didn't. I needed a lucky break, and I got one. Plus, I promised to double the rate if I arrived safely. I think that went a long way toward making things go smoothly."

Sam nodded. "Who says you can't buy morality?"

"Certainly not me," Severn said. "I'm now a believer."

Sam smiled. "So, now for the obvious question," she said. "What the hell were you working on that got people so pissed off?"

Severn looked at Davenport, who looked at Farrar. Farrar nodded, as if giving permission.

"Do you remember anyone named Janice Everman?" Severn asked.

Sam shook her head. "Name's vaguely familiar," she said, "but I really couldn't pick her out of a lineup."

"Nobody could," Severn said, "until she died a year ago."

"Violent death?" Sam asked.

"Not at first," Severn said. "I mean, it just looked like a rare food-borne illness. She was in her mid-forties, single, a hard-charging career type at the Department of Justice. She went out to dinner by herself after work, ate a salad, and was dead by noon the next day. Her cleaning lady found her, curled up in a ball on the bathroom floor."

"Holy smokes," Sam said. "Rotten lettuce?"

"That's what everyone assumed," Severn said. "People thought it was a tragedy, but nothing else."

"I assume it wasn't?"

"Well, that's the thing. They performed an autopsy. The official report said she died of food poisoning. She didn't have much family to speak of. Otherwise, I'm sure there would have been a lawsuit. It was in the newspapers. The reporter didn't mention the restaurant by name to avoid getting sued, and the thing just died away after a while."

Sam narrowed her eyes. "Until?"

"Until a month ago. We hired a new lead guitarist for the band. The guy wails. He's freaking awesome. He isn't much to look at, but he can play circles around the last guy we had."

"Relevant because?" Sam prodded.

"Right. Relevant because in his day job, the guy works in the coroner's office. He helps with autopsies."

"He worked on Janice Everman's autopsy," Sam guessed.

Severn nodded. "And it wasn't kosher. Janice Everman had barfed her guts out all night. Because they thought she had died of food poisoning, they took a close look at her stomach contents."

"Was there anything left to look at?" Sam asked.

"Not much. But there was something very interesting. Glass."

"Glass?"

"Glass powder, to be precise. They didn't find any big chunks of glass, but they found trace amounts of it, wedged into her stomach lining."

"How did they figure that out?"

"They got lucky, really," Severn said. "They cut out a piece of her stomach lining for analysis, and there was glass powder in the sample."

"What's the theory?"

"Her symptoms were inconsistent with any known acute-onset food-borne pathogens in regular human circulation," Severn said. "But they were very consistent with a rarer one."

"Ebola?" Sam ventured.

"No, but almost as fun. Botulism. Botulism on steroids, really."

"On steroids? An accelerated onset rate, you mean."

"Exactly," Severn said.

"Why did your guitar player talk to you about this particular autopsy, over a year later?"

"Because the shards of glass and the botulism diagnosis never made it into the report."

"And your guy has angst over that?"

"You could say so, yes," Severn said.

"Any chance his findings are wrong, and the official report is correct?"

Severn shrugged. "Who the hell knows, really," he said. "He just came to me because he found out I work at Homeland. Janice Everman worked in the Security and Public Policy Branch at Justice. My guy thought there might be a connection."

Sam nodded, a pensive frown on her brow. "So what took you to Budapest?"

"The money trail."

"Of course." It was always the money trail.

"There was a flurry of activity in a Slovenian and Russian gang out of Boston," Severn said. "And a retired assassin who leads a completely sedentary and solitary life suddenly came out of cloister around the same time. The funds flowed through a bank in Budapest."

"Coincidence?"

"Before Budapest," Severn said, "I would have said so. And a weak coincidence at that. So I thought I'd do the job right, go to Budapest, check things out, and put it to rest."

"But it got interesting in Budapest," Sam said.

"You could say that," Severn said. "Maybe I was paranoid, but it seemed like there were agents everywhere."

"I don't think you were paranoid. I think they had quite a team on the ground over there. Did you go back after your backpack?"

Severn shook his head. "It was full of bogus case notes."

"Nice," Sam said. "Throw them off the scent a bit."

"That was the idea."

"So you paid off the police and the hospital personnel to get out alive."

"That's right. It was much easier than I thought it was going to be. Took less than two hours to orchestrate."

Sam looked at Davenport and Farrar. "You knew about this?"

"Not nearly as quickly as we should have," Davenport said with a pointed glance at Severn.

"So Mark kicked over the hornet's nest, and I walked right into the swarm," Sam said.

Severn nodded, a sheepish look on his face. "I'm very sorry about that, Sam. I didn't realize they'd send someone over so quickly to tie up loose ends."

Sam shook her head. She shrugged. "Shit happens. And it's a tough business. All's well that ends well, I suppose."

She turned to look at Farrar. "So what now?" she asked.

"I went to school in Boston," Farrar said. "Early fall is pretty nice there. I think you'll enjoy it."

Chapter 25

David Swaringen went to work with a new sense of purpose following his discussion with Clark Barter. Gone was his vague sense of ethical disquiet, and in its place was a kind of moral equity, a quid pro quo, something more like the code Hammurabi espoused. An eye for an eye, and a tooth for a tooth.

He quieted any qualms he might have felt about watching other people die on screen at the hands of men with guns and helicopters. He had to, because the men with guns and helicopters were often following his commands. He wrapped it all in a rational cloak of prevention and service of the greater good, a doctrine of saving hundreds or thousands of lives, sometimes by taking a handful of them.

Conventional wisdom in the intelligence community was that some people just needed to die. Swaringen didn't know for sure, but he felt the sentiment was probably right. Some people were undoubtedly incorrigible. No amount of negotiation, education, or incarceration was going to change their minds. They were going to kill Americans at the earliest opportunity and in as grand and spectacular a fashion as possible, no matter what else happened.

In his more sanguine moments, Swaringen understood that the United States had provided plenty of hate fodder for the opposition. You didn't have to mow down too many neighborhoods for the remainder of the city to turn against you. Showing up in foreign lands with tanks, mortars, and Kevlar was a great way to influence people. But rarely was the influence entirely in the desired direction. People had a way of rising up against that kind of intervention. Hate and anger galvanized around ideology, and soon you had an insurrection on your hands. Like the insurrections the United States was currently bungling.

Hence the need for Penumbra, Swaringen figured.

Swaringen also paid greater attention to the litany of ID criteria that the technicians went through by rote during every situation response in the command center. This felt extremely important to Swaringen. He wanted to make sure they were using lethal force only against the right people, and never against the wrong people. Ensuring the IDs were correct obliged his innate sense of justice, of fair play. The gloves were off, but only against a certain crowd. Everyone else should be able to live in peace and tranquility, he reasoned.

It became evident as Swaringen paid closer attention to the ID criteria that there was some sort of a computerized system in use to help recognize people's faces at a distance. Swaringen wasn't quite certain what this technology entailed, but it was pretty impressive. The after-action reports that he had seen, where the individual's real face was compared to the database's parameterized representation, showed a remarkable degree of accuracy. "Advanced Adaptive Learning Algorithm," one of the technicians explained. "It runs in the background continuously. There are millions of video cameras all over the United States, and I think by now we're tapped into all of them. So there's plenty of video for the computer to chew on."

Desperate measures for desperate times, Swaringen guessed. Couldn't have another terror attack on US soil. Nobody would get reelected to office.

Several more incidents, or *situations* in the parlance, came and went. Clark Barter was there for some of them, but was gone for others. David Swaringen had the reins in Barter's absence. Swaringen was still not completely certain of his own ability and judgment, but he felt more confident. When people looked to him for guidance and direction, he felt slightly less like an impostor, slightly more capable of making good decisions.

It was a hard thing, to order the death of another person. But it would have been even harder to stomach another terrorist attack. At least, that's the way Swaringen assuaged the brief pangs of guilt he still occasionally felt as he watched people's innards splatter. Thermal imagery left little to the imagination. It was graphic, and the bowel-shaking reality could not be hidden behind jargon and euphemism. The bland technical terms — intercept, incapacitate, neutralize — did no justice to the splash of blood and guts. The feedback was immediate, visceral, unmistakable. David Swaringen was having people killed.

He didn't feel great about it, but neither did he feel all broken up, either. In his estimation, the people who were involved in the kinds of things that Clark Barter had described, peeling the skin off of other people's faces, slicing off their genitalia, beheading them while chanting religious slogans, those kinds of people deserved to have their innards aerated, to have their bodies laid open and left for the wild dogs and insects.

But a question remained in Swaringen's mind. It was an important question, but one that had so far been entirely taken for granted.

Who decided which names went on the list?

And how did they know they were putting the *right* names on the list?

The identification criteria in use on the operations center floor were rigid and rigorous, and Swaringen had little doubt about the accuracy and precision of the process of matching faces in the world to names in the database. But Swaringen could not vouch for the process used to identify people to be put on the list of "bad humans" in the first place.

Sure, some people just needed to die. But how did they know who fell in that category? Were there fringe cases? Line-straddlers? Could-go-either-way examples? If so, who made the life-or-death determination?

Swaringen gathered his gumption and asked Barter. The old man's reply was characteristically unhelpful. "That's protected under a different caveat." Which was security-speak for "You're not cleared for that information."

Which struck Swaringen as odd. He had the authority to kill people, but not the authority to understand why they were dying.

As the hours and days passed, and the body count climbed, and the number of people in detention rose, the question grew in prominence in Swaringen's mind: who's the mastermind behind the list, and what process do they follow?

How do we know we're killing the right people?

Swaringen decided to find out for himself.

* * *

Sometimes the best way to ask a sensitive question was not to ask it at all. Sometimes it was better to ask an oblique question instead, one that was related but not uncomfortably so. Like an administrative rather than substantive question, or a technical one, in lieu of a pricklier moral or philosophical one.

Sometimes it was better to aim for practical rather than political.

Swaringen took this tack in his effort to determine the origin of the list, the set of "bad human" names that lived in the biometric identification database. If one of the zillions of surveillance cameras on planet Earth found your face and matched it against the biometric data points in the system, the computer notified an operator on the command center floor. The operator notified his supervisor, who made phone calls, or radio calls, or sent commands via text or chat. And then you were investigated, prosecuted, and maybe even executed.

So the list was an important thing. Swaringen cringed to ponder the consequences if there was a flaw in the process.

And it wasn't an idle fear. America had done it before. At one time, US forces paid more than a year's salary to dirt-poor villagers in Iraq and Afghanistan in exchange for turning in their neighbors. Obviously, the quality of intelligence gleaned from such arrangements was even worse than abysmal. Guantánamo swelled as villagers ratted each other out to the Americans for princely sums.

Perhaps the effort did ensnare a legitimate terrorist or two, but in the main, the policy provided a terrific way for villagers to rid themselves of economic, social, and romantic rivals. Mountains of cash had been paid to place thousands of innocent people in detention, with no opportunity for a day in court.

Swaringen hoped it wasn't such a Gestapo-like arrangement that had produced the names on the list of people the drones were searching for. The whole thing had an Orwellian flavor to it. Worse, even.

Swaringen couldn't bear to think about what might've been going on behind the scenes. And he couldn't just let it rest.

He walked down the hall from the operations center after his shift, pausing at locked doors along the hallway to read the office placards. It didn't take long to arrive at his desired destination: the IT department. To most people, computer networks worked on the PFM principle. Pure Freaking Magic. But Swaringen knew it wasn't magic. It was human effort. The roomful of computers and video monitors in the operations center all required care and feeding. They required network connections, and network connections required servers, and servers required IT personnel to keep them running smoothly.

Swaringen knocked on the door.

"I'm still pretty new here," he said to the IT technician who answered, "and I'm hoping to understand things a bit better. I'd like to learn more about our process, about how things work."

The technician was eager to oblige. He walked Swaringen through a tour of the IT spaces, showing him the rack of servers that transferred data to and from the field, filtered it, prioritized it, and displayed it on the monitors in the command center.

Swaringen was surprised to learn that for every hour of video displayed on one of the monitors in the operations center, there were fifty more hours of undisplayed video. That tidbit dramatically changed his estimate of the number of drones airborne at any given time. The number had to be staggering. Well into the thousands. He supposed that he had read something about drone production programs in the newspaper at some point, but he hadn't paid much attention at the time. Now, however, Swaringen understood that the production scale had to rival the industrial mobilization during World War II.

"What happens to the unused video?" Swaringen asked.

"It isn't unused," the technician said. "Just because human eyes don't see everything, doesn't mean we're not looking at everything closely. We have over a hundred algorithms at work on every single second of video, looking for specific things. The high priority feeds are sent into the command center."

Swaringen pursed his lips, thinking. "How do you know the algorithms are looking for the right things?"

The tech smiled. "You never know, really. It's always a work in progress. We're constantly tweaking parameters, making adjustments, analyzing results."

"That's a high-stakes game," Swaringen said.

"Damn right it is." There was pride in the tech's voice.

"So really," Swaringen said, "the algorithms are running the show."

The IT tech held his palms up. "Whoa. I'm not allowed to say anything like that. Stuff like that could get me fired. But I can say that nobody on the command center floor ever sees a snippet of video that the algorithms don't screen for relevance and intelligence value."

"How does the machine know?"

The tech smiled. "Machines don't know. Just like humans don't know. Computers draw conclusions based on algorithms and heuristics, exactly like our brains do. The algorithms grade their own performance based on parameters we set, and they're constantly improving, training themselves for better performance."

"Artificial intelligence?"

The technician gave Swaringen a crooked smile. "No intelligence is artificial," he said. "We prefer to call it *nonbiological* intelligence."

Swaringen nodded. A troubled look crossed his face. "The algorithms aren't determining which names go on the wanted list, are they?"

The technician shook his head. "No, not yet. But obviously, with seven billion people on the planet, the algorithms are doing some pre-screening. Computers prioritize the people to watch. But analysts do the watching."

Swaringen frowned, pensive.

"At least, that's what I'm told," the tech said, palms raised again. "Really, the list just shows up."

"It just shows up?"

The technician nodded. "That's right. Once or twice a month, they hand-deliver a thumb drive to the ops center floor. It contains the names and associated biometric markers in a spreadsheet."

"What kind of biometric data?"

"Everything you can think of. The distance between a person's eyes. Between the corner of his mouth and his nostrils. The length and width of his chin. The length and width of his brow. The angle of his ears, the length of his neck. Fingerprint data, obviously. In some cases, unique patterns in the irises. It's beyond comprehensive, and it's the main reason the systems are so accurate."

Swaringen pondered. "These people aren't volunteering this information, I gather."

The tech laughed. "Sure they are. By walking around in public. NSA is tapped into every ATM in the country, and probably half the cash machines in the world. Every time anyone withdraws cash, their face is recorded. The biometrics are measured, categorized, and stored in the database. Same goes for all those traffic cameras you see."

"How in the hell did we get permission to do that?"

"I don't think we asked for permission," the technician said. "I think we figured out that we *could* do it, so we did."

Swaringen grimaced, uncomfortable. Not because he was a Luddite. He knew that computers made better medical decisions than doctors did. Computer-controlled robots performed better surgery than human surgeons did. He knew that computers made better flying decisions than pilots did. He knew that computerized robots made better assembly workers than humans. So there was no reason to think that computers couldn't be used to reliably identify behavior patterns.

The problem was making sure they were identifying the *right* behavior patterns. Humans were very complex. Behavior was not a monolithic thing. There were degrees and shades of gray, degrees and shades of intent. It was hard enough for humans, even with the brain's massively parallel processing, to accurately ascertain intent and affiliation. Swaringen hoped the computers were better at it than humans were, but he had his doubts.

But there were humans in the loop determining the list, according to the technician. Swaringen wanted to know more about how they did it. "Tell me who delivers the list every week."

The technician shrugged. "Just a courier. I should really learn her name, but I haven't."

"A female courier?"

"That's right. Same lady every time."

"Do you think she'll talk to me?"

"Couldn't hurt to ask."

* * *

Swaringen left the IT center with an uneasy feeling in the pit of his stomach. If anything, the technician's description of the way things worked at the NSA's command center generated more questions than answers. Sure, computers were smart. But you had to program them. You had to tell them what to look for. Which meant that you had to *know* what to look for. And you had to figure out how to turn that into machine language, to make sure nothing was lost in translation. The whole thing was fraught.

It was relatively easy to screen for intent in an email. You just looked for a particular set of words, in any language that you cared to exploit. And it was no longer a secret that NSA had been reading the world's email for a long time.

But even email analysis wasn't straightforward. People communicated with nuance, innuendo, metaphor, euphemism. Especially people who were planning illegal activities, who knew they were being watched. Those people were especially careful not to broadcast their intent. They used codes, indirect phrases, misdirection. So deciding the right words to look for wasn't nearly as straightforward as it seemed.

And Swaringen had a hunch that the problem of determining intent and affiliations was all the more fraught when information was sparser. As in video surveillance, for instance. Maybe you could figure out a person's circle of friends and acquaintances. Maybe some of those affiliations were so obviously "bad" that they were unambiguous. But Swaringen figured such circumstances were rare. Criminals and terrorists were careful. If not by nature, then by necessity. If you were a terrorist, the whole Western world was interested in hunting you down. Vast sums of treasure and talent had been invested to make you dead, as soon as possible.

Which led Swaringen back to the seminal question: who decided who lived and died, and how did they decide?

The IT technician had given him an important clue. The courier was female. Obviously, the courier had to be cleared for the information she was carrying, which meant she was on the Penumbra access list. Swaringen had only ever seen two or three females on the Penumbra ops center floor. It wouldn't take him too long to figure out which one was the courier.

He would approach her in much the same way he approached the IT technician. He would tell her, truthfully, that he wanted to understand more about the process, that he wanted to learn more about the intelligence gathering system.

Ultimately, Swaringen wanted to talk to the person who put the names on the list.

Chapter 26

Mark Severn had been yanked from the field. He had been 'made,' hunted down, even, in Budapest. Hence the fake death, in order to avoid a very real death. That meant that Mark Severn's duties had to fall to someone else.

Sam drew the short straw.

She pointed out the obvious: she had been made as well. They'd followed her all the way from DC to Hungary.

"Not the same," Davenport said. "You mopped up most of the muscle they sent after you."

"Most. But not all."

"They don't know you like they know Severn," Farrar said.

"Bullshit. They know me on sight."

"Some of them do, yes," Davenport said. "But as I mentioned, you thinned the herd considerably. I really think the risk is drastically reduced, especially since you're back on our home turf."

Sam frowned. "I'd really rather take that vacation," she said.

Davenport smiled. "Weren't you the one telling me just a couple of days ago that we couldn't possibly drop this case, that all sorts of messed-up things were happening that we needed to run to ground?"

"Yes," Sam said. "And I was right, as usual. I just don't want to be the one chasing it down. I'm tired, and I need a break."

"Unfortunately, Sam," Farrar said, "we're a bit thin at the moment."

"Bullshit," Sam said. "You have a floor full of monkeys sitting at computers instead of pounding the pavement."

Davenport and Farrar shared a look. "Not all assets are created equal," Farrar said.

"And you and Dan already have a number of hours invested in this," Davenport added. "You're making good headway. You made a few important discoveries. You have momentum. If you can hold out just a bit longer, get to the end of this thing, you'll be able to take that vacation."

"And then some," Farrar added. "I can authorize up to a week off with pay. It won't count against your annual leave."

"A bribe?" Sam asked.

"No, Sam. An expression of my genuine thanks for your effort and sacrifice."

Sam ultimately capitulated. Truth be told, she wanted to be the one to break the case. But she didn't want to want it. Because of Brock.

She thought about how to break the news to him. She didn't expect the conversation to go well.

* * *

Boston was definitely on her list, but not at the top. Because rarely in the counterespionage business was it easy to figure out who ordered a killing based on who had done the killing. Like nearly everything else in the modern world, assassinations were usually outsourced.

For that reason, and operating under the assumption that Janice Everman of the US Department of Justice was, in fact, a murder victim, Sam decided it would be important to figure out what she was working on immediately before her death. It sounded fairly obvious, but those kinds of simple questions usually led you in the right direction. Life was messy and chaotic and organic and nonlinear, but it was rarely overly complicated, when it came right down to it.

So she moseyed over to the Department of Justice, paused at the front desk, showed her badge, and asked the desk attendant whether he knew who had replaced Janice Everman. Sam figured Everman's replacement was as good a place as any to start.

"Do you mean in the Security and Public Policy division?"

"Is that where Janice Everman worked?"

"Janice Everman *was* the security and public policy department," the attendant said. "She was a force of nature, and we all miss her."

"Who replaced her?"

"Mr. France," the attendant said, making a face as if he'd just bitten into a lemon. Evidently, Mr. France wasn't well-liked, Sam surmised. The attendant gave her Jonathan France's office number, pointed the way to the elevator, and wished her luck. Which was strange, Sam thought.

She rode the elevator, pondering what might have happened to Janice Everman. It wasn't difficult to imagine a litany of enemies that anyone working in the Department of Justice might accumulate. Especially someone who could be characterized as a 'force of nature.'

And she was a lawyer, no less. Everyone hated lawyers. Even lawyers hated lawyers. A zealous lawyer could make enemies faster than a Jew in a mosque.

And the lawyers working in the Department of Justice found themselves in a curious predicament: they were ultimately appointed by the administration, to police the administration. Which produced an inherent conflict of interest. The Attorney General worked for the president, ostensibly to keep the president and his administrators from doing anything stupid or illegal. Or unconstitutional.

But in practice, Justice was just like any other watchdog agency. People in the Department of Justice served at the pleasure of the president. Everything else was secondary, tertiary, or utterly unimportant.

Which wasn't to say that everyone at Justice did the job the same way. It was entirely possible that one or two Justice employees took the job a little too seriously. Perhaps they got their priorities confused. Perhaps one of them placed the rule of law above the desires of the administration. Perhaps that's what happened to Janice Everman.

It would have to have been a serious misstep to have gotten her killed. The American system wasn't big on assassinations, except the political kind, not involving blood or body bags. Usually, getting sideways with one's political overlords merely resulted in a sacking, not a bagging.

Sam had already asked Dan Gable to look into Janice Everman's financials. Often, a person's money situation led to useful insights regarding their broader situation in life. A large debt, or a large sum of money suddenly deposited into an account, was usually a red flag from a security perspective. Sam wanted to rule out any security concerns, worst case. Best case, maybe Dan would discover something actionable. Mark Severn's work on the Janice Everman case had obviously touched a nerve, so Sam was hoping for a break.

Sam exited the elevator onto a floor that didn't look anything like a normal government office space. There were no gunmetal gray cubicles. The carpet was new and clean. It looked like a real office, and an upscale one at that. People sat at real desks. There were real filing cabinets nearby. The furniture was made of real wood. It looked very genteel, not very government at all.

It looked like a place full of lawyers.

Sam found Jonathan France's desk. It was large, oaken, situated at an angle in a corner office, with a view out over the Potomac. On France's desk sat a number of photographs. Many of them contained France himself, presumably, shaking hands with people of importance. Sam recognized a few of them from the local DC scene. The photos were arranged in a way that visitors could see them. France himself spent the day looking at the back of the photo mounts. It was an odd arrangement. France was clearly a man interested in impressing people.

Sam reminded herself not to be impressed.

"May I help you?" Jonathan France asked. He was a bookish man, pudgy, with narrow eyes, a sharp nose, thin lips, and a dour expression on his face. His reading glasses threatened to tumble from the end of his nose. There was a pile of paper in front of him on the desk.

"I was hoping to talk to you for a moment about your predecessor," Sam said, showing her badge.

Sam noticed a slight roll of the eyes. It was clearly a subject that Jonathan France had been prevailed upon to talk about on more than one occasion.

"I suppose it's about time for another one of these conversations," France said. "It's been nearly a month since the last guy was here."

Mark Severn had probably been the last guy to stop by France's office to talk about the case, Sam surmised. "There's been a lot of interest in Janice Everman?" she asked.

"No. Not to be insensitive, but there's been a lot of interest in Janice Everman's death. When she was alive, she was a nice lady doing a job. Nobody paid much attention."

"I see. Well, I won't take up too much of your time, in that case. It's just routine stuff, really, just revisiting a few things in light of some new information."

France's eyes flashed.

Sam noticed. She filed it away.

"Please, have a seat," he said, gesturing halfheartedly to a chair in front of his desk.

Sam obliged. "This is a nice office," she said. "I should talk to my supervisor about an upgrade. My office is decorated in 'early cheapskate.'"

"Attorneys like to feel self-important," France said.

Sam kept her strong opinion on the subject to herself. "I'll take your word for it," she said. "Anyway, I know you're busy, so I'll get right to it. I was just wondering what Janice Everman might have been working on right before she died."

France shrugged. "The usual, I suppose," he said. "I mean, nothing out of the ordinary. Nothing remarkable."

Sam frowned. "I see. I don't have much sense for what normal might be, though. Could you give me an example or two?"

France smiled. The smile looked out of place on his face. "Of course," he said. "Someone in the administration wants to do something. Someone else in the administration tells them they can't do it, because it's of questionable legality. So they call us. We prepare a brief, which is a legal document that nobody reads. We also prepare a one-slide summary, which everybody ignores. Then, people do whatever it was they wanted to do in the first place."

Sam smiled. "Sounds terribly rewarding."

"Not so much. But it's not too bad, either. I'm not working eighty hours a week at a law firm. I get to see my wife and kids occasionally. These days, I think they even like having me around. That wasn't always the case when I was at the firm."

"Which firm?"

"Kellerman, Stein, Schwartz, and Markowski."

"Isn't that a lobbying firm?"

"Same thing."

"I thought you said you were at a law firm."

"It is a law firm," France said. "It's a dirty little secret that lawmakers don't actually write laws. Corporations hire lobbyists to write laws and hand them to congressmen. And for that, lobby firms need lawyers."

Sam sighed. The government was worse than she thought.

"Not to mention the trillion legal pitfalls associated with being a lobbyist," France went on. "Paying the right amount of money to the right people at the right time and in the right way. Staying out of trouble is half the business."

"What's the other half?" Sam asked.

"I really have no idea," France said. "They kept me in a dark room drafting legislation."

"What kind of legislation?"

"Defense Acquisitions stuff, mostly. Like watching paint dry."

Sam gestured toward the expansive view out the window. "This must be a significant step up for you, in that case," she said.

"Like I said," France said, "the job doesn't have to be all that satisfying to make for a much better life than I had before. And Connie can stay home with the kids now, too."

"So it was a good opportunity for you, then."

Sam saw anger flash on France's face. "Did I benefit from Janice Everman's death? Obviously, I did," he said, a little testily. "It's a good job in a good location, and it's a stepping stone to bigger and better. But am I happy that a person died? Absolutely not."

"I wasn't implying anything," Sam said, conciliation in her voice. "So what kind of issues were on her plate when you took over her workload?"

France shook his head. "There were *no* issues. Someone else had totally cleaned out her inbox. By the time I took over, it was a completely clean slate. In fact, it took a little bit of time before anyone would send any work my way, because they had gotten used to going elsewhere to get it done."

Sam nodded. "I see. Was there any water-cooler scuttlebutt about anything going on in Janice Everman's world, that you are aware of?"

"I have no idea. I wasn't here at the time."

"How about during the time when you were here?"

France shook his head. "Nothing about her, except what a great lady she was. Everyone loved her. They said she always had a stern look on her face, until you smiled at her, and then her face beamed. Everybody loved that about her. Other than that, nothing. I know next to nothing about the kinds of things she was handling at the time of her death, or any other time."

"Is there anyone here who might know more about that?"

France thought for a moment. "Same as in any office," he said. "The secretary knows everything."

* * *

Jonathan France was right. Executive assistants knew plenty. Sometimes more than the bigwigs they served. They certainly knew a lot more about the inner workings of the organization, and they usually had a keen awareness of the politics going on behind the scenes. Who liked whom, who slept with whom, and who couldn't stand being in the same room together.

They also tended to have a solid sense of the ongoing business issues at any particular time. Sam hoped she would find that to be the case with Sylvia Salisbury. Sylvia was the executive assistant to Jonathan France, and she was Janice Everman's executive assistant before that. In fact, no one could remember a time when Sylvia Salisbury wasn't an executive assistant at the Department of Justice. She knew where all the bodies were buried.

Sam approached her with a smile. "Good morning, Ms. Salisbury," she said.

The secretary looked up. Her face was kind but serious. She had quick, intelligent eyes. She looked like a person with a lot on her plate. She also looked like a person who could handle even more. "May I impose on you for a few minutes of your time?" Sam asked.

"Sure," Sylvia Salisbury said. "There's not much going on here at the moment."

"Is there someplace private we can talk?"

Sylvia Salisbury nodded, stood, motioned for Sam to follow, and walked to a conference room with a stunning view of downtown DC. She held the door for Sam and closed the door behind them.

Sam sat at the head of the table. Sylvia Salisbury sat next to her, on Sam's right, in a position of deference, a courtesy undoubtedly learned and probably subconsciously applied after years as an executive assistant. It wasn't a power play on Sam's part. It was an attempt to establish the natural order of things in Sylvia Salisbury's mind, to put her at ease, to put her in a familiar element.

"You're here about Janice Everman, aren't you?" Sylvia Salisbury said after viewing Sam's Homeland badge.

"I am. But what makes you say that?"

"Nothing in particular. But if there's an issue going on involving Homeland, usually I know about it in advance, to put it on the calendar for the right people. Your visit was unscheduled."

"I see," Sam said. "But I'm curious why you thought right away that my visit might pertain to Janice Everman. After all, it's been a little over a year now, hasn't it?"

The secretary's face fell a little bit. She nodded. "I guess it still doesn't feel quite right for many of us," she said.

"How so?"

"Well, she was in such good health. DC is a very fitness-conscious town, and Janice Everman fit the profile better than most people. She went on a run or bike ride every day. She always defended that fitness time on her calendar. I could never get her to move her workouts to take an appointment."

"So she took care of herself."

"Very much so," Sylvia Salisbury said. "She said it helped her to think more clearly. To get more work done, be more efficient. She said it helped her feel better about things, too."

"Was there a lot of work stress?" Sam asked.

"There really was," Sylvia Salisbury said. "There was a lot going on at the time."

"You mean at the time of her death."

"That's right. All the meetings were classified, so I didn't know exactly what it was all about, but I could tell there was something big going on. And I could tell that Ms. Everman took it all very seriously."

"Classified meetings?" Sam prodded.

"They had nonspecific meeting titles, and they never published an agenda beforehand. But that wasn't unusual. Since 9/11, things have gotten much more secretive, and a much larger percentage of our time is spent on classified issues."

"I see," Sam said. She jotted a note on her pad.

"Do you suspect something?" Sylvia Salisbury asked while Sam wrote.

"Not particularly. We're just following up on some new information right now. It may turn out to be nothing, or it may turn out to be significant. But we never know unless we do our job and ask all the normal questions."

"That's the way Janice felt about her work, too. Ms. Everman, I mean. It's not like we were on a first-name basis. She was always very professional, but very kind. We all miss her."

"It was a tragic thing," Sam said. "Probably very traumatic."

Salisbury nodded, a faraway look in her eye.

"So, back to those classified meetings," Sam said. "How did you schedule them?"

"I scheduled them the way anybody schedules anything, I suppose," the secretary said. "I checked to find an open time on the calendar, and I booked the meeting."

"On the computer?" Sam asked.

"Yes, that's right. On the computer."

"Do you think it would be possible for me to take a look at Ms. Everman's calendar for the two months leading up to her death?" Sam asked.

"Of course. Anything I can do to help. Everyone has looked at all of that stuff already, and they didn't find anything. But as you say, maybe there's some new information that pertains."

"Thank you," Sam said. She followed Sylvia Salisbury back to her desk. She looked over the secretary's shoulder, watched her call up the calendar program and use the arrows to move back in time by a year, thirteen months, fourteen months, until the weeks leading up to Janice Everman's death became visible. "Would you mind if I sat in your chair for just a moment, to take a few notes?" Sam asked.

"Please, be my guest. I'll just take a coffee break."

Sam thanked her and began scrolling through calendar appointments. There didn't appear to be anything remarkable. But there was a meeting that recurred, called the NSP. Under the list of participants, the calendar only listed the NSP Group. It didn't list any individual names.

Sam opened up Sylvia Salisbury's contact information in her email program. She typed *NSP group* into the address finder. Nothing.

That seemed unusual. If an executive assistant were going to schedule a meeting with a particular group, she would require insight into the calendars of the individuals belonging to that group, Sam surmised. Otherwise, how could she schedule the meeting?

Sam continued to scroll through the appointments. A new meeting popped up two weeks before Janice Everman's death. It too was identified only by its initials, SAG. Again, there were no individual meeting participants listed. Just a repeat of the meeting title.

Puzzling. An executive calendar was no place for ambiguous annotations. Sam had never seen it done that way before.

Sam wrote down the dates and times of those meetings, of the NSP group and the SAG meeting. Nothing else stood out to her as unusual.

Sylvia Salisbury returned to her desk, and Sam asked her what the two meetings were about.

"NSP was the national security policy meeting," the secretary said.

"Do you recall who participated?"

"I never knew who participated in that meeting," Sylvia Salisbury said. "They would just telephone with the meeting time and place, and Ms. Everman would show up."

"Was that meeting ever held here, at Justice?"

"Never, to my recollection," Sylvia Salisbury said.

"Do you know who called to tell you the meeting times and locations?"

"Usually an executive assistant from the National Security Policy Group."

Sam's brow furrowed. "National Security Policy Group? I've never heard of such an animal," she said. "Do you know who any of the players were?"

"Yes," Sylvia Salisbury said. "I had to prepare a cover sheet one time, for a classified briefing that Ms. Everman prepared."

"Ms. Everman delivered a briefing to the National Security Policy Group?"

Sylvia Salisbury nodded. "I don't know what it was about, but it seemed like a big deal. I sent copies to Homeland, CIA, NSA, FBI, and the Chief of Staff."

"The White House Chief of Staff?"

"That's right," Sylvia Salisbury said.

Sam's eyebrows arched. "That's very interesting," she said.

"It was all very interesting," the secretary said. "Usually, when we're asked to consult on an issue for a group like this, there's an agenda forwarded in advance. The attorneys have a chance to look it over, do some case law research, form an opinion, maybe even produce a briefing to present at the meetings, to help guide policy. But this particular set of meetings had nothing of the sort. It all seemed very hush-hush."

"Interesting," Sam repeated. "How was Janice Everman's demeanor when she returned from those meetings?"

Sylvia Salisbury frowned a little. "I remember her as being more serious than usual," she said. "More stressed. And she always had classified work to do afterward."

"Are you sure? I mean, if it was classified, how did you know about it?"

"I do have a security clearance, but I wasn't briefed to whatever she was working on at the time. I just know that she was working on something, and I assumed it was related to those meetings because she always went into the classified room after she came back. She usually spent a couple of hours in there."

Sam pondered. Her brow furrowed. She chewed on the end of her pen. "Is there anything that's bugging you about events surrounding Janice Everman's death? Anything that seemed strange?"

Sylvia Salisbury thought for a moment. An uneasy look crossed her face. She opened her mouth as if to speak, then closed it again, as if having thought better of it.

"It's okay," Sam said. "I'm not on a witch hunt. I'm just here following up some new information, and I want to make sure we tie up any loose ends."

Sylvia Salisbury hesitated. She pursed her lips. Then she spoke. "It's just that she was so healthy," she said. "Vibrant. It really doesn't seem right that a disease could kill her that quickly. Literally, it killed her overnight. I mean, you hear about people dying of diseases all the time. The elderly. People who have been sick for a while, who have weakened immune systems. You know, they catch pneumonia, and that's it. Sometimes young children, too. Underdeveloped immune systems. But that wasn't Janice. I don't know that she ever missed a day of work until the day she died."

"Do you think it could have been something other than a disease?"

"I'm trying not to draw any conclusions for you," Sylvia Salisbury said, a serious expression on her face. "I'm just saying, the whole thing seemed... not right."

Chapter 27

David Swaringen was troubled. He couldn't let it rest. It nagged at him. He was determined to figure out who was making life-and-death decisions for thousands of humans.

He pulled his regular shifts in the command center, then invented semi-plausible reasons to remain afterward, doing all he could to learn more about the way the NSA operation fit together. So far, he had learned about how the data was passed to and from the command center floor, and about the particular algorithms that helped handle the flow of information.

But each answer pointed to new questions. Each algorithm had its own set of parameters. Each of those parameters had to be finely tuned. Otherwise, the algorithms would produce junk. The list of potential terrorism suspects would be as long as the list of humans, if it were done wrong. Or there might be nobody on it at all. Or any combination of wrongs in between.

And Swaringen had still never seen the list. He had no idea how many names were on it. He knew only that the list showed up via courier in the ops center a couple of times every month, updated to reflect new changes. The biometric identification parameters associated with each person on the list were then fed into the automatic recognition systems that screened all of the video that streamed into the NSA command center.

That part Swaringen understood very well. It seemed very straightforward, if a little bit spooky. Orwell had no idea how right he was. And how wrong. The current surveillance establishment far surpassed any dystopian nightmares of yesteryear.

Swaringen's attempts to ask Barter about the list had failed miserably. Not only had he obtained no answers, but he had received decidedly frosty non-responses. Swaringen felt he had pushed Barter as far as was prudent. Further, maybe.

So it came down to the courier. She was the link. If he were to learn anything further about the list, it would have to be through her.

Swaringen got ahold of the list of Penumbra-cleared personnel. Penumbra was the name of the program, but Penumbra was also something called a security caveat, a compartmented administrative construct that contained all the classified information associated with the top-secret program that Clark Barter ran.

There were close to fifty names on the Penumbra access list. But only three of them were female names.

The first two were shift workers in the video center. They never saw the list, and they never handled any classified information outside of the command center's secure room.

The third name was Emily Green. She was a short lady, squat, overweight, besieged and beleaguered, with an air of being permanently overwhelmed by the activities of her daily life. She seemed frazzled, far less than put together.

She was the courier.

They found a secured room where they could talk about the classified information in the Penumbra program. Swaringen began the conversation as he had with the others. He told Emily Green that he wanted to understand more about the process, so that he could be better at his job, more efficient. Which was still mostly true. He told Emily that he had been into the IT center, to see how things worked, to see the server stacks that housed both the algorithms and the data that supported the ops center floor.

Emily Green's eyebrows arched a bit. She seemed surprised. Angered, maybe.

"Should I not have visited the IT people?" Swaringen asked.

"I think that was within your security clearance," the courier said.

"I'm certain that it was," Swaringen said. "But you seem surprised."

"It's just that we really discourage people from asking questions outside of our area of responsibility. It's a security risk."

"How so?" Swaringen asked. "I'm supposed to stand in for Clark Barter during the times he's called away. So I want to make sure that I thoroughly understand the operation. There's a lot at stake, and I don't want to make any mistakes. How is that a security risk?"

Emily Green looked conflicted. He could tell the conversation was making her uneasy. He got the sense that with her, secrecy was more than just process or necessity. It seemed more like a way of life for her, well beyond habit, maybe even a belief system. "I suppose it does make sense," she said reluctantly. "I mean, it is a lot of responsibility."

Swaringen nodded. "I've gained a lot of insight into how the system works, and how things fit together. But there's one area where I still feel very ignorant. And it feels like an important area to me. So I was hoping maybe you could help me understand it better."

"Maybe." Emily Green turned her head and narrowed her eyes ever so slightly. Wariness, Swaringen saw.

He made his tone as gentle as possible. "You carry the suspect list down to the ops center a couple of times a month."

The courier's eyes widened in obvious alarm.

"Was I not supposed to know that?"

"It's just not in your area of responsibility," Emily Green said.

"I think it's very much in my area of responsibility," Swaringen said, doing his best to conceal his mounting frustration. "Like I said, I just want to understand the process. Can you tell me, where do you get the list?"

Emily shook her head. Her cheeks jiggled. Her brow contracted into a frown. "I really can't talk about it."

"But you have to get the list from somewhere, right?"

"Yes, obviously. But I'm not allowed to talk about it. And these are questions you shouldn't be asking."

"But isn't it classified under Penumbra? I mean, we're both cleared for the program. So we can talk about it. There's nothing wrong with having a conversation about the process, right?"

Emily Green shook her head again. "You're making me very uncomfortable," she said. "There are layers within Penumbra. If you were allowed to know about this, about the list and where it comes from, we would both know that already. They would have told us. But you're not cleared for that information. That's why I can't talk about it."

The courier rose. "I'm sorry, but I really can't continue this conversation," she said. "If and when you're cleared for that level of information, I would be happy to explain everything to you. Until then, please don't ask me any more questions."

* * *

It was clear that David Swaringen was going to get nothing more out of the courier. She took security more than a little bit seriously. He had run into another brick wall.

Really, he had run into the same brick wall. Barter hadn't cleared him to view the information necessary to do his job correctly. There were layers upon layers within Penumbra. Swaringen was cleared to some of them, but not all.

He wasn't cleared to the most important one.

You could learn a lot just by paying attention, Swaringen decided. He decided to keep an eye on the courier. Obviously, Emily Green got the list from someplace. She didn't conjure it from thin air. He wanted to know where.

Swaringen took more frequent breaks from the command center. He used the time to wander the halls around the operations center, venturing down unexplored corridors in the enormous NSA facility. He walked quickly, with a stern look on his face. Better to look busy and occupied. It would arouse less suspicion that way.

He was beginning to think it was a fool's errand. The facility was staggeringly large. He could wander the hallways for months without intercepting Emily Green.

But he caught a lucky break. He spotted her leaving the

restroom, courier bag in hand. Swaringen recognized her short, squat frame and her decades-old hairstyle. Her fat, lumpy ass looked like two tigers fighting in a gunny sack as she walked to the water fountain and bent over for a drink.

The courier bag hung by her side as she sipped. It must have been empty, Swaringen surmised, because you weren't allowed to stop anyplace with a classified package on your person. You had to go directly between origin and destination, with no stops in between. It cut down on the likelihood that someone might lose a pouch full of classified information. Emily Green didn't strike him as the kind to violate protocol of any sort by stopping in the bathroom while carrying a classified package.

Swaringen snuck a closer look at the courier bag. The zipper was open, and the padlock was unfastened. As he suspected, there was nothing in the pouch.

Emily Green finished drinking, wiped her mouth with a pudgy palm, turned toward Swaringen, and walked quickly down the hallway. Swaringen smiled and said hello as they passed. Emily Green's greeting was a few notches below friendly. She oozed mistrust. She really did take her job seriously.

Swaringen turned down a side hallway, took a few steps, and stopped. He wanted to gain a little separation from the courier. He wanted to follow her unobserved. He counted to ten, hearing her heavy footfalls echo off of the hard floor tiles as she hustled down the main corridor.

He returned to the main hallway. He followed Emily Green at twenty paces, walking slowly and on the balls of his feet to avoid alerting her to his presence. The hall was otherwise unoccupied. Not unusual. The building housed thousands of employees, but never seemed crowded.

The courier stopped at a door on the left side of the corridor. There was a key-card reader fastened to the wall adjacent to the door, and a telephone on the wall above the keypad.

Swaringen expected Emily Green to swipe her badge, type in her PIN, and enter the vault. But she didn't. Instead, she picked up the telephone on the wall adjacent to the door, dialed a five-digit extension, identified herself to whoever answered on the other end, and waited. Which meant that Emily Green wasn't cleared to enter the room unescorted.

Interesting.

Layers upon layers.

The door opened. A hand extended from within. Swaringen's angle down the hallway prevented him from seeing its owner.

Emily Green passed the empty courier bag to the person in the doorway.

Swaringen picked up his pace. He needed to see who Emily Green was talking to. He needed to read the person's name on their ID badge, or at least to get a glimpse of their face before the door shut.

The hand disappeared, then reappeared. Swaringen saw more of the person within the secured room. A man. Tall and lanky. With a shiny, bald pate. He couldn't make out the face.

Swaringen's eye went to the man's hand. It contained another courier pouch. This one was sealed and locked.

It contained classified information.

Emily Green signed a form and handed it to the tall, skinny man in the doorway.

She turned and continued down the hallway.

The door swung shut.

The man retreated within the secured room.

But not before Swaringen saw his face. Hawkish. Severe.

Familiar.

Someone Swaringen had met before.

The name escaped him, as did the context of their prior meeting. It was just beneath the surface of his consciousness. If someone had spoken the man's name, Swaringen would have recognized it immediately.

Swaringen took note of the room number as he walked by. The placard next to the phone said Current Operations. As if there might have been a room somewhere else called Future Operations. Or Past Operations. It was the kind of nondescript non-name that spoke volumes.

He looked forward down the corridor. Emily Green had disappeared around a corner up ahead, but he could hear her heavy, plodding footfalls.

He had a good idea where she was headed next. At least, he thought he did. And if he was right, it would confirm the contents of the sealed bag. She was headed to the basement.

Emily Green would undoubtedly take the elevator. She was overweight and didn't move very well.

Swaringen took the stairs. He bounded down two at a time. He was timing things in his head, and he figured he had a good twenty seconds on her. The elevators weren't fast, and while the courier had a head start, he figured he'd already more than made up for it.

He emerged from the stairwell onto the below-ground floor, maneuvered down a short hallway, crossed another long corridor, and finally arrived at the operations center doorway.

He badged himself in, took his seat next to Clark Barter, and waited.

Which was when it came to him. James Alcorn. That was the man's name. It arrived in his brain in a flash. Swaringen had met the hawkish, severe, unfriendly guy with the dead-fish handshake before.

In Clark Barter's office.

Where James Alcorn had retrieved something from Barter, something marked TOP SECRET.

Less than a minute later, the courier appeared, classified document pouch clutched in her plump hand like a prized possession. She handed it to a technician, who unlocked and unzipped it.

Inside was an envelope. Bright red, with TOP SECRET written on it in large, serious letters.

The technician sliced open the envelope. A data drive fell out.

Swaringen's heart pounded in his chest.

The list.

From the courier. Via James Alcorn.

Who got it from Clark Barter.

Which made Swaringen feel sick.

Because it made Clark Barter judge, jury, and executioner.

Chapter 28

Sam turned the pieces over in her head. A national security group, ostensibly meeting about national security items, had Janice Everman hopping during the weeks leading up to her death. She was summoned to various meetings, and afterward, she had many hours of computer work to do in a classified vault.

Undoubtedly, she had been asked to render a legal opinion regarding a particular classified program, or maybe a collection of them. It was the only plausible explanation. Why else would the Department of Justice have anything to do with NSA, CIA, and the Department of Homeland Security?

Sam frowned. It bothered her that there were no individuals associated with any of the meetings. Bureaucrats senior enough to rate an executive assistant invariably knew how to play the game. You were promoted only if people — important people — knew your name. People learned your name by seeing it, over and over again. So seasoned bureaucrats never missed an opportunity to associate their name with high-profile work. And anything involving a handful of three-letter agencies was undoubtedly big. Bigger than big, in fact.

So why weren't people's names plastered all over each others' calendars? Why weren't they marketing themselves, posturing for the next big job?

Maybe they couldn't. Maybe they weren't allowed to associate themselves with the effort due to security concerns.

Or maybe they were afraid to be associated with whatever was going on. Maybe it was controversial. Toxic, or radioactive, as the bureaucrats said. Dirty work, with the potential for big, ugly, messy blowback.

If that were the case, then nobody would want to be caught within a mile of any of the meetings. Movers and shakers would launder the evidence of their participation. Not much would be said about the gatherings, no minutes would circulate before or after, and the calendar coordination would happen very discreetly. Maybe even secretly.

Sam pursed her lips.

Maybe it was nothing. Maybe it was just administrative laziness that kept all those names off of the attendee lists. A kind of administrative shorthand. Maybe Sylvia Salisbury didn't put any names on that list because it just wasn't necessary. The National Security Policy Group was just another set of drumbeat meetings in an endless stream of drumbeat meetings. You had to have an iron ass to be a bureaucrat. You spent all day sitting on it, shuffling papers or listening to people reading from their slide presentations. Maybe it was just business as usual, too unremarkable for specifics.

But probably not. Self-promotion was a powerful motivator. People wanted to see and be seen. They wanted their names circulated. They wanted to be talked about, associated with big things, groomed for big things, hired for big things.

Sam sighed. "Hell if I know," she said to no one in particular as she unlocked her car.

She drove home. Brock was taking a nap. She took off her clothes, climbed in bed next to him, climbed on top of him. She woke him up and had her way with him.

She dozed fitfully for an hour afterward.

And then she rose, packed her bag, kissed Brock on the lips, and bade him farewell.

"Boston?"

"Just for a couple of days," Sam said.

"Promise me you'll be careful," he said. "No risks."

"I promise," Sam lied.

* * *

The flight was uneventful. Sam spotted no watchers. Dan Gable accompanied her on the trip. They took separate flights, to lower the probability of being tracked, to complicate the problem for the opposition.

Since her return from Budapest, Sam had noticed no surveillance. But DC was a horrendously crowded city, and surveillance was much harder to spot.

And there was also the matter of all of those video cameras. Hack into the right system, and there was no need to hire a goon in sunglasses to keep tabs on someone. There were enough video cameras around the city to do the job much more efficiently, and with a much lower probability of being caught.

Sam figured Boston was much the same, although she knew the camera density was significantly lower than in the nation's capital. There were fewer self-important people in Boston. At least, the self-important people in Boston didn't have their fingers on the nation's purse strings. They'd have to buy their own security.

Still, it wouldn't be hard for someone to track their movements, Sam figured. It didn't matter where you went. Odds were better than even that you'd be caught on at least one video camera, and probably many more.

She met up with Dan near the concourse exit. They hailed a cab and rode to a car rental place on the other side of town. It would've been much easier just to rent a car at the airport, but they figured there was liable to be less surveillance in an out-of-the-way place.

They wasted no time. They drove to the floral shop. The address was on the Russian business card that Sam found in the sock of the man she killed on the banks of the Danube. Asshole number three, she reminded herself. The third man she'd smoked in Budapest.

The shop was near the city's center, on a long block full of buildings built in a different era, when bricks were more expensive than the people who laid them. It was the closest thing any American city had to authentic charm, to a permanent sense of history, uncontrived and genuine and real. Sam loved it. She made a mental note to book a weekend in Boston with Brock. Sex and sightseeing would be the only items on their agenda.

"You with me?" Dan asked.

"I'm sorry. Did you say something?"

"Yes. I said that I don't like the vibe."

"Are you serious? It's gorgeous here."

"I wasn't referring to the tourist appeal. I don't have a good feeling about our plan. Sure you won't reconsider?"

Sam shook her head. "We could watch this place 24/7 for a year and not learn anything. These aren't stupid people."

"Even with everything that happened in Hungary? You mowed a few of them down."

Sam chuckled. *"Especially* with everything that happened in Hungary. They're going to lay lower than ever. They don't want trouble. They're in business, just like everyone else. They want to get paid, not arrested. It's tough to make a profit from prison."

"So our plan is to waltz in and say 'take me to your leader'?"

"Pretty much. Unless you have a better idea."

"Surveillance. Read their email. Listen to their phone conversations."

Sam shook her head. "These are old school knee-cappers. And they're licking their wounds. They're not going to be tweeting about their next hit, or posting shit on Facebook. They're going to stay hunkered down."

"If you say so, boss," Dan said, doing a respectable job of parallel parking in a narrow slot half a block away and across the street from the floral shop. "But aren't you afraid they'll recognize you?"

Sam smiled. "I'm counting on it," she said. "Just keep your phone on and your pistol handy."

Sam checked her own gun. One in the chamber, eight more in the magazine, safety clicked off, a spare magazine tight against her ass in her jeans pocket.

She opened the door and climbed out of the car, tossing her Homeland ID onto the empty seat behind her.

"Sam, please be careful," Dan admonished.

"What is it with you guys?" she asked. "What makes you think I'm not going to be careful?"

"I don't know," Dan said. "Had any near-death experiences lately?"

"Smartass."

"How long?"

"How long what?"

"How many minutes do you want me to wait until I come after you?" Dan asked.

Sam eyed him. She considered a testy retort, then reconsidered. It wasn't a bad idea. Russian gangsters weren't nice people. "Thirty minutes," she said.

"Fifteen."

"Fine."

Sam closed the car door and crossed the street.

* * *

Sam walked into the floral shop. It was just like all the other floral shops Sam had visited. Which wasn't a large number. She wasn't really into flowers. They reminded her of weddings and funerals and half-assed apologies.

She made a show of looking around, affected a frown, and moved forward to talk to the clerk. "I haven't really found what I'm looking for," she said.

"What are you looking for, ma'am?" the clerk asked. Her

accent was thick, as Russian as borscht, murky as the Caspian Sea. The woman had Slavic cheekbones, just like the goon in seat 32A.

Sam smiled. It felt like the right place. "I'm looking for something very specific," she said.

"Are you sure we carry it?" the clerk asked, turning her head sideways and squinting her eyes slightly, the universal sign of wariness.

"Maybe you don't," Sam said, "but my friend was very specific."

"Your friend recommended us?" The words were delivered in English via Moscow, just on the edge of intelligibility.

"Very highly," Sam said, turning to face the video camera. She wanted to be sure they knew.

"What is it that you need?"

"I need help solving a particular problem," Sam said.

"Wedding? Funeral?"

Sam shook her head. "Nothing that simple," she said. "Something more complicated. Something requiring... Strength. And resolve."

The clerk shook her head. "I cannot help you." The *h* in *help* was hard and comical. Like an old Communist caricature.

Sam put a look of disappointment on her face. "That's very upsetting," she said. "I was told that you would be able to help me, that you were the people I needed to see."

She let the silence ring out.

"I can't help you," the clerk repeated.

"I brought cash." Sam peeled off a hundred from a roll of bills in her pocket. She laid the money on the countertop.

Sam watched the battle behind the woman's eyes. The clerk wanted the money, but didn't want the strings it came with.

Sam used silence as a weapon.

Ultimately, the woman took the bill and stuffed it into the cash register. An employee, Sam thought. Not an owner. Not empowered to pocket any proceeds from the side business. Which was really the main business. Flowers were a show. Plausible deniability.

"Thank you," Sam said. "I was told I could count on you."

"Go out the front door. Turn left, walk three doors down, and go inside. It will be unlocked. You will wait there. Someone will find you."

"Thank you very much," Sam said. She walked out the door.

She looked nonchalantly down the street, toward the parking spot Dan had found.

But Dan was gone. The rental car was nowhere in sight.

It could be either good or bad, she decided. Maybe he was doing a damn good job staying out of sight. Too good, maybe. So far out of sight that he wouldn't be able to respond to a situation in time to make any positive difference.

Or maybe something had happened. Dan was as reliable as the sunrise, as certain as death and taxes. He wouldn't screw up.

Or maybe she had just looked in the wrong spot. Maybe he had repositioned. If so, he'd surely have let her know. She checked her phone.

No messages.

There's never any reason to worry until there's a real reason to worry, someone had once told her. And even then, worrying was counterproductive. It made you tense, which made you slow and stupid and vulnerable. Sam took a deep breath and continued down the street.

She counted the doorways on her left as she passed. The first two were shops, similar to the floral shop in vibe and disposition. Immigrant-owned. Maybe controlled by the same Russian gang. Those things tended to be territorial. Parochial. Organized crime wasn't a socially inclusive enterprise.

The third doorway was nondescript. There was no sign above it. Just a number: 1037. She texted the address to Dan, which made her feel a little silly. Asking for help clashed with the self-sufficient ass-kicker self-image she had constructed and cultivated, but she was entering a building full of an unknown number of assholes, and you really couldn't argue with the numbers. Especially unknown ones.

Sam tried the door. It opened into a long hallway that wrapped around the side of the building to the back. The only door was at the far end, on the left side of the hallway. She surmised that a cluster of residences lined the backside of the shopping center. The building was made of brick, classic Boston, and probably zoned for mixed-use. Shops in front, apartments in back, maybe apartments overhead as well.

Sam's footfalls echoed in the hallway. The interior was bare, sparse, dark, and dingy. It smelled of dirt and mold. The floorboards creaked beneath her. The gloom was already gnawing away at her confidence, and she felt fear nibble at the edges of her thoughts. A human thing. Inconvenient and uncomfortable, but largely unavoidable. She walked quickly and confidently to overcome the effect.

She arrived at the end of the hall and tried the door. Also unlocked. Sam turned the handle and walked in.

She waited. She checked her watch. Patience was certainly a virtue, but it wasn't one of hers.

She busied herself studying her surroundings. The room was unfurnished but for a table and two chairs. The windows were new. Other windows on the street had old glass in them, wavy and uneven from the inexorable assault of time. But not these windows. New, straight, and thick. Sam rapped her knuckles against the glass. Three-quarters of an inch thick. Bulletproof.

Escape proof.

Sam's pulse quickened.

She surveyed the rest of the room. There was a door on each side. She'd walked in through the door on her left. The one on the right was closed.

Both doors opened inwards, which was unusual. Security demanded that external doors swing outward, so the bulk of the door frame stood between an intruder and the inside of the room. You'd have to kick the doorframe free of the wall to break in, or hack all the way through the door itself.

But the effect was the opposite in this particular room. Break-ins weren't the concern, because the doors were mounted the opposite way. They were designed to prevent people from breaking *out*.

Well, Sam figured, gangs didn't take over the neighborhood by being nice. Overt resistance was bad for business. Therefore, it was dealt with harshly. Probably in rooms just like this one, Sam thought. Built to keep both people and noise inside. Scream all you want, the Russians probably taunted their guests, because nobody can hear you.

Five minutes passed, then ten. Sam checked and rechecked her sidearm, making sure the pancake holster under her jacket was unfastened, allowing the fastest draw her neural speed would allow. She controlled her pulse by controlling her breathing. Deep and slow, over and over, clearing her mind of fear and bullshit. Only this moment exists, she told herself. Be awake and aware. Not afraid.

Finally, footsteps. Heavy. Made by a large person with long strides, maybe wearing boots.

The door handle turned, the door squeaked open, and a small giant walked in. Six and a half feet tall, Sam guessed, probably two-fifty. Slavic cheekbones. Just like 32A. A family business.

"You asked for help." It was a statement, not a question. The man's voice was low, gravelly, barely more than a growl. Thuggish. Again by way of Moscow.

Sam gathered herself. "Yes, that's right. I hope I've come to the right place."

"What is your problem?"

Sam smiled. "I have a number of them. But only one of them needs your help."

The big Russian didn't say anything. If he was amused in the slightest by Sam's attempt at humor, he hid it well. His face remained impassive, inscrutable, big and foreign. Mean, in an innate way.

"I'm interested in a particular kind of physical labor," Sam said.

"With guns?"

Sam shook her head. "Blunt objects would be best," she said.

"How many people?"

"Just one."

"A man?"

"How did you guess?"

"Pretty woman always have man trouble. Hold your hands up. I check for a wire."

Sam did as commanded. The big Russian did as threatened. His thick, meaty paws spared no inch of Sam's body. He touched her in sexual places, but his touch wasn't lascivious. It was professional. He liberated her Kimber and her cell phone and her wad of cash and her spare magazine. He placed them all on the table.

"Satisfied?" Sam asked.

"Who sent you?"

"No one."

"Who told you to come here?"

"A friend. Someone I trust. Someone who had a problem like mine. They said you handled it quite well."

"What is the name of this friend?"

"They asked me to keep them out of it," Sam said.

"How do I know you are not cop?"

"I suppose you don't."

The big Russian eyed her carefully. "You have gun."

Sam nodded. "For protection."

"From your problem," the Russian concluded.

"That's right."

"Why not take care of problem yourself?" the big man asked in his thick accent, nodding at her gun.

Sam shook her head. "I can't. It wouldn't be self-defense."

She could see the wheels turning inside the Russian's head. His face lost a little of its impassivity. He was calculating, ciphering, weighing pros and cons and risks and rewards.

She nodded toward the roll of cash. "I can pay you."

The Russian nodded. "Of course. Everyone can pay."

She had no idea what he meant by that.

She also had no idea whether her story was compelling. It wasn't much of a story at all, really. A friend sent me. People in the Russian's line of work probably heard that line an awful lot. But it was probably true more often than not. Goon squads couldn't exactly advertise in the paper. Or on Google. It all had to be by word of mouth.

The Russian reached a decision. "Wait here," he said. "I will talk to my boss, and he will talk to you."

In one swift, practiced motion, the man collected Sam's cash, pistol, and phone from the table. "Boss has very strict rules for meeting," he said. "No gun, no phone."

Sam stared at him. Not an unexpected set of conditions, all things considered. Meeting with a mid-level manager in a crime syndicate wasn't an insignificant event for either party. If you were in the life, your life was in danger by definition. Nobody in his right mind would accept a meeting with an armed stranger.

Still, her heart rate jumped. She couldn't help but wonder whether she had miscalculated.

The big man left the room, closed the door behind him, and left Sam in silence.

Five minutes passed, then ten. Perhaps the boss was in a meeting. Perhaps he was indisposed. Perhaps they were debating internally about whether to take on the business.

Fifteen minutes went by, then twenty. Sam grew restless.

At thirty minutes, she decided to leave.

She tried one door, and then the other.

They were both locked.

Sealed like a tomb.

Chapter 29

It was a foolish idea and Nero knew it. But there weren't any good ideas floating around, and he had to do something. He had no money, no place to stay, no clothes, no food. And he had no friends he could call upon for help, because the feds undoubtedly had everyone in his life staked out and under surveillance.

So he waited until dark. He hopped back on his stolen motorcycle, chose a serpentine path to the highway, accelerated up the on-ramp, and headed north toward downtown Denver. He exited at the loop, C-470, which wrapped around the city. He took it west and exited at a street called Santa Fe, named for the railroad tracks laid in the Wild West days, which paralleled the street all the way through town.

Traffic was sparse, particularly by large city standards, but there were still too many cars out for Nero's liking. He was driving without a helmet. It wasn't illegal in Colorado. But it was stupid, and it left his face exposed, which made him feel vulnerable. Like somebody might recognize him. Or like he might be caught on camera, like the kind at every intersection.

Nero's time on Santa Fe Boulevard lasted until a street named Bowles, which he took west to a boulevard called Federal, which he followed further north. The neighborhood had been suburban at one point. But no longer. It had changed color, from middle-class white to lower-class brown. Nero could see the change as he traveled further north, further toward the center of the city, further toward the old section of town.

He was headed for his uncle's house. His uncle was a drunk and a degenerate. The old bastard sipped away his unemployment check, watching the Price is Right, trying to solve the Wheel of Fortune, shouting out answers to Jeopardy questions. Nero had every expectation that his uncle would be passed out, drunk. Which suited Nero's plans perfectly.

He turned west off of Federal onto a street called Arizona. The houses were small, built in the forties and fifties, made of brick, with small yards, large satellite dishes, and an assortment of disused cars and appliances strewn haphazardly about.

He drove past a religious high school. It had also opened in the fifties, ostensibly during the time when the neighborhood was nice, white, and suburban. But the middle-class white kids had evidently grown tired of a thirty-minute commute from suburbia to the barrio for math and dogma. Either that or God had fallen on hard times, Nero surmised, noting the graffiti on the walls and the faded "closed" sign on the fence.

Nothing stays the same. Everything changes. And rarely for the better. The neighborhood suited his drunken uncle perfectly, Nero figured.

He stopped one block west of his uncle's house. Nero had no intention of approaching from the front. He figured doing so would be the height of stupidity.

He figured the whole thing was the height of stupidity, really.

Stupid, but necessary.

But he vowed not to take any unnecessary risks. The last thing he wanted was to find himself back in captivity. As a detainee, as Special Agent America had said. No way out. Nero shuddered at the thought.

He wasn't interested in his uncle's house nearly as much as he was interested in the backyard. Or more precisely, what was buried in the backyard. A coffee can. Containing no coffee.

Nero disconnected the ignition wires, killing the motorcycle engine. He parked the bike on the curb, behind a shiny new truck, itself parked next to a dilapidated hovel. Nero shook his head. He never understood the lower-class penchant for squalid living conditions and beautiful, shiny cars.

Nero walked down the block, looking between houses to spot the telltale 1980s satellite television dish that had always dominated his uncle's backyard. It was a perfect landmark. And a necessary one for Nero, because he had never bothered to learn his uncle's address.

He didn't spot the dish right away. He worried momentarily that he was on the wrong block. He double-checked the street sign. He was pretty sure he was in the right place, but doubt nagged at him. He continued down the block, head craned and eyes straining to glimpse the big white disk sticking up from the ground. He grew more nervous by the second, felt more and more exposed with each passing moment.

Had his uncle taken the dish out of the yard?

Did his uncle still live there?

Was the old bastard still alive?

Nero fought a strange combination of despair and panic. He had rested his hopes on successfully recovering the coffee can from his uncle's place. It had taken on extreme importance in Nero's mind. Because it *was* extremely important. He was dead in the water without it.

He kept walking, searching, worrying about how suspicious he must have looked, like he was casing the place. Which, of course, he was.

Finally, he found the dish, big and ugly and anachronistic, protruding from a weed-filled yard around the other side of the block. Nero felt equal parts relief and tension. Because now he had to go dig up the coffee can.

He couldn't be spotted walking toward someone's house in the middle of the night. Great way to get shot, in such a neighborhood. He needed to find a stealthy avenue of approach.

He walked back up the block until he found a house with a row of waist-high bushes arranged in a line perpendicular to the street. Precisely the cover Nero was looking for. He bent down as if to tie his shoe, then Army-crawled on his hands and knees between the hedgerow and a parked pickup truck, heading away from the street and toward the backyard fence.

When he judged himself to be out of the line of sight from the street, he took a deep breath and stood, peering over the fence into the yard.

He heard the rattle of a chain. A low growl followed. A watchdog. His innards clenched in instant fright. He hated dogs. And it would do no good to sneak around like a ninja, only to wake up a guard dog by hopping a fence. It would alert everyone in the neighborhood, not to mention the bored feds who were undoubtedly sitting in a car someplace on the other side of the block watching his uncle's house.

He snuck one house to the north.

Another dog.

He tried the other direction. He fought his nerves as he made his way south, wondering who might have been watching him from a window. It wasn't smart to wander around back and forth in front of people's houses at midnight. Someone was liable to walk outside with a shotgun, interested in having a wordless conversation.

Nero peered over the fence into the backyard.

No dog. "Hallelujah," he breathed. He shook the fence a little bit, just to be sure. Nothing stirred.

His heart raced. Go time.

Nero scaled the fence, feeling the rotting wood creak and groan beneath his weight. He swung one leg over the top, then the other one, then lowered himself slowly and carefully to the earth.

Mud. Nero felt his shoes sink. He cursed softly beneath his breath. Mud was great for a lot of things, but not stealth. Mud left footprints. He stepped out of the puddle and did his best to scrape the mud off his shoes onto the grass. But it was dark, and he couldn't tell how successful he had been. He had no idea whether he would leave footprints en route to his uncle's backyard.

And he still had another fence to scale. Slippery shoes would be a hazard.

He cursed, shook his head, and took his shoes off, setting them near the fence. He hoped he wouldn't be called on to win a footrace. He doubted he could outrun even the fattest donut-munching flatfoot while barefoot.

Nero low-crawled toward the fence separating the neighbor's house from his uncle's.

Except that it wasn't his uncle's house. Avoiding the guard dogs had forced Nero to move further down the block than he had realized. Two more fences separated him from his uncle's yard. The realization left him even more nervous. Adrenaline coursed through his veins, and he felt the blood pounding in his temples.

Nero peered over the fence, praying there would be no angry animal on the other side.

All clear. He scaled the fence gingerly, taking care not to injure his bare feet on the old, rotting fence wood. It took forever. Maybe even longer than that.

Despite his care, despite the slow pace that he used to get over the fence, he had to suppress yelps of pain on several occasions as his foot slipped. He jammed his toe into the rail, and the pressure from his body weight dug the pad of his feet painfully against the thin strip of wood. Shoes were a damn fine invention, Nero reflected, gritting his teeth. Life really must have sucked before them.

He lowered himself down to the earth on the opposite side of the fence, and stepped into a nasty surprise. A thicket of weeds. Thorns. Thistles. Whatever the hell you were supposed to call them. He felt them biting into the skin of his feet. "*Goddamn,*" he groaned. It felt like things kept getting worse with each passing moment, like he was in some kind of a stupid television comedy. It wasn't much of a plan to begin with, and it felt like it was unraveling.

Nero stepped gingerly out from the weeds, praying for grass. Instead, he got rocks, small and sharp and jagged. He stepped gingerly across, wincing as the sharp edges bored into the bottom of his feet, biting his lip as his foot slipped painfully off of a large, jagged stone.

He fell. His body slammed into the ground. The air rushed from his lungs. An involuntary *ooof* escaped his throat, loud and unmistakably human. His foot hurt like hell. He felt it with his hand. It felt warm and slick. Blood. "Shit," Nero mouthed silently. What on earth had possessed him to take his shoes off?

He heard a noise. It came from inside the house. A light switched on. Footfalls sounded from within.

Nero flattened himself on the ground. He looked around for shelter. He was almost smack in the middle of the tiny yard, he realized. There was no cover anywhere. No place to hide. He held his breath, forcing himself to remain still, fighting an overwhelming urge to get up and run.

The light went out inside the house. More footsteps, but growing fainter, moving away.

Nero started breathing again.

He crawled onward, aiming for a tall tree on the far side of the yard, planning to use it for shelter while he peered over the fence into his uncle's backyard, hoping to stay hidden from any watchers in the front of his uncle's house.

He rose slowly, his eyes peeking just above the top of the fence, and spied the giant, ancient satellite dish, bought and paid for by honest taxpayers, by way of his uncle's unemployment benefit. It looked just like Nero remembered it, stark and trashy, just like it looked on those rare occasions decades ago when he and his mother would trek out from Ohio to see her deadbeat brother, for reasons Nero still didn't understand.

It looked the same, but more dilapidated, more decayed. Waist-high weeds dominated the yard. Disused lawn furniture was strewn about, lumps of rotting plastic punctuating the feral landscape.

Nero scaled the fence. He dropped into the weeds on the other side. A stabbing pain roared from his foot, through his leg, into his brain. Shards of broken glass dug into his heel. He stifled a cry.

It fucking *hurt*.

He dropped to the ground, the weeds now over his head. He examined his foot, pulled a broken shard from the fleshy part just in front of his heel.

He sat still for a moment, letting the pain subside, regaining control of his thoughts, cursing the moment of utter stupidity that had prompted his barefoot midnight foray.

Then he crawled to the far side of the satellite dish. He wasn't interested in the dish itself, but the support structure that held it up. The legs were built to last. Concrete anchored the metal posts. Colorado could get some impressive windstorms, and the satellite TV company didn't want to have to come back out after every storm to replace hundreds of dishes.

At least, that's what Nero guessed as he searched in the darkness for the area just to the south of the southeastern-most support post, the one directly opposite the large tree. One hand's distance away from the edge of the concrete. Always the same, with every hiding spot. One hand's distance away from a major landmark, something with some staying power. That's where he buried all his coffee cans.

He used his hands to start digging. He pulled a couple of weeds up by their stalks, leaving loosened dirt in their wake, which made for slightly easier digging. He had a long way to dig, and he had only his bare hands. Six to nine inches. It was a lot, with no shovel.

He kept working, conscious of the noise he was making, suddenly paranoid that it would wake his drunken uncle, that it would alert the cops sitting in the cars across the street, that it would cause dozens of searchlights to be trained on his face. The unhelpful workings of a frightened mind.

Nero forced those thoughts out of his consciousness and focused on getting the job done.

It was dark, and he couldn't tell how far down he'd dug. It felt like he had been shoveling dirt with his fingers forever, like the hole had to be seven feet deep.

Where the hell was the can?

A moment of panic seized him. What if it wasn't there? What if his uncle had found it? Blown all the cash on vodka and hookers? Sold the gun to a pawnshop, for more vodka and hookers?

Nero felt rage swelling up in his chest. He rose to his knees, used both hands to scrape deeper and deeper into the earth, flinging the detritus out of the way. Sand wedged painfully beneath his fingernails. He felt layers of skin scraping from his fingertips. It hurt like hell, but he kept going, faster than before, digging with a grim, manic determination, thinking of the things he would do to his uncle if the coffee can was gone. He thought of breaking into the house, of choking the skinny bastard with his bare hands, of breaking his skinny little neck. Worthless old coot.

Nero's hand hit something hard. Metallic.

His irrational rage turned instantly to glee. He accelerated his pace yet again, exposing the sides of the can, clearing dirt off the top. He ran his fingers around the lip of the can, building space, rocking it back and forth, loosening the soil, feeling the sides of the can flex under the strain.

Nero worked faster, harder. Would everything still be inside? Could someone have played a cruel trick? Could they have removed the contents but replaced the can?

Nero shook his head. He had to get ahold of himself. The strain was getting to him. He felt like he was losing his mind.

Finally, he freed the can from the ground. His fingers protested as he lodged them beneath the plastic lid, gritted his teeth, and peeled it up from the lip of the can.

Nero shoved his hand down inside. He felt hard, cold metal. Old, but familiar. The snub-nosed .38 revolver. He wrapped his hand around the grip, liberated the gun from the coffee can. The shiny barrel gleamed in the starlight.

Nero had mixed feelings about the gun. If he were apprehended again, it wouldn't look good at all. Particularly since the serial number had been filed off.

On the other hand, life on the streets was no picnic.

He tucked the gun into his belt.

He reached his hand back into the coffee can. He felt a cylinder, made of paper, held together by a rubber band around the center. He felt his eyes well with joy. The money was still there. Four big wads of cash. Twenty-five hundred each. Ten grand, total.

Salvation.

He shoved the cash in his pockets, replaced the can, replaced the dirt, tamped it down, hoping the lingering signs of his presence weren't too obvious. It was impossible to tell in the darkness, but he wanted to leave no trace of his midnight foray.

Nero stood, slowly, pausing at a crouch, keeping his head below the height of the fence to make surveillance from the street difficult.

He heard a car engine. He turned to look.

His blood turned to ice.

A cop car. Moving slowly, deliberately, right to left.

Nero's bowels threatened a frightened revolt.

A searchlight switched on, an inferno of painful white brilliance, originating above the mirror on the driver's side of the cop car. It played over the front of the house, then meandered to the sides.

Nero flattened himself against the earth, praying the sudden motion hadn't given him away. He felt sick with adrenaline. His heart pounded. He felt certain it was audible from a block away. His breath came in short gasps.

The searchlight bathed the side of the house, then invaded the backyard. It paused on the satellite dish.

Nero's fingers curled around the earth and weeds. He whispered silent prayers.

The searchlight stayed over him an eternity, moving over the big dish.

Then the light moved down, intruding all the way into the backyard through an open gate next to the house.

Nero thought he might piss himself.

He could see his own shadow reflected in the tall weeds behind him.

Surely, they saw him. They had to have seen him.

Nero contemplated standing up, hands in the air. He was armed. He didn't want to be shot. His muscles tensed, ready to push his torso upright, ready to surrender.

Not yet, a voice said inside his head. Don't give up yet. Make them come get you. Don't do anything stupid.

He lay there, inhaling the scent of the earth, willing himself to slow his breathing, to calm himself, to stay still. His chest heaved with each panicked breath. He closed his eyes. His panicked mind pictured the cell at Homeland, pictured Special Agent America and that smug smirk of his, pictured the slack-jawed lackey and his open-faced, dead-eyed meanness, thought of the throwaway phrase that said it all: *in cases like yours, we take the gloves off.*

He thought of Penny, and the kids. He thought of his favorite chair at home, the one in front of the TV, where he sat to watch the game.

Nero closed his eyes tighter, willing himself to stay calm, to stay still.

Surely they had seen him. Certainly they were coming for him. It was only a matter of time. There would be footsteps and shouts, imperious commands, the sounds of pistols being drawn, racked, and leveled at him. Nero was certain of it. He was going back to prison.

But they didn't come.

One minute passed. Maybe two. Maybe more.

Nero opened his eyes.

Darkness. A cool breeze. Weeds and leaves rustling. Nothing else.

The cop car had moved on. The searchlight was no longer blazing over his uncle's house.

Was it possible? Had they really not seen him? Had he really pulled it off? Nero's arms and legs shook. He felt terrified and giddy, minuscule and giant all at once.

He waited a few minutes longer, just to be sure. Then he stood, unsteady on rubbery legs, never straightening above a crouch, remaining beneath the fence line, moving toward the side of the house, back the way he had come.

He realized that he was crying. He wiped his eyes.

Then he scaled the fences, tiptoed through the rocks and weeds and broken glass, found his shoes, put them back on, climbed over the last fence, crawled along the hedgerow to the sidewalk. He stood, walked as confidently as possible to the motorcycle, reconnected the ignition wires, started the engine, and drove away.

He had made it.

At least, that's how it seemed.

Chapter 30

As the minutes passed, Sam became more and more certain she had miscalculated. She had not expected the response to be warm and welcoming, but she'd been counting on the element of surprise to catch them off guard, back on their heels.

She looked at her watch. Forty-five minutes. Any surprise the Russian gangsters might have felt had surely dissipated. They were forming a plan. Probably getting ready to execute it. Maybe getting ready to execute *her*.

Forty-five minutes. Thirty minutes longer than she had given Dan to come after her. "Where are you?" she said aloud.

She felt a sudden sense of dread. Dan was never late. Especially in an operational environment. She began to wonder if her inability to locate the rental car earlier wasn't due to something other than good tradecraft on Dan's part. Clearly, they had made her. Maybe they had also made him.

She looked around the room for the zillionth time. No change. It was still a prison cell, designed from the floor up to keep people in, undoubtedly used for pulling fingernails out and gouging eyeballs to win turf, intimidate rivals, ensure compliance, enforce loyalty.

Time to get resourceful. Sam surveyed the contents of the room. It was a short survey. Two chairs and a table. The chairs were wooden, with little metal discs on the bottoms of the legs. There were scuff marks on the floor from years of use. Sam lifted the chair and looked at it, felt its heft, assessed its construction. It felt light enough to wield but sturdy enough to do some damage.

She re-examined the glass, wondering for a brief second whether she could get the chair through it. Not a chance. The glass was designed to stop bullets. A chair had no prayer.

She re-examined the door frames, thinking maybe she had missed something earlier, some way out, some crack she could exploit, a lock she could pick. But there were no weaknesses. There was no lock on the inside. There was clearly a deadbolt on both doors, but the latch was accessible only from the outside, and only with a key. On the inside was only a brass faceplate. No keyhole. No way to take advantage of her lock-picking prowess.

She looked closely at the door frame. Metal. Out of place in the ancient building. Installed with a clear purpose. Sam couldn't tell for sure, but she figured the doors would also be made of steel, to prevent anyone from kicking their way out.

She examined the hinges. She wondered whether she might be able to tap the hinge rods out of them, then pull the door free of the jamb. But the hinges were partially recessed, and the long hinge rod was itself held in place by a small screw. The screw head faced the wrong way. To get the screw out, the door had to be open already.

Trapped. Non-negotiably and completely.

Forty-eight minutes. Whatever the goons had in mind, they were well on their way to making it a reality. She had killed a few of their own. They were probably more than a little pissed off about it. She was probably on their list anyway. Now was probably as good a time as any for them to take her out, Sam reasoned. They were probably more than a little eager to scratch her off their list.

And she had undoubtedly upset whatever uneasy detente had existed between the gang and the local law enforcement. She didn't expect a robust response from the locals. Maybe not even the Boston FBI field office.

No way she was going to wait around for the Russians to serve her sentence, like a death row prisoner. She needed a plan.

Two chairs and a table. Not much to work with. But it was better than nothing at all. She wasn't tied up, wasn't bound and gagged, wasn't suffering from a debilitating injury, and wasn't staring down the barrel of a gun.

Yet.

Sam picked up a chair, climbed atop the table, and stood upright. She inverted the chair over her head, so that the legs pointed up, toward the ceiling. She pressed her hands upward, accelerating the chair legs into the plaster overhead. She pounded once, twice, three times.

She listened. No movement, no noise.

She pounded harder. Flakes of plaster fell to the floor, shattering into small pieces.

She listened again. Again nothing.

She pounded again, then listened hard.

Movement. Heavy footfalls, moving rapidly, then a rhythmic, metallic staccato. Someone was running down the steps on the outside of the building. Sam felt the vibrations through the room. She pounded a few more times against the ceiling for good measure, just to make sure they didn't lose energy or interest. Just to make the point.

More footsteps upstairs. Heavy. Men wearing boots.

Sam climbed down from the table. Adrenaline crashed in her stomach. It was not the manufactured, vestigial, misplaced fear that modern humans felt in situations of contrived importance. It was the real thing, appropriate to a real life-or-death situation. Fight or flee. Do or die.

Sam took a position adjacent to the west door, the one she had entered nearly an hour before. It was a gamble. She didn't know if they would come in through that door, or the one on the opposite side of the room. But she couldn't be in both places at once. Either she would have the benefit of surprise, or she wouldn't. Fifty-fifty.

She bent her legs in a low crouch. She lifted the chair and held it by the seat, close to her chest. The legs pointed forward, out away from her body. Like a lion tamer. If you wanted to hurt somebody with a chair, you didn't do it by swinging it around, like in the movies. You concentrated all of your force, all of your body weight, all of your muscular strength, driving through one chair leg, one small point, less than an inch in diameter. Force divided by area. Basic physics. Lethal.

Sam waited, tense, heart thudding in her chest. She forced herself to inhale and exhale, to breathe calmly. No use getting fatigued before the fight even started.

She closed her eyes, listened for footsteps.

She felt vibrations in the floor. She couldn't tell where they were coming from, and she couldn't tell which door the men would likely burst through. She moved her head from side to side, hoping to triangulate the source of the sound. But it was diffuse, spread out through the building structure, nondescript and non-directional.

Would she get lucky?

Or would she get hurt?

The door rattled.

The wrong door.

Sam sprinted across the room, dodging the table and holding the chair out in front of her as she ran, arriving just as the door swung open.

She was on the wrong side of the opening. The door swung into her.

But she made it work. She crouched, forearms flexing as she gripped the chair, tensing her arms, coiling her legs, storing up her fury, waiting for the moment.

The tall guy rounded the corner. Same thug from before.

She aimed above the distinctive cheekbones, and a little aft, centering her focus on the slight depression that marked the goon's temple, a soft, vulnerable spot in an otherwise impenetrable skull.

Sam howled. She drove the chair legs forward with all of her strength, all the leverage she could muster, all the skill and accuracy she had available.

Her strike found its mark. Sam felt a wet crunch, felt the foot of the chair leg meet biological resistance, then punch through, then slow to a stop deep inside the man's brain.

He fell forward, onto his face, another sick, wet crunch announcing the end of his fall.

One down.

The chair leg was stuck inside his skull. Sam wedged her foot on the dead man's neck and pulled, jerking the chair from side to side, trying to pull it free, feeling rather than seeing the onrush from the next guy through the door.

She got the chair free just in time to duck beneath a wicked left cross. Number Two's meaty fist grazed the hair on the top of Sam's head. Close call. She ended up in a defensive crouch, in no position to take a shot at the man's face or head.

So she aimed for the next best place. She let loose another banshee howl, driving the chair forward with all of the considerable power her athletic body could deliver.

Again her attack found the mark: Number Two's nuts. She felt something give, something soft and fleshy. He screamed in instant agony. He doubled over. Right into Sam's knee. She drove it upward, accelerating through the man's face, trying to touch her shoulder with her thigh, delivering all the force and fury in her power.

And it was quite a lot of force and fury. The man's nose exploded. Blood splattered, and shards of bone and cartilage launched into his brain. It was probably over for him, but Sam was taking no chances. She cocked her elbow, drew it down from shoulder height like a scythe, her eyes focused just below the man's brain stem.

The blow connected. She felt something give catastrophically in the man's neck. He fell to the floor, face shattering against the hard surface, arms awkward and akimbo. Definitely dead.

Two down.

And the count was going to stay at two. Because the next guy had a gun, pointed at her. A black-barreled FNX, Sam saw. Chambered in 9mm, or maybe .40 caliber. A very nice weapon. Nice enough to get the job done, without a doubt.

Number Three stood too close to Sam to miss, but too far away to be vulnerable.

Checkmate.

Sam stood up, raised her arms above her head, a defeated look settling over her face. She could try something, but she would be dead almost before the thoughts reached her muscles. He was maybe eight feet away. Only a complete baboon would miss from that distance. She could see the safety lever was off, and she could see the round indicator sticking out just a hair on the right side of the weapon. There was a bullet in the chamber, loaded and ready to fire.

The man motioned for Sam to turn around. She complied. "Hands on table," he said in a thick Russian accent, stereotypically deleting articles of speech essential in English but with no direct Russian parallel.

Sam leaned against the table. She took care to keep her weight balanced on the balls of her feet. Her mind weighed options. She was breathing heavily, but she prepared her body for action. She formulated a plan.

Which Number Three thwarted immediately. "Each foot, three steps back," he said.

There was a reason cops used this technique while apprehending suspects. It was nearly impossible to move quickly or athletically with your weight forward on your hands. That made it extremely tough to cause trouble, which was exactly what was on Sam's mind.

She stalled. "I don't understand."

"Each foot! Three steps back!" The universal cross-lingual technique. If at first you're not understood, yell louder.

Sam debated whether to stall again. She glanced at the gun. It was still trained on her skull, still eight feet away. Still close enough that he probably wouldn't miss. Still far enough away that she could do nothing about it.

She complied, but minimally. She took three small steps backward, away from the table. Sam glanced again at the big Russian. He looked just as goon-like as his counterparts. He had a low forehead, angled eyes, a thick protrusion of bone above his eyebrows, the overall effect reminiscent of some kind of pre-human. He probably wasn't the bookkeeper, or the strategic mastermind. But he was probably perfectly adept at breaking kneecaps.

Sam saw him reach into his pocket. He pulled out zip-ties. Easier and more secure than handcuffs. Not a good sign.

"Each foot. One more step back," the man said. The words were thick and guttural, as if they had escaped from some route other than his mouth.

Sam inched her feet further back, feeling her weight move further forward onto her hands, making any kind of resistance or sudden movement beyond problematic.

But not impossible.

And the Russian was giving her a break. He should have shot

her. He should have ended it, right then and there. Sam didn't know why he hadn't already pulled the trigger. Two of his comrades lay dead or dying, blood and brains oozing onto the floor. Number Three had watched them die, watched her kill them with nothing but a chair and an elbow.

Obviously, they had orders. Bring her alive. They had plans to exploit her in some way. Maybe they planned to make an example of her.

Or maybe they just wanted to ensure they gave her the most painful death possible.

Number Three drew closer, moving slowly and warily, gun trained on her head. Which was a mistake. Center of mass, always. Even the best shooters missed in the heat of the moment. You wanted to aim for the biggest target possible. And shoot twice. Odds were good that one of the bullets would hit something important, like heart or lung. Maybe both.

The man drew closer. Sam tensed her muscles. She slowly, imperceptibly leaned her weight further forward onto her hands.

Always do what they don't expect, Sam coached herself silently. Breathe. Relax.

The man with the prehistoric face drew closer, approaching cautiously from Sam's side. Four feet. Three feet. Pistol in his right hand. Left hand reaching out, as if to grab her wrist.

Two feet.

He leaned forward, reaching to grab her arm and subdue her.

Now.

Sam leaned further forward, pressing her hands into the

tabletop. Her knee shot upward and forward with lightning speed, catching the Russian in the side. She heard the breath leave him in a loud grunt. She swore she felt one or two of his ribs break. She drove her knee upward and forward, aiming for maximum damage, hoping to send him sprawling over the table.

He didn't sprawl. His big, muscular body took the blow. He swallowed the pain. He was still in the game.

Sam sensed the blow before he threw it. He swung right-handed. The same hand that held the gun. If it landed, the steel and rosewood gun butt would surely fracture her skull.

Sam dropped and whipped around, moving with desperate abandon, throwing her right leg in a vicious kick toward his knee.

He moved.

She missed.

But so did he. The gun sailed in front of her face, close enough for her to smell the steel and oil and sweat.

She twisted again, coiling her other leg, readying for an attack.

She should have been readying a defense. She never saw the left cross. It landed with a bolt of lightning on the side of her head.

Lights out.

Her body hit the floor in a heap.

Chapter 31

There was a deafening explosion. It rang through the hollow room, loud, vicious, angry. But it barely penetrated the edges of Sam's consciousness. She swam in a murky neverland, vaguely aware, yet not comprehending at all.

There was another sound. A slap. Then another one, and another. More smacks. This too had difficulty penetrating Sam's mind.

Something else, too. A stinging sensation, on her cheek.

And a voice. Calling her name.

She inhaled, fighting to stay under, to stay asleep.

Cordite burned her nostrils, the unmistakable smell of gunplay. The smoke in the air penetrated the fog in her mind. She opened her eyes.

Her head hurt, both outside and in. She felt faintly nauseous, like the time she'd fallen from a tree, and the time she'd been knocked out during martial arts training. Clearly a concussion.

There was a face in front of her. Familiar, friendly, but urgent. "We have to go," Dan Gable said.

She felt herself being hoisted up. Dan's thick, athletic arms lifted her bodily from the floor. She stood, shaky and groggy on rubbery legs. "Sam, come on," Dan urged, starting for the door. "We have to get the hell out of here."

Sam looked around. There were two dead guys on the floor, faces smashed into the hard surface. A third dead guy lay behind her, a gaping hole in his side. That must have accounted for the deafening explosion and the smell of gunpowder. "How did you find me?"

"You sent me the address, remember?"

"I guess I did."

"I guess he hit you pretty hard," Dan said.

"I guess he did." Sam felt her head. A bruise was already forming. Her temple barked with an angry pain. The residual fog pervaded her thoughts, lifting slowly.

"Follow me," Dan said.

"Wait," Sam said. "We need pictures to ID these guys. Fingerprints, too."

"No time for prints," Dan said. "This place is like a prairie dog town full of gangsters. But I already took pictures of all of them for the facial recognition software."

"Any paperwork on them?"

"None. Foot soldiers, probably," Dan said. He led Sam out the door and down the hallway.

Sam slowly regained her faculties. Her legs still felt shaky and weak, side effects of the mad rush of adrenaline from a few moments before, and also of the neurological trauma she had suffered.

Sam looked around. "This place is a warren," she said.

"Now you know why it took me so long to get here."

"Thank you. You saved my ass."

"You're welcome. But your ass isn't saved yet."

They walked quickly but quietly down the dank, dark, grimy hallway. Dan paused at a closed door. He held his hand up, urging silence, then pointed to the door.

Sam heard voices from within. She nodded. They tiptoed, taking care not to disturb the ancient floorboards, holding their breath, aware that at any moment the door might burst open and emit more assholes.

Sam instinctively felt for her pistol. It wasn't there. She had surrendered it to the tall knee-capper, who now lay dead in a pool of his own blood. She felt naked. She had no weapon but her feet and elbows, knees and hands. They would be enough for one or two adversaries, but probably not more. She'd much rather have had the option of sending a slug of hot metal to do the dirty work for her. It was much more efficient, particularly given her current state, exhausted and groggy and not altogether at her best.

Sam inched forward, stepping wide, following Dan, nearly past the door, nearly ready to accelerate again and get the hell out of the building.

The floor creaked.

The voices in the room went silent.

Dan shook his head. He raised his pistol and pointed it at the door.

Sam moved aside, flattening herself against the wall on the other side of the opening, preparing her right elbow to deliver a crushing blow to the bridge of someone's nose.

The door creaked open.

A little bit at first, then more. Sam tensed her arm and shoulder muscles, anchored herself with her legs, got ready to swing her elbow.

Dan trained the weapon at the opening.

The door opened wide. A Russian woman. Stout, stocky, tough. She was dressed in an ankle-length smock. It was dirty and bloody, as if she had just slaughtered an animal.

Sam withheld her elbow. Dan withheld the bullet.

But they shouldn't have. The woman lunged, teeth bared, right arm tracing an arc, something shiny and silver and long and sharp in her hand. A meat cleaver.

The woman charged through the doorway, swinging wildly, growling like an animal, creating a terrific racket. Sam flattened her hand and swung her arm. The back of her hand connected with the woman's neck. Sam felt structure and sinew give way, heard the unmistakable pop of important things giving way inside the woman's neck. The howling turned to a gurgle. The woman fell to the floor with a heavy thud.

An explosion assaulted Sam's ears. She ducked instinctively. She threw herself back behind the doorjamb for cover.

Light flashed in front of her, and another vicious boom filled the small space. Dan's gun. He fired again, then once more.

He lunged into the room. "Clear," he announced a moment later.

Sam peeked through the doorway. Another dead Russian woman, bloody holes in her body from Dan's .40 caliber hollow-point bullets. There was a shotgun in the woman's hands. A long twelve-gauge. It would've done some serious damage. "Nice work,"

Sam said.

Sam looked down. The large woman stirred at Sam's feet, pudgy hand tightening around the meat cleaver, breath coming in labored gasps through her shattered windpipe.

Sam cocked her right foot and delivered a devastating blow. Her foot landed on the fat Russian lady's forehead. The woman's head snapped back. Her eyes rolled back in her head, and her body went limp. Sam grabbed the meat cleaver and followed Dan at a run.

She heard doorways opening up in the hallway behind her. She heard loud Russian voices. She heard palpable anger and alarm.

She heard the unmistakable crunch-crunch of a shotgun shell being racked into the chamber.

She looked over her shoulder. Thirty paces away down the long hall stood another giant of a man. He leveled the gun at her and pulled the trigger.

Another unbelievably loud roar filled the tiny space. Sam flattened herself against the hardwood. She felt the floor and walls vibrate as the pellets buried themselves in the ancient plaster. She heard a few of them bounce off the floor in front of her.

She felt a sting in her right calf.

She heard the shotgun crunch-crunch again. The man ejected the spent shell and chambered the next round.

Sam didn't wait. She sprang up, sprinted around the corner, spotting Dan several paces ahead in the gloomy hallway. There were doors on either side. None of them were marked. She was looking for an exit sign, but there was none. Only dark, dirty doors in a dark, dirty hall.

She sprinted down the hallway, a strange sensation with each step, as if her calf wasn't quite working properly. As if there was a shotgun pellet lodged in her muscle. It was undoubtedly going to hurt like hell, once the adrenaline wore off.

One of the hallway doors flew open. A tall man. Buzz cut. Anger on his face. Bear-like jowls. Arms like tree trunks.

Decision time.

Sam accelerated. She angled closer to the wall. She readied her elbow. She swung it from her hip. Up, out, and around. Throat-height.

The man turned. Perfect timing. His eyes registered alarm, a bit of anger, and a lot of surprise.

Sam's elbow landed with a crunch, crushing his windpipe, as hard a blow as she'd ever delivered. It was all over but the dying. He fell to the floor and thrashed around, hands clutched around his throat, suffocating, the beginning of a truly horrific death, which Sam didn't hang around to watch.

She looked up, forward down the hall. She saw Dan's stocky, muscular frame. He was airborne, flying across the hallway, shoulder lowered, arm curled by his side. His shoulder crashed into a doorway. It exploded inward. Shards of wood flew everywhere. Daylight burst into the gloom.

"This way!" Dan shouted.

Sam charged headlong down the hallway to the shattered door. She heard the sound of breaking glass. She used the doorjamb to help her round the corner into the room.

A child's room.

With a child in it.

A boy of about nine, staring open-mouthed. Sam held a finger to her lips, urging silence. The child said nothing, did nothing. Just observed, with a kind of reserved anger and resignation. Not the first time he'd been in the crossfire. Wouldn't be the last, either, Sam guessed.

Dan snatched a pillow from the boy's bed and used it to clear out the remaining shards of glass from the windowsill. He helped Sam through the broken window, then followed.

They emerged into an alleyway, full of garbage. Tall brick buildings rose on either side of them. It reminded her of Budapest, of the alleyways she'd snuck through, both chasing and evading. She felt small, exposed, frightened. Budapest wasn't a good experience.

Boston hadn't been a barrel of laughs, either.

"Where's the car?" Sam asked.

"This way," Dan said, taking off at a run. They sprinted out of the alleyway, emerging back onto the sidewalk, instantly out of place, bloody and breathless and brandishing a gun in the middle of civilized society.

They drew stares from passersby. Someone screamed. Dan raised his Homeland badge aloft over his head. "Federal agents! Back away, please!"

The crowd parted like the Red Sea. Dan holstered his weapon, charged forward, then turned west at the corner. Sam followed at a run. She spotted the rental car.

There was somebody in it.

"Going to have to ride in back," Dan said. "Somebody else

already called shotgun."

"Friend of yours?"

"Nobody's friend anymore," Dan said.

Sam looked into the window. A gentleman of Slavic descent. In fact a very familiar gentleman.

32A.

Extremely dead, torso covered in blood from a gaping hole in his neck.

"He tried to carjack me," Dan said.

"Looks like he did it wrong," Sam said with a chuckle, climbing into the backseat.

"That's the other reason I was late to your party. They were right on us, instantly. I don't even think you were inside the floral shop before this guy jumped in the car."

"Like they knew we were coming," Sam said.

Dan nodded gravely. "Exactly."

* * *

The Boston police cordoned off the area around the building full of Russian gangsters. The local FBI office responded as well, taking command of the scene.

There was jurisdictional angst regarding who ought to be in charge. Local cops never liked it when the feds showed up. The Bureau stiffs never liked it when Homeland ran an operation under their noses without telling them. Sam conceded the point. In light of the way things turned out, more help from the local FBI office wouldn't have killed anyone. Except she didn't have six months to plan and six more months to tap-dance her way through the Bureau's infinite layers of middle management. But she kept that to herself, and offered a genuine apology to the local agent-in-charge.

"Are we good here?" the agent asked. "I mean, you aren't taking over this scene, are you?"

"Not on your life," Sam said. "I'll leave the forensics and the tidying up in your capable hands. But I do need my gun and my phone."

The FBI boss motioned to an underling, spoke a few words, and sent him off.

The agent-in-charge said nothing until the lackey returned with Sam's Kimber .45 and her cell phone. He handed them to her. "What you did was extremely stupid," he said.

"Maybe a little stupid," Sam said with a smile.

He didn't return the smile. "There's been an uneasy truce between these gangs and the authorities. You've upset that."

"Truce?" Sam asked with a derisive laugh. "You don't mean a truce. You mean a payoff. These assholes bribed the local precinct assholes. Birds of a VCVC feather."

"I would never make such an accusation," the agent said.

"You just did."

The agent said nothing.

"Names, fingerprints, background checks on everyone in this building, please," Sam said.

She watched the FBI man's jaw tighten.

"An issue of national security," she said before he could protest. "Non-negotiable. I don't care if the mayor of Boston is on the take. I don't give a rat's ass if the President of the United States is on this gang's payroll. This place gets a good old-fashioned shakedown."

The FBI man shook his head. "You have no idea the trouble you're causing," he said.

Sam laughed. "That's not true at all," she said. "I have an extremely good idea of the trouble I'm causing. But I don't give a shit."

Chapter 32

David Swaringen's palms were sweating. He felt the acute discomfort associated with excess amygdala activity in the brain, the kind of anxiety that had no productive outlet.

His physical unease was progeny of a vague sense of dread. He paced back and forth outside Clark Barter's office door.

It was something in the old man's eyes, something dark, bottomless, unfathomable. It was a look that Swaringen had never seen on Barter's face before.

It had come when Swaringen asked to talk with Barter in private. Swaringen didn't know how, but he had the sense that Barter already knew exactly what was on his mind.

Perhaps it was just in his imagination, but Swaringen felt as though Barter had been peering over his shoulder while he was gathering clues about the suspect list and its origin, as if Barter knew exactly what Swaringen knew.

Maybe it was in the way the old man's look was surlier than usual, more direct, more openly truculent. Not an inner-circle kind of look, the kind Swaringen would have expected after having heard the gut-wrenching details of how Barter's son had been murdered. That had clearly been a bonding moment between the two men, superior and subordinate, but the bond had evidently been short-lived. There was nothing but frosty distance in Barter's eyes recently.

The door opened. Barter's secretary emerged. "Mr. Barter will see you now."

Swaringen nodded, stomach knotting anew. Time to man up.

He walked into Barter's office. There was a glass of scotch on Barter's desk, but Barter didn't offer one to Swaringen. Instead, the old man sat back in his chair, crossed his hands over his ample lap, and waited, an expectant look on his face.

Swaringen sat, unbidden.

"Make yourself at home," Barter said, eyes hard, clearly calling Swaringen's presumption, putting the younger man in his place.

Swaringen swallowed.

Barter shrugged, raised his eyebrows, shook his head. "To what do I owe the pleasure?" he finally asked.

Swaringen took a deep breath. "Mr. Barter," he began. "This job is a huge opportunity, and I've learned a great deal."

Barter snorted. "But?"

"No 'but.' I've learned a great deal, and I'm enjoying the challenge," Swaringen said.

The old man eyed him for a long moment. "I'm glad you're feeling challenged and fulfilled, David."

Swaringen paused, unsure of himself, unsure of Barter's reception.

"Say it," Barter said.

Swaringen took a breath. "I've had a concern," he continued. He studied Barter's face carefully. It registered no surprise whatsoever. The old man had been expecting this conversation, Swaringen surmised.

"You want to know more than you already know," Barter said. It was a statement, not a question.

Swaringen nodded. "I have the sense that I could do a much better job for you if I had a little more understanding of where the list came from, what factors we use to determine which people to put on it. You know, a more complete picture of the operation. I feel like I could be more effective as your deputy, and especially as your stand-in when you're not available, if I had a little more insight into how things fit together."

"You've been asking around." It sounded like an accusation.

"Like I said," Swaringen said, "I want to get better at my job, and to do that I need to understand how the operation works."

"Asking questions is poor form, in a security environment like this one," Barter said.

Swaringen bristled. "Bad form? What about throwing your deputy to the wolves with almost no information?"

Barter looked amused. "You think I threw you to the wolves?"

"No doubt about it. Which is why I started asking questions. Lives are at stake, and I didn't want to screw it up."

Barter pursed his lips, sipped his scotch, nodded his head. "Understandable," he finally said. "But trust me a little bit here. I'm not new to this game. Some things are highly classified because they reveal sensitive technical capabilities. Other things are highly classified because the information is politically sensitive. Toxic, even, in the wrong hands. In the wrong context. You understand what I'm saying, don't you, David."

The two men eyed each other. Barter's expression was arrogant, patrician, mildly bemused. Menacing.

It pissed Swaringen off.

"These operations are occurring on US soil. Aren't they."

Barter's mouth hardened into a line. "That information is above your clearance."

"We've got thousands of drones flying circles over US cities, watching US citizens."

"Pure speculation on your part," Barter said, a bit of menace in his mien. "And way above your clearance."

"But it didn't take a Rhodes Scholar to figure it out," Swaringen said.

"What makes you think that's the case?" Barter asked, switching tactics, eyebrows raised.

Swaringen played along. "A few things. First was the secrecy. We're blowing shit up in a dozen countries. Most of it's on the evening news. Not a secret at all. Which got me to wondering, what the hell might we be doing that could possibly warrant that level of sensitivity?"

Barter took a long pull of scotch from his glass. He eyed Swaringen, a cold, inscrutable expression on his face. No human warmth whatsoever.

"What else?" Barter asked.

"The roads," Swaringen said.

"Excuse me?"

"Well, the roads, and also the time zones. It's always daylight on the video when it's daylight here. It's always nighttime on the monitors when it's nighttime here. I thought at first maybe it was all tape-delayed, and being viewed and examined in retrospect. After the fact. But it's not. We're exercising real-time command and control of field operations. The key being *real-time*. So the raids were happening someplace in the Western Hemisphere. From there, it wasn't tough to figure out. Surely I can't have been the first guy to notice the world's best interstate highway system on camera. Better than the autobahn. Sure as hell better than any of the roads in Mexico, Central America, or South America."

Barter said nothing.

Swaringen eyed the old man. "So that narrowed things down pretty fast," he said. "Not the kind of thing you can keep secret for long."

Barter lit a cigarette and poured more scotch. A new expression settled over his face. Tiredness.

Then resolve.

"Clever boy," he said.

"So it's true, then."

Barter shook his head. "Above your clearance level," he repeated. "Have you spoken to anyone else about this?"

Swaringen shook his head.

"Don't lie to me, David," Barter said. "I have spies everywhere in this building. You've been asking around about the program."

Swaringen's face flushed with anger. "Absolutely I've been asking around. Just like I told you. I want to understand the process.

I want to be better at my job. I've asked relevant, responsible questions. And I've kept my suspicions and my speculations to myself. Until right now."

Barter pondered a moment. Then he pursed his lips and nodded his head quickly, as if he'd reached a decision. "Fair enough."

He took a drag of his cigarette. "I'll put you in for extra clearances. The paperwork may take a few days. But you're absolutely right. If you're going to act on my behalf when I'm gone, you'll need to understand exactly what's going on, and why. You need to have full confidence in what you're doing, and in what we are doing here."

The old man sat back in his chair. Still no warmth, Swaringen noticed. Something was still off.

But he decided to take the old man at his word. He felt relieved. He had doubted himself, doubted his sanity and his desire to understand things, wondered why he couldn't just trust the process and trust the system like everyone else seemed to do. But Barter's conciliation was validation of his instincts. He had been right to pursue answers to his questions, and he had been even more right to come forward to Barter and air his misgivings.

He breathed deeply, relaxing for the first time in days. "Thank you, Mr. Barter."

"Think nothing of it," Barter said. "Now, beat it. I have a lot of bullshit to catch up on. I'll see you tomorrow."

Swaringen rose and left.

Before the door shut in Swaringen's wake, Barter picked up

the phone and dialed. It was a number he hadn't used in quite some time. It was a call he never relished making.

But it had to be done.

And above all, Clark Barter was the kind of man who did what had to be done.

Chapter 33

Nero Jefferson Chiligiris was a new man, in spirit if not in body. He had just shy of ten grand in cash in his possession. It was enough to see to his basic needs. And it was enough to rent a storage facility. He slept there. He couldn't risk renting a hotel room, or an apartment. Couldn't take any chances on a background check. As it was, renting the storage unit had been beyond nerve-wracking. The clerk had given him a hairy eyeball when he told her he wanted to pay in cash. But money talks, and everything seemed to work out.

He sat in the gloomy storage unit. Thin bed clothes purchased from a chain store did a poor job of insulating his backside from the cold concrete floor. He recalled the foray to his uncle's house, the bowel-shaking terror he felt when the police searchlight hovered over him for what seemed like an eternity. His feet still hurt from scaling the fences without his shoes.

But those hardships made him smile now. They represented a milestone achieved. Progress. A challenge overcome.

The first of many on the way to clearing his name.

Nero wasn't dirty, but the feds thought he was. That had to be on account of Money. Which was a problem. If the feds hadn't already nabbed Money, they surely had him under surveillance. He wanted to see Money, to confront him, to figure out which cookie jars his former boss had stuck his paws in, to figure out how to disentangle himself from the crazy Arab.

But that would have been an even dumber move than going home to see Penny and the kids. It would be leaping out of the frying pan and into the fire.

And there was no safe way to find any of Money's underlings, either. Nero had made it a point not to become entangled with any of them. There were a few faces that he would undoubtedly recognize, if he saw them again, but he would never know where to begin looking for them. Nero had no names, no addresses, no phone numbers. He dealt with and through Money, exclusively.

He shook his head. It had seemed like a smart play, like he was mitigating risk by limiting his exposure to potentially shady characters. But it was obvious in retrospect that he had been a fool. De facto, he had placed all of his faith in Money. And it had evidently come back to bite him in the ass.

Dire circumstances notwithstanding, the successful midnight foray to his uncle's backyard had suffused Nero with a degree of optimism. He was determined to figure out what Money was involved in. Otherwise, he would simply have to forfeit his life. Sure, he could run somewhere, maybe hide out in a faraway place, but he'd always be looking over his shoulder, always waiting for the other shoe to drop. Without Penny, and without the kids.

Not an option.

Nero was determined to get his life back, to get back on track, to live life in broad daylight, to go completely legit, to have no worries about anything coming back around on him.

It was a lofty goal, from where he sat. He needed a lucky

break.

He needed a clever way into Money's affairs, a way the feds hadn't thought of, or hadn't had the time or resources to take advantage of yet.

It was certainly a daunting task. There were more federal agents on the payroll now than at any other time in history. It was just the law of averages, he figured, that at least a few of them had to be fantastically good at their jobs. They probably knew cyber security, computer hacking, airborne surveillance, all kinds of crazy shit. So what could Nero possibly know about Money that the feds didn't already know? What aspect of Money's life could Nero infiltrate that the feds hadn't already exploited?

Money had no personal or business associations that the feds couldn't trace, Nero decided. Money was careful, but he was nowhere near as paranoid as Nero had been. And Nero had been nabbed.

So the connections would have to be subtle. Nero would have to be able to access them without anyone else knowing.

There was only one idea that came to mind.

Chapter 34

The on-scene medic patched up Sam's wounded leg. They left the scene in the hands of the disgruntled FBI agent, after ensuring he'd received explicit instructions from the Hoover building in DC. It helped to have friends in high places.

The return flight from Boston was completely uneventful. Sam was able to grab a cat nap, which she sorely needed. Her head throbbed, and the aspirin hadn't helped much.

Sam and Dan were back in the office at Homeland by early evening. They sat in Dan's office, poring over the stream of data arriving from the Boston FBI office. They'd already received a long list of names taken from the Russian gangster house, and plenty of associated fingerprints and mug shots. Despite the FBI man's posturing, he had done a thorough job.

At least, that's how it appeared to Sam. But you never knew what you didn't know, and it was entirely possible the FBI man was also on the take.

But everybody was connected in one way or another, and Sam felt confident there would be enough leads to point her in the right direction. She was more than a little anxious to find the assholes who had hired the Russian gangsters to take her out.

From the names, Dan began assembling email and IP addresses. It was a wired, digital world, and the most productive sleuthing efforts were almost always electronic.

Sure, the foot soldiers and knee-cappers in the Russian establishment were not likely exchanging business emails with one another, or prospecting for clients electronically, or discussing details of crimes over a medium that kept a permanent and perfect record. Nobody was that dumb. It was the mere connections Sam and Dan sought. Who emailed whom? How often? What was the context of those emails? Did they make sense, or did they seem too vague, too innocuous, too meaningless?

It was the meaningless communications that were often most meaningful. Because they frequently contained codes. So Dan's snooping algorithm was programmed to highlight overly innocuous emails, overly vapid, overly banal, the kind of stuff that nobody would ever email anyone else about. The kind of stuff that nobody cared about or wanted to hear about. Because banal content often highlighted exceptionally interesting connections.

There was little hope of finding and breaking any kind of code embedded in the emails, so Dan didn't even try. People were too smart for that. Every code was theoretically breakable, but criminals were sufficiently cyber-savvy to realize that almost no code was completely secure. So they often used a one-time cipher, a pre-coordinated code that both parties had in advance. It was used only once, generated randomly and then destroyed after the message was sent and received. Such messages required physical tradecraft in order to pass the code's key to both sender and recipient. But that was accomplished easily enough. There were seven billion people on the planet. It was relatively easy to blend in, even in a world full of cameras.

Unless you were on the watch list. Then, God help you. No chance.

It was vitally important not to stop searching after the first layer of communications. Often, one email made its way unadulterated between four, five, six, a dozen different email accounts. The idea was to launder the source prior to arriving at the recipient's inbox. It wasn't terribly effective, but it did require extra computing power to chase down zillions of extra emails. It just meant that the system had to grind away for a few more hours to index and catalog all the correspondence.

Dan selected all of the appropriate options to locate an email from its source, record all of the intermediary email accounts, associate them with names and criminal records, if applicable, and spit the whole thing out in a neatly-correlated report, complete with a cloud diagram showing each individual as a node in a network, just like a diagram of the Internet. In just a few hours of computer time, it was possible to see the entirety of a network hundreds or even thousands of people strong.

Brave new world.

Of course, all of this data had to be filtered, sifted, processed. It had to be evaluated for significance, and it had to be bounced against a list of known or suspected bad actors. Computers were very helpful there as well. They could do in a minute what it would take a human a week to accomplish.

But the trick was bouncing the newly-found network goons against the *right* list of people. And they didn't have to just be bad actors. Sam and Dan made sure to include everyone with any involvement whatsoever in any aspect of the Janice Everman/Budapest thug case. They even added their own names, and Mark Severn's, and Tom Davenport's, and Deputy Director Farrar's, and everybody Sam met at Justice, even Sam's new Israeli friends, the ones who had saved her life in Budapest. It wasn't that everyone was a suspect. It was just that everyone with any involvement in the case was a potential hit in the giant new network schema produced by all of the data the FBI had gathered from the Russian gangster house.

Sam and Dan perused the list. Satisfied, Dan clicked on an icon, and the computer began grinding away.

There was a knock on the door. Mark Severn. "Exciting afternoon in Bean Town?"

Sam nodded. "Killer," she said.

"So, I've had a watch on a few folks from the Janice Everman case," Severn said. "Something significant has come up."

"Do tell," Sam said. "I didn't want to go home tonight, anyway."

Severn chuckled. "Carl Ivan Edgar Frankel," he said with a sarcastically formal affectation, handing Sam a photograph of an old man, clearly taken at an airport.

"We know this guy?"

Severn nodded. "Old-school Cold War assassin. Retired."

"From the Agency?" Sam asked.

Severn nodded. "Freelance now."

"Freelance? I thought the CIA was supposed to keep an eye on their retirees. Can't have pit bulls running around schoolyards."

Severn nodded. "They're supposed to keep them under wraps. But the way it looks to me, if I'm being honest, is that few of them ever really retire. Sure, they go dormant for a while. But then their handlers call, they take a short trip, and then fade away again after the hit."

"This is the guy you think had something to do with Janice Everman's death?" Dan asked.

Severn nodded. "He lived the life of a monk, holed up in his apartment, flipping channels for years on end. We know this because we back-doored a list of former wet men. Current ones, too, but they're harder to track. CIA expends more resources to keep them under the radar. Anyway, this guy turned off his TV and took a trip to DC just in time for Janice Everman's death. He was back home the next afternoon."

Sam frowned. "Highly circumstantial."

"Absolutely," Severn said. "But I'm not a district attorney. I'm just a guy running an investigation. So I put Frankel on the watch list and threw him into the computer."

"When was this photo taken?" Sam asked.

"Today. Reagan International Airport. Our Mr. Frankel flew into town from New York."

"How many trips has this guy taken since we've been watching him?" Dan asked.

"None. Before today, that is."

"Do you have somebody on him?" Sam asked.

Severn nodded. "Team of four, two cars."

Sam shook her head. "Nowhere near enough people. If this guy is who we think he is, he'll spot a two-car tail in no time flat."

"Those are all the resources I had," Severn said.

"Thanks, Mark," Sam said. "Dan and I will join the fun."

"Me too?" Severn asked.

Sam shook her head. "Sorry. You're still a wanted man. There's still a price on your head."

"And there's not a price on *your* head?" Severn asked pointedly.

"That's different."

"How, exactly?"

Sam rose, gathered her phone and keys. "Just is."

Dan shrugged his shoulders at Severn, giving him a man-to-man look, as if to say there's no reasoning with her when she gets like this.

"Dan and I just started a network analysis from the floral shop in Boston," Sam said, by way of a consolation prize, "and the house full of Russian rats behind it. Should be done in a couple of hours. Feel free to take a look at it as soon as it spits out the answers."

Severn nodded, slightly dejected, unhappy at being relegated to desk work when something was happening out in the real world.

Sam patted him on the shoulder. "Next time," she said.

Chapter 35

The old man felt giddy with anticipation. He loved nothing more than work. Especially this kind of work. None of that biological bullshit. This was the real deal.

Sure, there would be no blood, no gore, no shootout. Those days had long passed. He was too old for that kind of shit anyway. Too slow. Old age was tough on the reflexes, and that continuous tremor in his hands was murder on his aim.

But he would do the deed. He would break the skin of his mark, deliver death up close and personal. He would do it himself, like real men did. It would require skill and timing and tradecraft and risk and danger and adrenaline and excitement.

The things most missing from his life of late.

He studied the photograph one more time. Youngish guy, polished, with a business-school look about him. Nobody would miss him, Frankel figured. Dime a dozen. Totally replaceable. There was probably already another bullshit artist in the corporate breech, ready to take this guy's place tomorrow. Nobody would even know the difference.

Carl Ivan Edgar Frankel smiled to himself. He had no idea what the guy had done. But it didn't matter. His was not to reason why, Frankel reflected. His was just to make them die. He smiled at the clever turn of phrase, that old assassin's saw, progeny of the false bravado necessary to survive in a world filled with death, and also necessary to survive one's conscience, to keep one's soul from rotting away.

But Frankel's soul had long since rotted away, he figured. Which was okay. Souls were burdensome things, anyway. Full of doubts and second-guesses, worries and hang-ups. Better to be a simple creature, with simple goals, fundamental ones. Taking lives need not be overly complicated. In fact, it was best not to overthink things. Second thoughts were an occupational hazard, and could be lethal.

The old assassin looked at his watch. Almost time.

* * *

"Where is he?" Sam asked the lead agent on the tail detail.

"Metro, on the yellow line." The agent spoke softly into his phone. "Airport station. Waiting for the northbound train."

"Do you have anybody down there?"

"Two guys. Good ones. He's an old guy, not moving too fast. It won't be too hard to keep up with him."

"Be sure to get somebody on the train with him," Sam said. "And tell me if he changes direction."

* * *

That didn't take long, the old man thought, eyeing his tail.

He figured it might be an issue. The last case had turned a little bit nuclear, and they were undoubtedly watching him.

He smiled. It wouldn't matter. He was prepared. There could be an army of agents following him around, and it wouldn't make any difference. No way they would figure it out in time.

* * *

David Swaringen left his car at the park-and-ride on the northeast side of town. He paid for his ticket, waited on the platform, and caught the 451 MARC train away from Baltimore and toward Washington.

He needed to let his hair down, have a drink. Or five.

He needed to get laid.

He couldn't remember the last time he'd had sex. Weeks? Months? He wasn't into paying for it, but the thought had briefly crossed his mind. But he had decided to give his libido his undivided attention first, to see if he couldn't seal the deal with a nubile young corporate cubicle ornament on the strength of his charms. DC had more young, ambitious, attractive female consultants per capita than any other city on earth. At least, that's what Swaringen had heard, and he found the claim plausible enough. There was a lot of talent in DC, and he was determined to find a pretty young lady willing to spend some quality time with him.

He deserved it. His start at NSA had been rocky. He had been completely focused on his new job, to the detriment of every other aspect of his life, and it was taking its toll on his psyche. "Me time," he muttered to himself as the train left the station bound for downtown DC. Georgetown was his destination. A great area, with lively nightlife. And he had a great salary, which bought him a great suit, which made him a more attractive sexual partner for an ambitious, pretty young thing.

He wasn't exactly a player, but neither was he a wallflower. Especially after a couple of drinks. He had a sense of humor, an athletic build, a strong pocketbook, all the right indicators of social and genetic success. No reason to think that tonight wouldn't be a memorable night.

He finally felt able to relax after airing his misgivings to Clark Barter. He hadn't realized how heavily the whole situation had weighed on him. But now that things were over and out in the open, he felt much better. He felt strong, optimistic, in charge, like the future was bright again.

It was going to be a great night.

* * *

Carl Ivan Edgar Frankel headed away from the city. The subway train rocked and clattered, and the noxious fumes made him slightly nauseous. He had never enjoyed the subway, particularly in DC. But he did what needed doing.

He stared down at the page of his book, an old Russian crime novel, more thinly-veiled polemic than anything else, wrapped in an angst-ridden literary cloak. Frankel loved the layers of meaning, loved the forlorn aesthetic, loved the cold, wintry, dreary settings, loved the intrigue. They might have been bitter enemies for years, but the Russian culture was not without its redeeming qualities, Frankel decided.

And, of late, he found himself on the same side as a few Russians. Life took crazy turns.

Another watcher. This one was a short, stocky guy, with short, black hair and thick, meaty hands.

Frankel smiled to himself. Watch all you want, he thought. You've got no prayer.

* * *

"I'm eyes-on," Dan texted.

"Where?" Sam asked.

"Red line now, Metro Center Station, heading east toward Chinatown."

"I'll take the beltway around," Sam replied. "Keep me posted."

* * *

Swaringen leaned his head back and closed his eyes. The train wasn't fast, and it wasn't especially comfortable, but it involved infinitely less aggravation than driving in the DC area. And it was a great way to get home after a few cocktails, if the night didn't quite go as hoped. His plan was to fall momentarily but madly in love with a sweet young thing, preferably with an apartment in town. They'd make beautiful music, and whatnot. Naked. He smiled to himself.

He looked up. He felt the intensity of someone's focus. Someone was looking at him.

A female someone, across the aisle from him. Late twenties, lithe, long hair, short skirt, long legs, expensive shoes, pretty face, bright, exotic eyes, inviting neck, shy but with a hint of mischief.

She smiled.

Swaringen smiled back.

She wasn't headed to or from work, he surmised. Working women commuting to DC wore clunky tennis shoes and power suits. The girl with the great smile wore heels, and she carried a bright red clutch, too small to accommodate any of the normal paraphernalia associated with an office job in DC.

All signs pointed to pleasure rather than business.

Swaringen looked again. His eyes wandered to her legs. Long and athletic. He imagined what they might feel like wrapped around the small of his back. He felt that familiar male ache, desperation and exhilaration, echoes of the reptile brain chanting *sex! sex! sex! sex!* deep down in his skull.

Busted. She caught him staring. He looked away, cursing his overeager clumsiness. He felt his face flush. Such a klutz. He wondered whether she had read his lascivious thoughts.

He looked down at the newspaper in his hand, a studious expression on his face, making no sense of the words, wallowing in his embarrassment.

Motion caught his eye. He looked up.

She crossed the aisle and sat next to him. "Eva," she said.

"Excuse me?"

"Eva," she repeated. "It's my name." Her voice was like heavy silk, sexy but not sultry, seductive but not over the top.

"I'm David," he said, taking her offered hand. "David Swaringen."

"It's nice to meet you, David Swaringen," she said.

Things were looking up, he decided.

* * *

The old assassin looked at his watch, then looked at the subway map. He readied his old bones for motion.

The train screeched to a halt at the Union Station stop. Frankel rose, leaning heavily on his cane for support. He looked at his watcher, the stocky dark-haired guy sitting across the aisle, and fought the urge to wave as he got off the train.

His tail rose and exited onto the platform, doing an admirable job, Frankel thought, of avoiding eye contact. The man was clearly competent. But he was too aware of his surroundings, which didn't fit with the rest of the DC crowd, an arrogant, self-important, self-absorbed populace as a rule, which was what had tipped Frankel off in the first place.

Didn't matter. They could bring an army of watchers. It wouldn't change the outcome, Frankel thought.

The old assassin tottered slowly to the escalator, exited at the top, made his way deliberately and unhurriedly to the opposite escalator, which he rode back down to the train platform he had just left, except now on the other side of the tracks. Trains on this side of the rails headed back into town, opposite the direction Frankel had just traveled.

Retracing his steps.

A train arrived. Frankel didn't take it. Wasn't the right train.

So he waited, a bemused, satisfied look on his face.

It was great to be working again.

* * *

"He reversed direction," Dan said quietly into his phone. "He's waiting on the inbound platform at Union now."

"Balls," Sam said, driving on the highway shoulder with her emergency lights on, passing a sea of stationary cars, five lanes of misery, thousands of people lined up like cattle, sealed inside their metal boxes, rolling forward slower than they could walk. "I'm stuck in rush hour going the wrong way."

"I can still follow him," Dan said. "But he'll make me for sure."

Sam pondered. She weighed pros and cons. An old assassin, probably not all that light on his feet, probably not as slippery or dangerous as he used to be, probably not all that inclined to kill in front of an audience. They'd probably ruin their chances to discover who had hired him and why, but on the other hand, they'd probably prevent him from killing whoever he was sent to kill.

Not a hard choice, all things considered. "Do it," Sam said. "Keep me posted."

"Will do," Dan said. "Looks like he's getting on this train, heading back into town."

"Go with him. I'll get the rest of the team turned around."

* * *

David Swaringen felt alive. It had been way too long since he'd been with a woman, but Eva was giving off all of the signs, laughing at his jokes, touching her hair, touching his arm, even indulging in a bit of innuendo, inviting him to join her for a pre-dinner drink at her favorite spot.

The stressful situation at the NSA was a distant memory. Drones over American cities, armed assaults on American citizens, countless hours spent watching countless video feeds; those things all seemed far away, part of a different reality. Or surreality, maybe. Too crazy to be true, yet too true to ignore.

But it was all a universe away from Union Station, from the pretty girl of Eastern European descent named Eva on his arm, waiting for a train with him, heading for a sleek and chic

Georgetown watering hole, nothing but possibility ahead, all signals in the green.

She was intelligent, pretty, worldly, the opposite of an ingénue. She had an enticing lilt to her speech, a sexy feminine strength in her voice, and a thin, fit body that would feel incredible underneath his own.

And she seemed interested in him. Which made her twice as attractive.

She laughed at an offhanded joke of his, a strong, sexy laugh, and it made him wonder what she might sound like in bed. Would she moan? Wail? Howl? All exhilarating possibilities.

The train stopped, the doors opened, people spilled out, and Swaringen started toward the nearest car.

Eva tugged his arm. "This one," she said, leading him further down the platform.

He shrugged. He'd have followed her anywhere. He didn't care which subway car they boarded, as long as they boarded together.

* * *

Carl Ivan Edgar Frankel, ancient assassin, gave no sign of recognition as his backup team entered his subway car.

Not really a backup team as much as a backup woman. Tall, slender, Russian, eminently desirable, which was the whole point.

Her arm was looped through the mark's elbow. Mr. MBA. Or a lawyer, maybe. Everybody hated lawyers.

They walked toward the empty seats next to him.

But they were in the wrong places. The girl was nearest to

Frankel. The mark was on the opposite side of her.

It wouldn't work. The assassin was momentarily alarmed.

But the girl was sharp. She leaned in and kissed the mark's cheek. Frankel saw a surprised smile grow on the man's face. Something else was probably growing, too, Frankel thought with a smirk. The girl used the cascade of emotions and hormones coursing through the man's veins to mask a subtle manipulation. She turned him slightly, to put him in the right position, just enough to make it seem like he had chosen his own seat, the one next to the old man, when in fact he hadn't really chosen it at all.

The mark sat down. His leg brushed against the back of Frankel's hand. He murmured an apology.

Frankel smiled and nodded in return. No apology necessary.

The needle was too small for the mark to feel. Like a mosquito. It penetrated his thigh.

And that was that.

Child's play.

In full view of the stocky, dark-haired watcher. Could have been a hundred men tailing him, Frankel thought again, and it wouldn't have mattered.

The old assassin returned to his Russian novel, a satisfied smile on his face.

* * *

The gray-haired assassin sat next to his already-dying mark on the subway car for several more stops.

Another watcher joined them, he noted, a tall man with graying temples and a serious look on his face. It gave Frankel satisfaction. He felt happy to still be noteworthy. Or maybe to be noteworthy again. To be a person of interest. Which for a man of Frankel's ego was much better than being a person of *no* interest, a person sequestered in a New York apartment for years on end without so much as a phone call from anyone important.

The train screeched to a halt at Metro Center Station. Frankel rose. He nodded to the amorous couple to his right, comprised of the mark and the honey trap. She was gazing deeply into his eyes, sending all the right signals, keeping him interested, keeping his thoughts on anything but what he should have been thinking about.

Frankel hobbled to the escalator and rode it up to street level, pausing in a restroom, where he flushed a particular item down the toilet.

He walked south on Twelfth, just one block to F Street Northwest. He turned right, toward the setting sun, marveling at the high, wispy, crimson clouds arrayed before him like exotic jewels on a deep blue blanket. He inhaled the early fall air. It had just a hint of crispness, just a note of the coming chill, but was still full of the scent of life, verdant and earthy. It felt good to be alive.

He spotted the third and fourth watchers on the short two-block stretch to his destination. There was one on either side of the street. There was nothing in particular about them that was obvious. It was just a feeling that Frankel got, progeny of decades on the job. He could just tell. They weren't Bureau guys, and they definitely weren't Agency thugs. Didn't look the type. He didn't think they had any association with the Russians, either, but it was hard to be sure.

And it didn't matter. His job was done. The evidence was

already in the sewer system. They had nothing.

It didn't take him too long to reach his destination, the Intercontinental Hotel. He walked up the stately steps, opened the ancient doors, took in the self-important decor. He was impressed in spite of himself by the long list of luminaries who had dined and rested, plotted and fornicated, conspired and stolen and usurped and even murdered while staying at the Intercontinental. Presidents, ambassadors, congressmen, senators, foreign dignitaries, prostitutes, gangsters, titans, captains of industry. An august crowd. Frankel smiled to himself. His kind of place, he fancied.

He had no luggage to speak of. The check-in process consisted of a cash transaction, prearranged, no questions asked, no paperwork, no home address or driver's license, in exchange for a key. His name would never appear on the hotel registry. And in spite of the modern Big Brother video camera obsession, the Intercontinental was above all a discreet place. Cameras were positioned only to monitor the hotel staff, to keep them from stealing from the register. Guests were not photographed. Frankel's face was on a hundred video cameras throughout the city, maybe more, but the Intercontinental Hotel's camera was not among their number.

He ambled slowly back outside from the registration desk, down the marble steps, rounded from decades of use, and turned right at the bottom. Several steps further took him to the reception podium of the sidewalk café attached to the Intercontinental. The Café du Parc.

A significant location, to the savvy observer.

Frankel smiled, smug and superior. It was a fitting spot for a celebratory dinner, particularly in light of the crowd of watchers he had attracted. A small crowd, now swelled to five with the addition of a tall, pretty redhead.

He smiled. He ordered a salad. Arugula. Overpriced. Not his normal fare. But symbolic.

He enjoyed a glass of Cabernet Sauvignon, doctors be damned. Took in the sunset, ate at a leisurely pace, soaked in the atmosphere, a little bit of the old days.

He loved the game.

His salad complete, the night air turning chilly, Carl Ivan Edgar Frankel, former and current assassin, decided it was time to retire for the evening. He rose and leaned on his cane as he walked out of the sidewalk café, pausing to wink at the tall, pretty redhead stationed at the table nearest the maître d'.

Chapter 36

Sam and Dan regrouped back in Sam's office at Homeland. They shared a pizza. Neither had felt inclined to indulge in a thirty-dollar meal while on the job. So they'd settled for a cup of coffee at the Café du Parc, eyeing the retired CIA asset with wary nonchalance.

Sam was still a little bit livid over the brazen wink the old assassin had given her on his way out of the café. Clearly, he knew he was being followed.

Clearly, he knew something else they didn't.

Sam checked her phone. Nothing. She had stationed three members of Frankel's surveillance detail to monitor him through the night, to stay with him until he returned home to his apartment in New York, whenever that might be. He hadn't moved since dinner. He was in his room, probably fast asleep.

She pondered. "Maybe he's just here on vacation," she said.

Dan shook his head. "Frankel doesn't take vacations."

"Surely he wasn't just here for the subway experience."

"Right," Dan said. "But he didn't do anything else. He sat his ass on the subway train, rode halfway out of town, then turned around and caught a train heading back in the opposite direction. Then he went to dinner."

"I don't know what to make of it," Sam said. "Maybe Frankel

was a diversion. Maybe the main show was someplace else."

"Maybe," Dan said with a nod and an arch of his brow. "I wonder if there has been any activity at local hospitals."

"It's DC," Sam said. "Probably a thousand drug overdoses and armed robberies."

"But we wouldn't care about those," Dan said, "unless they had a national security angle."

Sam nodded. "But how would we define 'national security angle'?"

Dan shook his head. "Maybe anything involving employees at any of the security agencies, or known persons of interest in Homeland investigations."

"Feels like a long shot," Sam said. "Besides, Janice Everman wasn't working at one of the security agencies. She was a lawyer at Justice."

Dan nodded. "But I suppose we don't have a choice but to put feelers out there," he said. "Maybe just a list of people reasonably high up in the government agencies for starters."

"It'd be a long list."

Dan shook his head. "It would take five minutes to assemble."

"I suppose it's better than nothing."

Mark Severn entered the room. He looked tired and bleary-eyed. He had a stack of papers in his hand. It looked like a list of names, telephone numbers, and email addresses. A dozen names had been highlighted in yellow. One name had pink highlighting. "Arts and crafts?" Sam asked, nodding toward the sheaf of papers in his hand.

"Exactly," Severn said. "Your network analysis from the Boston gang." He handed the papers to Sam.

"What did you highlight?"

"Connections that I thought might be of interest," Severn said. "How did it go with our semi-retired assassin?"

Sam shook her head. "We chased him around the city for a couple of hours. He did nothing but ride the subway, and then go to dinner at a sidewalk café."

A funny look crossed Mark Severn's face. "What sidewalk café?"

"Café du something," Sam said. "Long on pretense, short on portion sizes."

"Café du what?" Severn pressed.

"I don't remember," Sam said. "Next to a hotel."

"The Intercontinental?" Mark Severn asked, a dark look on his face.

Sam's eyes registered surprise. "How did you know?"

"The Café du Parc?"

"Sounds right. Why?"

Severn shook his head. "He's rubbing our noses in it. That brazen son of a bitch."

"What are you talking about?"

"Did he order a salad?"

"How did you know?" Sam asked again.

Severn grimaced. "A salad at Café du Parc."

Sam shook her head. "If you're trying to confuse and annoy me, you're succeeding."

Severn looked at her, wearing a grave expression. "Arugula salad at Café du Parc. That was Janice Everman's last meal."

Chapter 37

Nero still hadn't thought of a way to contact Penny and the kids. It was taking a terrible toll on him. Retrieving the cash from his uncle's backyard had been a significant morale booster, and had allowed him to buy a few essentials. But with food, clothes and shelter taken care of, the next item on Maslow's hierarchy of needs came into play. The meaningful relationships in his life were deteriorating moment by moment in his absence.

He had no idea what his family thought. Maybe they thought he'd died in an accident, or maybe they feared that he had skipped out on them. Perhaps they thought he had saved some money in secret, that he had run off, maybe with some floozy, someone whose body hadn't been battered by childbirth and middle age.

Those were unbearable thoughts for Nero. He wanted desperately to get in contact with Penny and the kids, to hold them, to tell them everything was okay, to commiserate, to tell them all of the crazy things that had happened to him.

He was also going stir crazy. He'd been hiding out inside his rented storage unit for hours on end, staring at the same cramped, closed-in walls. He had considered buying a small television for entertainment, to while away the hours as he worked to clear his name while staying under the DHS radar. But he had ultimately decided against it. The noise would certainly have attracted unwanted attention. The rental agreement was quite clear about residing in the storage facility. Strictly verboten.

So he had picked up a book from a secondhand store. Ray Bradbury. Fahrenheit 451. As if Nero needed anything else to be paranoid about. He was living his own private dystopian nightmare. He identified with the protagonist in a visceral way. The light reading was meant as a diversion, but it was too close to his own reality, and he found his stomach in knots as he read.

He opened the door to the storage shed for a glimpse at the sun, to figure out what time it was. Almost late enough. But not quite.

Nero thought the plan through one more time. It was a plan born of paranoia. He needed to make inroads into Money's life, to figure out what kind of business Money was mixed up in. But Nero wasn't computer-savvy. He couldn't hack into Money's cell phone or bank accounts. He couldn't invade Money's email accounts, either. Plus, he was pretty sure the feds would be able to find anyone who tried.

He would have loved to see Money's correspondence. Nero was betting there was something incriminating, something he could use to figure out why his association with Money had produced such a virulent reaction from the feds.

Then there were the physical facilities Money used. Nero was aware of a small rented warehouse, a low, squat building in the industrial section of town, not far from the train station, not far from a defunct rubber factory, recently razed to make room for a shiny new condominium complex. There was likely to be evidence laying around the warehouse, Nero figured, something that could point him in the right direction. Something he could bring to the feds to convince them that he was innocent, and that while he might have worked for Money, he had no idea what Money was really up to.

But that was also an impossibility, for the same reasons that he couldn't visit Penny and the kids. The feds would have it completely staked out. Likewise, he couldn't call any of the telephone numbers he had used to get ahold of Money. Homeland would undoubtedly have those under surveillance as well. Nero didn't know much about electronic surveillance, but he knew enough to be scared shitless of it. He knew they would be able to triangulate the location of any phone used to call any of the numbers in Money's rotation. It would take them a matter of seconds to figure out where he was. If they had agents in the area, Nero would be nabbed again. Even if there weren't agents nearby, Homeland would have confirmation of his general whereabouts. Still in Denver. Lacking the good sense to run away to a foreign country, change his name, change his face, disappear.

Which was an option, but not one that Nero entertained. He loved his family. A life without them was no life for him.

Which brought him back to square one, back to the problem. How to move toward the center of Money's business without the feds getting wise.

The dead drops, of course.

Nero had serviced a number of them over the course of his employment. They were an old trick taken from espionage annals. To reduce the risk of capture and exploitation, spies left information, weapons, instructions, and other valuables in hiding places. They used signals to tell each other when an item was ready for pickup. The signals were usually hidden in plain sight, innocuous and nondescript, like a chalk mark on a park bench, or maybe a small, nearly imperceptible mark on a graffiti-covered wall. It didn't have to be much, as long as both sides knew what to look for.

It had always given Nero a bit of a thrill to service the dead drops on Money's behalf. Usually, he retrieved and delivered sealed envelopes. Paper. He had no idea what was written on the paper, or who was on the other end of the clandestine transactions. He never wanted to know.

Until now.

The plan wasn't without risk. If Money had indeed been captured, there was every possibility that he had given Homeland the locations and codes for all of the dead drops he and Nero had used over the years. In fact, there was a remarkably strong chance that was the case, Nero surmised.

But it had been a few days since Nero's escape from the wrecked prison van. While Homeland had nearly unlimited resources, Nero was counting on the normal human tendency toward reduced effort over time, particularly toward a fruitless task. He was betting that if Homeland had indeed watched the dead drop locations for a few days, they would likely have lost interest.

Of course, it was entirely possible they had not. It was entirely possible there was a small army of Special Agent America-like people, sitting in confiscated cars with binoculars and infrared night vision devices, keeping watch over a dozen dead drop locations.

Maybe even more. Maybe Money had other couriers, each with their own dead drop locations. Maybe dozens of them. Even so, a surveillance agent for every dead drop was not beyond the realm of the possible. So there was risk involved.

But he couldn't do nothing. He was going out of his mind.

He ran through the details one last time as he watched the sun set over the horizon.

Then it was time to go. Time to get his life back.

* * *

Nero connected the old motorcycle's ignition wires. He flipped the kick starter out, placed his heel on top, drove his foot down, and gave the motorcycle a little throttle as it sputtered to life. It ran like a charm. A huge blessing. Well worth the trouble to find and fix it.

He rounded the corner out of the long aisle of storage units. He turned west, toward the highway, stunned again by the beauty of the sunset. There was nothing like a Denver twilight. He saw wild, unfathomable mountains in deep indigo, cutting a jagged silhouette into the blazing reds and yellows of the sky. There was an invigorating bite in the air. It was impossible not to feel good about being alive, no matter the circumstances.

The sunset brought momentary calm to his butterfly-filled stomach. He worked hard to keep his mind clear and alert, but he felt worry cloud his thinking. A chill passed through him, a certain knowledge that he was on borrowed time.

Perhaps that was true. Perhaps it was impossible for one man to hide indefinitely in the modern world from the Establishment, from the Machine, from Big Brother.

But Nero didn't have to hide forever. He only needed to remain free long enough to gather the evidence he needed to clear his name.

Which was another worry. A fool's errand, maybe. Suppose he found something of use, something that might help convince people of his innocence. Then what? Would Special Agent America listen? Would he care?

Or maybe Special Agent America had a quota, a certain number of people he had to capture and detain, to prove he was doing a good job, to prove he was keeping the country safe, to prove he was winning the war on terror, whatever that meant.

There was another nagging worry, one Nero had thought about previously. How the hell was he going to prove his non-knowledge and non-involvement? Especially when it looked so clearly like he *was* involved. He was, after all, Money's deliveryman. His pleas of deliberate ignorance didn't sound terribly compelling, even to him.

So he had no idea what to expect.

And he had no idea what he was looking for. He just had the vague sense that it all began and ended with Money. Money had to be the key. Because outside of Money, Nero's life was squeaky clean.

Nero merged onto the highway. He headed south, spectacular sunset off his right shoulder, traffic still heavy but moving. He planned to start in the south end of town and work his way north, visiting every dead drop location in the city, one by one.

He didn't expect to find a smoking gun. But it was the only thing he knew to do, the only starting point that didn't seem like a certain trip back to the slammer, the only course of action with any prayer of yielding results.

He took the exit for I-225, dodged slower traffic in the right lane, exited at Parker Road, just past a gargantuan man-made dam, and looped back around to the south.

The Emerald Isle Tavern appeared after a mile or two on his right. His first stop. Nero had no idea how many years the place had been in business. Over thirty, at least. Maybe forty or fifty. He had no idea if it was under the original management, either. He just knew that the place hadn't changed much over the years. Decent food, a great view, and all the alcohol you could drink. A winning, timeless combination.

Nero parked his motorcycle, disengaged the ignition wires, set the kickstand, and went inside. Despite his growing hunger, he didn't stop to order anything. He didn't want to be recognized.

He walked through the restaurant. It looked and smelled familiar. He had been there many times before. It had a mom-and-pop feel to it, not like one of those big chains. Nero liked that. Real character, not manufactured pseudo-culture.

He found his way to the restroom. The door was equipped with a sliding lock. Nero clicked it into place, sealing himself off from the rest of the restaurant and bar. He climbed atop the counter, taking care not to slip on the wet, slick countertop. He placed his hands on the mirror to steady himself as he stood upright, his head just a few inches below the ceiling tile.

He splayed his fingers and pressed upward on the ceiling tile, lifting it out of its seating. He moved it off to the side, creating just enough room to snake his arm up into the space. He bent his elbow and wrist, feeling the top of the adjacent tiles.

Nothing.

Nero cursed softly to himself. The dead drop was empty. There was nothing there.

Someone jostled the lock and pounded on the bathroom door.

Nero jumped. Adrenaline flooded his body. He jerked, nearly fell.

"Pinch it off, buddy!" a drunken voice yelled.

Nero breathed a sigh of relief. Just a drunk in need of relief. "Just a minute," he said.

He moved the ceiling tile back into place, hopped down from the counter, wiped his boot prints from the countertop, washed his hands, and opened the door.

"About damn time, buddy. Were you giving birth in there?" A giant of a man, in a biker's jacket, with neck tattoos.

Nero muttered an apology. He made his way back out the front of the pub. He was tempted to stop, to grab a bite to eat, to have a beer. But he fought the temptation. If Money had squealed to the feds about all of his dead drop locations, it wouldn't make sense to spend any longer than necessary at the Emerald Isle.

He opened the front door, stepped out into the cool night air, looked all around him. No cops. No big, ugly Fords, the kind that only grandparents and feds drove. It was all pickup trucks and motorcycles and a few out-of-place imports in the parking lot.

Nero heard no helicopters, either. A good sign. He looked up in the sky, just to be sure.

Just a single bird circled overhead. Big, graceful, never even flapping its wings. Riding a thermal, maybe. He wondered idly if there were thermals at night. Probably. Residual heat from the asphalt, maybe. Maybe it was enough to keep a big bird with a big wingspan aloft, with no effort.

He heard a strange sound, kind of like a tiny propeller, like there was a model airplane flying around nearby. He only heard it when there was a break in the stream of traffic flowing along the road. He couldn't place the sound. It seemed far off, spread out, coming from everywhere and nowhere, bouncing off nearby buildings. He shrugged it off.

Nero reconnected the ignition wires, kick-started the bike, waited for a hole in traffic, and turned left, northbound on Parker Road, back the way he had come. The next location was only a couple of miles away.

He drove there automatically, mind wandering, arriving suddenly and without recollection of the journey. It was a playground, with big, bright, plastic playthings bolted into the sand. There was a metal bench, with wooden slats. The oldest dead-drop trick in the book, Nero figured.

He sat down at the bench, ran his right hand underneath, and moved it back and forth, searching for an envelope taped to the underside of the bench.

Nothing.

He bent over, looked beneath the bench, obvious as the nose on his face, violating every rule of tradecraft.

But Nero wasn't a spy. He was a courier. He ran his hand

deeper beneath the bench, further and further, just to be sure he hadn't missed anything.

He *had* missed something.

Something very important.

"Looking for something, Mr. Chiligiris?"

Nero froze. His gut spasmed with fear. His eyes grew wide as quarters. He whipped his head toward the sound. A large man. Tall, athletic, buzzed hair, bulletproof vest, pistol drawn.

"It's nice to see you again, Mr. Chiligiris."

A familiar voice.

Ominous.

"Now put your hands in the air," Special Agent America said.

Chapter 38

"I think the prudent call is to treat it as though Frankel was here in town on business," Dan said.

"Obviously," Sam said, a little too testily. "But what does that mean for us?"

Dan shook his head. "I suppose the local hospital alert is as good a start as any."

Sam grimaced. "We're only going to find anything out after the fact."

"Obviously," Dan responded in kind. He shrugged. "We could always roll him."

"But we watched him the whole time," Severn said. "He didn't *do* anything."

"He didn't *appear* to do anything," Sam corrected. "But as a profession, assassination has come a long way over the years. And our man Frankel has had plenty of time on his hands to stay up-to-date with the latest techniques."

Mark Severn nodded. "Biological weapons," he said. "Just like Janice Everman."

"That's a giant logical leap," Sam said. "Nothing more than a hunch."

"True," Severn said. "But you believe it, too, don't you?"

Sam pondered a moment. "I suppose I do. Healthy people like

Janice Everman don't die of food poisoning inside of a day," she said. "Hell, people don't die of Ebola in a day. I don't know what the hell Frankel used on her, assuming it was him, but it must have been in a league of its own."

Dan nodded. "But like you said, science has come a long way. And it's anyone's guess who hired this guy, and how connected they might be."

"You're thinking of a foreign government?" Severn asked.

"It would fit. Given the Budapest angle, and the Russian gangsters in Boston."

"Speaking of which," Sam said. She waved the sheaf of papers that Mark Severn brought with him. "I need to dig into this network analysis. Dan, can you head up the hospital search? Also, let's assemble all of the surveillance camera footage we have on Frankel over the last twenty-four hours. Run it all through the software, spectral detection algorithms, anything we can throw at this to shed some light on what he was doing in town."

"Roger, boss," Dan said. He turned to Severn. "Can you help?"

Severn nodded. "Nothing on my agenda tonight."

"Excellent. I'll leave this in your capable hands," Sam said.

She retreated to her office, where she called Brock, to tell him goodnight, and to tell him that something had broken in the Budapest case, and that it demanded her full attention, probably until dawn.

"You're lucky I'm not the jealous type," Brock said. "And you're lucky I have my bitches to keep me warm in your absence."

Sam laughed. "Make sure you clean up the glitter when they

leave."

"Always," Brock said. "I don't know what you're doing, Sam, but please be careful."

"Always," she lied.

* * *

Sam started with the highlighted names, email addresses, and telephone numbers that Severn had annotated on the network analysis report. The computer had identified all known connections between the house full of Russian gangsters and anyone with any remote attachment to the current happenings. The computer had identified connections originating from anything related to Janice Everman's death, then constructed a network analysis using financial transactions, airline tickets, cell phone records, tax returns, property titles, automobile loans, anything at all that might establish a tie between the Russians and whoever had hired them.

The list of connections was staggering. There were first-order links, of course, generated when A called B, or C called D. There were also second order connections, where A called B, who then called C. The computer continued to identify affiliations all the way out to the seventh layer, which produced a nearly unfathomable list of possible connections. Far too many to sift through, and entirely too many to even contemplate investigating.

The computer's results required a computer to understand, so the report also included a meta-analysis. Many of the higher-order network connections shared common nodes with some lower-order connections, and it was possible to cross-reference them to figure out who the major movers and shakers were in the game. Those individuals appeared toward the center of the network diagram, with the most connections leading to and from them, signifying the greatest number of people with whom they kept ties. Sam focused her efforts on the major players. They would be the ones finding business, doing deals, taking payments, ordering the goons around.

They were a very active bunch. They had their hands in a lot of different things. Undoubtedly, the vast majority of their activities were of the questionable variety. But Sam didn't have time to sift through them all, so she quickly switched tactics.

She found the names of the three dead goons in Budapest. She analyzed their connection activity. It was sparse. Clearly, they were foot soldiers. They didn't make decisions, they didn't recruit new business, and they weren't critical nodes in the network.

But that worked to Sam's advantage. She analyzed their email and telephone activity over the preceding weeks. Not much activity. There were a few calls to and from a well-known and well-protected whorehouse. Perhaps it was one of the Russian gang's businesses, and the goons were charged with making sure the madam paid the proper protection fee. Or maybe they liked to taste the wares on a regular basis. It wasn't like they were handsome men. And the women that Sam and Dan had encountered in the house in Boston were even less handsome. So it was not inconceivable that if the thugs wanted to spend time in the company of beautiful women, they would have to pay for it. Sam jotted the whorehouse down as a possibility, in case nothing else panned out.

There was another set of interesting phone calls. The number corresponded with one of the phones used by Viktor Markov.

Markov was one of the big shots, one of the names with a lot of lines leading to and from it on the network diagram. A boss of some sort, maybe an upper-level manager.

Sam checked the dates of the calls between Markov and the foot soldiers.

Bingo.

They corresponded to Mark Severn's time in Hungary. And also to her own time in Budapest.

Sam's first instinct was to pay a visit to Mr. Markov. But that was the old-school investigator in her. It was the digital age, the brave new world. There was a much more efficient way to go about things. She simply dug deeper into the network analysis report, centering her search around Markov.

A weak connection caught her eye. It caught her eye because Mark Severn had highlighted it. It was the one in pink. Sam followed the highlighter through the columns until she found the man's name.

Jonathan France.

Janice Everman's replacement at the Department of Justice.

The man who benefited most directly from Janice Everman's death. At least, the one who benefited most obviously from her demise.

Sam looked at her watch. Almost ten p.m. DC time.

Perfect time for a house call.

* * *

Sam left Dan and Mark Severn working to assemble the video footage of the assassin, and to cross-reference any suspicious, security-related injuries in the local hospitals.

Both seemed like long shots. But both needed doing. No two ways about it.

And Jonathan France needed a friendly visit. No two ways about that, either. So Sam went alone. She waved off Dan's offer to go along, ignoring the look he gave her.

She drove her usual speed en route to Jonathan France's house, which was to say she was a hazard to other motorists. But the DC streets weren't crowded, which made Sam happy. She wasn't in the mood for traffic. She had found herself in bumper-to-bumper snarls at midnight, for no apparent reason, and she was pleased to be making solid progress on this particular night.

Because it felt like something was brewing. Something was about to happen. Things felt perched on a precipice of some sort, like an avalanche biding its time.

Jonathan France lived at a tony address in Georgetown. Sam parked her car at the curb in front of his apartment building, showed her badge to the doorman, found the France residence in the registry, and took the elevator to the fourth floor.

The place was simple, elegant, high-end, tasteful.

Expensive, Sam noted. She was sure that the lawyers on the Department of Justice payroll earned more than the average government employee. But she wasn't sure they earned nearly enough to live in a place like this. And France had told her that his wife stayed home with the kids. So either France had come into some money, or he was earning stacks of dead presidents on the side, Sam decided.

She found the right apartment, rapped on the door, the kind of authoritative knock that rarely spelled good news an hour before midnight.

Nothing stirred inside. She knocked louder.

Still no movement. She pounded a third time, announced herself as a federal agent, and listened.

Nothing.

She produced from her purse what looked like a standard key card, but with computer wires attached to one end of the card. The wires converged to form a cable, which fit perfectly into the receptacle on Sam's Blackberry. She called up an application on the phone called Cypher King. She scrolled to the green button, pressed it, inserted the key card into the slot in Jonathan France's door, and waited.

It took just shy of a dozen seconds. Sam heard a definitive click as the lock retreated from the jamb. Sam opened the door, marveling again at how far surveillance technology had come.

The smell hit her immediately.

Sweet, metallic, moist, sickening.

She had smelled it more times than she could count. It still made her stomach turn. She drew her weapon, crouched, searched the apartment one room at a time.

Empty.

Except for the body of Jonathan France. She found him fully clothed in the bathtub. His face was drawn, gray, slack. Extremely dead. Both wrists were slit.

Sam sighed. She snapped photos of the scene, then leaned in close to examine his wounds. Most suicides had hesitation marks, small, probing cuts next to the lethal wound, as the victim worked up the gumption to make the big cut. But Jonathan France's arms had none. The wounds were deep, definitive, confident, determined. He was either extremely eager to die, or he had help making his way to the afterlife.

Sam's money was on the latter. She looked around the apartment for a suicide note. She didn't find one.

Dead-end. No signs of forced entry, no signs of struggle, and a fully clothed victim lying in a pool of his own blood in the bathtub. Lots of different ways to interpret the scene. Had the old assassin been here? And where were France's wife and kids?

And France's computer was missing.

She dialed Dan's number. He picked up on the third ring. "How did it go with our friend the lawyer?" Dan asked.

"He's permanently taciturn," Sam said.

"Jesus," Dan said. "It got serious all of the sudden, didn't it?" He thought for a moment. "You're wondering if our man Frankel didn't pay him a visit, aren't you?" he asked.

"Among other things," Sam said. "No forced entry, no struggle, two wrists with deep gashes in them, no hesitation marks."

Dan whistled. "A pro."

"I think so too. I was hoping you had some ideas," Sam said.

"It wasn't our favorite semi-retired Agency man," Dan said. "We've pieced enough of the video together to account for his whereabouts since arriving in DC."

"It didn't seem like Frankel's MO," Sam said. "He's too frail to manhandle anyone. Any other ideas?"

"Well, let's figure out who was in the apartment. I can cross reference all the cell phone networks for their location data."

Sam heard a keyboard clacking away in the background.

"What the...?" Dan said absently.

More clicking.

"Those bastards," Dan finally said.

"What is it?"

"Those assholes have denied me access to the cell phone records."

"Which assholes?"

More clicking. More cursing. "Unbelievable."

"NSA?"

"Yep. It's their surveillance system and database. Homeland has a subscription to it, but they control access."

"Policy change?" Sam asked.

"No way," Dan said. "I stay up to date on all of that kind of stuff. No policy changes at all. Let me make a phone call and I'll call you right back." Dan clicked off.

Sam took another look around France's apartment. She didn't find anything useful. She phoned in his death to the DC Metro police, and to the local FBI office. She left her business card on the counter in case they needed to get ahold of her, then she got back into her car and drove to downtown DC.

To the Department of Justice.

* * *

The gigantic Justice edifice was deserted. It was dark and gray, more than a little ominous. Sam used her Homeland badge to gain access. The rent-a-cop seemed happy for the diversion from what was otherwise a mind-numbing evening. "Are you sure I can't help you, ma'am?" the pudgy guard asked.

"Matter of fact, you *can* help me," Sam said, handing her card to him. "Anyone else comes to that door, you hold them and give me a call right away, okay?"

The guard nodded, eager to help, unaware that he had been sidelined.

Sam made her way to Jonathan France's office. She turned on the light. She pulled out a small antenna from her purse, again with a cord attached to it. Again, she called up an application on her government-issued Blackberry, plugged in the antenna from her purse, and began walking slowly around the room, looking at the display.

There were a couple of false alarms. The equipment was terrific, sensitive and reliable, but the designers had erred on the side of caution, and it reported a few false positives.

But the third time was the charm. The signal was loud and strong, coming from a clear acrylic obelisk on the edge of Jonathan France's desk. With great appreciation for a job well done, the inscription said. An award of some sort. From France's last law firm. Maybe a going-away gift. Sam turned it upside down. There were no visible openings. It appeared just to be a solid piece of acrylic. Nothing out of the ordinary.

Except that it transmitted a signal.

Sam captured and copied the signal using her phone. She stored it as a graphics file and sent it in a text to Dan Gable.

"Somebody's been spying on our man France," she typed.

Chapter 39

Sam went home. There wasn't much left for her to do. Dan and Mark Severn were working on decoding the messages sent by the listening device she found in Jonathan France's office at Justice. DC Metro and the local Bureau office were busy working the scene at France's apartment.

The scene was conditionally classified as a crime scene, on Sam's insistence. She was sure there would eventually be overwhelming pressure from somewhere else in the government to classify France's death as a suicide. And it may very well have been. But probably not. Whoever slashed France's wrists had more than a little experience digging knives into flesh. Suicide victims rarely had that kind of experience.

Sam left her clothes in a heap and crawled into bed next to Brock. She snuggled close, feeling his warmth, feeling the instant comfort of his scent, enjoying the familiarity of his soft snores. He felt like home.

She fell asleep moments later, exhausted from an extremely long day.

Then the phone rang. She fumbled in the dark, looking for it. Her office Blackberry. She found the device, pressed the green button, held the handset to her ear. "The hospital feelers came through," Dan said.

"Someone checked in?" Sam asked groggily.

"Quite the opposite. Someone checked out."

"Of the hospital?"

"Of life."

"Someone we know, I take it?"

"No, but someone maybe we should know. NSA employee, name of David Swaringen."

"Doesn't ring any bells," Sam said, rubbing her eyes.

"He's on the list of executives at NSA," Dan said. "That's why we got the call from the hospital, after our request last night."

"What happened?"

"Girlfriend made the 911 call," Dan said. "Apparently, he just keeled over in bed."

"That's how I want to die," Sam said. "How old was he?"

"Early forties."

"Heart attack?"

"For the moment," Dan said. "But that's mostly because they haven't been able to find any other cause of death."

"Was he overweight? Cholesterol issues?"

"Fit as a fiddle. Except he up and died."

"Like Janice Everman," Sam said. "Okay, text me his address and I'll take a look around. You can go home and get some sleep."

"I won't argue with you. The computer's analyzing the signal from the bug in the lawyer's office at Justice. Should be done in an hour or so. And we've completely traced Frankel's whereabouts since his arrival, but we've learned nothing new."

"Thanks, Dan. Get some rest."

Sam dressed, kissed Brock lightly on the cheek, and left.

* * *

Sam set out for David Swaringen's apartment. It was about halfway between DC and Fort Meade. Undoubtedly chosen for its proximity to both places. Work in one direction, fun in the other.

Along the way, Dan filled her in on Swaringen's last evening. The NSA exec took the train into town, had dinner and drinks with a new flame, then took the girl back to his apartment for conjugal delights.

Eva something-or-other was the girlfriend's name. Not a long-term relationship — only a few hours old, to be precise, which piqued Sam's interest. But the girl seemed genuinely distraught, Metro had said. Swaringen hadn't died during intercourse, evidently, but he expired not long after. It was undoubtedly unnerving for the girl, who'd accompanied Swaringen to the hospital, then gone home from there.

Sam parked in the parking garage and took the elevator to the twelfth floor. Swaringen's place wasn't considered a crime scene, and Sam took advantage of an unlocked door left by the medical technicians to gain entry. She looked around. The decor was consistent with mid-life bachelorhood. Minimalist, a few status symbols laying around, nice furniture but not too nice, all hardwood and hard edges. Very masculine.

She looked at the pictures on the wall. Handsome guy, she thought. Good job, good salary, good looks. Probably a bit of a player.

She looked again at his face. Something in his smile. A lack of confidence, maybe. A little bit of self-doubt. Maybe he wasn't a player after all. Maybe he had just gotten lucky with Eva.

Her phone buzzed. A photograph, sent by Dan Gable, which he evidently received from the Metro police. Of Eva. She was young, beautiful, exotic. Slavic. Sam typed the question that popped immediately into her mind. "A hooker?"

"LOL," Dan replied. "I thought so too. But evidently not."

At least not a hooker with a record, Sam thought darkly. Maybe an in-house hooker. Maybe employed for particular purposes. It was the Russian face that kept giving Sam pause.

Of course, there were a lot of Russians in the world, but it seemed like a hell of a coincidence. You could go months without seeing a single one of them, but Sam had seen a dozen in the last week. It made her suspicious.

She searched Swaringen's bedroom. His clothes still lay on the floor, strewn haphazardly, as if they were shed during the heat of the moment, leading up to the Big Moment. Which was duly documented by the presence of a used condom, drying on the carpet. At least he went out with a bang, Sam mused.

She searched his drawers and closet. Nothing unusual.

On to the bathroom. A Xanax prescription was the only thing of note, sitting next to a bottle of Viagra. Anxiety and flaccidity. She wondered if Swaringen's angst was real or imagined. She wondered if there was any way to know the difference. An NSA executive on anti-anxiety medication probably wasn't all that uncommon, but it was a data point, and she made a note. Job stress, maybe. Or maybe his anxiety was caused by erectile dysfunction, Sam thought with an inner smirk.

She wandered into his office. A pair of diplomas hung on the wall, from schools with impressive names. Swaringen had an executive MBA from one of them. Harvard.

Sam wondered if that was how he had landed the job at NSA, by rubbing elbows with up-and-comers. Technician jobs were a dime a dozen at NSA. In fact, there were very few employers in the world with a larger number of tech-savvy employees than the NSA. But executive jobs were another matter. Executives got the keys to the kingdom.

NSA was one of the most secretive organizations on the planet. It had been beaten up badly in the press, and probably rightly so. A series of high-profile leaks had left no plausible doubt that NSA had overreached its charter by light years, trampling on basic privacy rights and pissing off everyone on the globe who possessed an email account. Sam wondered what kind of enticement NSA had to offer in order to attract new talent in the aftermath of all the drama.

Specifically, she wondered what attracted David Swaringen. He was a recent hire, according to Dan. His position was high enough to place him on the list of potential terror targets, which also placed him on the list of persons of interest in the previous evening's hospital and police query.

Sam continued her methodical search through Swaringen's apartment. She hadn't found anything unexpected, but she still had a hard time shaking the feeling that something was amiss. Young, healthy people rarely keeled over dead.

Sure, it did happen on occasion. Sometimes there were hidden medical conditions. But it was starting to smell like a pattern was emerging. And then there was the Russian girl, the maybe-hooker. Those things made Sam think there was something else going on.

She searched through David Swaringen's desk. There were old bills, paid and unpaid. There was a copy of a divorce decree. It contained child support provisions. Strange, because Sam saw no pictures of children in the apartment. Maybe they were too painful of a reminder, or maybe they slowed things down with the young ladies Swaringen might have managed to lure back to his bachelor pad.

She turned on his computer. She wasn't a forensics expert by any stretch, but she knew the basics of what to look for. She perused the file index, looking for anything of interest. It didn't take long to find his bank statements. He downloaded them onto his hard drive every month, evidently paranoid about a data loss at the bank itself. Sam noticed nothing out of the ordinary. It didn't look like he was receiving large deposits, and his only outrageous expenditure over the past several years, other than alimony, was for graduate school. And it was an outrageous expenditure. Sam wondered if it had been worth it.

After bank statements, there was no more informative a place on a person's computer then the browser history. Sam saw the usual. Lots of pornographic searches. Swaringen liked brunettes, evidently, with manicured nethers, bending over while nude. Blondes, too. An equal-opportunity self-flagellator, it appeared. Years ago, it would have been a solid basis for blackmail. But not any longer. The chief function of the Internet, some argued, was to indulge the universal voyeuristic dark side.

There were some strange searches that caught her eye. "Drones over US territory" was one of them. "US surveillance laws" was another. There was a dictionary word, an obscure one. Penumbra. Maybe Swaringen had run across it in a book and wanted to know the definition. Probably nothing at all, but Sam wrote the word down, along with the notes on the surveillance searches. They were potentially noteworthy, particularly given that Swaringen worked at the National Security Agency. Why would an executive at the world's largest surveillance apparatus be researching surveillance legalities on his home computer?

And why would that person die at the ripe old age of forty-something?

Maybe he should have asked his doctor whether he was healthy enough to engage in sexual activity.

Or maybe there was something else going on.

* * *

The sun threatened to take over the horizon by the time Sam left Swaringen's apartment.

She had closed her eyes for a little less than an hour in the past day, and she wasn't quite on her game.

Which was why she saw the tail so late.

Too late.

Caucasian this time, not Slavic, dressed in jeans and a leather jacket and a black ball cap. Cliché. Young. Fit. Late twenties, maybe. He joined her in the elevator as she descended to the parking garage. She heard the faint crackle of an earpiece.

Interesting.

Unnerving.

Sam smiled and nodded at him.

He reciprocated, but it was pained. He was definitely on the job, she surmised. She snuck her hand into her purse.

The elevator dinged. Sam motioned for the guy to exit first. "After you," she said.

The man extended his arm, reversing the invitation. "I insist," he said.

Sam didn't want to make it awkward. She exited the elevator, walked quickly to her car, hand still in her purse.

The man followed.

She stopped, turned, looked.

"Hands up," the man said. A large-caliber pistol stared Sam in the face.

* * *

Sam tried never to overcomplicate things.

She asked to see the man's badge.

The man didn't produce a badge.

Sam shot him.

She didn't bother to pull the pistol free from her purse. She just shot right through the side. The bullet made a little hole in the side of her Prada bag, a small tragedy, but it made a significantly larger hole in the man's gut. Loud, noisy, messy, and effective.

Gut shots were excruciatingly painful. It was difficult to describe how much they hurt. They were good for taking all the fight out of a person. The man didn't try reaching for his gun. He was done. He offered no further resistance, no further antisocial behavior.

Sam kicked away his pistol, just to be sure. Then she knelt down to talk with him.

"You know how this goes," she said. "This is the part where I ask you who the hell you're working for."

The man shook his head.

"My suggestion is that you skip the tough-guy act. I may take it the wrong way, like maybe you're resisting a federal officer."

He groaned, regarded his gut, then looked back at Sam with anger and defiance on his face.

"I may decide that your actions are placing my safety in question," Sam said. "I may not feel comfortable bringing an ambulance into this kind of situation. Which would be unfortunate, given the size of your leak."

The man gritted his teeth, wincing in pain. "You have no idea what kind of shit you're in," he said, voice strained.

Sam looked at him. Dark, purple blood spewed from his gut. His insides made a gurgling sound. Sam guessed her bullet had maybe nicked a lung. It made death by suffocation a real possibility. She pointed that out to the young gentleman.

He didn't reply.

She studied his face. He looked young, hard, lean, professional. Close-cropped hair. He didn't look like a thug. He looked well trained. Like a fed.

"CIA?" Sam asked.

The man shook his head. The pain on his face gave way momentarily to insult. "I'm not permitted to divulge my affiliation."

"Do you want to die for a secret?"

"I'm already dead."

"Nobody likes a drama queen," Sam said. "It's not becoming. Man up. You just pulled a gun on a federal agent. That's a federal bullet in your gut. I think it's probably going to kill you, if we don't call someone soon. I'll do that as soon as you give me a name."

The man shook his head. "You have no idea," he said.

"Obviously. Enlighten me."

The man shook his head again, stared at the profuse bleeding from his midsection, cursed.

"You're going to wait me out, aren't you?" Sam asked. "You're going to hurry up and die. Pussy."

The man shook his head again, groaning, red foam forming on the edges of his lips. "They're listening."

"Who?" Sam asked. "Who's listening?"

He shook his head more vigorously. "I'm not allowed…"

"You're crooked, aren't you?"

The man shook his head. "Not even close," he gasped. "I'm following orders."

"You can't possibly be following orders," Sam said. "Nobody would ever give you orders to pull a gun on a federal agent.

The man shook his head. "You don't understand," he said again. "You have… no idea."

His eyes glazed. His gaze lost focus. Sam provided compression on his wound with one hand and slapped his face with the other. "Wake up, asshole," she said.

He didn't wake up.

Sam dialed 911. She spoke to the operator, got medical help on the way. But she knew it was a lost cause.

Sam took a picture of the man's face.

She got into her car, started the engine, pulled out of the parking space, turned toward the garage exit.

It was blocked by a man with a gun.

Sam's mind raced. She weighed her options. Bad and worse. She should have taken Dan up on his offer to accompany her. She shouldn't have been running around out in the wild all by herself.

She made her decision.

She slammed on the brakes, squealed to a stop, opened the door, grabbed her keys, and ran back into the building. She heard no footsteps behind her. That was a bad sign. It meant a disciplined team. Some agents had perimeter duty, and others undoubtedly had search duty.

Sam bounded up the steps of the mid-rise apartment building. She burst through the door, found a janitor's closet, picked the lock, sealed herself inside.

She took a moment to catch her breath.

Then she called Dan, after texting a picture of the dead agent to him.

"It's a dirty trick," Dan said. "Sending me home to sleep, only to wake me up again with a phone call."

"Misery loves company," Sam said. "I need you to work your magic, please."

"Don't I always?"

"Did you get the picture?"

"You made another new friend, I see," Dan said.

"I think he was a fed of some sort. He pulled a gun, wouldn't show me a badge, so I shot him. He kept talking about following orders. I didn't find any ID on him, but he had a federal vibe."

"Is that your scientific diagnosis?"

"You can just tell after a while. I need to know who he is, affiliations, the whole nine."

"I'm already on it."

"You're at your computer?"

"No," Dan said. "I'm in bed. But I have system access on my phone."

"He brought friends," Sam said. "So I'll need a clever way out."

"Sorry, boss," Dan said after a brief silence. "I think you might be screwed."

"What gives you such unbridled optimism?"

"The system just returned an ID on your newest dead guy."

"And?"

"Deleted."

"You mean it didn't find a match?"

"No. It definitely found a match. The guy has been deleted from the database entirely."

"Balls," Sam said.

"So he's a battered spouse, a protected witness, or an asshole working for one of the clandestine services."

"I asked him if he was CIA," Sam said. "He gave me a look like I had insulted him."

"No chance he was FBI?"

Sam shook her head. "No way."

"I think we know who that leaves, then," Dan said.

Sam took a deep breath. "I think we do."

Chapter 40

Sam pondered the situation in the darkness of the janitor's closet.

The dead agent's voice echoed in her ears. They're listening, he had said.

David Swaringen had been an NSA executive.

Janice Everman had been working on national security policy. With the NSA, among others.

They were all dead.

And NSA had switched off Homeland's access to pirated telecom information.

All of it meant that there was no effective way for Sam to coordinate any kind of measured response to stop the bloodshed. NSA was among the world's elite electronic surveillance agencies. There was no electronic communication that Sam could trust to be free from prying eyes.

It didn't matter what she tried. They would always be one step ahead of her. Because they would always know exactly what she had planned.

NSA also had access to the same video camera network that Homeland had. There was virtually no stoplight in America that didn't feature a video camera of some sort. The cameras fed video to a massive database. Even if she destroyed her phone, her face would trigger a response. She would be instantly recognized, and more paramilitary NSA trigger-pullers would descend on her like locusts.

But there had to be a way.

There was always a way.

It usually involved seeking an answer to the right question.

So what would cause the NSA to call off the dogs? What would cause them to stand down?

The answer, when it came to her, seemed obvious.

Obvious, and terrifying.

* * *

If your opponent has overwhelming strength, maybe it can be used against him. Maybe all of his momentum can be turned to work in your favor, rather than his.

There was no way to win in a strength-on-strength confrontation, Sam knew. So it would all come down to art and guile and a little bit of skullduggery.

She destroyed her cell phone. Because there was no sense in making things too obvious. No reason to give them any suspicion. She was going to have to communicate with Dan, which meant they were going to listen in — his phone was undoubtedly tapped just like hers — but she had to make it look like she was attempting to be stealthy.

She sprinted to the seventh floor, using the stairs, avoiding elevators and hallways, running on her toes to keep the sound down. She figured the seventh floor of the apartment building was as good as any, far away from the muscle on the ground floor, and several floors away from David Swaringen's apartment on the twelfth floor.

Sam wasn't sure how many NSA agents were on the scene, but she felt fairly confident it wasn't a large enough number to station a team on every floor.

Sam put her ear to the hallway door and listened. No sounds. She peeked through the little glass window. No movement in the corridor.

She took a breath, turned the handle, looked both directions down the hall, and walked toward the nearest apartment door.

She rapped loudly. "Federal agent!" she shouted in an authoritative tone. "Open up, please."

It was early in the morning, and Sam didn't expect an immediate response. She repeated the knocking and yelling procedure a couple more times before she heard the latch retreat.

"Can I help you?" asked a groggy young man, dressed only in boxer shorts. He was trim, athletic, handsome. His nearly-naked body made her think of Brock, lying naked at home in their bed. She longed to go home, to see him, feel him, touch him.

"Sorry to disturb you," she said, showing her badge. "I just need to borrow your cell phone."

The man stared blankly, blinked a few times, shook his head. "My cell phone?"

"That's right," she said. "And maybe a cup of coffee, if it wouldn't be too much trouble. It's been one of those days."

More staring and blinking. "I'm not in trouble?" the man finally asked.

"Not that I'm aware of," Sam said with a smile. "But I haven't tasted your coffee yet."

The man smiled. He opened the door and motioned her in. Sam thanked him.

He handed her his iPhone and padded off to the kitchen. He had a nice ass, Sam noticed. Broad shoulders. Well endowed, if the jiggle in his boxers was any indication. It was also evident that he was circumcised. Her thoughts turned briefly to mischief. But only briefly. She wasn't into straying.

She dialed Dan Gable's number for what had to have been the hundredth time in the past day. He didn't answer. Not unexpected. It wasn't a number he'd recognize.

She called a second time, and then a third. Dan picked up on the fourth ring. "Special Agent Dan Gable," he said.

"Hi, Special Agent Dan Gable."

There was a long pause. "Sam?"

"Who were you expecting?"

"Whose phone is this?"

"Belongs to a guy in boxers. Cougar bait."

"What are you doing?"

"I need to pass on some investigation direction," she said slowly and deliberately, sounding official and officious.

The statement was clearly stilted. It didn't sound like Sam at all. Which, Sam hoped, Dan would understand as her way of telling him that she was engaging in a bit of theater.

It took Dan a moment to wrap his mind around things, but he played along. "I'm ready," he said.

"First, I need you to send me something. Those results you were waiting for."

Dan thought for a moment. "The computer is done analyzing. I have a name and address."

"Send it in an iMessage to this number," Sam said.

Dan immediately realized why. NSA had strong-armed all of the telecom companies into giving up all of their information, but Apple had fought back by encrypting its users' messages. From one iPhone to another, text messages were sent with strong encryption. Hackable, of course, but it would take NSA a bit of time to break the code and decrypt the information Sam was asking for. "I'll send it as soon as we hang up," Dan said.

"Great. Here's the plan," Sam said.

She spoke for a while. Dan listened.

"That's a terrible plan," Dan said when she had finished. Not because he was playing a part in her charade. Because it *was* a terrible plan.

But it wasn't really *the* plan. Sam had just laid out a pseudo-plan. A curveball. Sleight of hand.

The real plan was even worse.

* * *

Sam sipped coffee as she waited for Dan's text. It arrived with a ding-ding. It contained a name, title, and address.

She read the man's title. Her heart sank as realization dawned. It was worse than she thought. Much worse.

She felt waves of exhaustion wash through her mind, bringing fear and despair. She tried to clear them with a deep breath, and more coffee.

She wrote the name and address on the back of an envelope

and stuffed it in her pocket. She thought about the address. She was familiar with the area and had a good idea how to get there without using the map function on a telephone. Avoiding electronic navigation aids would help keep the goons at bay for a little longer. Maybe it would allow enough time for her misdirection to take hold.

But she didn't have much time.

Sam finished her coffee and thanked the handsome young man with the athletic body and the enviable bulge in his pants. She left him her business card. "If you ever need anything," she said.

"I very well might," he said with a coy smile.

Sam caught his meaning. She winked. "Next life, maybe."

She closed the door behind her, checked her pistol, steeled herself, walked toward the elevators.

It had all the makings of a long and painful morning.

* * *

The National Security Agency processed more data than Google. It processed more data than Facebook. In fact, NSA processed all of Google's and Facebook's data. NSA obtained this data by stealing it.

And they processed even more data than that.

The FBI, CIA, and Homeland had some pretty impressive tools. Surveillance was no problem for any of America's federal agencies. But none of them had anything on the NSA. There really was no place to hide. They had tapped into every camera in the United States. They had tapped into every Internet pipe. They had tapped into every telephone, and, effectively, every computer with an internet connection.

And, evidently, they also employed a team of trigger-pullers. This was news to Sam.

Not a terribly competent team, if the dead guy on the parking garage floor was any indication, but NSA's omniscience was a tactical advantage that could never be overestimated.

In effect, Sam was outnumbered by about a billion.

But the pieces had started to come together for her. She finally understood why they were after her.

It wasn't about her. At least, it hadn't started out that way. That was clear.

And it wasn't about Mark Severn, either.

It wasn't even related to Swaringen, the dead NSA employee, or France, the non-suicide, or Janice Everman, the Justice lawyer whose death had sparked Mark Severn's investigation.

It wasn't personal in the least, Sam realized as she pushed the elevator call button.

Except for one man. The man whose name, title, and address were written on the envelope in her pocket. It was probably always personal for him.

If he wasn't the guy, then he knew the guy. That much was certain, with a title like his.

It was about secrets, scandals, and still-healing wounds. It was about blowback. And fallout.

It was about a nation gone rogue.

Which explained why they'd hired Russian thugs. Plausible deniability. Misdirection. The United States of America wouldn't possibly do those things, people would think. *Couldn't* possibly.

Because it was un-American, against everything America stood for.

Except they could.

And they had.

And they *still were* doing those things.

We are doing those things, Sam thought. Us. Doing it to ourselves.

The elevator arrived. The doors opened. The immediacy of the situation descended upon her. She had to get away from the apartment building, put some distance between her and the thugs surrounding her.

But she had to do it extremely carefully. She had no idea how many more shooters might be lying in wait for her.

A familiar, asphyxiating sensation descended. Fear, with a healthy dose of panic mixed in. The odds were ridiculously bad. Even with Dan's help, and all the help she hoped he would have the good sense to rally. It was just a hope, because she couldn't be specific with him on the phone. They were listening. So she had left a lot unsaid. Which left a lot open to interpretation. Or misinterpretation.

In a sense, it didn't matter whether Dan could read between the lines of her instructions. Because it all came down to her, for reasons that were immediate and inescapable. For them, at that moment in time, Sam personified an existential threat. She had decimated their Budapest team. She'd poked around at Justice. She had tossed the Boston gang's nest. She'd led the team that followed Frankel through the city. She'd investigated France's murder scene. She'd nosed through Swaringen's apartment.

And, ultimately, she'd traced the problem to its source. Or very near to the source, she reasoned. Within one or two people on an organizational chart.

Which was close enough to be more than a little lethal.

Because it didn't start out personal. But it sure as hell was now.

The elevator stopped. Ground floor.

She held her breath and her gun. Her heart hammered. She felt sick with adrenaline.

The doors crept open.

She exploded through them. She caught the sentry completely by surprise. He faltered, unable to decide whether to raise his weapon to shoot her or raise his forearm to block her wild attack. In the end, he did neither, and the butt of Sam's pistol caught him square on the side of the head. His body folded up underneath him, and he crumpled to the floor. "Nighty-night," Sam muttered.

She commandeered his weapon, a Walther PPK. Compact, accurate, chambered in 380 ACP. Not a huge punch, but enough to grab someone's undivided attention. James Bond's gun, Sam thought with a chuckle. But this guy was no James Bond. She checked it, set the safety, and tucked it into her sock.

She dashed down a darkened hallway. She didn't want to emerge from the front or back doors, for fear an ambush awaited her.

A laundry room, sauna, and mechanical room dominated the ground floor. She checked each in turn.

The laundry room and sauna didn't contain what she was looking for.

She shouldered the door open into the mechanical room. It smelled of oil and grease and a carcinogen whose name Sam couldn't conjure. It was hot and humid. Sweat instantly formed on her brow.

She heard voices in the hallway, terse and clipped. And footfalls, heavy and determined. They'd undoubtedly found the unconscious sentry, probably bleeding out his ear and well on his way to permanent brain damage.

She was running out of time.

She glanced around the backside of the furnace.

Bingo. A small window, chest high, opening to the cool morning air.

She tried the window. Locked, and bolted shut.

Breaking the glass was a bad idea. She didn't want to attract attention. But in the absence of a giant wrench to unscrew the window from its housing, she didn't have much choice. She used the muzzle of her pistol to spider the pane. Then she used her purse to push against it, hoping to flex the window outward, maybe remove the whole thing from its housing without shattering it to pieces.

She failed miserably. The cheap window glass flew everywhere, shattering on the concrete outside. She cursed.

But there was no turning back now. She used her pistol to clear away the shards of glass around the edge of the window frame, leaped up, pulled her body into the opening, and squeezed out of the window. Glass pierced her forearms and midsection as she wriggled free. Her wounded side registered its strident protest. She cursed softly under her breath.

She looked around. Dumpsters, accumulated trash, loose paper, a stray cat or two. Just like alleys the world over.

Sam crept to the corner of the building and paused, fighting to control her breathing, listening intently for signs of motion. She peered around the corner of the building.

Another agent. Tall, short hair, curly wire protruding from an earpiece, handgun drawn, watching the front entrance of the building. His back faced Sam. His head swiveled about, alert and searching.

Sam studied the movement of his head as it scanned back and forth.

Almost.

Not yet.

Now.

When his scan was furthest from her, she darted across the alleyway. She took cover behind an adjacent building, pistol trained at the corner, forcing herself to take deep, quiet breaths.

One minute passed, then two. No one rounded the corner after her.

Sam backed away carefully, making her way along the back wall of the building adjacent to Swaringen's, weapon ready, head on a swivel.

After a brief eternity, a door appeared on her left. To a parking garage.

Sam tried the door. It opened, and she breathed a sigh of relief. She crept inside the garage, searching for a particular kind of vehicle, a late-model domestic, her hand sifting through items in her

Prada bag until it closed around the object she wanted: a universal key fob. Not truly universal, because Homeland had only been able to strong-arm domestic automakers into surrendering entry codes. Foreign manufacturers had told DHS to get stuffed. Hence her search for an American car, which she otherwise wouldn't be caught dead driving.

She sidled up next to a ridiculously large pickup truck and pushed the button on her device. The truck chirped, flashed its lights, unlocked its doors.

Sam looked around, climbed in, pushed the keyless start button, and held her breath. The big diesel engine came to life.

Sam put the truck in gear, drove out of the garage, turned away from Swaringen's building, checked her mirrors.

Safe.

For the moment.

Chapter 41

The Baltimore-Washington Parkway was rarely a pleasant experience. It connected some of the worst sections of DC to some of the worst sections of Baltimore, and it did so via a pothole-riddled span of ancient asphalt that was nothing short of hazardous. There were too few lanes, access was poorly designed, and sharp on-ramps meant merging traffic met the speeding flow at a crawl. The road sucked, and there had been a time when Sam had made a major life decision or two to avoid it.

But today's major life decision had the opposite effect. She found herself stuck in a line of crawling cars.

It was murder on her psyche. She checked the truck's dashboard clock about twice a minute, calculating and recalculating the time it might take for NSA to decrypt the iMessage Dan had sent her, wondering how long it would take the facial recognition algorithms to alert NSA watchers of her whereabouts, wondering whether the truck's rightful owner had yet noticed its absence, and if so, how long it might take for the registration number to show up in the automated license plate monitoring system.

She turned on the hazard lights, moved over onto the left shoulder, and put her foot down, honking intermittently. Half an hour, she estimated, moving at the improved pace available by driving half off the road, barring unforeseen holdups, such as traffic cops and mentally-challenged commuters.

She wanted desperately to confer with Dan, to confirm his understanding of her plan, to iron out the details, to make sure the right people were heading to the right places. She also wanted confirmation of her educated guesses. She felt an acute need for what every field agent craves: sound intelligence and solid backup.

She felt extremely alone. Which was often what she preferred. But today it made her feel naked, exposed, vulnerable. It felt like extreme, raw risk. The kind she'd promised Brock she'd no longer take. The kind she'd decided had no place in her post-death life.

"Hell," she said by way of summary, uncomfortably aware of the storm of butterflies in her stomach, uncomfortably aware that she hadn't worn her bulletproof vest when she left Homeland the previous evening, uncomfortably aware of the seconds ticking away.

Because it really came down to timing. She needed them to decode Dan's message quickly, but not too quickly. She needed them to mount a response, which would take time, but she needed that response to be less than overwhelming, less than insurmountable, which implied less preparation time rather than more.

She needed a little bit of surprise, but not too much.

She also needed them to take the bait.

And she needed to give Dan enough time to get things together on his end.

She looked at the clock again, its inexorable march mocking her, competing factors weighing in her head, a hundred unknowable variables swarming through her calculus like pests, acutely aware that chaos would weigh just as heavily on the outcome as skill, effort, and cunning.

She put a little more pressure on the gas pedal and barreled onward, toward the belly of the beast.

* * *

Preparations were indeed underway. A stern-faced man of stocky build supervised them.

The sun was up. He was unaccustomed to being home during daylight. He normally went to work well before sunrise and returned home well after sunset. Because he believed in what he was doing. Because he did it well. And because it was that important.

And it was under attack, by people who didn't understand what they were doing, who didn't know what was at stake, who weren't qualified to make the kinds of decisions they were trying to make.

His men had established a perimeter. A wall separated the building from the world, and another wall of highly trained, supremely skilled, unquestioningly loyal citizen-soldiers provided further buffer. Half a dozen of them, his on-call rapid response force, with more on the way.

They guarded a residence. His residence.

But on this day, it felt more like a fortress.

There would be no quarter given. It would end today. And things would return to normal. Business as usual.

Because it was a business of supreme importance.

* * *

Sam's mind raced through contingencies as her stolen truck

raced through traffic on Highway 50. The mental exercise was meant to reduce her anxiety, to increase her feeling of preparedness, but it had the opposite effect. Her thoughts blitzed through punches and counterpunches, possibilities and probabilities, scenarios, branches, and sequels. Her stomach knotted tighter with each spin through her possible futures, evidence of the horrendous odds she knew awaited.

But there was no other option.

If she succeeded, she would likely decapitate the beast.

If she failed, they would sense victory. Which would be the mechanism of their defeat.

But only if Dan came through, in either case.

Total victory on one hand.

Pyrrhic victory on the other. The kind of win she probably wouldn't survive.

So events had conspired to re-order her life priorities once again. As in, events had prioritized themselves over her life.

The Powder Mill Road exit snuck up on her. It jolted her from theory to reality, from abstract to in-your-face. A fresh wave of sickening adrenaline landed in her gut.

She steered the giant truck toward the exit, plowing across lanes of traffic frozen in place, earning honks and gestures and curses, which failed to pierce her focus. She made the exit, but barely, and only by driving across the grass.

She turned east. The road took her around a gentle arc to the north, circumscribing Snowden Pond, a mid-level yuppie haven. It was familiar territory. She'd dated a man once who lived here. He was her boss, and he was also married, but it was a long time ago and she wasn't terribly sober or terribly hung up on details. At the time, she'd never have guessed that her lack of judgment and restraint would provide her with critical terrain knowledge for a future op.

Crazy life, she thought idly, rechecking the magazine in her hefty .45, accelerating the big truck around the wide bend. Dense Maryland forest flashed by on either side.

An intersection loomed. Laurel Bowie Road. Getting closer. Her heart beat fast and hard. More butterflies tore up her insides.

She made a cursory check for traffic and careened left, slowing just enough to keep the truck on the pavement. Mostly.

She hammered down on the accelerator, hearing the beastly rattle of the unnecessarily large engine, grateful for the first time in her life that giant penis-extender pickup trucks had become vogue. She was going to need every last pound of steel, and every last pound-foot of torque under the hood.

A church appeared ahead on the right. It had been a signpost in a previous life, a harbinger of forbidden flesh, a reminder that she wasn't living a family values kind of life as she snuck to her boss's house while his wife was away.

Today, the church was again a signpost, but a more pragmatic one. She slowed the truck, peeled her eye for the semi-hidden lane on the left, and turned onto a narrow, winding, brick-lined drive leading up into the forest.

Sam knew the street name. Old Laurel Springfield Road. Where the rich people lived. Big houses, with gates and fences around them, modern nobility, isolated from the hoi polloi, as if the proletarian condition were beyond merely distasteful, but also contagious.

Executives, stock market winners, surgeons, lawyers.

And tyrants.

She had memorized the house number, but just as she expected, it wasn't necessary. Because this particular tyrant's fortress was surrounded by eager young men with guns and training and a keen desire to use both.

She drove at a normal speed up the lane, until she was just a hundred yards from her target's front gate, which was tall and iron and undoubtedly expensive, but insufficient to the task ahead.

Sam matted the accelerator and reefed the hulking behemoth hard to the left, ignoring the shouts of the agents flanking the drive, aligning the nose of the truck with the center of the gate, where the two pieces swung together and latched.

She tensed her body, braced for impact.

It was anticlimactic. The gates exploded from their hinges, no match for the giant stolen man-toy.

But Sam wasn't finished. She had no intention of ringing the doorbell. She kept the accelerator on the floor, searched for a weak spot in the structure, cursed its solid stone construction. She steered toward an oversized bay window, flanked by roof-high evergreens, hoping she'd picked up enough speed, hoping the impact wouldn't kill her.

She held her breath and closed her eyes.

Then the world exploded.

Chapter 42

Sam smelled pulverized rock, drywall powder, and sawdust. She had a metallic taste in her mouth. Blood. From her lip, split open by the air bag. The big diesel engine still banged away, unfazed by the calamity that had befallen the grille, now a rumpled mess of twisted metal.

Shouts sounded over the idling engine.

Sam snapped to her senses. She scanned frantically for her Kimber. On the floor, over on the passenger side. She twisted her head to see out the back of the truck. The two agents at the gate were charging across the lawn, pistols drawn, yelling commands.

She cursed. No time to fetch her pistol from the floor. The stopping power of the big handgun would have been extremely handy.

She reached down, lifted her right pant leg, slipped her hand inside her sock, and retrieved the Walther PPK she'd borrowed from the young man whose skull she'd cracked earlier in the morning. Her thumb found the safety lever, and her finger found the trigger.

Then she unlatched her seat belt, slumped her chin onto her chest, and played dead.

The first guard approached, gun drawn, barking at her to exit the vehicle with her hands up, or something similarly asinine.

Sam didn't move.

The guard shouted some more.

Sam waited.

More shouting. Exasperation and waning patience were evident in the man's tone. Which was perfect.

He shattered the driver's side window with the butt of his pistol.

Sam waited for the glass to stop flying.

Then she flung her body away from the window, flattened herself onto the wide bench seat, twisted her torso to free the pistol in her right hand, and shot the man in the face.

One down.

The second guy fired indiscriminately into the cab, running forward toward the open window.

Sam rolled her body onto the floor, twisted onto her back, and curled into a tight somersault, coming to rest on her knees on the floorboard in front of the passenger seat. Her hands slapped at the mat, searching.

Her left hand found it. Her fingers closed around the grip. She felt its gorgeous weight as she lifted it, aimed it toward the sound of the guard's gunfire. How many rounds had he shot? She hadn't been counting.

Silence. The man stopped shooting.

Sam heard the click of a magazine release, then the clatter of an empty clip hitting the ground.

Dumbass.

She rose, aimed, and fired.

She wasn't a great left-handed shot, but she wasn't terrible, either. A nontrivial portion of the man's head disappeared in a cloud of red mist.

Sam twisted, pulled the passenger door latch, kicked open the door, and burst through the opening. She rolled through the debris on the floor and came to a halt in a crouch, pistol ready, in the middle of a posh dining room.

The stolen pickup truck had made it halfway inside.

A number of guards had evidently made it all the way inside. Because Sam found herself staring down the barrels of several assault rifles.

Four of them.

Balls.

She dropped her pistol and raised her hands.

A deep, authoritative voice broke the uneasy silence. "Jesus Christ, have you become a pain in my ass."

Sam regarded the man as she rose to her feet. Large, powerfully built, florid face, fat gut, late fifties or early sixties.

"Deputy Director Clark Barter, I presume," she said. "Sorry to barge in on you like this."

* * *

Barter raised his pistol. It was an old .38 Special, a dual-action revolver, all brute force and gleaming metal. Plenty of charge behind the slug. Tough to survive if it hit near anything important.

"Think it through, Clark," Sam said, her voice cool and low, which she found a pleasant surprise under the circumstances.

The race had ended. She had gotten there in time, before NSA could mount a serious response.

Now it was time to slow things down. Because now it was a waiting game.

"Right now it's just my word against yours," Sam said. "One fed against another. Nothing to get all bent out of shape over. A beef like this might never even see the light of day."

Barter cocked the hammer and brought the sight to his eye. She saw the dark abyss inside the barrel of his gun, and a darker abyss in his eyes. He clearly had it in his mind to shoot her in the face.

"But if you kill me," she went on, "then it becomes something different." She motioned to the guards — hard and lean and out of breath from their dash inside — and counted them off on her fingers. "One, two, three, four of them, Clark. Four witnesses."

Barter chuckled, derision on his face. "You have no idea what you've stepped in."

Sam smiled. "I've been hearing that a lot lately. Maybe you'd care to explain."

Barter's face hardened. "I would not," he said. Sam saw his index finger whiten between the second and third knuckles. He was applying pressure to the trigger.

Sam noticed something else. Something important. Critical, maybe, depending on which way things went.

Her next words had every possibility of being her last.

"You're aiming in the wrong place, Clark," she said.

Barter looked confused.

"You're too far away to risk a head shot," Sam said. "Especially with that old thing. Stubby little barrel like that, heavy trigger, you'd be lucky to hit the wall behind me."

Barter's eyes narrowed.

"And when's the last time you practiced?" Sam asked. "Perishable skill, you know."

Barter bared his teeth in something that bore no resemblance to a smile. "Thank you," he said with exaggerated courtesy. "I see the error of my ways." He moved the barrel downward, pointed it at the center of her chest.

Sam's heart pounded. Her knees felt weak. Her hands shook a little. She hoped no one noticed. "That's better, Clark," she said, surprised again at how calm her voice sounded. "But there's still that tiny little problem."

Barter's eyebrows raised in mock curiosity.

"Of murdering a federal agent in front of four witnesses. Four witnesses who are also military servicemen, no less. Subject to a court martial. Am I right?"

Barter sneered. "These men know their duty," he said, tossing his head toward the guards.

Which told Sam something. It told her that her hunch was right, about his ego. He would rather make a point than make a move.

"Let me guess," she said. "To support and defend the Constitution?"

Barter didn't reply.

"Against all enemies…" Sam prodded.

Barter was silent.

"Against all enemies…" Sam said again.

Barter said nothing.

"Foreign, and…"

"And fucking domestic, Goddammit!"

A small smile found its way to Sam's lips. A line had been crossed. It was as much of a mea culpa as she'd ever need.

She looked at his face. Red, flushed cheeks, eyes narrowed, mouth set with renewed resolve.

"Foreign and domestic," Sam repeated slowly. "I'm curious. Which category was Janice Everman?"

A quizzical look crossed Barter's face, but just for a fraction of a second. It evaporated, leaving anger and hardness in its wake.

Sam turned to the nearest guard. "Your boss ordered a hit on a federal employee," she said in a stage whisper.

The guard's eyes darted between Sam and Barter. Sam saw uncertainty in his eyes. Which was important. It meant that the men guarding Barter's house were mere watch dogs, not privy to the dirtier truths, not trusted to perform the assassinations Barter had ordered.

"You're misinformed, I'm afraid," Barter said, menace in his voice.

"Really?" Sam asked, affected surprise on her face. "So Janice Everman didn't oppose your little operation? Threaten to voice her opinion to Congress, out in the open where all the liberals and appeasers and pussies would get their panties all bunched up? Maybe shut down your private little war?"

"You have no idea what you're talking about," Barter hissed.

Sam turned to the guard again. "He's probably right," she said.

"I probably just showed up here on a hunch. And you guys just happened to be standing guard in the street. Makes perfect sense."

Confusion registered on the guard's face. Which was progress.

Barter shifted his weight, re-gripped the pistol, steeled himself. "You have no idea what's at stake here," he growled.

Sam ignored him. "And there's probably no backup on the way," she said, still talking to the guard. "Just little old me, alone in the big bad world. Completely at your mercy."

"Shut your goddamned mouth!" Barter roared.

Silence followed.

Then Sam laughed. She looked back at Barter. "No sense getting riled up, Clark. You're the one with the gun. You even have it aimed at the right spot now. Fire away."

He shook his head. "You have no idea the damage you're causing."

Sam smiled. She was staring at the business end of a lot of firepower, but she was winning. Because Barter was talking instead of shooting.

"Maybe you're right, Clark. Maybe I have no idea what's going on. But I bet Jonathan France did. And David Swaringen, too."

"Where the *fuck* do you get off, accusing *me*?" Barter shouted.

Sam chuckled. Cornering egos was always entertaining. They followed a predictable script. Bluff, bluster, deny, make counter-accusations. So far, Barter was hitting all the notes.

Which was a good thing. Because she was betting her life.

"Maybe they got cold feet," she said. "Or maybe you were

afraid they might let something slip. Loose ends."

Barter eyed her. The pistol shook in his grip. Just a little bit. But every little bit helped. He tightened his finger around the trigger.

"Did you notice anything?" she asked the guard in her stage whisper, her eyes still locked on Barter's. "No surprise on your boss's face. None whatsoever. Those two men died just a few hours ago. I don't think their families have even been notified yet. But your boss already knew about it."

The guard's eyes shot to Barter's face.

Barter's finger tightened on the trigger.

Sam noticed something, the same detail about Barter's grip she had seen earlier. Seeing it once was encouraging, but it wasn't a reliable indicator. Maybe it was something, or maybe it was nothing at all.

But twice was a pattern.

"I get it," Sam said, calmness in her voice, gently taking control of the conversation. "Sometimes the enemies aren't foreign. Right, Clark?"

Barter didn't reply.

"Sometimes they're domestic. Right here among us. Driving on our streets, shopping in our stores, plotting against us, ready to strap a bomb to their chests. Right?"

Barter's face tightened. "What the hell would you know about it?"

"You might be surprised."

"It takes courage to deal with this kind of threat," Barter said. "Resolve. Commitment. Courage."

Sam got the sense he was talking to his guards, reassuring them, restoring their confidence. Shoring up his flanks.

Maybe reassuring himself, too.

"Courage?" Sam asked. "What would a guy like you know about courage?"

Barter's face reddened. His fingers flexed around his gun.

His eyes drifted to something behind her. They focused there. Studied something.

"It's easy to play God," Sam pressed, "jerking off behind a desk in some office."

Barter's eyes didn't move. They stayed fixed on the wall behind her, looking at something, taking in its details.

"Maybe you can order death like something off a menu," she said. "But do you have the stones to do it yourself?"

Barter didn't move. Neither did his eyes. They stayed fixed, far away but focused.

Sam turned her head to follow them, all the way around to the far wall, directly behind her.

And it suddenly became clear.

She wasn't fighting wayward ideology. She wasn't up against some zealot who'd wandered off the reservation.

She was up against a man who was sickened, hobbled, crippled by wounds that would never heal.

And she wasn't going to win.

On the wall was a portrait of a young man. An American soldier, standing in the desert sunlight, wearing Kevlar and a full beard, brandishing a camouflaged carbine, wearing sunglasses and a smile too old for his years, weariness and wariness in his stance.

And an American flag, folded in the shape of a triangle, ensconced behind glass and oak in a display case, white stars against a blue background. It had last been unfurled when it was draped across the young man's casket. Sam was sure of it.

It was over. Sam had guessed wrong. She had gambled and lost.

Because Barter had no limits.

Because he had nothing left to lose.

She looked back at him, at his eyes.

They returned to her. Calmness settled over him. And certainty. A sort of transcendent peace softened his face as he met her gaze.

He pulled the trigger.

Chapter 43

There was no time for thought. Sam's subconscious mind moved her body before her frontal cortex even knew why.

And it moved her in the proper direction.

To her right.

To Barter's left.

Opposite the direction he pulled the barrel of the stubby little revolver, every time he applied pressure to the trigger.

Once, you couldn't be sure. But twice was a pattern.

And the third time was for all the marbles.

Sam had been wrong about Barter. But she was right about his trigger finger. It's what saved her life.

The big, angry slug grazed the flesh of her left arm as she dove to the right.

Then chaos.

The guards' uncertainty bought her a precious second. She hit the ground, skidded across the floor to the nearest guard's feet, rolled onto her back, and scissored her legs around his arms. She arched her back, crossed her ankles together for leverage, extended her hips, twisted. Her legs met resistance, which gave way in a sudden, sickening crunch as she dislocated the man's elbow.

He howled. His weapon fell from his hands and dangled from the strap around his neck.

She twisted harder, pressing her palms into the floor, sliding her torso into his lower legs, curling him in on himself, bringing him down to the floor.

He fell on her. She grabbed his torso and rolled beneath him.

His body absorbed the first volley of shots. Some impacted his bulletproof vest. Others definitely did not. She heard his breath leave in a gasp, and heard a nauseating, familiar gurgling.

She ripped the rifle from around his neck and wrapped him in an embrace, her hands clasped around the rifle, behind the dying man's back. She released the safety and fired unaimed bursts in the vicinity of the other three guards.

She got lucky. One screamed. His knee exploded, and his leg folded the wrong way. He fell to the floor.

Sam aimed at a moving shadow, her arms still gripping the rifle around the torso of the dying guard, her human shield.

She squeezed the trigger. Miss.

The lame guard rolled toward her. He raised his weapon. Flame spat from the muzzle. Sam retreated beneath her human shield, felt the rounds impact his torso.

She aimed again, held her breath, pulled the trigger, hit the lame guard in the upper thigh.

A fountain of blood gushed from the new wound. Femoral artery. Certain death. But not fast enough, under the circumstances. Sam finished him with a burst to his head.

Two down.

Motion caught her eye. Barter, lumbering from the room, his large frame disappearing down a hallway.

More gunfire. Rounds peppered the hardwood floor beyond Sam's head, walked their way back toward her. She slid beneath the dead guard and held her breath.

The dead man's head exploded just inches from her face. With surreal clarity, she saw it stretch, expand, deform, shatter as a 5.56mm NATO round tore its way through his skull. Blood and brains and bone and gore splattered her face, filled her mouth and nostrils. She howled and spat in fear and disgust, threw her body out from underneath the corpse with panicked abandon, scrambled away, slipped and fell on the blood-soaked gore.

Which saved her life again. An angry squadron of hot, supersonic slugs tore above her, through the space she'd just occupied.

She rolled toward the gunshots, squeezed the trigger, eyes still blinded by shards of the dead man's face. She wiped her face with her sleeve, aimed, fired again.

And hit. A third man, short and wiry, dropped to the floor, clutching desperately at his throat, suffering unspeakable agony. Sam squeezed the trigger again and put him out of his misery.

Three down.

Silence.

There might have been footsteps upstairs, heavy and hurried, reverberating through the floorboards beneath her.

Or not.

Sam couldn't be sure either way. She heard nothing but the ringing in her ears.

She rose, took stock. No wounds, as far as she could tell,

which was less of a miracle than it seemed. A firefight was much different than a leisurely day at the firing range, and missing your target was a lot more common than hitting, especially if you were green and untested. Like Barter's guards.

Three of them lay dead on the floor, leaking goop and fluid.

Two more lay dead outside, next to the truck.

Which left one guard, by Sam's count. And Clark Barter.

She heard motion upstairs. This time, it was unambiguous. Like someone was moving furniture around. Which they probably were.

But Sam took no chances. She took her time clearing the bottom floor, heart still pounding, senses still on high alert despite her growing nausea, caused by the stench of blood and guts turning to paste all over her head and torso.

It had been a race, and then a waiting game, and now it was a race again. She needed to clear the house before Barter's reinforcements arrived. They'd take one look at the scene and decide to shoot first and ask questions later.

She needed Dan to hurry the hell up. She was beginning to wonder if he was coming, if he was bringing help. And she had no way to get in touch with him.

Which left her in an absurd position. Her own Little Bighorn. Waterloo, maybe. About to be surrounded and grossly outnumbered, unless things broke just right.

She wished she was a bigger believer in teamwork, because it would have given her a bit more hope.

She checked the magazine in the assault rifle she'd stolen from her human shield. She counted six rounds left. Six singles, or two bursts of three. She selected singles and started up the stairs.

It was a wide staircase, with a landing halfway up. Sam cursed beneath her breath. The geometry meant that she would be exposed long before she was in any position to return fire.

She laid down on the stairs. She climbed slowly, feet, knees, elbows, one step at a time, stopping to look and listen with each step.

She made it to the landing.

She could go no further. It felt too exposed. Too foolhardy. Like a great way to die.

She retreated back down.

And stopped dead in her tracks. Voices. Coming from outside. And car engines. And the unmistakable sound of ammunition slamming into place in large-caliber weapons.

Barter's reinforcements.

Or hers.

Or someone had called the cops, and a SWAT team had shown up.

Or the FBI.

Too many possibilities. Lots of ways to make a wrong decision. Too hard to make a right one. If it was Barter's thug brigade assembling out in front, peeking through a window would be a quick ticket to martyrdom.

She hesitated. No good decision presented itself. She was trapped. More than a little bit screwed.

Then she heard more voices. They came from upstairs this time, muffled, sealed off, far away.

Not near the stairs.

Sam made up her mind.

* * *

Sam walked quietly up the stairs and peered around the corner into the long, wide hallway. Every doorway was open, except for the one at the far end of the hall.

Sam tiptoed toward the closed door.

She paused to check each opening along the way.

Empty.

Until the last open doorway. Which was where she found the muzzle of an assault rifle, and guard number four, young and inexperienced and obviously shaken.

"It's over," he said, trying to sound brave. "They're here. They're getting ready to come inside."

Sam felt weariness. And defeat. "Where's Barter?"

The guard didn't respond, but his eyes betrayed him. They snapped to the closed bedroom door.

"You don't have to do this," she said, grateful again that Barter's troops were untested and unseasoned. The guard should have shot her, no questions asked. Instead, he was letting her make small talk.

The foot soldier shook his head. "Yes, I do."

"There's still time. I can help you."

The guard chortled, bitterness on his face. "I don't think you can."

"Last chance," Sam said.

She saw hesitation in his eyes, but it passed. "I don't think so," he said.

Sam shrugged. "Have it your way."

Her foot moved with lightning speed. It traveled from the floor in a blur. It crashed into the guard's balls, arriving with all sorts of energy, sounding alarms and triggering ancient biological failsafes. He collapsed to the floor, in too much pain to scream.

Sam smashed the butt of her rifle against the back of his head. And once more. And again, for good measure, because a man who'd just received a devastating kick to the stones was not apt to negotiate when he regained his senses.

She took a deep breath.

No time to screw around.

On to Barter.

She faced the closed door, backed away five paces, tightened her grip on the rifle, and charged.

She slammed her heel into the door, just inside the doorknob.

The jamb shattered.

The door flew inward, crashed into the wall, and rebounded. The chair Barter had shoved beneath the doorknob skittered across the carpet.

Sam didn't pause. She charged into the room, rolled, flattened, and came to rest in the prone firing position, rifle trained on Clark Barter's chest.

He was seated, back against the wall, legs straight out, pistol raised.

"I'm sorry for your loss," Sam said.

"Fuck you."

"You were right. I have no idea. No clue what that must be like."

Barter stared, silent.

"I imagine it's the worst thing a man can live through. Losing a son."

He blinked, started to speak, then changed his mind.

"No need for it to end badly," Sam said. "Sure, you could pull the trigger. But then what? What's your next move?"

Barter said nothing.

"You could have your troops swarming all over your front lawn right now, and it wouldn't matter. Because I'm not here alone," Sam said. "No matter how many men you brought, it won't be enough."

And she desperately hoped it was true.

Barter shook his head. "You're jeopardizing lives," he said.

"And you're taking lives. And keeping secrets from the people you're spying on, the ones you're supposed to be protecting. Who's more wrong?"

"You don't understand," Barter said. "You have no idea what needs to be done, what it takes to keep this country safe."

Sam pondered, keeping Barter's heart in her sights, up and left a little bit from dead center.

"Maybe that's true," she finally said. "But what kind of nation do you want it to be when you're done saving it?"

Barter shook his head, a response on his lips. But he didn't speak it. Because he heard something.

Sam heard it, too.

A deep, throbbing, wall-shaking thrum. Rattling doors, windows, rafters, teeth, and innards.

Rotor blades, pounding the air into submission. A helicopter, and not a small one. Close by. Dangerously, terrifyingly loud.

And another, on the opposite side of the house.

They grew louder until the noise was impossibly intense, their deep throb vibrating every cell in Sam's body. The walls thumped and flexed against the onslaught.

More NSA muscle?

Did Barter have access to military hardware?

Had he ordered air support?

Or was it Dan, maybe with Homeland's hostage rescue team?

Or someone else, maybe? FBI? Metro PD? The TV news gawkers?

Sam had no idea. But she didn't like the development. Lots of ways for the situation to turn plaid.

She shifted her focus from his chest to his face. What she saw there surprised her.

Uncertainty.

Fear.

Then she understood.

Barter didn't know whose choppers were hovering over his house, either.

But he knew whose helicopters they weren't.

They weren't his.

She watched his eyes. Turmoil, weight, and sadness registered, but only for a moment. Then clarity and focus returned.

And peace.

"May you have the will to do what needs doing, Ms. Jameson," he said.

Which were his last words.

He raised the old revolver to his temple and squeezed the trigger.

Epilogue

In the end, Nero Jefferson Chiligiris remained a guest of the Department of Homeland Security for seventeen weeks.

It wasn't the dead drops that got him captured.

It was the drones. The little ones, bird-sized, powered by a little hobby motor. Made by the thousands in a factory in Ohio. Deployed everywhere the Stars and Stripes waved, and many places it didn't.

He wasn't allowed a telephone call until the middle of the third month. By then, Penny wasn't interested in accepting telephone calls from Nero. Nero wasn't even sure whether Penny still lived at their address. He'd had no contact with her since that fateful day near the Kansas border.

His next telephone call had been to a lawyer. Not one he knew, because Nero wasn't the kind of guy who knew any lawyers. He picked one out of the phone book.

Nero didn't exactly have orthodox legal needs. There wasn't much precedent for fighting terrorism charges in New America, where you're guilty because someone thought you might be, and case closed, so Nero's guy was grossly under-qualified. But together, Nero and his overmatched lawyer put up a good fight. They filed motions, petitioned courts, wrote letters, contacted news agencies.

Nero wasn't squeaky clean, with jail time in his background

and a long list of questionable associates, and that made it much more difficult to garner sympathy. But he and his lawyer hammered away at the civil rights issues, which were many and egregious. The lawyer gave an earful to anyone and everyone who would listen, and many who wouldn't. A US citizen was detained at gunpoint, he would howl in a nasal voice. Charged with no crimes, presented with no evidence against him, afforded no opportunity to defend himself, given no chance to secure legal counsel, and thrown in jail without recourse for a permanently damaging length of time.

It was the kind of thing that happened in third-world dictatorships, in old Iron Curtain countries, in Vladimir Putin's New Soviet Union, the lawyer said. It wasn't the kind of thing that was supposed to happen in America. You weren't supposed to have your life ruined by the feds without a damn good reason.

The Department of Homeland Security, of course, believed they had a damn good reason. They believed Nero's association with the man known on the street as Money was evidence enough that Nero was a terrorist.

It didn't come out until later that Money was not, in fact, a terrorist. Money was a thief. He stole cell phones. Rather, he worked in the upper-middle layer of an organization full of petty thieves who stole cell phones. Money was the wholesaler. The guy near the top, moving volume.

As such, Money had particular needs, such as a need for firearms without serial numbers or paper trails, storage for large quantities of cash, and a plausible, legal fence to launder that cash.

That, evidently, was where Nero had come in. Nero's courier

duties had facilitated the logistical operations necessary for Money's enterprise.

So how had Money ended up on the terror watch list? It was an answer that Nero never obtained. But it wasn't too difficult to imagine what kind of needs a terror cell might have. Clandestine communication was chief among them. The feds had grown wise to the use of internet chat rooms, and there wasn't a telecommunications company on earth that wasn't in bed with the US security apparatus, either by choice or by force, so it was difficult for Ahmed the Asshole to make calls on his personal cell phone to his asshole friends to iron out the details of a terror attack.

So maybe one of Money's clients had harbored Islamist sympathies. Maybe Money had inadvertently sold stolen cell phones to a terrorist. Maybe more than once. Occupational hazard. Doing business on the shady side of the line attracted shady people. Not all of them were mere petty criminals. Odds were good that at least a few of them were ideologues. Zealots. Religious criminals.

None of it mattered in the end, other than as an idle curiosity. Because Nero's life, such as it was, had been thoroughly devastated.

It wasn't Nero's lawyer who had ultimately secured his freedom. It was a high-profile scandal that had done the trick. One federal agency had evidently started a shootout with another federal agency. The left hand had gone to war with the right hand. One police-state juggernaut started duking it out with a rival bureaucracy. It made headlines the world over.

Heads were evidently rolling. The President of the United States claimed ignorance, then claimed a national security prerogative. Flip-flopper, the press wailed.

The American Civil Liberties Union crawled so far up the federal government's backside that the security agencies had no choice but to demonstrate some degree of reform.

Not because it was the right thing to do. Merely because it was what had to be done for those in power to remain in power. Because the big companies with deep pockets who owned the politicians could not afford to support liberty-trashing fascist warmongers, which was one of the catchier euphemisms to find its way into print. Corporations threatened to pull their campaign donations. And without corporate cash, the Washington illuminati had nothing. They couldn't buy votes by themselves. Too damn expensive.

The whole thing went down remarkably quickly, particularly by Washington standards. Senators began losing donations, which meant that telephones lit up like Christmas trees at Homeland, NSA, FBI, CIA, DIA, and any other federal agency that even remotely smelled like a surveillance apparatus.

The heads of all of those agencies served at the pleasure of the President of the United States. And the President had become increasingly displeased. A flurry of mea culpas and resignations ensued.

The press caught on to stories like Nero's, of lives shattered without the benefit of due process. Even more egregious episodes eventually came to light. American paramilitary teams had assaulted, shot, and killed dozens of American citizens. Judge, jury, and executioner. Not the kind of thing the public was willing to tolerate from the nation's powerful, secretive intelligence giants.

One man had come to symbolize the degree to which America had become a rogue state. That man's name was Clark Barter.

He had been an enthusiastic participant, a zealous ringleader, some said. He was guilty as hell, they claimed. And he was also dead, which made him a perfect scapegoat. Duplicitous politicians joined the Barter-bashing, desperate to distance themselves from the crisis. His suicide was evidence of his guilt, they said, though deep down they thanked Barter for making the ultimate sacrifice for his nation. It allowed them to preserve the lie just a little longer. Agitators and watchdogs gradually shifted their howls from "rogue nation" to "rogue agency" to "rogue actor."

And life went on.

But not completely as before. Operation Penumbra ceased to exist.

The blatant self-interest at play in the aftermath of the scandal worked in Nero's favor. Cell doors sprung wide open in federal detention facilities all across the globe. Nero's cell door was one of them.

But when Nero finally stepped back into daylight, it was to face a painfully uncertain future.

He arranged transportation to the home he and Penny had shared for years with their kids.

There were no cars parked in the drive. Nobody answered the door. There was no furniture in the house.

Only silence greeted him.

The helicopters over Clark Barter's house had indeed belonged to Homeland. They were the cavalry, and they arrived just in time to save the day, thanks once again to Dan Gable's brains and balls. They rounded up the sparse NSA reinforcements on Barter's front lawn.

When she emerged from Barter's house, shaken and bloody, Sam gave Dan the grateful hug he richly deserved.

Homeland also rounded up the rest of Barter's men, who were nabbed as they waited outside Mark Severn's house. Severn wasn't home. He was with Dan. But the NSA goons didn't know that, because Sam's ruse had worked. And it had saved her life.

The dust eventually settled, but not in a completely satisfying way. In keeping with the grand American tradition of punishing the lowest-ranking asshole available, Clark Barter's foot soldiers, all military members detailed for special duty, were placed on trial. Many were convicted. Several became destined to die in prison.

Carl Ivan Edgar Frankel, semi-retired CIA assassin, remained a free man. No evidence.

Sam faced mountains of paperwork, tedious after-action interviews, and stressful administrative reviews at the hands of hindsight heroes who had long ago gone soft in the middle. But she endured it all with uncharacteristic good humor, because it felt good to be alive, and it felt good to be home with Brock. She cleared everything off her plate at work, and showed up only when required. She and Brock spent the extra time joined at the pelvis.

They also booked vacation time and airline tickets. To the Caribbean. Europe could wait, maybe until a few of the nightmares about men with Slavic cheekbones lost their intensity.

The real, ugly, nearly-unbearable truth about Operation Penumbra came out over time. Sam was appalled at the details, as was the rest of the human population.

She watched in cynical amusement as the administration's movers and shakers shimmied and shuffled away from the radioactive calamity NSA had wrought.

There was even talk of abolishing the NSA altogether. Sam wasn't sure it was such a bad idea, all things considered.

But she knew NSA was the scapegoat. Sure, they were bald-faced tyrants, but they weren't operating in a vacuum. Odds were better than even that the President of the United States had authorized the whole operation. The big man himself had ordered the assassination of at least one American citizen without trial or tribunal. What would stop him from scaling up? And Sam knew from Janice Everman's calendar at Justice that the president's chief of staff knew all about Penumbra. It was a smoking gun, but it would never see the light of day.

And all indications were that the president stood a solid chance of reelection.

Which was disheartening. Because her calling was to rid the world of the bastards, to make things a little bit less unbearable for the weak and powerless. But what kind of dent could she really make, when the biggest bastards ran the whole damn world?

The futility got to her. She considered leaving Homeland. She discussed it with Brock, and together they debated, vacillated, calculated, raged, furied, fumed, wavered. They decided, undecided, then re-decided. They talked late into the night, many nights in a row.

And ultimately, she stayed.

Because the one battle you should never fight is the battle against yourself.

What's next?

Get Lars' **#1 Bestseller,**

DEVOLUTION

What readers say:

"**The best writing in decades. Move over, Lee Child.**"

"**Some of the best action and spy thriller fiction you will ever read.**"

"**Right up there with Patterson, Baldacci, Forsyth, and DeMille.**"

"**The best thriller I've ever read.**"

"**LOVE LOVE LOVE this series!**"

Become part of Lars Emmerich's book launch team

WANT TO GET A **free** advanced e-copy of every new thriller Amazon #1 Bestselling Author Lars Emmerich releases?

Just visit www.larsemmerichbooks.com/landingpage/launch-team/.

Books by Amazon #1 Bestselling Author Lars Emmerich

The Incident: Inferno Rising

The Incident: Reckoning

Fallout

Descent

Devolution

Meltdown

Mindscrew

Blowback

Excerpt from #1 Bestseller DEVOLUTION

Prologue

Crystal City, Virginia. Wednesday, 3:47 p.m. ET.

A gloved hand pressed hard against the priest's mouth and nose. He felt a fast tearing sensation rip across his neck. Jets of deep crimson flew in front of his face as his own blood splattered to the floor.

His vision began to dim. He didn't feel his knees buckle, but felt the cold tile flatten his cheek as his face hit the floor. Shallow, frantic breaths caused ripples in the growing pool of red.

It was over in a few seconds.

The killer watched as the priest exhaled his last breath. *Vaya con Dios, Monsignor.*

* * *

A phone rang on Capitol Hill. Senator Frank Higgs picked up the receiver.

"Curmudgeon has been retired," said the disembodied voice on the other end of the line.

Senator Higgs was struck dumb. "What?"

Silence.

"*Retired*? How? Who?"

"You know better than to ask. The usual time and place, please. No mistakes."

The dial tone interrupted Higgs's reply.

* * *

Somewhere north of Las Vegas, Nevada. Wednesday, 10:58 p.m. PT.

"Clear the line!" the laboratory safety chief bellowed with far more force than necessary. His amplified voice exploded from a dozen loudspeakers spaced out over the eight-mile expanse of the Nevada desert.

With the exception of the fifteen officials and technicians gathered in the control room with the safety officer, no one heard the announcement. The weapons test range was in one of the most desolate locations in the United States, and every person involved in the test that evening had gathered in the control room to either conduct or witness the event.

Large high-definition monitors displayed infrared, ultraviolet, and low-light versions of the same image. An automobile, parked out in the middle of nowhere, engine idling.

Sensitive to temperature differences, the infrared images clearly showed the exhaust escaping from the tailpipe and the deep red outline of the engine, warm and idling.

Next to the sedan was a table, which looked exceptionally out of place in the middle of the desert. On the table's surface were four television sets, arranged in a line from front to back. All four television sets were on, with images flashing in the darkness.

"Let's zoom in on the engine compartment." Art Levitow's basso resonated in the small room over the hum of machinery. As the director of Senior Quantum, an unacknowledged government program that had consumed just shy of three billion dollars over the past seven years, Levitow's was a voice that commanded respect. His deft political leadership was matched by equally impressive technical and scientific credibility. Despite the stakes, he wasn't nervous in the least.

The same couldn't be said for the technician operating the cameras, whose initial attempt to zoom in on the car's engine compartment resulted in a close-up of the desert floor.

The Vice President of the United States chuckled. "Now you look like me, hunting geese."

Secretary of Defense Bill Pomerantine grinned. "No, sir, that's not quite true. He's still aiming in the right county."

Vice President Arquist's chuckle turned into a good-natured laugh. "Bill, if you keep that up, you may be the first man in history to go from Secretary of Defense to coffee barista in a single night."

Laughter tittered through the room as the technician slewed the cameras in the target area over the engine compartment of the late-model sedan.

"Let's expand out just a little bit. I'd like Vice President Arquist to see the dashboard electronics as well." The camera operator zoomed out slightly in response to Levitow's request.

Levitow continued. "Mr. Vice President, as you know, three years ago we made the breakthrough that enabled us to reliably and consistently demonstrate the fundamental physics, but the major technical hurdle has been to project and localize the effects. In other words, we had to figure out how to shoot the beam, and how to aim the shot. That problem has consumed the bulk of our effort, and it didn't go as smoothly as we had hoped. But we've figured out how to do it."

Arquist smiled. "I was relieved when Bill told me the news, and the president insisted I go see for myself."

"We think you'll like what we've put together, sir. Keep your eye on the engine compartment, and we'll begin the demonstration. Go ahead, Amber."

An attractive technician moved a mouse pointer over an icon, clicked the button, and answered "OK" at the warning that popped up. The lights dimmed in the control room, and a deep, throbbing hum rose above the usual computer noise.

Ten meters to the south of the control center, in a drab two-story concrete structure surrounded by concertina wire, an electric current began to flow through large coils of copper wire. The coils were attached to a circular array of six small dish-shaped antennae, all aimed in the same direction, parallel with the desert floor. The air around the antennae crackled for a brief second, and had anyone been in the vicinity of the apparatus, they would undoubtedly have noticed the unmistakable odor of ozone in the air.

"Keep your eye on the infrared monitor," Levitow instructed. The small crowd in the control room saw numerous bright spots appear inside the sedan's engine compartment and dashboard. A bright flash also appeared on the ultraviolet display monitor, adjacent to the infrared monitor. The flash dissipated in less than a second.

Seven miles away, the idling vehicle suddenly stopped.

"Mr. Vice President, you'll notice that the exhaust is no longer coming out the tailpipe, and no lights are on inside the car. We've completely disabled the vehicle. Despite the brief infrared and ultraviolet emission, there is no fire or other noticeable physical damage."

Arquist raised his eyebrows and let out a low whistle. "I'll take a thousand of 'em."

"We're not finished yet. Amber, let's move on to the second part of the demonstration."

The technician's mouse raced across several screens, and a crosshairs appeared on the main display. The cameras showed a grainy picture of the four television sets, all arranged in a row, one behind the other. All four flat screen televisions were powered on. The technician slewed the crosshairs, and they came to rest on the third television from the front.

Levitow continued his narration. "No sports addict would ever arrange his televisions this way, with three TVs hidden behind the front one, but we've set things up to show you just how precisely we've been able to refine the targeting solution. Keep your eye on the third television screen in line from the front. We're going to pass the beams through the first two televisions without any effect whatsoever, disable the third TV, and leave the fourth one completely alone. Go ahead, Amber."

Two clicks later, the third television began to glow and spark on the infrared camera. A brief, bright light flashed again on the ultraviolet display, and the visible spectrum monitor confirmed that the third TV went dark. The adjacent televisions droned on, completely unaffected by the weapon.

Arquist turned to the Secretary of Defense with a smile. "I like your new toy, Bill. When's Christmas?"

"We think we'll be ready for Santa's sleigh by October of this year."

"Good. Don't get behind. I think you're all probably aware that there's a great deal riding on this program." Vice President Arquist rose and extended his hand to Levitow. "Damn fine work, Art. Thank you."

* * *

Vice President Arquist motioned for Levitow to join himself and Secretary Bill Pomerantine on their long walk through the weapons-testing bunker, back to the waiting helicopter that would take the two officials and their Secret Service agents to the relative civilization of Las Vegas.

Arquist spoke over the click of heels on concrete. "As you know, Art, there is no shortage of naysayers. Now that you've shown me the magic, I want you to help me understand how it works. I've got to put my salesman hat on when I get back to DC, and I want to be able to explain just a little about what the hell this thing does."

Levitow's eyes sparkled. Arquist was reminded that despite his cold administrative efficiency, Senior Quantum's director was a scientist and academic at heart. He felt himself responding to Levitow's genuine enthusiasm for the minor miracles the team had pulled off.

"When you boil the geekery down, it's really fairly simple," Levitow said. "Electrons are lazy. Inside an atom, they hang out in the lowest energy state possible. It takes energy to move away from the atom's nucleus, and like my teenager, electrons need a very good reason to expend any energy at all…"

* * *

At the tail end of the small entourage, a large, fair-skinned and blue-eyed Secret Service agent, known as Whitey in the most important circle, extended two fingers on his right hand. Pinched between them was a small piece of paper. As his right arm swung forward on the next step, a tall, lanky scientist named Jonathan Cooper surreptitiously retrieved the piece of paper from the Secret Service agent.

Then, while his right hand scratched his nose, Cooper's left hand deftly placed the small strip of paper into his lab coat pocket.

The exchange had been carefully planned so that Whitey's bulk blocked the nearest security camera's view. The next-nearest camera, at the far end of the long concrete hallway, was blocked by the mass of people, including the Vice President of the United States walking down the hallway in front of the two spies.

It was a seriously ballsy pass, one that Cooper was certain would be talked about for years to come. It had gone off without a hitch.

* * *

The small entourage wound its way through the labyrinthine network of low concrete hallways. Levitow's voice echoed up and down the narrow corridors, as the vice president listened intently.

"With a strong enough magnetic field, you can temporarily stop a circuit or device from functioning. Or, by reversing the magnetic field, you can free up so many electrons that you fry critical connections within every semiconductor. It's a handy trick."

"Sounds pretty simple. What's the catch?" Arquist was used to playing the straight man, which was also a subtle way of letting people know that he was following along closely and they should skip as much fluff as possible.

"There are two major problems. First, it takes a ton of power to make this happen. More importantly, at the beginning, we could only have these kinds of effects if we placed the target object inside a specially built magnetic field generator. That obviously doesn't work well in a weapons application—if we can get our hands on the object, we may as well just stomp on it with our boot heel. It took us forever to figure out how to affect targets that were some distance away from the field generator."

As the heavy concrete door opened into the hot desert night, Arquist gave Levitow a warm smile and extended his hand. He spoke loudly, but was barely audible over the whine of the helicopter engines. "I'm interested in learning how you ended up cracking that nut. Join me for dinner out east. My chief of staff will be in touch to set things up."

Levitow's reply went unheard as the vice president walked quickly onto the helipad. Levitow felt Pomerantine's pat on the back, and watched as the rest of the group made their way to the aircraft, ducking instinctively to avoid the rotor wash.

Seconds later, the helicopter was out of sight.

Chapter 1

The Pentagon, Crystal City, Virginia. Thursday, 9:46 a.m. ET.

A tall, lanky man left the Pentagon's Metro entrance and ambled across the vast parking lot, beneath the highway bridge, and across Army-Navy Drive to his office building in Crystal City.

People knew him by several different names.

His wife called him Mike. His friends from a twenty-year career as a fighter pilot knew him as Buster, a tongue-in-cheek homage to an episode involving an inadvertent sonic boom and dozens of broken windows.

And he was Mr. Charles to the eight hundred people in the Department of Defense's Mobile Anti-Satellite Targeting System program office, a name usually shortened in bureaucratic circles to the almost-accurate ASAT acronym, under his charge.

But in the most important circle, he was known simply as Stalwart.

Stalwart had left the Pentagon meeting deeply satisfied. Things in the ASAT program were a mess. Nobody seemed to have any sense of what to do next. Nobody but Stalwart, that is, and he kept his thoughts to himself.

He loved opacity. Fog was so much more useful than clarity. It allowed him to declare confident certainties to the murmuring bureaucrats who were castrated by their own timidity. Forever in search of decisiveness, an exotic bird in the fatuous forest of any large, stagnant organization, the pencil pushers fell all over themselves to fall in line behind him. He was guidance and shelter.

But that was not to say he was a charlatan. Quite the opposite, really. A natural strategist, he could easily see and articulate simple connections between complex things.

He stood out enough already, but a confusing environment – and military weapons development programs were anything but straightforward – made him appear godlike next to his counterparts, whom he dubbed the self-herding sheep.

Many such sheep worked for him. They were a nuisance. He delegated only those things he didn't care about. If a task was important, he did it himself.

And Stalwart worked for a few sheep himself. They provided nearly endless entertainment as they struggled to masquerade his trademark clarity and vision as their own.

In this way, he manipulated the Machine. When he chose to advance a cause, major or minor, his skill and personality allowed rapid movement through layers of grinding bureaucracy. But there were many serious issues that he simply allowed the befuddled bureaucrats to bludgeon with their ineptitude.

He did this because the system deserved it, and so did the system's perpetrators.

Even the sheep.

Especially the sheep.

He was a patriot in the truest sense. He had long ago taken an oath to support and defend the Constitution of the United States against all enemies, foreign and domestic. The Constitution, he believed, represented man's highest organizational attainment, the best mechanism yet devised to balance the benefits of collective effort with man's innate freedom. It wasn't perfect, but Stalwart believed it was worthy of defense.

But the Machine had manipulated and twisted that oath, slowly substituting loyalty to an insipid self-serving organization in place of loyalty to the liberties enshrined in the Constitution. He had the clarity, as he saw it, to understand the difference.

With that vision came the clear belief that the great governmental bureaucracy, the lumbering parasite of public treasure, was itself functioning at odds with the Constitution.

This was a hard realization, from which there could be no retreat for a man like Mr. Mike Charles, Co-Director of the ASAT program.

His adoption of this belief was a byproduct of his insatiable curiosity, which took him to the dark corners of the institution. There, buried beneath bromides and false assumptions, he found gleaming fragments of reality. He gradually pieced these fragments together.

What he learned had demanded action.

The final piece of the puzzle had been the hardest for Stalwart to place. Something had nagged at him, a vague, inchoate perception that something significant was amiss. He had the sense that it was right in front of him, maybe even clubbing him over the head, yet he couldn't quite place it.

He was right. It *was* something enormous, glaring, pervasive, and with a prominent public face. Yet it was also absolutely secret.

It started to click into place for Stalwart when he accidentally heard a sentence uttered on television by a thoroughly marginalized congressman and erstwhile presidential hopeful. The hapless politician meant well, but was relegated to crackpot status because of his predilection for publicly disagreeing with what the mainstream considered to be self-evident economic truths.

The politician felt that many of the commonly revered economic precepts most people believed weren't in fact true, and were, instead, little more than unexamined dogma.

But the poor fellow just couldn't speak in public without harping on currency inflation as an insidious and dishonest method of wealth redistribution. His time on the national stage was brief, and since his decisive defeat in the most recent primary, every picture shown of him seemed to have captured his face in a strange, cartoonish contortion.

The politician's name didn't help. "Arvin Duff" didn't roll off of most tongues without a snigger.

Stalwart made it his practice to studiously ignore the politics staged for public consumption in the news media. But on one particular occasion, he was trapped in a clinic waiting room, his ears assaulted by loud, compressed audio from a cheap television tuned to the "Inside Washington" segment of the high-pitched, hard-right daily news agency.

He felt his annoyance growing with each salvo of anti-left invective that invaded his senses. He wasn't annoyed because he leaned left—he was long past picking sides in the Kabuki Theater otherwise known as American politics, and he thought there were sufficient idiots in both camps to make "None of the Above" the only viable choice. He was just irritated because he was forced to listen.

At half past one, Stalwart had asked the receptionist sardonically whether she knew what time his one o'clock appointment would begin. He had smiled at her to take the edge off his sarcasm, and she muttered an officious apology for his inconvenience.

Politely, he had made it clear that they were within ten minutes of losing his appointment and his patronage. He didn't have anywhere in particular he needed to be, but he had decided that he was finished waiting. Life was short.

His message delivered, Stalwart had been on his way back to his seat in the waiting room when Arvin Duff, the crackpot anti-inflation guy, appeared in a television interview. "In 1933, the US government banned the ownership of gold. It was punishable by ten years in prison and up to a $10,000 fine," Duff's nasal voice squawked.

Stalwart stopped in his tracks. Could that be true? The US had banned the ownership of gold? *We—the United States of America— had forbidden American citizens from owning . . . gold?*

Assault weapons, vicious animals, and nuclear weapons he could understand.

But gold?

One might expect something like that from Stalin's Soviet

Union or Mao's China, but never in his life would Stalwart have guessed that the United States government, bastion of liberty and justice, would ban the ownership of a precious metal. It seemed so . . . out of character.

His curiosity was piqued, and Stalwart had turned to his smart phone for answers. As he waited for the browser page to load, he found himself thinking that someone must have lost his mind temporarily and instituted this bit of one-off governmental quackery, only to be corrected by more clear-thinking successors. How could it be otherwise?

But he was wrong.

By executive order number 6102, President Franklin Delano Roosevelt had banned the ownership of gold and ordered that all bullion, coins, and gold certificates be surrendered to the US Treasury no later than May 1, 1933, for which citizens were to be compensated $20.67 per troy ounce.

Eight months later, Congress passed the Gold Reserve Act of 1934, which outlawed the ownership of gold by any US citizen anywhere in the world.

This law also arbitrarily raised the price of gold to $35 per ounce, almost doubling the value of the confiscated gold that by now had accumulated in enormous quantities in the national treasury.

The government had taken all of the citizenry's gold, and then, months later, had arbitrarily declared the confiscated gold to be almost twice as valuable.

In effect, Stalwart mused, the government had scooped up all the gold, then declared the dollar to be half as valuable by comparison. A chilling thought.

The law remained in effect until 1977. Forty-three years was too long for temporary insanity, Stalwart decided.

That revelation had marked an inflection point for Stalwart. Over the following year, he had slowly gained the insight and resolve that would ultimately lead to action.

His fellow bureaucrats had a name for the kind of action he took.

Treason.

The elevator took Stalwart to the top floor of the mid-rise Crystal City office building. He stepped past the secretaries and into his large office, with its incredible view of the Washington Monument, and settled in for a long afternoon of meetings.

He also prepared for some other activity, the kind that could never be put on a calendar at work.

Chapter 2

Somewhere in the Adirondack Mountains. Thursday, 10:24 a.m. ET.

The slight, athletic young man wasn't particularly nervous, but the gravity of what lay ahead of him was never far from his mind. His training had been lengthy and thorough, and he felt confident in his abilities. Soon Chaim would prove his mettle.

He settled his cheek against his rifle, centered his attention on the target, and calmed his breathing.

He was a recent graduate of a lengthy and rigorous training syllabus. Throughout the yearlong course, he had focused on the martial aspects of his regimen, and as young men tended to be, he was quite oblivious of the more important result of his time at the training camp: he had emerged thoroughly indoctrinated.

Extremist groups and mainstream militaries have long known that the most effective indoctrination methods didn't involve hours of dogmatic instruction or rote memorization of political or religious precepts.

Instead of preaching, the most thorough indoctrination efforts merely provided skills training. When done well, the curriculum rarely, and only peripherally, addressed the ultimate purposes to which the newly acquired skills were to be employed. The ideology was taken for granted. It was counterintuitive, but remarkably effective.

Chaim had emerged from his extensive training with an embarrassment of praise and accolades from his superiors. He had been handpicked for his upcoming assignment.

He adjusted his aim for both wind and gravity, exhaled slowly, silenced his mind, and slowly added pressure to the trigger with his index finger. The rifle's report echoed off the far Adirondack hills.

He trained his sight back on the target and discovered that he had missed the center circle by a little more than an inch. Not bad for a 420-yard shot.

He was ready.

It was time for Chaim, now just over twenty years old, to live up to his promises to God.

Over the past weeks, to prepare for his upcoming duty, he had learned of many atrocities committed against peoples of faith in Southwest Asia and North Africa. He had watched hours of grisly footage, and had seen countless grief-stricken survivors laid low in their misery. Bloody mothers clutched dead infants, and husbands tore at their hair in grief at the loss of their families.

Along with a more senior member of the Faithful, he had also flown to see the gruesome aftermath of one of these attacks with his own eyes.

He saw the maimed and grotesquely disfigured children struggling to function normally, and he felt the seething rage of heartbroken parents helpless to remove the pain from their young ones' lives.

He was Jewish, born in Tel Aviv. The disfigured child he had held was Arab, born in Iraq. It didn't matter to him. Humanity was his family, Earth his home, as God had designed.

He was angry in his bones, stricken in his soul. The atrocities were ordered by men in suits and executed by men in uniforms under a banner of justice and freedom.

He had seen the footage and aftermath of many attacks, but they were all linked by a common thread. The weapons that had both cruelly ended some lives, and cruelly failed to fully end others, were all guided by components made by a single company, Langston Marlin.

This company reported to shareholders and was run by a board of directors. Its employees lived in modest homes not altogether unlike the homes their products had decimated.

For the moment, this company also had a chief executive officer, John Averett.

But it would not have one for long.

The young sharpshooter was not looking forward to ending a man's life. The suffering wrought by violent death was all too real to him now, and he loathed bringing this heartbreak upon anyone's wife, children, and grandchildren.

If there was another way, he had pleaded, it would be so much better, so much more righteous.

His superiors had not attempted to justify their strategy. They had merely invited him to help them find a better way, if one could be found.

Together, they had worked through myriad ideas, each dashed by the same limitation the weak always had when they wished to stop the tyranny of the strong.

None of the other ideas had a prayer of working.

In the end, Chaim had concluded, it was simply a matter of mathematics. If he and his comrades did nothing, the mass killings on the other side of the globe would continue.

But if he did *something*, a thing so significant, powerful, frightening, and serious that it couldn't be ignored, then things just might change.

There was no guarantee that his efforts, his sacrifice, the rending of his soul with the guilt of murder, would bring about any change whatsoever.

But Chaim knew with a calm, bottomless clarity that he no

longer had the ability to do nothing.

He had held the blinded and legless child in his arms, and through his own tears, he had promised God with the full force and depth of himself that he would expend everything, including his last breath, if need be, to stop the barbarism.

He would sacrifice the purity of his conscience. He would descend to savagery himself.

This price he was willing to pay. He was already broken, indelibly altered, by the horrible things he had seen. There was no turning back.

He heard footsteps behind him and turned to see a familiar face. "I am told that Mullah has confirmed it. It is time, my brother."

Get Lars' #1 Bestselling Thriller:

DEVOLUTION

What readers say:

"The best writing in decades. Move over, Lee Child."

"Some of the best thriller fiction you will ever read."

"Right up there with Patterson, Baldacci, Forsyth, and DeMille."

"The best thriller I've ever read."

"LOVE LOVE LOVE this series!"